Gareth Joseph has liv

Homegrown

Gareth Joseph

HEADLINE

First published in 2001
by HEADLINE BOOK PUBLISHING

10 9 8 7 6 5 4 3 2

ISBN 0 7472 6665 4

Typeset by Avon Dataset Ltd, Bidford-on-Avon, Warks

Printed and bound in Great Britain by
Mackays of Chatham plc, Chatham, Kent

HEADLINE BOOK PUBLISHING
A division of Hodder Headline
338 Euston Road
London NW1 3BH

www.headline.co.uk
www.hodderheadline.com

**Mummy, it could
only be for you**

The middle-aged woman struggled with her pillow and sat up flustered. She handed the telephone to her husband on the other side of the bed. He noted her scowl of disapproval at the lateness of the call and shrugged. She huffed, lay down and turned her back towards him.

'Barrett,' he stated flatly.

'I want to see you, soon,' the caller replied.

He wanted to ask the caller what he thought he was doing, calling him at that time. Didn't he know there were other methods and more sociable times to make contact? He glanced across at his wife and held his tongue. 'How soon?' he asked.

'Tomorrow morning. The car park.'

'I'll try,' said Barrett. 'I'll call if I can't make it.'

'Don't call,' the caller advised. 'Just be there.' He hung up.

Barrett frowned and reached over his wife to replace the receiver. He switched off the lamp on the night stand beside him, but he wasn't able to sleep. Things were getting out of hand and something had to be done, before everything he had worked so hard for came crashing down.

He slid out of bed, knowing that his wife was awake but pretending not to be, and made his way downstairs to his study. He closed the door behind him, strode to the expansive leather-topped desk and from a drawer produced a large cigar. He clipped the end, lit it and puffed as he poured himself a large Scotch. Then he grasped the receiver of an old-fashioned telephone and dialled, confident that the call would be answered despite the time.

'It's me,' he announced. 'With a problem.'

'I can tell that. What's the matter? Didn't the appointment turn up?'

'Yes,' said Barrett. 'The appointment did turn up, but he took something from me. Something I need back.'

'Well, I did warn you about that from the very beginning. Told you to be careful. It's a problem we've been trying to work on for a good while now.'

'I don't care how long you've been working on anything, you little Yid runt,' Barrett hissed with a glance at the ceiling, imagining his wife stirring above. 'Your light-fingered friend has something that belongs to me, and I want it back.'

'What was it?'

'A tape.'

'A tape? Are you serious?'

'It's not any tape, you prat!' He lowered his voice:

'It's of the appointment and me. The first time.'

A weary sigh and an exasperated chuckle came down the line. 'Believe me, I've tried before, different circumstances obviously, but it was a waste of time. I assure you, I won't be able to get it for you. If it's that important, you're going to have to get it yourself.'

'Are you serious?' demanded Barrett, placing his tumbler on the desk. 'Do you know who I am? *What* I am?'

'I certainly do. That's why you need to get it back. And anyway, who's better placed than you?'

There was a pause as Barrett grasped the glass and emptied its contents in one gulp. 'Tomorrow morning,' he growled. 'Where's he likely to be?'

MONDAY

CHAPTER ONE

Vaughn made his way reluctantly along the balcony of the block of flats, noting each door as he looked for number thirteen but secretly hoping that he wouldn't find it. The block was grey and dismal. The walls were a depressing grey-brown, the balcony a darker, even more disheartening colour – a typical south London housing estate. He stopped in front of a peeling, faded red door centred with a frosted-glass square – number thirteen. He knocked and waited, hoping that no one would answer. A few seconds later, from inside the flat, a child's sing-song voice asked, 'Who is it?' and the visitor groaned.

He explained his presence and there was silence. A few moments later the door opened to reveal a small, scrawny blond boy, no older than five, who stood there wearing nothing but a pair of oversized Chelsea shorts and a lot of ingrained dirt.

'Hello there,' beamed Vaughn with such false verve that he impressed even himself. He tried to ignore the smell wafting out from behind the boy. 'Is your mum in?'

The little boy didn't answer but gazed at the visitor for a second before he turned and trotted into the flat, leaving the door open behind him and shouting, 'Mum! It's a black man!'

Vaughn frowned. He *was* black and had no problem with that, but was always on his guard when he was introduced as such.

He didn't have to wait long. The boy trotted back and stood at the door peering at him. The young man felt forced to communicate so he crouched down. 'Well,' he said grinning, 'what's your name? Mine's Vaughn.'

'Kevin William Keeler,' announced the boy and almost stood to attention as he did so.

'Nice name,' said the visitor. He already knew who Kevin was. 'Well, Kevin, what did your mum say? Can I come in?'

'You're black, aren't you?' asked Kevin. 'My brother says black people are like monkeys. Are you like a monkey?'

Vaughn smiled weakly; it wasn't the kid's fault that his brother was an idiot. It probably wasn't even the brother's fault. 'No, I'm no more like a monkey than you are. Now, what did your mum say?'

'She's sleeping.'

'Are you sure?'

Kevin nodded.

'Is there anyone else in the house?'

Kevin nodded again.

'Who?'

'Me.'

Vaughn sighed, scratched his head and pushed a stray lock of hair behind his ear. Kevin then told him that his brother said dreadlocks were dead worms. In two minds about whether to leave and ring social services, or enter the flat, the visitor informed the boy that this was not the case.

As an education welfare officer he had read a number of Social Services reports about the family and knew that the home was dysfunctional. Mum – Mrs Keeler – was a drinker, and her children had been bounced on and off the Child Protection Register with more regularity than kids on an inflatable castle. The categories of registration varied like the seasons – neglect, emotional abuse and suspected sexual abuse. If and when the Keeler kids got put on for physical abuse, the trophy cabinet would be complete. For all he knew Mrs Keeler could have drowned in her own puke and left Kevin to fend for himself. He sighed again and thought, why am I doing this? A brief spell in the Careers Service in a particularly run-down corner of south-east London had shown Vaughn that if he was really to help the young people he worked with, he needed to become involved earlier. So when he saw adverts for education welfare officers he had applied with enthusiasm and a desire to really make a difference. The desire remained, but the enthusiasm was long gone. And although he repeatedly told himself that he didn't care about these crap families and their crap kids, it wasn't true.

The house was by no means the worst that Vaughn had seen in his two and a half years in the job, but it was one of them. What amazed him more than the stench, the dirt and the general state of disrepair, decay and neglect was that he hadn't read about it in the social worker's reports. A flat couldn't have got like this in three months, which was when the last Social Services case conference was held. He picked his way behind Kevin, over all manner of clothes and other, unrecognisable things on the floor.

Vaughn forced himself to glance into the kitchen as he passed the open door. The sink and surrounding work surface was piled high with dishes that were encrusted with food. A black bin bag on the floor in front of the sink was packed with and surrounded by rubbish of all kinds. The smell was unbelievable and Vaughn found himself involuntarily placing his hand over his mouth and retching. Eyes smarting from the stench, he followed Kevin into what had to be the living room. The room was bare except for a dirty, worn brown velour settee and matching armchair. A television doubled up as a shelf for lottery papers, a couple of plates and an apple core. Those were the recognisable things. The walls were in the same state as the passage – ripped paper, smudges and oily marks. Vaughn couldn't identify what colour they had been originally. They may have been white or magnolia, maybe even a pale green or blue, but now they were just grimy, a grey-brown blend the colour of London pavements. The linoleum floor had obviously been covered by a foam-backed carpet in the past, but only the foam remained and there were clumps of it dotted around the room. They had become so black and hardened that they resembled blobs of chewing gum on the street.

The living room had another repulsive odour, the smell of filthy human flesh. Looking at Mrs Keeler in the armchair, obese, dirty, covered in sores and bruises, appearing to have been poured in to the armchair in order to perform a brilliant impersonation of Jabba the Hut, Vaughn thought he could understand why the room smelled the way it did. He took a deep breath, regretted it and introduced himself.

Mrs Keeler's breath came frequently and heavily, and her massive bosom rose and fell dramatically as each intake and expulsion of air crackled through her lungs. Her eyes were barely open or were simply hidden by her fatty eyelids. Vaughn was impressed by how grotesque she was, and had to suppress a chuckle.

He perched on the edge of the sofa refusing to sit on the cushions. The memory of sitting in baby piss and shit on one visit would haunt him forever, and he was adamant it wouldn't happen again. Mrs Keeler hadn't said anything yet and Vaughn speculated that that might be where Kevin got his reticence from.

Throughout the visit Mrs Keeler sent Kevin to the kitchen for beer after beer, belched, scratched and tried to answer Vaughn's questions about the school attendance of her sons. Vaughn eventually gave up when Mrs Keeler refused to accept that Christopher could be in danger when out of school and was doing his chances of success in the future no good at all. Following procedure, Vaughn then informed her that if Christopher's attendance did not improve he would have to issue her with a first court warning.

He thought he heard her snoring before he was out of the room.

Marcus Irving Lucas Kerr, known to most by his initials as 'Milk', showed no surprise or displeasure when he awoke at seven forty-five in the morning to find his reproductive organ wrapped in a small fist. The fist ended in long, colourful nails and was moving rhythmically up and down the shaft. When the owner of the fist realised that Milk was awake, she smiled and unwrapped some protection with her teeth, then slipped it on and swung herself aboard. She lit a left-over joint that had been parked in the ashtray overnight – in reality only three hours because they hadn't really gone to sleep, just sort of napped in between courses – then took a puff and stuck the joint into Milk's mouth. He in turn took a puff, longer and deeper than hers, keeping the smoke in his lungs to gain the maximum benefit. He then put the weed back into the ashtray, admired the fine breasts and nipples suspended in front of his face, felt the firm body and legs squeezing his, and nobly had no other thought in his mind than to do the girl justice.

By the time he finished here, this girl was going to know that there was no one else like him.

Milk started to work with concentration. Nodding to the tune on the radio, he began rocking and rolling, riding and gliding, making sure the girl knew the score and regretted leaving it for a week before she'd phoned him. He could see that if she didn't know now, as soon as she recovered enough she would recognise her mistake. Although she rode high and proud, dark breasts pert and pristine, she was in a state, covering her face in distraction, moaning and whimpering, biting her lips and pulling at her hair. Milk couldn't suppress his grin. He loved it.

A short while later, while the girl was still astride quivering in a post-orgasmic state, Milk thought he heard something outside the bedroom door. It disturbed him because he liked to be in total control of his immediate environment. Past experiences had taught him to make sure that he knew what was coming at all times. He reached for the remote control and lowered the volume of the radio, pulled himself up so that his back was against the cheap pink velour headboard, and reached under the pillow. The girl moved up with him, her trembling beginning to subside.

The bedroom door swung open, quickly but quietly, and Milk locked eyeballs with a dark, angry-faced guy who stood in the doorway. He sported a goatee around dry, cracked red lips, and looked like the kind of person that scowled twenty-four hours a day. He was big, not particularly tall, but thick and solid. The impression was increased by the black puffa jacket and woolly hat on his large head. Milk thought the guy was slightly younger than him, a couple of years or so, but that didn't affect his intentions. So when the guy lunged towards him on the bed, still not having said a word or made a noise, Milk had no option but to bring his hand from under the pillow and land the pistol butt on the guy's temple. The new arrival folded in the air and crashed into the bedside cabinet, bringing the pink lamp and ashtray crashing to the floor. The girl screamed. When she saw what had happened she screamed even louder until Milk asked, 'What the fuck you making noise now for? He's out cold. What's the problem?'

She stopped and stared wide-eyed at the guy lying peacefully on the pink carpet, a lump growing on his head.

'Who is he?' asked Milk, turning the radio back up. 'Your man?'

She struggled to find her voice and said, 'No, not my man, just some guy I kind of know.'

Milk frowned. 'So how come he's got a key? And how come he tried to jump me?'

'I don't know,' she said. 'I must have given it to him the other day when he was going to the shop. I just forgot to get it back off him. He's just a guy. I don't know where he gets off rushing you like that.'

Milk looked thoughtful. 'I hope you're telling the truth, because it could look to me like you've just gone and called me up to come here and get jacked by your boyfriend there. Now that's not the case, is it?'

She shook her head.

'Good. I hope not.'

'I haven't got a *boyfriend*,' she said suggestively.

Milk's ears pricked up and he raised an eyebrow and sneered. 'Well, you ain't finding one here, but when you want it done properly, call me.'

Milk checked the prone figure on the floor, making sure that he wouldn't be regaining consciousness too soon. He was satisfied, but just in case, he bound the guy's wrists behind his back with the pink cord from the girl's dressing gown. Milk glanced at her and thought to himself that it was ironic that in recent months he had begun to think seriously about a permanent, full-time girl that he could call his own. It had taken him a long time to get with the fact that that was actually what he wanted. A very long time indeed. He found it hard to believe that he was beginning to tire of his sleazing, where anything and everything was fair game. He was getting too old for that stuff, and needed to revise his thinking. Milk knew it was going to be hard to find someone that could keep him on the straight and narrow, a girl that he wasn't prepared to drop at a moment's notice to move on to something new. This one was a good shag, no doubt, but she had nothing else going for her, and although this start to Milk's day had been fun and different, it proved that she was not for him. On top of that, the pink theme was making him feel nauseous.

Having carried out the bare hygiene essentials he came back into the room and began to dress.

'So, what are you going to do with him?' she asked.

Milk feigned confusion. 'What am *I* going to do
with him? Sorry, mate, but I don't know him, you do.
You brought him into your house and gave him your
keys. I think the question should be what are *you* going
to do with him?'

Aghast, the girl suddenly decided to cover herself
with the pink duvet, as though she had any modesty
left to be protected. 'But you can't leave him here.
What do I do when he wakes up?'

'I don't know,' said Milk, buttoning up his jeans.
'You can try what you just did to me. I liked it, so he
probably will.'

She glared and clenched her jaw, which only served
to make Milk laugh, do a little pirouette, and shuffle to
the garage tune that was now on the radio.

'So? What's that mean then?' Milk quizzed. 'What
you pulling that face for? You gone off me?'

She refused to answer, and instead reached for
the packet of cigarettes on the bedside cabinet. She
realised that the cigarettes had been knocked to
the floor and reluctantly raised the intruder's hand
to retrieve the packet. She lit one and smoked in silence.

'So what, then? You're not going to call me again?'
asked Milk, trying to keep a straight face. 'Is that us
over? Short and sweet?'

She still refused to answer and continued to smoke
in silence. Milk shrugged, but on his way out he jigged
around to her, pulled the sheet down and scooped up
a breast. He sucked a nipple into his mouth and put a
hand somewhere sensitive. All her composure and

aloofness suddenly went out the window like smoke on an air current. Not long afterwards she gasped and shuddered.

'Phone me,' said Milk.

She nodded, shuddered again and said, 'By the way, you've been calling me Nadine. My name's Nicole.'

'Oops,' said Milk. 'Sorry.'

The week started with a dream – *the* dream. He knew what it was about but not what it meant, nor why he was having it now, after being free of it for so long. He sat up with a start, drenched in sweat and effectively lashed to the bed by twisted sheets. It took a while for him to compose himself and find his bearings. The bulldozers were screaming their way into the building site behind the terraced house, and the next-door neighbours wailed, banged and stamped their way around their flat as part of their early-morning pre-work ritual. He couldn't be certain of what had woken him, the bulldozers or the neighbours, but he didn't care. For once he was glad.

It was always the same. The young black man curled up on the floor in a foetal position screaming and pleading for mercy as the blows rain down on his head, arms, back and legs. He soon realises that it's futile and stops. The only sounds then are the thuds of the blows on his body, the wet, snapping sounds as bones are broken in his hands and arms, and the grunts of exertion from the uniformed assailants, enthusiastic about their work.

Ditton reached for the ashtray at the side of the bed and retrieved a half-smoked joint. Knowing what the dream was about didn't make it any easier to deal with. He hadn't realised he had been sweating until he shivered as the beads of perspiration across his body did their job. He held his head in his hands for a few seconds, listening to the clip-clop of feet from next door's kitchen and a curse as someone dropped a plate and dragged a chair across the floor.

Frustrated, he looked at his watch. It was only seven and he didn't have to be at Tyrone's until eleven at the earliest. He hadn't gone to bed until after twelve, and then because of the neighbours hadn't been able to sleep until way after two. He was tired and needed to rest, just an hour or so.

Not for the first time, Ditton fantasised about kicking down their door with a couple of guys and spraying the whole house with bullets. At first it had just been the four guys upstairs. Ditton had given up trying to get them to realise that in his bedroom he could hear them sneeze, drop a spoon and even fart. They didn't seem to understand that if they slammed their front door Ditton's teeth would rattle in his head, or that their constant repetitive music was worse than dripping-tap torture.

But then the French-speaking African girls had moved in downstairs and the guys in the upstairs flat became mutes in comparison. Ditton had never met a more raucous, rowdy, uncouth bunch of bitches in his life. He hoped he never would again. On every occasion he had gone to complain about the volume of their music they had been too drunk or stoned to be capable of responding to his requests.

Ditton groaned and tossed the pillow to the end of the bed. He turned on the television and studied a presenter on breakfast TV. He wondered where her parents were from as she didn't look English, whatever that meant nowadays. Her skin was too dark and she looked like an oriental or Arab mix. Not bad, though, whatever her ancestry was.

His imaginings were rudely interrupted by one of the empty-headed neighbours slamming the front door. He waited for the ringing in his ears to stop, wondering whether he might be able to get another hour's sleep before he had to get up and drive to his 'cousin's'. Tyrone had phoned the night before and asked him to stop by in the morning to discuss something. There weren't many things Tyrone could need to talk to him about, and definitely not with any urgency. In fact there was really only one thing it was likely to be, and unfortunately Ditton thought he knew what it was.

Some time later, just as Ditton had managed to put the dream out of his mind and the weed was beginning to drag him down into the bed like insistent hands, as he lay debating whether to get up and make a drink or try to get back to sleep, he suddenly realised that there was no noise. No JCBs, no neighbours. He sighed, a mixture of apprehension and exhilaration. He reached for the pillow to cover his head, hoping that if he managed to nod off before anything started again, he would have a good chance of staying asleep. The thought was just *too* nice and he was beginning to believe it possible when a distant telephone began ringing. He knew that it was from next door and waited with bated breath, hoping against hope that they were all out of the house or too stoned to hear the phone. It kept ringing, and just as he was almost certain that it wouldn't be answered, it stopped. The suspense was too much. Had the caller rung off, or had it been picked up? He soon had his answer – a grunt, a direction to 'Ecoute!' followed by some guttural sounds and wailing that meant the main bitch had answered the phone. He cursed and swung himself out of bed. As was his way, Ditton found something positive, and was grateful that for differing reasons his brother and father who also lived in the house hadn't been disturbed.

Michelle didn't lose control often, if ever, but that morning she woke above the covers with a splitting headache and a serious thirst that had her dreaming about pints of water. Her head hurt but she didn't care; her heart was in more pain and she wasn't sure that it could or should recover. How could she have been so stupid again?

She had always had bad luck with men. One boy-friend had given her a son, Dale, her pride and joy, and then disappeared. She had never seen or heard from him again. The next one, Carl, had initially been an angel, but things had soured steadily until one day he turned nasty, forcing her to place a carving knife so forcefully against his Adam's apple that she cut him every time he swallowed. After that experience Michelle was convinced that if there were any good black men in the world they were nowhere near her, and she wasn't even going to bother looking for one. As she wasn't going to get on the white-man bandwagon, she would have to manage without.

She had been working evenings in the supermarket for a couple of months, earning a pittance, when Patrick had approached her at the checkout and tried talking to her. She wasn't hostile or aggressive, she just wasn't interested and was sure that she never would be. Finally, she got so fed up of seeing him standing there looking pitiful that she gave in and reluctantly agreed to meet him after work. She made no effort to look glamorous. She simply put her coat over her red-and-white supermarket overalls and walked out not caring if he was there or not. He was. They spent an hour or so in Pizza Hut in Brixton and Michelle eventually agreed to see him again. He didn't seem too bad, a bit short and stumpy, not particularly good-looking but not *ugly* ugly. A year later, his look hadn't improved but their relationship had. Patrick was Michelle's man and she didn't want it any other way.

Last night, at Brixton Water Lane, she'd spotted Patrick's car while driving to her friend's and flashed him but he hadn't seen her. As they were going in the same direction she'd followed, curious about the girl who looked so comfortable in the passenger seat. Later he'd stopped for petrol and she'd parked opposite, watching him. He came out looking miffed, stuffing a packet of blue Rizla into his pocket and trying to conceal a packet of sanitary towels. Michelle knew she wasn't on, so they had to be for the girl. What man bought sanitary towels for a friend? For that matter, what man bought sanitary towels for his beloved?

Amazingly, Patrick hadn't seen her even though she'd wanted him to, and she'd ended up following him all the way to Thornton Health, to a quiet terraced street around the corner from Selhurst Park stadium. Patrick had parked the car and both he and the girl got out, the girl letting herself into the house adjacent. She left the front door open and Michelle watched her trot straight upstairs to the top flat while Patrick disappeared from sight, pottering about in the boot of the car. He'd reappeared holding a lovely brown leather holdall. Michelle couldn't believe her eyes and actually found herself blinking a couple of times to make sure her lenses weren't playing tricks on her. The bag was exactly the same as the one that had been stolen from her flat in a burglary a few months previously. Patrick had explained that burglars often used a bag from inside the house to carry away items. It had made perfect sense until she saw the bag in Patrick's hand. It had to be the same one but it was all too much to take in.

The girl had made her way upstairs and was drawing the curtains. Michelle looked up at the window and saw a tall standing lamp, exactly the same as one she had lost in the burglary. She really couldn't believe it, didn't want to believe it. By now, Patrick had gone inside and was standing behind the girl, his arms around her waist as he had done with Michelle so often. The curtains had closed and Michelle was distraught.

She had stayed outside for three hours, waiting for she didn't know what. Finally she was rewarded by the sight of Patrick coming out of the house with his I-just-fucked swagger. She recognised it, and it hit her like the one and only smack in the mouth she had taken from Carl. She had naively thought it was only her that made Patrick swagger like that and she felt so stupid and gullible as she watched him get into his car and drive off. Michelle had remained where she was, immobile and stunned. Five minutes later, at ten minutes to twelve, her mobile phone rang and the display screen lit up to tell her that the call was from Patrick. She knew that he was calling to see if she was in so that he could stop by. He regularly did at that time of night and usually she didn't object, she wanted to see him. But now she wondered how many times he had come round to her after leaving this girl, or any number of others because that had to be a possibility. She didn't answer the call.

Michelle had driven straight home, showered thoroughly and drank the bottle of wine that she had bought earlier. When that was finished she began on a bottle of brandy that had been half empty for months, then went on to a bottle of Bailey's. She got no further, but must have woken up at some point during the night and dragged herself off to bed. There she remained until the morning where she woke up hung-over, thirsty and hungry. Last night she'd felt desperate, stupid and dirty. Now she just felt angry.

By midday Michelle had calmed herself. She had spent the morning thinking about what had happened the night before, and looking at herself in the mirror while she listened to Aretha crooning in her inimitable style, telling her that despite the weakness of her man, she was still strong and beautiful.

It had taken some time, some serious soul-searching and a lot of tears, but finally Michelle had made some decisions. First of all, she was not to blame. Secondly, her long-held belief that all men were bastards was true and the only mistake she had made was in beginning to think that maybe a few of them were not. She wouldn't make that mistake again.

She was still angry and she needed a way to make Patrick hurt. She wanted something to knock him back hard, like he had done to her. Nothing paltry like acid on his car; she wanted more than that – this rose had thorns. But although she gave it serious thought for a couple of hours, she couldn't come up with any idea, that satisfied her sufficiently to act upon it.

One thing she *was* certain about was that she wanted sex. Not a man, just sex. Uncomplicated, non-binding, adult sex, full of grunts and groans and finished with a fag and a 'let's do that again sometime'. She wasn't sure why, as it wasn't a feeling she recognised. Whatever the reason, Michelle knew who to call. Someone that had been offering her respite for a considerable time, and who may well have had the opportunity if Patrick hadn't got there first. She smiled and picked up the phone.

CHAPTER TWO

Having been forced out of bed, Ditton spent an hour in the bath with the radio. He flicked from station to station, finding out the morning's grim details. Clinton pleading with the Unionists, Pakistan preparing to test their nuclear device, Sinatra's family squabbling over his millions. He bathed, creamed his skin and greased his hair. The ritual made him feel slightly more awake, if not totally refreshed, and he proceeded to make a breakfast from the previous day's leftovers, frying rice with onions, chicken and corn. His older brother Rodney hadn't surfaced yet, but Ditton knocked on his bedroom door and called out that there was food in the kitchen. If his dad found it, he found it. Ditton wasn't going to tell him.

Ditton chose to speak very little to his father. He also spoke very little to Rodney but this wasn't through choice. Rodney had had an accident some years previously and had suffered relatively serious brain damage as a result. Although he wasn't a complete vegetable, he was far from the man he used to be and complex conversations were no longer possible. Rodney Ditton – *the* Ditton–Gary's senior by six years had made his life from crime and was good at it, possessing the ability and charisma to lead and organise others. He was very careful, very successful, motivated, intelligent, and destined for big things until one day, according to the police, he was arrested, taken in for questioning and released – his signature was there for the world to see. However, some time after the alleged release, Rodney was found unconscious in a dilapidated disused factory. His skull had been fractured, his ribs and hands broken, and he had a very slim chance of survival. The police were adamant that they were not responsible; they had released him and whatever had happened after that was unfortunate, but nothing to do with them. There had been uproar in the community, protests, marches and a mini-riot; but as usual nothing came of it. No suspensions, no prosecutions – just another black man to add to the list of those who had suffered at the hands of the constabulary.

Communication with Mr Ditton senior was hampered by a very different reason. As far as his youngest son was concerned, the man was a shameless, hopeless, strong-lager-drinking fuck-up, and his son loathed him with a passion that was missing from most other areas of his life.

At half ten Ditton left the house, got into his little 205 GTi and set off for Croydon and Tyrone's flat. The roads were fairly clear at that time of the morning, and he parked outside Tyrone's block twenty-five minutes after leaving home. It was a nice little council flat that Tyrone had registered in some girl's name. Ditton had been dealing for a couple of years, Tyrone however, had been selling heroin, 'brown', for about six years and was making a pile of money. The rumours said that he had about ten guys working for him, and had millions stashed around the world. It wouldn't have surprised Ditton at all. Tyrone had always been the kind of guy who sought the quickest route to everything. He didn't like having to answer to people, and his overbearing, domineering nature made it an ideal vocation for him. Tyrone had become so big that he no longer touched the stuff himself, just raked in the cash and gave his boys their cut. Ditton had a feeling that one of those employees was likely to be the topic of conversation.

'You want to try going to bed at night,' Tyrone remarked gruffly, sitting down opposite Ditton. 'You look like shit.'

'Cheers, you really know how to make someone feel good, don't you?'

Tyrone settled his big, muscular frame into the plush leather armchair, which squeaked in protest. He frowned. 'Well, it's true. You look like you haven't slept for weeks, man.'

Ditton yawned. 'Something like that.'

Tyrone raised an eyebrow on his big dark face. 'What? Not them neighbours still?'

Ditton yawned again and nodded.

Tyrone sat forward, shaking his head. 'You've got to

29

be joking. Look, I can send some guys round there who'll make sure they stop that shit straight away. What do you say?'

Ditton smiled. 'Believe me, I've thought about it, but I don't think it's come to that yet. I've just got to get round to talking to them properly. It shouldn't be a problem.'

'And if that doesn't work?'

Ditton stretched out on the sofa like a cat and shrugged. 'Who knows? We'll see.' He held back a smile at the thought of Tyrone offering to send guys round to sort out a problem like some Mafia don. Who would have imagined it twenty years ago when they first became friends and their mothers, consequently, just as close?

Ditton glanced at Tyrone in his white underpants and vest. He looked like the classic male catalogue model, except that he would have been considered too black in complexion and features to sell clothes. A field nigger who had found his way into the house to terrify and excite the master's wife simultaneously.

'How's your mum?' asked Ditton, sincerely, but also to pre-empt Tyrone, who was guaranteed to wind him up about not seeing his 'aunt' for so long.

'She's all right. Still complaining about her blood pressure and joints. You know how it goes.'

Ditton did, because Tyrone's mother had always complained about ailments. She wasn't a hypochondriac but that was probably only because she didn't know the word, and if she had, she would have added it to her list of complaints. When Ditton's mother had died and he and Rodney had gone to live with Tyrone's family, he'd been amazed at how much time Mrs Gayle, Tyrone's mother, had spent complaining about her aches and pains. He loved her dearly and had to see her soon, but he had enough problems of his own and was sure that Tyrone was going to give him another one now.

'That'll be Babbler,' declared Tyrone in response to the buzz from the intercom. 'I asked him to come too.'

'Who's Babbler?' asked Ditton, puzzled.

Tyrone looked surprised. 'Earl. Earl Carlyle. You never knew he was called Babbler? Yeah, it's some name those Junction boys gave him. You know he's from Junction, though?'

Ditton shook his head and remained silent. He wasn't going to ask what this was all about; he could wait to be told. Instead, he enjoyed a quick daydream about taking up Tyrone's offer and being out of the way while the neighbours got a visit from some thugs in balaclavas. He opened one eye as Tyrone came back into the room and sat down, followed by an inordinately gaunt light-skinned guy. The newcomer was so skinny that he looked positively unhealthy, as though the thick gold bracelet on his wrist was likely to slip up his forearm and shatter his elbow. His knees looked ready to slice through his black jeans, and his shoulder blades were too evident despite the jumper he was wearing.

31

Ditton couldn't explain what it was about Earl
Carlyle that got to him, just a feeling that he had
expressed to Tyrone in the past. Tyrone said if Ditton
gave himself the chance to get to know Earl, he'd see
that he was an all right guy, dependable. Ditton had
never found the enthusiasm to try to find out.

'D.' Earl nodded. 'What's happening?'

Ditton held out a fist for Earl to meet with his own.
'Yeah, mate. Long time no see. What's up?'

'Just earning,' said Earl with a small grin. 'Just
earning.'

'Too much fucking money, that's what he's earning.
He's only gone and bought himself an M-reg Prelude,'
interrupted Tyrone. 'Wanker signs on, claims housing
benefit, and he's driving a fucking M-reg Prelude. I
told him, "On your head be it," but he doesn't want to
listen.'

Earl grinned at Ditton and rolled his eyes. 'Do
you know how much this wog earns? Do you know
how many guys he's got running around selling his
gear?'

'No need to go there,' said Tyrone holding up a big
hand. 'No need to go there.'

'I haven't seen you for ages,' said Earl as he fell on to
the sofa next to Ditton. He narrowed his eyes as if in
serious thought, and asked, 'Where was it the last time?'

Ditton hesitated. Earl knew the answer. 'Henrietta's,'
replied Ditton. 'The bar.'

'Yeah, Henrietta's,' agreed Earl. 'That's where it was.
You still go there?'

Ditton shrugged. 'Sometimes.'

Earl raised his eyebrows. 'I haven't been there for a while. Normally only go there to meet for business, you know how it goes.'

Ditton felt like saying that the only thing he knew for sure was that Earl was full of shit. But instead, as usual, he stayed quiet, pragmatic and calm.

Tyrone stood up and offered drinks. Ditton nodded at tea.

'And as for you, Earl,' declared Tyrone, 'you need some of my mum's soup with yam and dumplings and green banana. If you can't get hold of that you need to live on fucking Nurishment.'

Earl's response was less than polite.

Ditton closed his eyes as Tyrone walked out to the kitchen. He propped himself up on one elbow and made what he hoped was a good attempt at looking as though he was asleep. Earl babbled on, regardless, about who he had and hadn't seen. Ditton was forced to listen until Tyrone came back with a cup of tea and an orange juice. He put the drinks down on the coffee table that separated him from Ditton and Earl.

They sat in silence for a while, except for the sound of lips sipping and the rustle of paper as Tyrone rolled a small, neat joint that looked ridiculous in his big black hands. When he had finished, he lit it, sat back and said to Ditton, 'I guess you've been wondering why I asked you to come here?'

Ditton shrugged. 'Well, I haven't been going mad trying to figure it out, but I've wondered.'

Tyrone glanced at Earl before declaring, 'It's about Jonah.'

Ditton's guess had been right and he groaned. 'Ty, man. What now? And anyway, what's it got to do with me?'

'You know what it's got to do with you, *consigliere*. He's your boy, man. Everybody knows that.'

Ditton frowned. 'I'm no one's *consigliere*,' he pointed out, but didn't disagree with the rest of Tyrone's statement.

Tyrone continued: 'The guy's out of order, he's making me hot and he's making me nervous. Everywhere I go there's talk about what Jonah's done, who Jonah's shot at, and who Jonah's going to stick up next. It's fucking crazy, and it could get me in trouble. I don't want him or his madness near me. If I'm standing next to Jonah, I could have any number of people taking pot shots at him and hitting me. Now I hear the latest one is some Peckham guy, Kevin Hill. I heard that he wants blood after what Jonah did to him in that club. I mean, shit! What's wrong with the boy?'

Tyrone sat back and Ditton waited for the rest, but it didn't come. 'Is that it? You called me here for that?' he asked. 'So what? Are you saying you want to cut him off? You don't want him working for you?'

Tyrone shrugged. 'Maybe.'

Ditton spread his hands. 'Well, cut him off then. Why do you have to consult with me?'

'You asked me to take Jonah on, remember? Because he didn't want to work for his brother. All that stuff about wanting to do it on his own.'

Earl's gold bracelet clanked as he raised his pipe-cleaner of an arm to cough. 'Tell him the rest, Ty.'

Ditton glanced at Earl, and then at Tyrone. 'What rest?'

'Vincent,' Tyrone stated flatly.

Slowly, Ditton placed his mug on the coffee table and sat up straight. 'What about Vincent?'

'He's trying to put pressure on me, trying to treat me like a boy, and I'm not having it.'

Ditton didn't want to ask but he had to know. 'What's he done?'

'He's threatened a couple of my guys, worked over Jerry and put a gun to Barry's head. The flat where I stash the gear got done over, and the gear was trashed. Not taken, you hear? Trashed. I had the flat for three weeks before I put anything in there, and the day that I did, it gets done. How's that?'

Ditton didn't like what he was hearing. 'Do you know that Vincent did the flat?'

'Who else is it going to be? If the gear got taken, then I might think it could have been anybody, but to put it down the fucking toilet had to be Vincent trying to prove a point. And I saw him outside the Ritzy and confronted him about it. He didn't admit it, but I know he knew.'

Ditton shook his head in disbelief. 'You confronted him? What the fuck are you playing at, Ty? This is Vincent we're talking about here, not some silly little school kid, or your average one-a-penny hustler.'

Tyrone scowled hard. 'Look, I'm not scared of Vincent and I told him that. If he tries anything again, I'm going to have to go for him. I told him that too.'

Ditton was stunned. Tyrone actually sounded serious. It was time to establish facts. 'All right,' he said, holding up a hand. 'Barry and Jerry. Was that actually Vincent?'

Tyrone shook his head. 'Nah, that was Popeye, one of Vincent's wankers, but that means Vincent ordered it done, doesn't it?'

Ditton found it hard to disagree. 'So if it was Vincent that did the flat, how did he know where it was?'

Tyrone raised an eyebrow. 'Good question. I've been wondering about that too.'

Suddenly Ditton realised what Tyrone had decided, and the real reason his presence had been requested. 'No! Jonah wouldn't do that,' he exclaimed.

Tyrone scowled and took a long puff of the joint, making the tip glow bright orange. He blew the smoke out and from behind the cloud growled, 'He better not have done it, because if I find out he did, I'm going to kill him with a fucking smile on my face.'

'Easy, Ty,' Ditton warned. 'You're talking about Jonah. You're talking about Vincent's brother. You don't want to be talking like that.'

'Fuck Jonah, and fuck Vincent. I'll talk about whoever and whatever, you get me? Who the fuck does he think he is? He's the only person allowed to make money? Bollocks! If he wants to bring it to me, he's going to get a fuck of a lot more than he bargained for.'

'All right,' said Ditton, trying to soothe. 'Who else knew about the flat?'

'Jerry, Barry and Jonah, that's it. I didn't tell any of the others. *You* don't even know where it is.'

Earl leaned forward and cleared his throat. 'And me,' he said, sounding slightly embarrassed.

'Fuck you,' growled Tyrone irritably. 'You don't count.'

Ditton reached for the Rizla and the weed and began rolling a joint for himself. He rarely smoked during the day, and never this early, preferring to keep his head clear until darkness descended. He didn't like what he was hearing and had a bad feeling that this thing was likely to get out of hand. Tyrone's temper and violence were well known, but they were nothing compared to Vincent's. Vincent had started out with Rodney, Ditton's brother, and the two of them had threatened to sweep everyone and everything aside in their pursuit of riches. They had been a good team, awesome and rightly feared, until Rodney's accident removed him from the equation. As a result Vincent Carty had been The Man for years. In his early thirties now, Vincent had a hand in everything. Drugs, protection, prostitution, you name it, Vincent did it, and did it successfully. No one took Vincent on, no one was crazy enough. Folklore had it that even the police were scared of Vincent. They certainly never managed to make anything stick on him, and he had become Brixton's very own Teflon Don. His violence was legendary and his lack of compassion notorious. Tyrone didn't stand a chance.

Rolled and ready, Ditton lit the joint. 'I don't think Jonah would do that. I don't think Jonah would do anything against you for Vincent.'

'Come on,' Tyrone protested. 'Vincent's his older brother. He can get him to do anything, man. Look at Rodney. You'd do whatever he told you to.'

'Maybe,' Ditton conceded, 'but me and Rodney isn't the same as Vincent and Jonah. Don't ask me why, but I know that Jonah wouldn't do that. He's not like that.' He took another puff and exhaled through his nose like a medieval dragon. 'Don't get me wrong. I don't think he'd go against Vincent, but I don't think he'd go against you either.'

Tyrone spread his hands. 'So how do you explain the flat then? There's no way Jerry or Barry would have been involved.'

'Can I say something?' asked Earl. Tyrone shot him a withering look signifying that the question was stupid. 'I also find it kinda hard to believe that Jonah would do that. He's wild, but I don't think he's a bastard.'

Tyrone stood and strode to the window. 'Are you lot crazy? Was it me who told Vincent where to get my gear? Eh? Was it me?'

Despite the seriousness of the situation, Ditton felt the urge to laugh. All of them spoke with south London accents; they had to, that was what they were and where they were from. And as Ditton had never seen Jamaica he didn't try to speak like he had. However, when

Tyrone became upset or excited he sounded as though he had been born within six feet of the Bow bells. Ditton kept a straight face.

'Why not test him?' suggested Earl.

Tyrone turned from the window and looked at his emaciated associate. 'What do you mean? How?'

'You said that you needed to make a pick-up from that guy in Bermondsey, yeah? Derek? Well, send Jonah. If nothing goes wrong, fine. If something happens, well . . .'

Tyrone folded his big arms and stared off into space. 'I don't know,' he said. 'Derek won't be happy. The last time I sent Jonah to pick up from him, he parked in Derek's neighbour's space. When the guy came out to talk to Jonah about it, Jonah broke his fucking nose.'

This time Ditton laughed; he couldn't help it.

'That's not fucking funny, man. Derek had to clear everything out of the flat sharpish 'cos he knew the guy was going to call the police.' Tyrone shook his head. 'Jonah's fucking crazy.'

Earl smiled. 'So are you going to go with that, then?'

Tyrone looked at Ditton. 'D? What do you think, *consigliere*?'

Ditton shrugged and frowned. 'It's your call. It's your gear, your business – and I'm no one's *consigliere*.'

Tyrone grinned at Ditton's scowl. 'All right, we'll go with that. But D, you had better talk to that boy today, show him the score, because I'll be giving him twenty grand cash and he better bring back the fucking goods, or so help me God, I will kill him. And if his brother, big bad Vincent, wants some too, he can fucking have it.'

Ditton nodded but kept silent, even though his head was filled with a myriad of thoughts and emotions. That was his way.

CHAPTER THREE

Vaughn had been sitting in his car in the forecourt of the Keelers' drab block of flats for five minutes, killing time. He allowed himself an hour for each visit but very rarely stayed that long in one house. As he had spent so little time with Mrs Keeler, he had forty-five minutes to kill, and since the next visit was in sight of the Keelers' block, there was no travelling time involved.

He sat in the car with the windows up and lit his second cigarette, having decided that the smell of smoke in his hair and clothes was preferable to that of the Keeler household. Remembering the flat, he scratched himself and wondered if he had time to race home and have a shower. That led him into thinking about what he was having to do for a living, and produced a heavy sigh. Fortunately, before he was able to depress himself further, a small figure came speeding into the flats from the direction of the main road. Vaughn sat up and took note. He turned the radio off and listened for sirens. The figure looked familiar, with his shaven head, oversized school uniform and rucksack trailing behind him as he sprinted. His name was Darryl Buckle, and Vaughn groaned.

Darryl was a twelve-year-old mixed-race boy who exasperated everyone he came into contact with. He had never met his father and Social Services had removed him from the care of his heroin-addict mother. Along with his other problems, Darryl was a compulsive thief who stole the most inexplicable things. The staff at the children's home had no control over him, and case conference after case conference had identified that Vaughn was the only professional Darryl was prepared to relate to in any form.

Vaughn stepped out of the car and waved to the boy, who turned, still running at the same speed, reached the car and tried to yank the passenger door open in a frenzied manner. Vaughn didn't ask any questions, just got back into the car and reached across to open the door for the excited boy. Darryl threw himself in and sank as low down in the seat as possible, all the while glancing across to his left and the entrance to the flats. He didn't say anything, simply nodded at Vaughn and turned again to look out of the window as if expecting marauding hordes to appear on the horizon.

Vaughn was no longer surprised by any of Darryl's behaviour, and calmly asked what was going on.

The boy's small voice matched his small body, and he chirped, 'Nothing. Why?'

As usual when dealing with Darryl, Vaughn was unsure whether to laugh or cry. He decided to laugh.

'*Why?* Because you're supposed to be at school, but I see you here tearing through the flats like a nutter with the devil on his tail. Then when I call you over, you jump into my car without saying a word and stare out of the window as if you're expecting someone to come after you with an axe. That's why.'

Darryl grinned and scratched his head. 'I guess I know what you mean. But it's still nothing.'

'Then why are you still looking out of the window?'

'I like the view, don't I?' snapped Darryl.

Years of abuse had made Darryl one of the most rude and belligerent people Vaughn had met. However, he very rarely directed this hostility at Vaughn, and on the occasions that he did, Vaughn had learnt to overlook the comment or action, rationalising that it was Darryl and that Darryl was special. So Vaughn clenched his jaw and counted to five.

'What's happening with school? You haven't been in for almost three weeks.'

Darryl shrugged and was probably about to produce another insolent reply when a black Rover swung into the flats at speed. The windows were heavily tinted, making it impossible for Vaughn to identify the race or sex of the driver. It wouldn't have been an issue if he hadn't noticed Darryl disappear on to the floor of the car and heard him hiss, 'What's he doing?'

'Who?' asked Vaughn, genuinely surprised.

'Him! In the car. Has he seen me?'

The diminutive boy looked comical, curled into a ball with his head below the glove compartment.

Vaughn tried not to laugh. 'How's he going to see you down there? Who is he, Darryl? Is that why you were running?'

'Is he still there?'

Securing significant answers to any question was always difficult with Darryl. He often seemed to resent having to say anything more than yes or no, and Vaughn had learnt to treat conversations with him like a game of Twenty Questions.

'Why's he after you?'

'He thinks it was me that scratched his car the other day, but it wasn't. Honest. I saw him at the bus stop just now and turned back, then I heard him put his foot down, so I didn't look back.'

'I can't see any scratches on his car,' lied Vaughn. If the owner of the Rover was actually after Darryl for scratching his car, the likelihood was that the boy was guilty. However, Vaughn doubted that the answer would be so simple, and he rarely expected to get the truth from Darryl, who operated on a strict need-to-know basis.

'So who is he?'

'I don't know, some geezer I've seen a few times when I've been on the estate. I don't know his name or anything. He's just a face.'

'All right,' suggested Vaughn playfully. 'Why don't we just get out of the car, go and talk to him and sort this out?'

Darryl grabbed Vaughn's leg and hissed, 'No! He can't see me. I don't want to sort anything. OK?'

The Rover idled past Vaughn's battered old Renault and although Vaughn couldn't see inside, he knew the driver was looking straight at him. Despite himself, he felt slightly unnerved and was pleased when the car reversed and drove out of the flats at speed.

'You can get up off the floor now,' offered Vaughn. 'He's gone.'

Darryl rose warily and said without a hint of humour, 'Good. This car's a state. When was the last time you cleaned in here?'

Although he had to agree with the boy, Vaughn again counted to five before turning the key in the ignition.

'Where're we going then?' asked Darryl.

'I'm going to work. You're going to school. I'm taking you. Put your seat belt on.'

'You can't do that,' said Darryl with an impish grin that belied the distressed state he had just been in. 'That's kidnapping, that is. You're abducting me.'

Vaughn checked his mirrors, put the car into gear and pulled off. 'Well, how about I chase down that Rover and let him abduct you?'

Vaughn thought it odd that Darryl didn't reply with some kind of wisecrack. Instead he sighed, frowned and played absent-mindedly with the lapel of his blazer. He must be worried, thought Vaughn, but there was no point in pursuing the reason. If Darryl hadn't volunteered the information already, he wasn't likely to now.

Three minutes later Vaughn swung the car in

through the gates of the school car park. Out of the corner of his eye, he saw Darryl shrink at the sight of the four-storeyed expanse of glass that made up his school. Suddenly he felt compassionate, a bad idea for someone in his profession. He applied the hand-brake and turned to Darryl, but before he had a chance to speak, his client declared, 'You know I'm not going to go, don't you?'

Vaughn turned the engine off, and they sat there for five minutes talking about school and why Darryl had such a problem with it. Eventually the child reluctantly agreed that he would give it a try, but wasn't going to make any promises. Vaughn didn't expect any.

'Do me a favour then, Vaughn,' asked Darryl as he got out of the car. 'Look after this for me?' He had taken a video out of his bag and held it under Vaughn's nose.

Vaughn was wary. Experience with Darryl had taught him to be. 'What is it?'

'A video, of course.'

'I can see that, can't I? I meant what's on it?'

The boy shrugged, suddenly looking much younger than his twelve years. 'This and that. Music and stuff.'

Vaughn was still wary. 'Why do you want me to look after it?'

'You know what it's like in here,' said Darryl, motioning behind him towards the double glass doors of the school entrance. 'Them Year Elevens will take it off me, or it'll get stolen or something.'

Vaughn raised a sceptical eyebrow, finding it hard to

imagine Darryl allowing anyone to take anything from him without a lot of hassle. He didn't comment. He wanted Darryl in school as soon as possible. 'So why did you bring it with you, then?'

Darryl sighed and grinned. 'I wasn't coming to school, was I?'

Vaughn couldn't help laughing as he took the video Darryl had wrapped in a carrier bag and stuffed it underneath the front passenger seat. 'So how are you going to get it back?' he asked.

Darryl shrugged. 'I can get someone to phone your office. Or if that doesn't work, I'll just stay away from school again and get you to come looking for me.'

Vaughn had to concede that the boy's logic was sound. He got out of the car and pushed Darryl playfully but forcefully towards the school doors. Darryl turned around in good humour and told Vaughn to behave. Vaughn lifted him off the ground and placed him in front of the doors. Feeling strangely paternal, he prepared to watch Darryl walk slowly into school, wait for someone in the office to buzz him through the security doors, and disappear into the bowels of the building. Instead, the boy turned around, shouted, 'I've just got to go to the shop,' and bolted past Vaughn and back out through the school gates.

As he pulled out of the car park and waited for a gap in the traffic, Vaughn asked himself why he had ever believed that he would get Darryl into school that easily. He resolved that later that afternoon he would return to check if the kid had attended, and if he hadn't, he would hunt him down tomorrow and give him a piece of his mind.

CHAPTER FOUR

The three men sat in the car in the car park of the supermarket, a couple of hundred metres from Lambeth Town Hall. Two of the men sat in the front and one in the back. All three were silent and looked straight ahead until the man in the back spoke. He was black, about medium height, with a powerful chest and shoulders that seemed to take up most of the back seat of the car. He was dressed casually, but expensively.

The two men in the front were both white. The driver was in his late twenties. His build was big, but in a loose, unfit way. He sat with his hands resting on the wheel, continually fiddling with the big Rolex Oyster on his wrist. It looked new, real and cherished. Next to the driver was an older man in his early fifties. He was big also, but extremely tall, and had his seat so far back that the black man in the back seat had to sit behind the driver. The tall man had thick black hair, and a craggy, rugged face with a large hooked nose. His dark hooded eyes were stationed below prominent brows that were pure black despite the flecks of grey in his hair. He also had a small scar on his chin. It was him that broke the silence. 'Well, what can I do for you?' he asked in a deep, resonant voice. 'You sounded like it was pretty urgent.'

The driver continued fiddling with his watch and looking out of the window at the early shoppers.

'What can you do for me?' asked the black guy, his lip curling with sarcasm. 'You can start with what you *said* you were going to do. What happened to "You scratch my back and I scratch yours?" I feel like I'm doing all the scratching, and that wasn't the deal.'

The passenger was silent for a second as though thinking carefully about what he wanted to say. 'That's hardly the case, is it? Anyway, did you mean the young bloke we talked about last time?'

'Exactly. So what's happening about it?'

'Unfortunately, he's smart. It's not as easy as you think it is.'

'You said that you would – you could. Now I'm expecting you to stick to your side of the deal.'

The tall man reached up and turned the rear-view mirror towards him so that he could make eye contact. 'And if I don't?' he asked quietly. 'What then?'

Without hesitation, the black man looked directly into the mirror and answered, 'Then there's going to be at least one body rolling around soon with a nine-millimetre hole in its head.'

'You can't do that, son,' the passenger declared with a chuckle. 'That would be very bad for everybody. And it's because you were talking about doing that last time that I agreed to do it my way. Now calm down, stop being hysterical, and let's work something out.'

The black guy smiled and stroked his dusting of beard. 'Firstly,' he said, 'I'm not your fucking son. Secondly, I am very calm. A long, long way from being fucking hysterical. Thirdly, who says the body I was talking about will be his? How do you know I wasn't talking about yours?'

The tall man turned to the driver, who shrugged, breathed on the face of his watch and gave it a brisk polish. 'Did you hear that, Dave?' the passenger asked. 'Do you think he's threatening me?'

Dave shrugged again. 'Dunno, boss. I heard something, but I don't know what it was.'

'I think he was,' continued the tall man, removing a speck of something from his lapel. 'But I'll ignore it. The competition's getting to him, it can be a bit of a strain.'

'The only strain comes from people who don't stick to what they say they're going to do,' said the black man. 'Now, I might be a lot of things, but if I say I'm going to do something, that's what I do. This thing's got nothing to do with the competition. It's personal now, and I will sort it with or without you. Understand?'

The black man's head turned sharply to look out of the window to his right. 'Hold on,' he said quickly. 'I've seen someone I need to talk to. I'll be back.' He didn't wait for acknowledgement as he stepped out of the car to stand twenty metres away, awaiting the arrival of someone he had hailed. The two remaining occupants of the car watched him talking to a younger, slim black man in his mid twenties.

'He's a bit full of himself, ain't he, boss?' asked Dave.

His companion nodded and growled, 'He's got a right to be. He's top dog round here. Earned it too.'

'Fair enough, but talking to you like that, it's not on. I was in two minds about getting out and putting one on him.'

The older man chuckled and lit a cigarette. He offered one to the driver, who declined with a wave of his hand. 'I appreciate the gesture, Dave, but he would have probably had your head off before you touched him. He's vicious.'

Dave watched with more interest now, although he refused to believe that the black guy could have had him. Dave refused to believe that any black bastard could have him; they were all mouth and arm-waving. In his twenty-eight years alive in this great country he had never met a wog who could row, really go for it, fist to fist. As far as he was concerned they were nothing if they weren't part of a mob or armed with shooters or knives.

The conversation outside the car was brief, and the black guy sauntered back and eased himself into the car. 'So where were we?' he asked. 'Weren't you about to sort something out?'

The tall man nodded and stroked the scar on his chin. 'All right, I'll have a look at him this week, and if I get the opportunity I'll have a little chat with him.'

'You've got to be joking. Little chat?' said the black guy in disbelief. 'Fuck little chats. I'm after the same arrangement as last time.'

The tall man frowned. 'Which time?'

'The delivery at the factory.'

No longer content with eye contact via the mirror, the older man turned around quickly. 'Now hold on a minute. You've got to be joking. That can't happen again. Look at the stink it caused then. If it happened again there'd be hell to pay.'

The black man shrugged. 'Fair enough, but that's what I was expecting, that's what I was talking about. So now I'm going to have to do it my way, which is going to be messy, you get me? It's going to cause you headaches and it's going to be the end of our business dealings. If that's how you want it, fine. But don't try and come after me from any angle, because I can and will hang you in a number of ways. Don't ever forget that. Remember, apart from everything else, I know all about your disgusting extramarital tastes.'

He opened the door and was about to step out when the older man halted him, seemingly eager to placate him.

'Hold on, what's your rush? I suppose we could manage the delivery again. It might be a bit tricky, but we should be able to do it. But you've got to do your bit properly. No half-arsed job like last time. OK?'

'No problem. This week?'

'Christ! You're pushing it now,' exploded the big

man. 'I don't know about this week, that'll leave me short of time.'

The black guy put one foot out of the car and said, 'It's only Monday; you've got six days to sort it out, nonce. Call me to let me know when.'

At about the same time, in a council flat off Loughborough Road, Brixton, Jonah Carty's sleep was being disturbed. His first thought was that someone was shooting at him, and he tossed and bucked in the bed as he fired a return fusillade at his dream assailants. Suddenly he sat bolt upright, forcing himself awake, and tried to assemble his sleep-muddled thoughts. The shots were still reverberating around his head, but he didn't realise what was happening until three more loud knocks resounded along the passage to his bedroom.

Jonah rubbed his eyes, yawned and stretched, hard, then cursed, and swung himself out of bed, snatching the little .22 from the bedside cabinet as he padded barefoot out to the front door. He had been out at a club the night before with Cannibal and some of the others, and had only managed to get to bed at nine thirty in the morning. Now, three hours later, some bastard was banging on his door trying to wake the dead. If it was that bitch from next door, to complain about the music he had been playing when he came in, he might have to smack her and deal with the boyfriend she had been threatening him with.

Outside on the balcony, Ditton was about to knock

again when he detected movement from inside the house. He wondered how many times he had stood outside this door in the last ten years. Too many. Jonah still lived in the same flat that he had lived in with his family as a child. After the second riots, in '85, his parents had found enough money to join the mass exodus from Brixton and buy a small cottage in Thornton Heath, complete with double glazing, central heating and a little paved yard at the back. They took Jonah, the youngest, and his older siblings Esther and Saul to live with them. But Jonah caused so much grief and got into so much trouble that they sent him back to live in the flat with his older brother Vincent. If he was wild before he left, he became totally uncontrollable once he moved back.

Jonah yanked the door open with a snarl, and one hand behind his back holding the pistol. Ditton pointed to the small television screen next to the door that allowed each occupant in the block to see who was outside their front door. 'You're supposed to ask who it is, or at least use that screen to have a look.' The blocks had recently been spruced up but they remained run down and the occupants as impoverished as ever.

Jonah stepped back, opening the door wider, and grimaced while rubbing his eyes. In a croaky, still-asleep voice he said, 'It's more exciting this way, like Russian roulette, *Deer Hunter* and that shit, you get me? There's no point doing things the sensible way. It's too boring.'

Ditton stepped in shaking his head, noting that the

last statement just about summed Jonah up. 'You're one sick guy, you know that? And you'd better go and wash that sleep off your face. That stuff's caked on, man.'

Ditton watched Jonah amble off to the bathroom, and marvelled at how many people were terrified by him. The number of people who would rejoice if they heard that Jonah had suffered a gruesome death did not square with the Jonah that Ditton had known for so long. It was roughly ten years earlier that he had been at home in his room minding his own business when a car had hooted outside. Rodney had gone out to investigate. That was how it always was then. People coming up to see Rodney, business and plans being conducted on the street. Everyone wanted to know Rodney Ditton then. Rodney had called up to him to come down and meet somebody; obediently he did, and met Jonah.

Actually, he met Vincent first. Vincent Carty had parked his brand new Golf GTi outside the house and was sitting on the bonnet speaking with Rodney. Ditton knew who Vincent was; everybody knew who Vincent was, just as they all knew Rodney. They were renowned even then. Vincent and Ditton had nodded to each other, and Rodney had explained that Vincent's younger brother was starting at Tulse Hill School. Vincent wanted someone to keep an eye on him, make sure he got off to a good start. Gary Ditton had been chosen. He didn't mind, he would have done anything Rodney asked, but it wasn't until he had agreed that Ditton actually saw Jonah sitting in the car and wondered what he had got himself into. The boy was sitting in the passenger seat, innocently licking an ice lolly, and he looked *bad*. Not mischievous or naughty, not roguish, but *bad*. There was no real reason for Ditton to come to that conclusion; just a feeling, but a strong one. Jonah had been polite and respectful when the introductions were made, but Ditton sensed another side to the boy that was potentially much more disagreeable. Time had proved how perceptive the fifteen-year-old Ditton was.

'And Jonah . . .'

Jonah stopped and turned just before entering the bathroom. 'What?'

'I don't think you need the gun.'

Vaughn parked the car and began the five-minute walk to the office. A woman came out of a newsagent's as he was passing, and stepped into his path. He stopped abruptly, to prevent a collision, and noticed the woman clutch her handbag and eye him suspiciously. Even after years of experiencing the same thing it still angered him. The woman apologised, reluctantly, and tottered off on her heels with Vaughn watching from behind. She was in her thirties, had a decent figure, and for a moment Vaughn found his mind wandering. He reined in his imagination quickly, annoyed that he had done it again, dismayed at the fact that he was paying too much attention to white women on the street, on television, anywhere. He couldn't understand why. It was beginning to concern him. What was worse was that most of them he didn't even find attractive. The mere fact that they were white seemed to make his head turn involuntarily.

It was confusing because he had Courtney, his beautiful, intelligent and creative Nubian princess who adored him. Consequently, he couldn't for the life of him understand why he kept looking at these women who couldn't have held a flame to her. But he did keep looking. It terrified him.

As he walked the last few yards to the office and buzzed himself in through the first security door, Vaughn wondered how much of it had to do with Janine, a work colleague. Half of him hoped she was in the office; the other half prayed that she wasn't. Out of the blue Janine had propositioned him. She'd made it plain that she knew about Courtney, but that it was no obstacle to them getting together and having a good time. Vaughn had choked so hard on his tea that Janine had been forced to bang his back to save him.

Vaughn hadn't managed to give her an answer – he hadn't known what to say. Deep down he wanted to take her up on her offer, that was obvious even to him, but how could he? There was Courtney to think about, and at the end of the day, Janine was white. So he had muddled along trying to avoid her but at the same time wanting to see her. And whenever they did meet she would say, 'I'm still waiting for an answer,' and he would smile weakly and shrug, annoyed at himself for being so pathetic, but at the same time trying to convince himself that he was doing the right thing. Again, deep down he knew that the right thing would have been to tell her that there was no way they could get together. He was in a loving relationship and had no intention of doing anything to jeopardise it. He didn't manage that either.

Janine was the first person Vaughn saw as he let himself in through the security door. She was coming out of the photocopying room and crossing the passage to the kitchen. She winked and held the door open for him, saying that the urn had just boiled.

Janine was about average height, with a slim but curvaceous figure. There was nothing flat on her, and Vaughn reflected that for a white girl she even had a reasonable behind. Her strong face bordered on stunning, she dressed with style and carried herself well, but at the end of the day she should have been no match for Courtney. Vaughn really couldn't understand the attraction.

'I'm still waiting for your answer,' said Janine mischievously.

Vaughn gave her a pained smile and asked, 'What was the question again?'

She shook her head. 'I know you haven't forgotten.'

'No, I haven't,' admitted Vaughn.

'I can be patient.'

Vaughn nodded graciously. 'They say that it's a virtue—'

'But not forever,' interrupted Janine. 'Everyone's patience has its limits.' And with that she switched out of the room, her shiny gold skirt catching the light and making her behind shimmer and glitter like something precious.

Back in the office he tried to ignore Janine as he told Sue, his team leader, about his visit to the Keelers' and his meeting with Darryl. Sue sat back, tossed her long, curly brown hair over her shoulders and proceeded to chew a biro to pieces while recommending that Vaughn contact the Keelers' social worker and pass on his concerns. There was little else he could do. Sue wasn't an admirer of Martin Green, the social worker in question, and as Vaughn got on well with Martin he was always amused to hear her talk about him with evident distaste.

Every now and then, Janine would pass Vaughn's desk on her way to her files or the fax. Whenever she did, Vaughn felt pangs akin to a nicotine craving. It got so bad that he switched off his computer, packed his bag and almost ran out of the office far earlier than he needed to. As he left, Sue reminded him that one of the councillors on the education committee would be sitting in on their staff meeting the next morning, and that it would be politic for him to do all he could to attend. He nodded, saw Janine wink again, and fled.

Milk's housing association fuck-pad comprised three bedrooms, communal kitchen and bathroom, and a large living room. Because Milk had been the first one to move in after the place had been refurbished, and because of the layout, the living room was effectively his. Normally Milk could tolerate the place and the other two occupants – droopy-shouldered, skulking, furtive Byron upstairs, and good-time girl Jackie below.

When she first moved in Milk had seen Jackie bending and stretching in front of the washing machine and knew she was as supple as a sapling. He had been tempted to try his luck but thought better of it; it was too close to home even for him. Apart from that, the succession of guys she had trooping in and out of her room was frightening. Milk often had to stop and ask himself if the girl was whoring in there, especially as he didn't see her in any kind of gainful employment, but always raving and dressed to the nines.

As he glanced in at the dirty kitchen Milk wondered if there was any scope in bribing his housing officer to jump the queue and get him his flat early. Everyone had their price. Having lost his appetite, he turned back from the kitchen and decided he would sleep for a couple of hours. But just as he was kicking off his trainers and tugging at his jeans, his mobile phone erupted. He checked the number – his mother. After speaking, Milk pulled his clothes back on in preparation to take his mum shopping. No problem, he'd take her to the supermarket, then back home and be fed properly there. Although Milk was trim and fit, he loved to eat. It was one of the few things that could keep him quiet.

Jackie happened to drift half-naked out of her room as Milk was on his way down the stairs and out of the house. She seemed determined to have a conversation, even though her heaving chest appeared to have a life of its own and was eager to escape her loose gown. To Jackie's obvious dismay Milk concluded the chat as quickly as possible; her face made it clear that she felt snubbed. That was all good to Milk. He couldn't have the girl thinking he was one of those young boys turned foolish by the sight of a bare breast, especially one suckled as often as hers by all those guys with rough lips.

Milk drove at breakneck speed from Balham to Tulse Hill, accompanied by a big bass-line from the tube in the boot of the car. He couldn't drive any other way; fast and loud, or not at all. To Milk, driving was about fun, and fun had to include music. In fact, as far as Milk was concerned, everything had to include music. He arrived at his mum's flat, the house in which he had grown up, lost his virginity, been arrested and returned to by police on many occasions. He had spent every Christmas of his life in that flat. It was his only home and he still called it that.

It was full of good memories, but there were equally as many bad ones. Mixed with those bad memories, though, were recollections of his mother's protection, direction and encouragement. Milk had always taken the brunt of his father's violence, although the others suffered occasionally. He didn't know why it happened, but he accepted it. A punch or a kick could only hurt so much, and the pain would leave eventually. And at the end of the day, if it meant that his mother was spared, it was for the best. The number of times Milk had thought about killing his father were too many to remember. He hated the man and knew that he would never let anybody abuse him again. Milk wasn't a psychopath, and could take a joke as well as the next man. But anybody foolish enough to overstep the mark had to be put straight, firmly and quickly.

When Milk arrived, breakfast was waiting and he stood in the tiny old-fashioned kitchen lapping up the saltfish and dumplings that no one could cook like his mother did.

Mrs Kerr answered the phone and Milk could tell that something wasn't right, from her tone and the frown that had set into her forehead like artex ripples on a ceiling. He raised an eyebrow for an indication of the concern.

'Shane's been excluded from school, and Sandra wants to know if you can take her up there to collect him.'

'Yeah,' Milk mumbled around a mouthful of saltfish. 'When we get back from shopping I'll run her up there. What's he done?'

Mrs Kerr held up a quieting hand as only mothers can, and continued talking to her daughter. 'But that's not like him, is it? . . . He did what? Never! Not Shane.' It went on like that for a while until Mrs Kerr snorted, 'Hunnhh!' and replaced the receiver. She turned to Milk. 'Your nephew's gone mad. He had a fight with his friend and started attacking teachers with his hands and feet when they tried to break it up. He kicked one teacher in her stomach, and slapped another one in the face.'

Milk's nine-year-old nephew was his mother's favourite grandchild, as to everyone's surprise Milk was still childless. Shane was a beautiful boy with thick, shiny eyebrows, long eyelashes and an intelligent smile. In that sense he reminded Milk of himself, but he was also a quiet, shy boy who rarely raised his voice or made demands – unlike Milk. Shane was the last child Milk or his mother would have expected to attack a teacher.

Milk looked up from his plate, astonished. 'Yeah? That's my boy. Nice one!'

'What you talking about? Eh?' snapped Mrs Kerr. 'You put ideas in his head? Is it you make him do this?'

Milk spread his hands in supplication. 'Nothing to do with me, Mummy, but I know I'm gonna get blamed anyway, I usually do. I don't know what you lot would do without me to blame for everything.'

All Mrs Kerr managed was another 'Hunnhh!' She was still trying to understand her grandson's out-of-character behaviour.

'Any more dumplings?' asked Milk.

CHAPTER FIVE

Sandra had left work and was already there when they got back to the flats. At thirty-seven she had experienced much more than she would have chosen. She had two children, an estranged nineteen-year-old daughter and Shane, her nine-year-old son. She had been through a divorce, a breakdown, borderline alcoholism and other troubles: redundancy, homelessness, domestic violence. Sandra had been a beauty in her younger years and although there were still signs of how stunning she had been, time combined with hardship had encouraged premature lines and an air of weariness that would never leave her. She was still slim and mobile, but her dynamism and confidence had been sapped. Her face and soul had hardened, and her once radiant, heart-stopping smile was now a rarity.

Milk noticed the brandy straight away. Sandra drained the glass and immediately turned her back to pour another, pausing to toss Milk a limp-wristed wave. The glass set alarm bells ringing in Milk's head, but the last time he had made a comment about her drinking, she had nearly bitten his head off, asking who the hell he thought he was? Her father?

'You ready then?' asked Milk.

Sandra nodded and finished her drink. She said, 'Bye, Daddy,' as she passed her father, who had returned from the betting shop, and 'Bye, Mummy,' as she squeezed past her mother in the small, dark passage. Milk ignored his father, looked at his mother and shrugged before following Sandra out of the front door and on to the balcony.

Milk's phone rang twice during the journey. The first call was from an employee, Theo, who Milk dealt with quickly and brusquely so that Theo didn't have time to annoy him. The second call made Milk smile. He had been after this girl for years, bumping into her every now and then, each time politely demanding to know when she was going to relent and allow herself to enjoy him. Milk couldn't understand how she had resisted, but then Milk found it hard to understand how any girl could resist him. Now she had phoned and made her change of heart clear. She wanted to see him as soon as possible and was ready to enjoy all he had to offer. Milk hadn't realised that she could talk that way, but he liked it and drove even faster.

The secretary buzzed them in through the school gates, and upon entering the building they saw Shane immediately, sitting in his electric-blue puffa jacket and woollen Chicago Bulls hat, swinging his legs, a disconsolate look on his face. Catching sight of his mother and uncle didn't improve his expression. He looked thoroughly miserable. Not worried or apprehensive, just miserable. Milk couldn't ever recall seeing his nephew like that. Shane was quiet and low-key, rarely smiling or laughing, as though he had forgotten how, but there was always a light in his eye that suggested he could remember, with help.

Upon seeing Milk and Sandra, the secretary notified the head teacher, who called them into her office and asked them to be seated. Milk declined and stood with a hand on Shane's shoulder while Mrs Nimmons, a tall, very slim woman in her late forties, with a greying blonde bob and pinched mouth and nose, recounted that Shane had gone wild, kicking and punching. Although it was very unlike Shane, Mrs Nimmons explained, she had no option but to exclude him for the rest of the week. Sandra sat through it all, nodding impassively, while Milk was enjoying the unique experience of being in a head teacher's office and not being in trouble himself.

Once Mrs Nimmons had outlined that Shane wasn't to return to school that week, she handed Sandra a pack of work and turning to the boy said, 'Well, Shane, I hope that you spend this week at home thinking and reflecting on what you did today. There's no place for that sort of behaviour in our school, and I hope that by next Monday you're ready to return with a good attitude and apologise to the pupils and teachers concerned.'

Shane didn't answer and Milk had to bite his tongue. He wasn't a teacher, he didn't work with kids, but he could see that there was something wrong here. Or was it that she thought this was how black families were? All black boys violent and out of control, their mothers morose and distant. Sandra was pissing him off as well. Couldn't she open her mouth and say something? Support her son like a mother was supposed to do?

Mrs Kerr knew something was wrong when the three of them trooped in silently. Her son was never quiet; now he was just about managing to answer direct questions. Shane walked into the living room and sat down. Sandra mumbled something about going back to work and her mother looking after Shane, then left the flat. Milk shook his head and sucked his teeth.

'Marcus, why don't you go and give her a lift?' suggested Mrs Kerr.

Milk shook his head. 'No. She's only going to Brixton. She can walk, or get the bus.'

Mrs Kerr didn't force the issue.

The bass was coursing through Ditton's chest, and the treble threatened to seriously damage his eardrums. Realising that Ditton wanted to talk, Jonah had set a bath and put on some music to listen to while he washed. The massive JAMO speakers meant that Jonah was able to hear and feel the music all the way down the corridor, even with the bathroom door closed, while Ditton stayed in the room and suffered. It wasn't until he reached the amplifier and turned the volume down that Ditton heard the banging on the wall from the flat next door. He understood and sympathised completely. The noise he had to put up with at home was bad, but he could never live next door to Jonah.

'What did you turn it down for?' asked Jonah in anguish, exiting the bathroom wrapped in a towel. 'I was listening to that.'

While Jonah dressed, Ditton stood at the window rolling a joint and looking north-east at the London skyline. It was something to do while he decided how to tell Jonah what had to be told. Jonah didn't always respond well to criticism or suggestions and there was a danger that he could end up confronting Tyrone. Ditton knew he had to be selective with what he told Jonah. It would be best for everybody. Jonah was typical of a disinherited generation, who had nothing and therefore had nothing to give. The only things the boy owned were his body, his reputation and his life. He used the first, worked hard on the second and as a result was reckless with the third. To guys like Jonah there was no point living if you were going to let people fuck you like a pussy.

The diminutive youth came back into the room and picked up the smoking joint from the ashtray, took a lug and fell into the tatty old orange-brown sofa that his parents had probably broken themselves to buy in the seventies. 'So what's up then? What brings you here so early?'

Ditton puffed out his cheeks, scratched his head and began. He didn't talk about Tyrone's death threats, or Tyrone's suspicion-cum-accusation that Jonah was working with his brother Vincent against Tyrone. He chose not to mention Tyrone's opinion of Jonah's wildness. Ditton simply informed Jonah that Tyrone was concerned about his attitude and professionalism, and was wondering whether the time had come for them to part company. He didn't want to, but if things continued the way they were, what with this Kevin Hill feud appearing to escalate, Tyrone might have to give some serious thought to distancing himself from Jonah.

Jonah was silent for a moment, then sat forward and asked, 'What's he really saying? I ain't stupid. What's he really saying?'

Ditton shrugged. 'That's about it. He wants you to pick up from some guy called Derek, is it? Yeah, tomorrow. And then see how things go. He just wants you to calm down a bit, for everybody's sake.'

Jonah nodded, but Ditton could see that he wasn't satisfied with the explanation. He was too quiet, too thoughtful, and that was always dangerous with Jonah, who, as he rightly said, was not stupid.

'So what is the situation with you and Kevin Hill?'

Jonah shrugged. 'He's a wanker. He reckons he wants to do me 'cos I broke a champagne bottle on his head at some rave, and his boys had to carry him out. What else can I say?'

Ditton smiled at Jonah's description of the current state of affairs. It was typically simplistic, the bare essentials. Apparently, Jonah and some of his boys had been at the club having a good time, terrorising girls, drinking champagne like it was going out of fashion and ingesting copious amounts of drugs. Jonah had been off his face, which wasn't unusual for him, and he had started talking with Kevin Hill, a guy from Peckham that he had done business with in the past. Something silly had been said, Kevin had been dismissive but not intentionally disrespectful, and Jonah, being Jonah, had taken exception. He'd hit Kevin once, with a bottle of champagne that had happened to be in his hand, and Kevin went down like a rag doll. Reports said that Kevin's people were too concerned about his injuries to consider taking retribution at the time, and that Jonah had had enough people with him to make it unwise. However, it was unlikely that it would be left like that. Kevin Hill had face to save.

'Have you seen him since?'

'A couple of times. He ain't tried nothing. I ain't even sure that he wants to, it's probably all hype. You know how it goes.'

Ditton sighed and took a puff. He knew all too well how it went and wasn't keen to be involved again. But if Jonah got himself into a major problem Ditton would have to be involved. His role of protector and mentor to Vincent's younger brother was still in place ten years after it had started, but now it was different. Now the boys had been through so much together Jonah was like family.

Ditton dropped the joint in the ashtray. 'So you're going to be calm tomorrow and deal with this collection and delivery properly. Yeah?'

Jonah smiled and said, 'I'm always calm.'

Ditton thought, yeah, right. Calm as a Caribbean cove in the middle of a hurricane.

Jonah followed him out on to the balcony and they stood there chatting for a while, Jonah punctuating each sentence by sending a gobful of spit over the balcony to splatter on the tarmac below. Music boomed out of the front door behind them, and echoed across the estate to mingle with the traffic and sirens in the distance. Ditton motioned over his shoulder and couldn't help asking, 'But what about the neighbours? Don't they have anything to say about the music?'

Jonah spat over the balcony again, managing to hit the windscreen of a red Fiesta parked directly below, and informing Ditton that the car belonged to 'the bitch next door'. 'What can they say, eh? The bitch has come round a couple of times and threatened me with her boyfriend, but there's been no sign of him yet. Sometimes she bangs on the walls and shit like that, but fuck her, I pay my rent, or at least the benefit does!'

'So this one with the boyfriend. You *ever* seen him?'

'Nah, he probably don't exist, or if he does he's a wanker. She's been going on for years and he still ain't shown up.'

'Maybe he's just got patience.'

'Maybe he's got no balls.'

Ditton shook his head in exasperation. 'Yeah, well just make sure you don't have to find out.'

* * *

Ditton trotted down the stairs, concerned about the Jonah, Tyrone and Vincent situation. Too many hot-heads in conflict wasn't desirable, but he had done what he said he would, up to a point. Jonah appeared to have taken it reasonably well, considering. Ditton had learned a long time ago that trying to please everybody was impossible, so his strategy was to try not to upset anybody. Sometimes it worked, other times it didn't, but that couldn't be helped. He did his best.

As he got to the last flight of stairs a short, stocky white man in his early thirties, with cropped fair hair, rounded the corner below and began to climb. He looked up at Ditton, who at first only saw a white guy in jeans, trainers and a light jacket. There was nothing special about that, they were everywhere, even Brixton. But by the time Ditton had taken that information in, he saw the man's eyes narrow as if with suspicion. Ditton didn't recognise him and didn't want trouble, so he kept on walking.

Just as they were about to pass each other, the white guy raised his head, stared directly at Ditton and frowned. 'So it's like that now, is it? Too grown up to say hello to me?'

Ditton stopped, puzzled, and almost stooped to look at the short man closely, purely to convince himself that the guy was either genuinely mistaken, or mad. But there was something familiar about him. The hair was shorter, the face looked older, and he was definitely bigger, the chest looking as though it had performed countless bench presses, but . . . 'Nash! It *is* you!' exclaimed Ditton in surprise.

Jimmy Nash smiled a boyish smile and laughed while Ditton apologised profusely for not recognising him. Nash explained that it had been at least five years since they last saw each other. His sentence for armed robbery had been eight but having behaved himself he had got out in five.

'So when? How long you actually been out?'

'Four weeks and three days, to be precise. Seems like a lot fucking longer than that, I promise you.'

Ditton knew Nash through Rodney. Nash and Rodney had knocked about when they were younger, and remained close until Nash was put away for a vicious post office robbery in which a cashier had his skull fractured by the butt of a sawn-off shotgun, and another had to have pellets removed from her back after a warning shot had gone astray. Nash was a nutter, and notorious. Once Ditton had asked his brother what a psycho actually was, Rodney had simply said, 'Nash,' and Ditton had understood instantly and completely.

As they stood there chatting, Nash eager to find out how the youngster had turned out, what he was doing, how he was earning, Ditton found it funny that someone as charming and harmless-looking as Nash could jump on the back of a six-foot-three monster and chew his ear off, and that was before Tyson v. Holyfield.

At the mention of 'Brown', Nash whistled and nodded appreciatively. 'Earning bundles, I bet?'

'Enough, I suppose,' answered Ditton with a smile. 'So what are you doing here then?' he asked.

Nash grinned and his trademark cracked upper incisor made him look about fifteen years old. Ditton wondered why he didn't get it fixed, it was a give-away for identification. 'I live here, don't I? The missus has got a flat up there.' Nash motioned up the stairs with his head. 'It ain't all that, but it's somewhere, innit?'

'Better than a lot of places, believe me.'

Nash nodded. 'Neighbours are full of shit, but that's life I suppose, innit? We've got one set who spend half the night either fighting or fucking, I ain't sure which one makes more noise. There's a sod who plays his music so loud he must think he's running a fucking sound system in Jamaica, and there's a couple of old dears, Alf and Maisie, who keep knocking on the door for a chat. The missus gave 'em the time of day, and now they expect me to as well. Bollocks, innit? It's a bit like being banged up really, having to deal with all sorts of sorry bastards. Only difference is that I lock myself in at night.'

Nash had lost none of his humour being inside. He had become more cynical, but he was still as funny.

In an instant, Nash's face changed and became solemn. He frowned and asked, 'So how's Rodney? I heard what happened from inside.'

Automatically, Ditton became sober too. It had been five years now, but the pain was still intense. He shrugged. 'What can I say? He's not the Rodney he used to be, but he's my brother.'

Nash hesitated as if trying to find the right words so as not to cause offence. 'But what's he like? What I mean is—'

Ditton nodded. 'It's all right, I know what you mean. He's not a total vegetable or anything like that. He can talk and understand; he's just in his own world most of the time, and he's got pills that slow him down a bit. But apart from that, I suppose he's all right.'

Nash looked thoughtful. 'I'm sorry about that. There's a few things I was hoping to find out from him, things from before I went inside. Things to do with me getting sent-down, know what I mean? Do you think he'd be able to remember back then?'

Ditton shrugged. 'I really don't know.' Although he didn't want anybody to treat Rodney like a charity case, he expected a bit more tact than Nash was showing.

'I wouldn't mind having a chat with him. Are you all in the same place, off Tulse Hill?'

Ditton was picking up bad vibes. Nash didn't sound concerned about Rodney or interested in his welfare; he only seemed interested in obtaining information. 'No, we've all split up since then,' he lied. 'But I'll be seeing him later. Give me a number, and I'll see if I can get him to call you.'

Nash flicked Ditton a probing look. Ditton returned it, unflinching. If Nash didn't believe Ditton's reply, he wasn't ready to pursue it. 'Give me yours as well, then. I might want to do a bit of Brown business with you this week. Can that happen?'

'No problem,' said Ditton.

They exchanged numbers and parted, shaking hands. 'Good to see you again, Nash.'

Nash grinned and nodded. 'I'm glad I bumped into you, stopped me having to come looking. It's better that way, innit?'

Ditton didn't understand Nash's statement, but smiled and shrugged. 'I suppose so,' he said, unsure. He stood for a moment watching Nash walk away up the stairs. Ditton hadn't woken in the best frame of mind, the dream saw to that, but it seemed that everything he had encountered so far was doing its damnedest to make sure his mood didn't improve.

CHAPTER SIX

The final bars of the theme tune of the lunchtime news were escaping from Rodney's room upstairs, so Ditton went straight into the kitchen.

Just as he'd finished unpacking the bags of shopping and put the kettle on, Ditton heard someone trying to open the front door, unsuccessfully, scratching and knocking the key plate. He wasn't alarmed and waited a while longer until he could take it no more and strode down the passage to yank the door open. He was faced by a small, dark, wiry black man, who was in his late fifties but could have passed for older. He wore brown trousers and a black blazer over a grey shirt and blue tank top. A little homburg sat perched at a rakish angle atop his head. All the clothing had seen better and cleaner days, as had the man.

Ditton looked into his father's unseeing, bloodshot eyes and stepped back to admit him. The old man tottered into the house, supporting himself on the wall, almost dislodging a cheap ornamental crucifix. He turned to speak to his son. Ditton swayed back, a reflex action designed to protect himself from the noxious alcohol fumes his father exuded, and because, although Mr Ditton was going to lean forward conspiratorially, he was bound to shout.

Ditton closed the front door and tried to slide past his father and up the stairs, but the drunkard caught his arm and beckoned him closer, breathing heavily and blinking involuntarily while trying to focus. 'Gary, you got a tenner for me?' he slurred. 'Eh?'

Ditton had learned long ago that there was no point in refusing to give his father money. Once Ditton had seen him stop a man on the street and ask him for change to make up enough for a Special Brew. Ditton had been so mad, he had pushed his father into the car and driven him home, finding out later that the old man did it regularly, was known for it, and was becoming one of those old drinkers that kids crossed the road to avoid.

He reached into his pocket and produced a twenty-pound note. It was the smallest he had, so he handed it to his father, who mumbled his thanks.

'You's a good boy. Good boy, not like the other one, no way! Not like the other one at all.'

Ditton released himself from his father's claw-like grip, and took himself upstairs to his room. He could hear the old man clattering about in the kitchen, but didn't know why. His father never seemed to eat, and he didn't keep any drink in there.

Rodney was moving about in his room, and Ditton was tempted to try to speak to him about Nash, but didn't want the frustration that often came with trying to talk to his brother nowadays. Instead, he resolved to speak to Clive, Rodney's friend, to find out what he knew, or could find out from Rodney. Something had to be done, because Ditton didn't like the idea of a nutter like Nash wanting something that his brother couldn't provide.

He lay on his bed, thoughts buzzing around in his head like flies over a Serengeti carcass, and was about to fall asleep when the music started from next door; a thud, thud, thud that he could feel as well as hear and thus couldn't ignore. He banged on the wall, hurting his hand in the process and making him wonder if he could ever take up Tyrone's offer.

Milk flew to Walworth as quickly as he could, as though he wanted to get there before he woke and realised it was all a dream. He couldn't remember looking forward to something so much. At least not since he had found out that some twin sisters he had been messing about with had each found out about the other and wanted to see him together. That was some night.

Michelle opened the front door wearing faded, well-worn 501s and a casual white shirt. She smiled at Milk, who returned the grin and followed her inside. Now Milk was nasty, he loved girls and he loved sex, but at the same time he was extremely selective. Any girl that wanted a piece of him had to at least look the part. The problem was that they all seemed to have the looks and not much else. So Milk was pleasantly surprised when

Michelle opened the front door and looked even better than he remembered her. He liked the way her naturally red lips stretched over her white teeth when she smiled, and he approved of the way her dark-toffee cheeks dimpled on either side of her perfectly sculpted nose. And, when she turned to lead him into the flat, and he noted the fine silver chain sparkling amid the light, downy hair on the back of her elegant neck, he thought this was truly turning out to be a good day. Michelle poured them both a drink, Milk rolled and lit a joint, and after some small talk and big petting, they found themselves in bed.

After all had been done, and that was a considerable amount, Milk finally thought to ask, 'So what made you change your mind? Don't get me wrong, I'm not complaining, I just wondered why. And what happened to Mr Wonderful I heard so much about?'

'Mr Wonderful isn't so wonderful any more, OK?' answered Michelle with a rueful smile. 'That's all you need to know.'

Milk lay back and stretched, suppressing a grin. 'Well, I have to say, it was worth waiting for, but you're lucky I kept after you, otherwise we wouldn't have done this.'

'I'm lucky? So what are you, then?'

'I'm just Milk, man.'

Michelle looked across at the slim young man lying in her bed. He was attractive in a golden-syrup kind of way. Golden skin, thick black eyebrows over slightly hooded eyes, almost no facial hair, just a slight moustache and a wisp on his chin. He was full of himself, but he was good. She rolled towards him and said, 'Well, show me your bottle again, Milkman.'

Milk raised an eyebrow. 'One pint or two?'

Courtney stepped inside, complaining about the cold and her day at work, and placed a cheek in front of Vaughn which he dutifully kissed. She then took out a packet of cigarettes, lit one, kicked her shoes off and flopped on to the sofa.

'I am *sooooo* fucked off with that place, you just wouldn't believe it.'

Yes I would, thought Vaughn, I'm always hearing it.

He handed her a glass of wine, poured one for himself, and sat next to her on the sofa, facing the television. He stared at the box while she jabbered on about who had annoyed her at work, and who wasn't pulling their weight. Vaughn tried to look interested in the television, hoping that Courtney would notice, believe it, and shut up. But in reality he was thinking about his own work situation, and how much he hated having to work with sad, crap people. How he hated being in the middle of everyone else's domestic, educational and professional fuck-ups. He was tired of having to wheel and deal constantly just to get a kid into a school. He was tired of having to threaten parents with court just so that they would do what they were supposed to. He was tired of visiting disgusting houses occupied by disgusting people, and having to be ingratiating because he was trying to remain professional.

Vaughn excused himself and went to the kitchen, where he spent longer than necessary preparing a culinary masterpiece, assuring Courtney that he didn't need any help, enjoying having a space to himself where he could function alone with no responsibility to behave a certain way. Maybe, he thought, he should just lock himself away and live in the kitchen.

Milk stood outside the car, on his phone, trying to negotiate with somebody while he jigged about, keeping the chill away and thinking that he shouldn't have to be wearing a jacket in May. Business concluded, he slid back into the car, behind the wheel, and said, 'We've got to stop off at the flat for some more. Theo's at the Queen wanting a bit extra. I told him I'll drop it off now.'

'What, is the punter there, waiting?'

'They're supposed to be meeting him there now.'

'Who is it?'

'Andy and Nigel.'

Andy and Nigel were customers and a couple. They were nice enough guys, but Ditton didn't like being seen with them because they looked like what they were – junkies.

Ditton groaned. 'Hurry up then. I don't want to be seen with either of those two freaks. And imagine, they say that vampires don't exist.'

Milk chuckled. 'Well, that's what Theo's getting paid for, isn't it? To deal with the customers.'

Ditton nodded. 'Yeah, but he's also getting paid so

that we don't have to be driving around with the gear on us. You know that if Andy or Nigel see us they're bound to start whining about something or other. And the state that those two are in, if I saw them talking to black guys like us, I'd probably reckon there was drugs involved.'

Milk shook his head. 'You think too much, man.'

Ditton nodded. 'And you don't think enough.'

'Perfect partnership then?'

The partnership had been going for just over a year, and after a rocky start had steadily improved to the situation they were now in, where Theo was employed to conduct business for them. In that short space of time their eyes had been opened to what heroin was really about. It was nasty, it twisted people, hurt people and killed people, but it generated fantastic amounts of money. Enough money to encourage people to overlook the seedier side of the business. Milk and Ditton weren't in Tyrone's league, and weren't looking for promotion to it, knowing that it could never happen because they didn't want it badly enough. Ditton was too cautious and Milk too reckless to ever aspire to anything like that.

The Queen was a large, good-looking pub on Beulah Hill. It served a number of local, hidden housing estates, and had a mixed clientele ranging from pensioners reminiscing about how it was during the war to kids brought up on Game Boys and Pot Noodle. Because it was mild enough, a group of guys, black and white, stood outside the pub chatting, laughing and puffing. Theo was instantly recognisable. He was short, and his light complexion made his large, rounded forehead glisten like a cue ball in the pub's halogen outside light. Milk turned left on to a side road opposite the pub and Theo made his way over to the car with a bottle of Pils clasped in his hand. He slid into the back seat with dexterity. 'What's up, Milk? D?'

The three exchanged quick greetings and handshakes, Theo handed over the day's takings and Milk counted quickly. He shot Ditton a brief look and nodded stiffly. Then, taking Ditton's concerns about Andy and Nigel into account, he asked, 'So what did you want?'

'I need another six. There are another couple of guys who want some.'

'Are they safe?' asked Ditton.

'Yeah, I've dealt with them before. They're just a couple of poofs.'

Milk and Ditton laughed at Theo's description, but exchanged glances. New clients needed to be vetted carefully.

'They're safe,' confirmed Theo. 'I've seen them about, and this guy Marty reckons they're all right.'

Milk turned in his seat to face Theo. 'Marty? Marty who? White guy? Marty McGinty?'

'I don't know his last name, but he's white. Arsenal Marty, they call him.'

'Arsenal youth team, to be precise. I didn't know you knew him. When did you see him last?'

'He's inside now, racking up pints and doing business.'

'Gear?'

'Yeah. Charlie.'

Milk produced two small parcels from beneath his seat and quickly passed them to Theo before turning to Ditton. 'I'm just going to pop in there a minute and talk to Marty. I haven't seen that nutter in years.'

As Milk trotted across the road behind Theo, Ditton closed his eyes and immediately saw Nash in his thoughts. He opened his eyes and saw Jonah, closed them again and saw Tyrone. He cursed and hoped Milk would hurry. Ditton didn't like being anywhere near the pub, feeling that he looked guilty just being near it. He knew that what he did was seen as heinous, knew the misery and anguish that drugs caused, the broken relationships, broken homes, crime and violence. But that was the drugs, not him or Milk. And anyway, if he wasn't selling, it wouldn't make the slightest bit of difference to the problem because there were countless others out there that would trample each other to take his place. Even though he wasn't as educated as those politicians and theorists that spouted about the drug problem when they didn't have the slightest clue what it was about, Ditton had enough sense to know that it was the reasons for drug use that needed to be addressed if anything was going to change. Having said that, he had no illusions about the risks and dangers involved, and he wanted to get out. He didn't want to lose the fast money or the free time, and he didn't know what else he was going to do, but his liberty and peace of mind were becoming increasingly important to him. The problem was that he had set himself a target figure to have stashed away before he quit. He was way short of that.

Milk was obsessed with sex, money and prestige. He liked food and music, but he was passionate about football. Wherever and whenever there was a match on, no matter who was playing, Milk could watch. Footie was footie. He was good at it, and he loved it. So when he heard from Theo that Marty McGinty was in the Queen, Milk had to go and see him. Marty was a villain, and they had played together in the Arsenal youth team years back, before both were released for different reasons: Milk because his attitude to training and authority was 'unacceptable', and he had 'personal differences' with the coach; and Marty because his convictions for assault, affray, and wounding with intent were too much for the club to risk being associated with.

Unlike Milk, Marty had persisted with football, signing for a succession of lower-league clubs and being released because of his off-the-field conduct. The last time Milk had seen him, Marty was playing for Lincoln, and they had eventually let him go just before he was convicted of possession with intent to supply. Knowing Marty, thought Milk, he was lucky that was all he got done for. He had probably masterminded the growing and importation of the gear too.

Theo had said that Marty was in the corner near the

toilets, and Milk saw him straight away, leaning against a wall with two other white guys, all holding pints. Marty looked the same as the last time Milk had seen him, short and thick, if a little harder and leaner, but definitely very healthy. He sported a fading tan beneath a dark crew-cut, jeans, pristine Reebok Classics and a black Stone Island jacket. His eyes darted around the pub, constantly probing, even while he smiled in response to something said by one of his companions.

'You little shit!' Marty exclaimed, grabbing Milk's hand and hugging him at the same time. 'How long's it been?'

'Not long enough to be away from a scamp like you. You still as bad as ever?'

'What?' asked Marty. 'I'm still trying to catch up with you!' He turned to his companions and explained, 'Steve, Dave, this is Marcus. Best left foot I ever saw, after Maradona. It's just a pity he couldn't keep his mouth shut and his dick in his pants. This is the one I was telling you about who shagged the coach's daughter at the Christmas party and then reckoned he couldn't understand why they released him from the club.'

Milk grinned and shook his head. 'The guy was a sick fucking paedophile. He was just mad because I had her before he got around to it.'

'You got time for a pint?' asked Marty.

Steve and Dave made their way to the bar, and Milk leaned next to Marty. 'So, Gints, how's it going? Theo told me you're back to your old business.'

After some chit-chat Milk asked, 'So who you playing for now?' That was the start.

When the bell rang Michelle adjusted her dressing gown, moved over to the door and looked through the peephole. The lens distorted her best friend's features, but it was her, shuffling outside on the balcony to some imaginary tune in her head. Natalie breezed into the flat like a dance-hall queen, long waist-length plaits piled on her head, short skirt just about covering an ample backside, long legs in knee-high, stiletto patent boots, and glided straight to the front room, leaving a scent trail of Moschino, or 'Mosheeno' as far as Natalie was concerned, behind her.

'Well? You didn't phone or anything,' complained Natalie. 'I was thinking something terrible must have happened. I had the Bailey's and the Martell ready too. So? What?'

Michelle retied the belt on her gown and tucked her legs beneath her. 'Get yourself a drink, I'll have one too. Then sit down, shut up and I'll tell you what happened.'

Natalie did as she was bid, sensing she was going to hear something juicy.

It didn't take long, but by the end of the tale Natalie was gaping through eyes made to look feline with creative eye-liner, and her jaw hung loose. Her expression of shock wouldn't have been much different had she been told her six numbers had come up on a double roll-over week. Michelle turned the television down and they drank brandy and put their heads together.

'You did what?' asked Ditton, incredulous. 'You made a bet with Marty on Sunday's match?'

Milk shrugged. 'Yeah, what's the big fucking deal?'

'For how much?'

Milk grinned and rubbed his chin. 'Well, there's sort of two bets, really. Whoever wins gets a grand, and if me or Marty score a hat-trick, that's another three grand.'

The look Ditton gave his friend was full of pity. 'So let me get this straight. If you lose the match, you owe Marty *one* thousand pounds. If you lose the match and Marty scores three, you owe him *four thousand pounds*!'

Milk nodded. 'Simple, eh? Only thing is that we're not going to lose, are we?'

'What makes you so certain about that?'

Milk grinned. 'Well, I'm playing, aren't I?'

Ditton threw his hands up in despair. 'Vaughn, talk to this boy, man. He's off his head. Totally gone.'

Vaughn had entered the kitchen, his kitchen, the first room Milk had headed for upon entering the flat, and said, 'I was coming to find out what damage this one was doing to my fridge.' He grabbed Milk by the ear and led him away from the cooker, where he had been eyeing rice in a pot and scouting for the accompanying meat. 'What's he done now?'

It seemed as though Milk had been taking Vaughn's food for as long as he could remember. When they had met in the first week of their first term at secondary school, Milk had tried to take a packet of crisps from Vaughn. Ditton had felt sorry for the timid kid who was just about ready to cry and didn't seem to realise that there were other options, like fighting. He had persuaded Milk to return the crisps; they were only ready salted anyway. From then on Vaughn had attached himself to Ditton like a leech, and regardless of how hard Ditton tried to shake him off he couldn't lose him. In the end he gave up and convinced Milk, his long-time friend, that Vaughn was OK. True, he was a bit brainy and spoilt, but he was all right. It had taken Milk a while to come around to the same way of thinking, but eventually he did, and from that day the three very different boys had been inseparable.

Milk sighed in mock frustration and explained that he had met an old colleague from Arsenal. They had got chatting about football, and by an amazing coincidence it turned out that they were both playing in the same Sunday league. An even bigger coincidence was that their teams were playing against each other in Sunday's cup final.

'So what's the problem?' asked Vaughn, putting a plate of rice and chicken in the microwave, and watching Milk's eyes light up.

'He's only gone and made a potential four-grand bet with the guy, hasn't he?'

Vaughn paused, set the timer for two and a half minutes, then said slowly, 'Yes, he is mad, definitely.

But it's his money. Let him throw it away.'

'Oh, nice one, V,' Ditton complained, laughing. 'Nice one. I ask you for help and you come out with that?'

'But what could I say? The boy's sick. We both know that.'

Milk grinned and continued counting down with the microwave timer. Ditton winked at Vaughn and asked Milk, 'So, if you win, and you score a hat-trick, you going to split the winnings eleven ways?'

Milk kissed his teeth. 'Get real, man. The others are only there to support me. I thought you knew that. I'm not splitting anything, but as long as they keep sending those through-balls, I might give them something.'

Ditton shook his head. 'One in a million. You're a one-off, Milk. You really are.' Vaughn nodded in agreement. 'Priceless.'

'That's more than I can say for this,' Milk stated, indicating the microwave. 'What's wrong with this nuclear gizmo? I'm starving, man. When's it going to fucking ping!'

Milk sat back and wiped his mouth and hands with a piece of kitchen roll. 'Yeah,' he said, easing out a belch. 'That was good.'

'Why're you so quiet, Gary?' asked Courtney. 'You look like you're not really here.'

Ditton frowned. 'Sorry, I've got a few things to think about.'

'What?' asked Vaughn and Milk in unison.

Ditton paused before recounting his meetings with both Tyrone and Earl, and Jonah. He didn't mention Nash; that was too personal, and anyway he wasn't even sure there was a problem. He finished, shrugged and declared, 'That's about it.'

Milk whistled. 'You think Tyrone's serious?'

'I don't know. He sounded serious, and he doesn't make idle threats.'

'Ah, that reminds me,' remembered Milk. 'I saw Vincent this morning. He told me to tell you he wants to see you. Sorry, *consigliere*.'

Ditton glared. 'What did he say?'

'Just that he wants to see you.' Milk grinned. 'That was it.'

Ditton nodded, suddenly weary. It was only to be expected, considering the circumstances, that Vincent would demand his time and counsel as well. He hoped, however, that it would only be time and counsel that Vincent wanted. He asked Milk what was funny, expecting it to be the way he had responded to being called *consigliere*.

'Hear what happened to me today, then?' said Milk. 'Amazing stuff.' He proceeded to narrate the events of his day, stressing the encounter at Nicole's in the morning, and the liaison with Michelle in the afternoon. Being Milk, he had no qualms about Courtney being present

'Let me get this straight,' said Vaughn. 'Today you've slept with two girls, both of whom have boyfriends – in fact, you knocked one of the boyfriends unconscious. Along with that, you've made a four-thousand-pound bet on a game of Sunday football. Is that about right?'

'Yeah,' grinned Milk, pleased with himself. 'That's about right.'

Courtney observed Milk with interest stemming from a slight revulsion. She would have liked Milk even if he wasn't one of Vaughn's closest friends, and although she could have been spared the gory details of the day's sexual exploits, she found that she had to respect Milk's honesty, both with the present company and the girls involved in his day.

Vaughn turned to her. 'You see how lucky you are? I could be like him.'

Courtney shook her head. 'You couldn't be like him and be with me.'

Milk held up his hand as though he was seeking assistance from a teacher, something he had rarely done in school. 'As everyone's talking about me, can I say something? If I was in a relationship like you two, I wouldn't do the things that I do. But I'm not, because I quite like doing the things that I do. And I don't lie to anybody. I lay it on the line and if the girl doesn't like it, that's it, her fucking loss. However, when I find the right girl, trust me, I'll be as faithful as a castrated nigger.'

While Vaughn, Milk and Courtney debated the rights and wrongs of Milk's sexual conduct, Ditton's thoughts wandered again and he asked himself if he would ever be in a relationship like Vaughn and

Courtney's. There was a time when he was sure, almost took it for granted, but it had evaporated, just like that, and up to this day he still wasn't sure how or why. Of course, there had been girls since. There were girls now that he would contact when he needed some comfort or release, but nobody special. Nobody that he cared about enough to take home and expose to his family, nobody that he felt was qualified to deal with his family. He wondered where she was now, what she was doing, and who with. It would be easy enough to find out, and he often thought about phoning to ask why she had ended it as and when she did. Why then, of all times? He had told himself over and over that he could do it without getting angry or emotional, he just wanted answers. But when all was said and done, he didn't trust himself, and he wasn't used to the feeling.

Ditton's reverie ended when he noticed Milk standing in front of him. 'D? You ready?' Milk was asking. 'All that talk about sex and stuff has got me going again.'

Just as they were leaving, when Courtney had been kissed and Vaughn stood waiting to follow them to the front door, a picture on the television, the south-east news, swung Vaughn's head around. 'I know where that is,' he said scrabbling around for the remote control. 'That's around the corner from my school. What's going on?'

Courtney turned up the volume and Vaughn watched transfixed. A reporter stood wearing an overcoat, at the entrance to the wasteground adjacent to the railway arches, behind the school where Vaughn had deposited Darryl that morning.

'The body of the young boy was found behind me, here, in a corner of this wasteground, by a group of children from the local secondary school who came here during their lunch hour. The police have revealed that the victim was beaten and strangled before the body was hidden under a piece of corrugated iron and covered in rubble. The police feel certain that the murder took place here, and evidence suggests that it must have been committed between nine in the morning and one in the afternoon, when the body was found. They are unable to reveal the victim's name at present, but are appealing to anyone who may have any information to contact the local CID.'

'That's right behind my secondary school,' cried Vaughn. 'That could be a kid I know. Imagine if it is.'

'Forget it,' said Milk flatly. 'The kid's dead. If you know him, you'll find out soon enough. And you didn't do it, so why're you worrying?'

It wasn't that simple for Vaughn, but he knew that sentiment and sensitivity rarely played a part in Milk's life. For Milk it was as simple as he had explained it. 'Yeah, you're right,' Vaughn conceded, exchanging knowing glances with Ditton. 'It's not my problem.'

'Good!' Milk grinned. 'Now, remember. We're going for a drink tomorrow, right? No excuses. Don't even try it.' He turned to Ditton. 'D? You heard him, yeah? He said he was coming.'

'I heard him,' confirmed Ditton.

And with that, Milk was out of the house, pulling Ditton behind him like a child dragging a parent towards the toy department.

Courtney rose and met Vaughn as he returned from the front door. She stood in front of him, placed a hand on each shoulder and kissed him three times, once on each cheek and once on the forehead. 'I'm glad you're not like that.'

'Like what?'

'Like Milk. Nasty. I mean, he's all right, I like him, you know that. But he does have a lot of faults.' Courtney stepped back and yawned. 'Right, I'm going to bed. You can meet me there if you want.'

Vaughn nodded and began to tidy up, well aware of what Courtney was suggesting but unsure how he felt about it. 'I'll be there in a minute.'

A bedside lamp was on, casting elongated shadows around the room and making it difficult for Vaughn to see Courtney's face as she lay on her back under the duvet, hands behind her head. She didn't say anything as Vaughn undressed, but as he slid under the covers and his weight tilted the bed, she snored lightly. 'Great,' muttered Vaughn. 'Great!' He put his dressing gown on and stalked to the kitchen to get a stiff drink, roll a joint and watch the television. He flicked through the channels and found nothing to watch. He checked the teletext for more information on the dead child, but got even less detail than on the news. He threw the remote control down in disgust and thought, Janine wouldn't have fallen asleep.

TUESDAY

CHAPTER SEVEN

When he arrived at his mother's flat in the morning, Milk was surprised and slightly perturbed to find that Shane was still there. Mrs Kerr shrugged and reported that Shane hadn't been anywhere since Milk and Sandra had collected him from school the previous day. Sandra having phoned the previous evening to ask if it was OK for the youngster to stay over. Milk made a face, but Mrs Kerr didn't comment or pass judgement on her daughter's actions. Instead, she turned her back on her son and busied herself with the dumplings frying in the pan.

Milk walked round to face his mother. 'You think Sandra's getting sick again?'

Mrs Kerr looked up abruptly from the frying pan. 'Yes, I think she might be getting sick again. But she won't talk about it to anyone. Yvonne and Beverley have tried to speak to her but she just shouts and says she's all right.'

Sandra's breakdown had been sudden and extreme. As far as the family were concerned, one day she had been fine, and the next she had alternated between babbling and incoherent, violent and voluble, and near catatonic. She had been hospitalised almost immediately. Fortunately Shane was too young to remember it in any detail. However, Sandra's daughter, Vanessa, had been at exactly the wrong age and couldn't appreciate that her mother wasn't capable of looking after herself, let alone her children. The teenager had become frustrated and angry, and their relationship had never recovered.

'Shane's not happy at all,' Milk reported. 'And I don't think it's because of what happened at school. I think that thing at school was because of that.'

They discussed Sandra for a while, Milk trying to dredge up all memories of Sandra's recent behaviour, searching for clues to her mental state, hoping not to see parallels from the past. But something occurred to him, and before he had time to give it serious thought, the question asked itself.

'He's not back there, is he?' asked Milk tentatively. 'Tell me he's not, because if he is we'll have the answer straight away.'

Mrs Kerr's jaw dropped and her eyes expressed alarm. 'I really don't know, but none of you have been there for weeks, have you?'

Milk shook his head, glared, and strode down the passage to the front room. He sat beside Shane and asked, 'When's the last time you saw your dad, mate?'

The boy swallowed and looked troubled. Milk was about to rejoice, assuming that Shane had been reminded of the painful fact that he hadn't seen his father for almost a year.

'Day before yesterday, Saturday,' said Shane. 'At home.'

Milk felt himself becoming dangerously angry, as though his personal fuse was just about burned down and the explosion was next, but he tried his best not to convey that to Shane. He took a deep breath, composed himself as best he could, and asked, 'When did you see him before that?'

The boy struggled with the concept of time and days of the week, but confirmed that his father had been at the flat almost every other day for the last three or four weeks.

Milk nodded, stood, and walked back to the kitchen. His jaw already ached from being clenched too tightly, and he could feel the tell-tale twitch in his right temple and the tightening of his right shoulder which signified that he was close to exploding. Mrs Kerr saw the signs as her son returned to stand in the kitchen doorway. She frowned and massaged the back of her neck.

'Yeah,' Milk muttered. 'It sounds like he's back. And if it's started again, I'll kill him this time.'

The town hall office was a hive of activity when Vaughn finally arrived in the late morning. The imminent visit of Councillor Goode meant that most of the Education Welfare Service staff were present. Paul, the principal, had made it clear that everyone was expected to attend, and that only a very good excuse would suffice to cover any absences. Obviously nobody had been able to come up with a good enough excuse.

Janine was perched on the end of Vaughn's desk talking to Debbie, her colleague and confidante, and she looked up as he entered, but continued chatting. She smiled as he approached, uncrossing and re-crossing her legs, but made no effort to move away. Vaughn didn't mind. He couldn't be bothered, and skirted past her to remove his coat and check his in-tray for messages. On top of the unwelcome pile was a message to phone Martin Green urgently.

Janine eased one cheek off the desk to allow Vaughn access to his telephone. The Social Services switchboard answered on about the fiftieth ring, an improvement. Vaughn was transferred to Martin Green's extension, where he was informed by another social worker that Martin was unavailable, but that he could leave a message if he wished. Upon hearing Vaughn's name, the social worker said, 'Wait right there, I'll get him. I know he's desperate to speak to you.'

Strange, thought Vaughn, but he waited for Martin to come to the phone, and at the same time surrep-titiously ogled Janine's thighs and breasts. The latter occasionally shook with her laughter, and to his annoy-ance Vaughn found himself imagining them in his hands and against his chest and face. He knew she was aware and not displeased, feeling that her seeds of seduction were slowly but surely taking root. He wanted to kick himself for being her fertile ground.

'Vaughn, is that you?' Martin cried down the line.

'Good God, I'm glad I was still here when you called. Something terrible has happened.'

Vaughn wasn't sure whether to laugh or to be concerned. It wasn't like Martin to be this serious, ever. So although the rarity of the event should have lent credence to his words, it only served to make them harder to believe.

'What have you done now?' asked Vaughn from behind a chuckle. 'What letter have you forgotten to send? What visit did you forget to do? Or was it a report you forgot to hand in on time?'

'It's nothing like that,' said Martin quietly. 'It's Darryl.'

Vaughn felt his heart stop. His stomach began to churn and his eyes began to sting. 'What now? Arrested? What?' It was the worst he could allow himself to think.

'Dead,' said Martin flatly. 'I'm sorry. Yesterday, the wasteground behind the school. It was on the news—'

'I know,' interrupted Vaughn. 'I heard it.' A million thoughts and emotions flooded his mind at once: panic, loss, numbness, guilt, anger. From somewhere else he heard his name being called, and realised that Martin was still talking to him.

'The police have been here already this morning to speak to me, and they'll probably want to see you too. In fact, I'm sure they will.'

'Me?' cried Vaughn in a cocktail of alarm and disbelief. 'What would they want to see me for?'

There was silence on the line until Martin admitted,

'I told them that we spoke yesterday. I think you might be the last person known to have seen Darryl alive. They're going to want to speak to you, believe me.'

Vaughn spent five or so minutes in the toilet, just sitting on the lid with his hand under running cold water in the adjacent sink. He didn't know why, he had never done it before, but it seemed like the right thing to do. After a while he felt stable enough to go back into the office, via the kitchen and a cigarette. He wished he had a joint and would have smoked it right there if he had. Instead he took one of Sue's cigarettes from her packet on the windowsill and lit it just as she walked in and gave him a bright smile. He didn't respond, his face just wasn't capable.

'Oi, oi, ducks!' Sue joked. 'What's the matter with you, then?'

In less than a second, all manner of possible replies flew into Vaughn's mind and then flew out again. He didn't want to talk about it, but maybe he did. He didn't want all the fuss, but again, maybe he did. 'Darryl's dead' found its way out of his mouth before he had decided to voice it. 'I just spoke to Martin. Killed yesterday, behind school.'

Sue's face dropped, and she mouthed nothings like a goldfish. 'I am *so* sorry,' she said eventually. 'Are you all right? Well, I can see now that you're not, but—'

'I'm all right,' said Vaughn with a shrug. 'I'm definitely better than him.'

Sue sighed, shook her head and lit up herself. 'So what happened? How? When? *Why?*'

Vaughn told her what he could, which wasn't much. She listened, flinching or frowning every time she heard Martin Green's name or a graphic detail. Despite the situation, Vaughn was still amused by Sue's aversion to the social worker, and her valiant attempt not to criticise him.

'Do you want to go home?' Sue asked. 'Just say the word and you can be out of here.'

Vaughn thought for a moment. He didn't want to be in the office with the noise, the phones, the work, but right then he really didn't want to be alone at home, alone with his thoughts and guilt. He shook his head. 'No thanks. I'll stay. I might leave a bit early, but I'll stay for now.'

'I really am so sorry,' said Sue again, just at the moment the doorbell rang. 'I bet that's the bloody councillor,' she mumbled. 'Doesn't he know the code is the same throughout the town hall? I ask you!'

Vaughn managed a feeble smile. 'I suppose I'd better go and try to look professional then.'

It wasn't the councillor at the door, which gave Debbie and Janine their opportunity to question him. He told them quietly, but they clucked and squawked like chickens sensing a fox, and soon the whole office knew what had happened. Paul, the principal, came bustling in offering sympathy and support as did other colleagues. Frankie, a Ghanaian EWO offered some of her medicinal Pimm's, which she kept in her bottom drawer, while Matthew tried to look serious but only succeeded in coming across as insincere. Vaughn wearied of repeating what little he knew.

The door furthest from Vaughn's desk opened and Katherine, the admin officer, poked her head around it. 'Councillor Goode has arrived,' she announced as though the man was royalty. 'He's in with Paul now.'

Janine stayed where she was on Vaughn's desk, asking questions about Darryl and Vaughn's feelings. It was painful but he was grateful, and when he finally got up he knew that his eyes had communicated that to her. He didn't bother to kick himself this time; he was too low.

Again the door swung open, and Paul bustled in followed by a tall, well-built man who may have been impressive when he was younger, but was now fat and unhealthy. He was in his early fifties, maybe older, and wore the obligatory navy-blue suit, and an expression that resembled a permanent sneer. Vaughn took an instant dislike. He caught Sue's eye and she raised her eyebrows to signal that her first impression was also negative.

The councillor sat down, removed his jacket and began to explain what had prompted him to invite himself to the Education Welfare Service meeting. He explained that he wanted to meet all education department staff to hear their views and concerns, and allay as many of their fears as possible. The service was always in the spotlight, but a recent report highlighting that a large percentage of street crime was committed by truants had given the spotlight a hundred-thousand-watt bulb. The councillor wanted to hear from the

EWOs what they felt would enable them to carry out their jobs more effectively. Slowly but surely the suggestions and complaints began to flow, until eventually Councillor Goode must have been ruing his decision to visit. Things became so heated that the councillor loosened his tie and removed his glasses, defending himself from attack on all sides. Finally he declared himself late for another appointment and rose to leave. Paul thanked him and was just about to escort him out when Katherine popped in and whispered something to Sue. Sue stood up, excused herself and beckoned for a puzzled Vaughn to follow her out of the room.

'What's the matter?' asked Vaughn.

Instead of answering, Sue motioned with her head. Vaughn peered through the glass in the security door to see a man and a woman standing at the top of the stairs. He wasn't sure what it was about them that he recognised, but there was something. 'Police?'

Sue nodded. She searched Vaughn's eyes. 'You all right?' He nodded. 'It's going to be routine,' continued Sue, 'but if you want I'm more than willing to come and sit in with you.'

Vaughn's instinct was to decline the offer, but he nodded. It wouldn't hurt to have Sue there. 'Please, if you don't mind. At the end of the day they are police, and I am what I am.'

Sue grinned. 'Sure. Come on then.'

They walked down the corridor to the police couple who Vaughn could see loitering outside the conference room. Vaughn suddenly felt apprehensive, the nausea returned, his legs felt weak and his head light.

'You sure you're all right?' Sue asked again.

Vaughn heard and felt his heart beating like a drummer on speed, and his queasy stomach felt ready to spew. 'Yeah, fine,' he lied.

CHAPTER EIGHT

Ditton sat in the passenger seat thinking about his visit to Clive's barber's shop first thing that morning. He had told Clive, Rodney's oldest and closest friend, about the meeting with Nash. Clive had tried to reassure him that there was nothing to worry about. Ditton wasn't so sure.

A glance at the rear-view mirror told Milk a police car was following them up East Hill. As they navigated the one-way system at Wandsworth Common, it stayed with them, sticking to a rigid thirty miles per hour.

'Guess what, D?' Milk warned. 'I think we're going to get a pull.'

Ditton tensed, glanced in the wing mirror and went silent.

'Don't worry about it,' Milk reassured. 'You're clean, I'm clean. All I can get is a producer.'

Ditton snorted, memories of Rodney lying unrecognisable in a hospital bed forcing their way into his mind. He balked at the memory of his brother's grotesquely swollen face hidden by tubes that protruded from every imaginable orifice, and hardware that bleeped and buzzed like R2D2 going through a major malfunction. 'Yeah, right,' he mumbled. 'You think it's always that simple?' Milk didn't answer.

The stop took place as expected. Ditton stayed in his seat, looking neither left nor right, but straight ahead, even when he was being addressed by the junior partner of the two constables. Eventually he wound the window down, answered the man and stepped out of the car when he was asked to. He stood there trying to remember when his dislike of the police had really begun, knowing that it was way before he saw Rodney in hospital. The first time he had been stopped and questioned he had been more surprised than anything else. He had been thirteen and standing at a bus stop, and couldn't understand what could have been suspicious about that.

In later years, when he was being stopped and searched almost daily, he hated them with a passion for taunting and belittling him, and having the power to lock him away and fabricate evidence whenever they felt like it. But it had begun even before that. One Saturday afternoon he had been walking in Brixton with Rodney when a large powerful car had pulled up alongside them. He had a feeling it was an old sloping hatchback Rover.

A white man had leaned out of the passenger window and doffed an imaginary hat to Rodney. The image that remained with Ditton was of a large man with jet-black hair, piercing black eyes, and a cruel hooked nose, who sneered maliciously. A jagged scar ran across his chin. The car had sped off and Rodney had cursed and walked faster. After insistent questions from a disturbed Ditton, Rodney had explained to his younger brother that the man was a policeman, a bent one, who was trying to get Rodney to pay him to overlook his activities. 'Like protection?' Ditton had asked in astonishment. 'He calls it business,' corrected Rodney.

Ditton had been young enough to struggle with the idea of a dishonest policeman. The ones in uniform that swore at him, called him names and gave him the odd slap or dig in the ribs when no one was looking, were just policemen as far as he was concerned. He honestly thought that was how they were supposed to behave, or at least that it was condoned because they were the guardians of law and order. But to hear Rodney telling him that a senior policeman was blatantly corrupt was hard for the youngster to take on board. He thought it must have started then, the realisation that they were no better or worse than any thugs on the street.

Meanwhile, Milk played the game and took their sarcasm and facetiousness with a forced smile. Even when the officer he was dealing with congratulated him on being so affable and said, 'You know, if more of you lot were like our Frank Bruno we'd all get along a lot better. He's the kind of fellow who knows his limitations, know what I mean? None of this attitude stuff, eh?'

As he got back into the car Milk grinned and said, 'Yeah, that's why he's *Your* Frank, and not ours.'

The policemen scowled and made their way back to their car. Milk outwaited them and finally the constables took off at speed.

'What a couple of boy-racing wankers,' observed Milk.

Ditton failed to answer. He was still remembering a hooked nose, scar, and those terrible black eyes.

Later, Ditton lay back on his bed smoking and closed his eyes. As usual he was tired and wanted to secure some sleep while there was nothing pressing that needed his attention. As he puffed he thought about yesterday and decided that he couldn't remember a day that had revealed so much potential conflict, and serious conflict at that. Years previously, when Milk had been in the middle of his wild, warrior stage, Ditton had been involved in the constant feuding. But that was through choice and he hadn't been too different himself. In those days he couldn't leave the house without a weapon, feeling naked unless he knew he had a blade or a bat handy. Looking back he could still feel the excitement and exhilaration, the crazy adrenaline rush that came from the knowledge that injury or even death was not far away. It meant that Ditton understood Jonah and his antics because he had been there years before, with Milk, who made Jonah look like a choirboy. Now that they had matured he hadn't expected to be mixed up in this sort of thing again, but Jonah had a way of spoiling the best-laid plans.

The weed began to take effect and Ditton felt himself relax. His limbs and eyelids grew heavy, and he tried to empty his troubled mind to allow himself to slip into sleep and a welcome escape from other people's problems. He was nearly there, floating in that ethereal void between consciousness and unconsciousness that couldn't have been so different from an out-of-body, near-death experience. But then a crash from next door shook the house and music began to thud. He sat up and cursed.

Milk had been hoping that Michelle would call again, but he didn't really expect it to be so soon. He knew it had been good for both of them, and she had made it clear that she wasn't after commitment or exclusivity, so maybe she would. Whatever, he wasn't chasing. As he pulled off from outside Ditton's house, the phone rang in the middle of a three-point turn. He caught sight of the dialler's number, completed the manoeuvre and pulled up on the other side of the road. Bingo! She wanted more. Could he come round in an hour or so? Milk ummed and ahhed, took a couple of sharp intakes of breath, trying to sound thoughtful, then said, 'Yes' as though he was doing her a favour. Milk was grinning like a Cheshire cat and squirmed in his seat like a kid with a bum rash at the thought of Michelle naked and willing. However, he sounded indifferent and said he had a few things to do, but would be round as soon as he could.

The hostel reeked of burgers when Milk let himself in, but Byron was nowhere to be seen. He crept past Jackie's door, as though it was the lair of some Homeric beast and let himself into his room. As she hadn't come out to waylay him, she either had to be asleep or on her back, paying her way.

Milk had a quick shower and sat on his bed naked, smoking a spliff and admiring what he was going to be giving the lucky Michelle soon. He was surprised to realise that he was more excited than he had been the day before. That was strange; Milk usually went off them after the deed had been done and another coup notched up. Michelle seemed different. How she could ever be with a wanker like Patrick, Milk just couldn't understand.

He dressed quickly, as usual, and opened his bedroom door, but heard movement from downstairs, Jackie's room. She was seeing someone out to the front door. Jackie shuffled back upstairs in her dressing gown and Milk locked his door and walked down towards her. Even with the smell of sex wafting out of her room and the gown clinging to her groin exposing vulva that looked like they had just had a couple of collagen shots, Jackie smiled and asked, 'When you gonna come see me so we can have some fun?'

Milk told her that she should spray her room, wash her body and take a look at her life before she came and made overtures like that to him. She carried on smiling and Milk shook his head in disappointment. 'If you were my sister—' He didn't finish and instead shuddered dramatically, making a big show of avoiding touching her as he squeezed past and trotted down the stairs.

'Don't worry,' said Jackie. 'You're going to want it one day and it won't be on offer any more. Then we'll see you begging for it.'

Milk stopped on the last step and turned to see Jackie at the top of the stairs, arms crossed and a haughty expression on her face. He sauntered back up with his hands in his pockets and stopped one step below Jackie so that he was her height. He cleared his throat and said quietly and calmly, 'If you were the last woman on earth I wouldn't want you. I'd say, "Thank God for hands," and wank myself silly.'

Jackie's chin quivered and a vein in her forehead twitched. 'All right,' she began, but couldn't manage more than a gurgling growl and had to settle for glaring at him with undisguised malevolence.

'What was that?' teased Milk. 'You said something? I couldn't quite understand it.'

Again Jackie's anger affected her speech and again she gurgled but managed to finish with 'Fucking bastard!'

Milk didn't pay her any mind and walked back down the stairs. When he got to the bottom he turned and beamed. 'Syphilis, that's what it is. That's why you're not making sense.'

Jackie scowled.

* * *

Again Michelle was astonished to find that she really enjoyed her afternoon with Milk, and found it more surprising than the day before. She realised that he actually made her laugh, and that some of the seductive, sleazy things that she did for him and to him came easily to her. There was no embarrassment or shyness, just a refreshingly open, adult relationship that she was quite disturbed to find she was enjoying.

Because she felt that things were open between them, she toyed with the idea of telling Milk why she wanted him to take her to Thornton Heath. Milk's reputation was legendary, and she felt that if she explained it to him he probably still wouldn't think twice about taking her there. In fact it would probably encourage him. But Michelle felt that it wasn't right. She wanted to keep him out of it, wanted to keep him in a different part of her life, private and new, not to be linked with the dreary, disappointing past. That realisation troubled her too.

She had asked him to drive her there after they had been at it for what seemed like hours, and he lay peacefully with his head on her stomach. He had put up a bit of resistance – 'What's wrong with your fucking car?' – but she guessed it was just for show. She had told him that she just wanted him to drive her because it was him. The lie rolled off her tongue so easily that she had to question the truth of the statement. She decided that she was undecided and didn't want to think about it right then. She was also beginning to realise that the notorious Milk wasn't as fearsome as he was portrayed to be, at least not with her.

Milk grumbled a bit – he was comfortable and cosy and didn't want to get up – but she promised him he could come back afterwards if he wanted to. From Michelle's point of view, the offer wasn't hard to make. It seemed to convince Milk, and he tidied himself while Michelle dressed in a pair of baggy jeans, trainers, hooded sweatshirt, black leather jacket and baseball cap.

'Do you think I look like a boy dressed like this?' she asked.

Milk looked her up and down, told her to turn around and looked her up and down again. 'Yep, you sure do.'

Michelle grinned. That should help. At least she looked the part. Now she just had to be able to play the part too. Milk didn't ask why she wanted him to drive her and that impressed her. However, she still volunteered the information that she had to go and collect a bag from a friend who had been promising it to her for years, but had only recently agreed to give it up. It was a lovely brown leather bag, and she really wanted it. Milk had nodded, seemingly disinterested, and directed the car where he was told to, hoping that this thing would be quick and he could get her back to her house as soon as possible. He had to admit that this girl was first class, even when she was dressed like a boy.

'Just here will do,' said Michelle as they got to the flat.

It had begun to rain, so Michelle didn't look *too* odd when she pulled her gloves on, removed her baseball cap, put her hood up, drew the strings tight and replaced the cap on top of that. She got out of the car carefully, making sure that Dale's rounders bat didn't fall out of the jacket and leave her in an embarrassing situation with some explanations to provide for Milk. She walked across the street to the girl's front door, looking left and right for any passers-by, and rang the bell, careful to stay under the porch so that she couldn't be seen from the upstairs window. Sure enough, Michelle heard a tap on the glass above her head but didn't step out to be identified. A few moments later, from the other side of the front door, she heard footsteps descending the stairs. When the girl asked who it was, Michelle answered, 'Me, Patrick,' in as gruff a voice as she could manage, hoping that the thickness of the door would do the rest for her.

She began to have second thoughts and nearly panicked, but her ruse seemed to have worked because the door opened and Michelle was confronted with a sleepy, confused girl trying in vain to ascertain the identity of the person at her door.

'You're not Patrick,' said the girl dumbly. 'Who are you?'

Michelle had been thinking about this moment since the morning. What would she do when she got in? She had the bat and an oblivious Milk outside, but she didn't need them. When she had realised earlier who the girl was – a bitch from a party that she had attended with Patrick about a year earlier – it had made everything so much easier. She had wondered why at the party Patrick had left her alone so often, claiming that he was going outside to smoke, or chat to a friend. Now she knew.

Sisterhood was out of the window, and while she still couldn't really blame the girl for what had happened, Michelle didn't feel that she was deserving of any respect or preferential treatment.

Michelle clenched her fist. She had always been a fighter, so without much anguish she punched the girl on the jaw, not particularly hard but hard enough to scare and stun her. The girl let out a little squeal and fell to her knees holding her face more in shock than in pain. 'Who are you? What do you want?' she appealed again, more insistent this time.

Michelle slid the rounders bat from her jacket, grabbed the girl by the scruff of her neck, raised her to her feet and steered her up the stairs towards her open front door. They entered. Everything was going well. The girl thought that Michelle was a guy, and was terrified.

'What do you want?' asked the girl again, fear causing her voice to crack.

Michelle was tempted to say 'Don't worry, not you', but she had to remember not to speak unless it was absolutely necessary. She directed the girl into the living room and forced her to the ground, making her lie flat on her stomach while she turned and took a look around to see if there was anywhere that her bag could have been concealed. She failed to identify any obvious places, but she did see her lamp. It was definitely hers, and she saw her CD midi system too. A mad, indignant rage threatened to descend on her but she remained calm and focused. She yanked the girl to her feet, demanding in a gruff voice. 'The bag. The leather bag. Where is it?'

The girl had begun to sob so much that she was incapable of answering, so Michelle knocked her on the back of the head with the rounders bat. Again, it wasn't hard, just the kind of rap a parent would give to admonish a child for some flippant remark that the parent secretly finds amusing. However, terror made the girl scream and blurt out, 'In the bedroom, under the bed!'

Michelle heaved her to her feet again and forced her out into the passage. She didn't know where the bedroom was so ordered, 'Go!' The terrified girl did as she was told.

'Where?' demanded Michelle, and the girl dropped to her knees, reached under the bed and pulled out Michelle's bag. She handed it over with fear-induced timidity. Michelle looked around the room again but could see nothing else that belonged to her. There was nothing in the room except the bed, a wardrobe and a chest of drawers. Suddenly, the enormity of what she was doing struck Michelle right between the eyes, and she had to fight the urge to run screaming out of the flat and down to Milk's car. She motioned for the girl to lie face down, then backed out of the bedroom. All that for a measly old bag, she thought, trying to get her bearings and find the front door. She yanked it open and took the stairs two at a time, thinking, I must be mad.

Meanwhile, Milk had been sitting in the car entertaining himself by playing music loud, experimenting with bass and treble to try to secure the roundest sound from the bass tube in the boot. Not satisfied, he got out to adjust the position of the tube, hoping to achieve a little more oomph. Michelle found him there with the boot open, and with as much composure as possible said, 'Come on, Milk, let's go. I've finished here.'

'Soon come,' said Milk. 'I'm just trying something.'

'Well hurry up,' said Michelle, with more urgency this time. 'You've got something to try back at my place, remember?'

Milk grinned. 'Get in the car then. I'm coming.' He didn't know why he looked up at the window. Whatever the reason, he glanced up, saw Michelle's friend, and grinned and waved. She didn't seem too friendly, though, failing to acknowledge him and instead dropping the curtain and disappearing from sight.

Upstairs, the girl, realising that her assailant was no longer on the premises, had made her way to the front room and peered out of the window. From there she could see the attacker speak to his accomplice and then get into the passenger seat of a car. The accomplice was casually doing something in the boot as if there was no need for haste at all. Finished, he strolled around to the driver's door and looked up at the window. She tried to move the net curtain a fraction to get a better look at him, but in her distressed state her actions were not quite as sure as usual, and she managed to knock down a vase and almost yank the curtain off the runner. However she got a look at the guy and, more importantly, she thought she recognised him.

The interview was an experience Vaughn was not keen to repeat. From the outset Detective Inspector Walker made him feel that he was the prime suspect, asking questions about his relationship with Darryl and implying that the playful scuffle with Darryl outside the school entrance had been something much more serious. During all of this the woman, Detective Sergeant Rose, had looked sympathetic and asked curious questions about Vaughn's relationship with Martin Green. Vaughn had answered as truthfully as his muddled mind would allow, recounting the visit to Mrs Keeler, the encounter with Darryl and the Rover, and the incident outside the school entrance. The two officers had glanced at each other at the mention of the Keeler family but nothing had been said by either. DI Walker advised Vaughn to be available for further contact, and on her way out DS Rose gave him a card with her number in case he remembered anything pertinent to the investigation.

So although eleven pounds for a bottle of Barbadian rum was exorbitant, Vaughn thought, to hell with it, and handed over his money to the Asian guy behind the protective wire-mesh screen in the off-licence.

Armed with enough packets of Rizla to redecorate his flat, the bottle of rum, a two-litre bottle of Coke, twenty cigarettes and the knowledge that a quarter of an ounce of weed was waiting in the ornamental box on the coffee table at home, Vaughn let himself into the flat at three in the afternoon, ready to knock himself out for the rest of the day. Before starting, he checked the answerphone for messages and found that the only one was from Courtney, just to let him know that if he wanted to see her he wouldn't be able to. She had to attend some fashion function somewhere or other.

'Yeah,' grumbled Vaughn aloud, walking back across the room, 'you go and do your stuff, I didn't expect to see you anyway. I never do.' He stopped in mid-stride, struck by a thought: why was he still with her? He never saw her and when he did she fell asleep; surely he could do better than that and find someone who truly appreciated him? He spent a few seconds trying to decide whether the question had been prompted by grief or common sense, gave up and started drinking. The end of the third joint had petered out between his fingers when he finally dozed off, curled up on the sofa. The bottle was half empty.

The telephone must have been ringing for ages but Vaughn had to gather his senses enough to find it, and then answer it with any amount of lucidity. However, it took him a while before he could manage to engage in conversation and he found himself mumbling incoherently in response to the entreaties, demands and directions of the frustrated caller, who was trying hard not to lose his patience. Vaughn hung up, looked at his watch – seven o'clock. He stretched and yawned, bumped into furniture a couple of times on his way out of the room, and stumbled to the bathroom, where he attempted to take a cold shower. It was a good idea in theory, but the combination of grief, rage, rum and weed made his body and skin feel so fragile and tender that he screamed and ran a bath.

When he heard the car beep outside he pulled back a curtain, checked and waved, scrambled around for his keys and wallet, pulled on his jacket and let himself out. After the bath he felt warm, even hot, and admitted to himself that much of the feeling was probably due to the excessive amount of rum he had drunk before passing out. He was clean but still too drunk for his own good. He felt better.

CHAPTER NINE

Michelle threw her keys on to the table in the passage and had a quick look at her disguise in the mirror. She did look like a boy but hoped that it was only because the clothes were big and her face couldn't be seen. The idea that she could pass for one of those wild, lawless kids was quite disconcerting.

She thought for a moment about Milk's response when she had asked if she looked like a boy. Maybe she had put him off, maybe that was why he hadn't returned with her. It bugged her for a while, but she wasn't about to dwell on it. She wasn't making that sort of mistake again.

In the kitchen she dropped the bag and heard it bang loudly as the four studs on the base hit the floor. She paused on her way to the kettle. The bag was heavy, it was good-quality leather, but if it was empty it shouldn't have hit the floor like that. She suddenly realised that she hadn't checked the contents of the bag since acquiring it. She crouched down and un-zipped it, apprehensive and excited, but not sure why.

There was nothing in the main compartment, so she checked the pockets and zippers inside – nothing. But as the bag was Michelle's she knew that it could expand and that there was a way to conceal small things in that section. She pulled the zip three hundred and sixty degrees around the holdall, straightened it out, and revealed a packet the size of a paperback book, wrapped in plastic and again in a carrier bag. She didn't need to touch the parcel to know what it was. It was wrapped and packed so neatly and tightly that she immediately knew it had to be drugs, and Class A at that. She sniffed. It couldn't have been weed, a packet that size would have reeked no matter how well wrapped it was. She put the parcel back into the bag and sat down in the living room, realising that she had some thinking to do. At times it seemed crazy to break into a house for a bag, a poxy leather bag that had seen better days and could be bought for half the price now. But she had been convinced that she had to get that bag for her pride, her self-respect, her sanity, and now that she had she really was not disappointed. A little nervous, perhaps, but not disappointed. She had wanted a way to hurt Patrick and unwittingly she had.

A quick guess told Michelle that she was sitting on a fair amount of money, twenty or thirty thousand pounds. Somebody somewhere was smiling on her. The only problem now, as she was no longer in touch with any of the people that could have helped her in the past, was selling the gear. Despite her elation, Michelle guessed that the hard part had only just begun.

* * *

Henrietta's was directly opposite the Cannon Cinema, in Streatham, between a building society and a restaurant that boasted a performing Elvis look-alike. It wasn't a special bar, it wasn't the in place to drink at, the clientele weren't happening people and the décor was nothing to write home about. It certainly wasn't a black bar, but it was out of the way, and the guys liked it.

Milk lounged in the corner of the dimly lit booth of dark wood and red velvet and reached for his White Russian. He took a mouthful, rolled his eyes in pleasure and put the glass next to the other two lined up in front of him on the table. It was happy hour, with half-priced drinks, so Milk had bought all his at the same time, just in case. He took another sip and said to Vaughn, 'You were really talking shit on the phone, you know that? I didn't know who the fuck I was talking to for a while. I was thinking, who is this wanker and what's he on?'

Vaughn showed Milk his middle finger and sucked so hard on his straw that in the gloomy lighting his cheeks disappeared.

Ditton nodded and began to peel the label off his bottle of beer. 'He's got a point, V, know what I mean? How comes you're so moody anyway? You knew we were coming, you had plenty of notice this time but you're still behaving like somebody's died or something.'

Vaughn swallowed his Long Island Iced Tea and felt

as though the alcohol was travelling from the glass, up the straw, into his mouth and straight to his brain. He was pleased. 'Somebody *has* died,' he said flatly.

The statement had been so level and routine that Ditton didn't take it in initially. After a few seconds he clicked, frowned and asked, 'Somebody's dead? Who's dead?'

'Darryl, one of my kids from work. Strangled and beaten beyond recognition. That's why I'm like this. That's why I drank a bottle of rum this afternoon and sounded like a village fucking idiot on the phone, and that's why I'm not saying much now. OK?'

Ditton's eyes narrowed. 'The kid on the news yesterday?'

Vaughn nodded and Milk sent Ditton an *Oh, shit* look, remembering his flippant remarks from the previous evening.

'I'm just going to keep my mouth shut from now on,' Milk declared.

Ditton nodded. 'I think that might be a good idea.' He turned to Vaughn. 'What happened?'

'There isn't much to talk about, except that it looks like I'm the number one if not the only suspect at the moment. I'm the last person known to have seen him alive, and they reckon that we had an argument and then I shot off after him.'

Ditton and Milk looked at each other, puzzled, and then both sat forward, their full attention gained.

'So what happened? Why do they think that?' demanded Ditton.

'It's a long story.'

Milk looked at his watch and held his hand up to attract one of the staff. 'We've got time.'

Vaughn told his tale and the other two tried to convince him that nothing was going to come of it. He was innocent and they didn't think the police really suspected him, it was just their normal full-of-shit procedure. Try to frighten everybody and see what comes to light as a result.

'Come on, V,' Ditton urged. 'You know they're bastards, don't let them get to you. Intimidation, bullying. That's what they're all about. They're thugs. They're just the biggest, most organised firm out there. That's all they are.'

Vaughn shrugged, remembering DS Rose. 'She seemed all right, though.'

'Yeah, she *seemed* all right,' snapped Ditton, out of character. 'Seemed is not the same as *is* or *was*. Don't let the fuckers fool you with the good-cop-bad-cop routine, don't let me think you're falling for their shit. OK? OK? Get real, for fuck's sake.'

Ditton sat back and drained his beer, his eyes ablaze and his breathing heavy. He continued to glower until he saw the expressions of curiosity on the faces of Milk and Vaughn, and realised that he must have sounded more passionate than he'd thought.

Milk grinned and enquired, 'So, do I take it that you're not too enthusiastic about our wonderful police force, then?'

They sat in silence for a while. Vaughn was on his

way to being drunk but still upset with himself for upsetting Ditton. Ditton was annoyed with himself for becoming upset and thus upsetting Vaughn even more in the process. Milk was just thinking what a sorry couple of wankers the two of them were. At some point during the subdued silence, Vaughn looked across the room and managed to focus properly for long enough to see a painfully skinny light-skinned young man enter the bar. He spoke briefly to one of the staff before heading straight for a group of tables around a corner in the most secluded section of the establishment.

'Hey,' Vaughn asked, pointing, 'isn't that your friend over there? There, in the green jacket.'

Milk and Ditton looked up, declared in unison, 'He's not *my* friend,' and snickered like children.

'But don't you know him?' persisted Vaughn. 'I'm sure you know him.'

'Put the drunkard out of his misery,' Milk instructed. 'It's fucking painful to watch.'

'His name's Earl,' Ditton informed Vaughn. 'I know him, but that's as far as it goes. He's Tyrone's mate. I hope he stays over there and doesn't see us.' Ditton kissed his teeth and shook his head like an old man who has seen it all, one time too many. 'I suppose he's here for *business.*'

A couple of minutes later three other guys filed in and headed for the same corner as Earl. They stood out for a number of reasons, not least because they all wore full-length black leather coats and baseball caps.

The one at the front of the line was very short, dark and squat. The second was very tall, light-skinned and massive, with little brown freckles on his nose that made him resemble a doll.

The last newcomer was also dark, also very tall, but he looked as gaunt as Earl, if that was possible, and mean, with thin straight lips and a long nose. If he had been wearing a low-crowned, wide-brimmed stetson he would have been the perfect spaghetti western bad guy.

'Junction boys,' stated Milk. 'I recognise the one at the end.'

'Shit,' exclaimed Ditton, referring to the tall, dark guy. 'That is the Grim Reaper, and nobody can tell me different.'

The three guys turned the corner, disappeared, and were forgotten.

'I hate this country,' declared Vaughn, out of the blue. 'I just want to pack my bags and piss off somewhere.'

Milk and Ditton exchanged knowing glances, feeling one of Vaughn's self-pitying, nobody-loves-me-nobody-appreciates-me rants about to start. The ingredients were there: grief, pressure and lots of alcohol.

'What's brought this on?' quizzed Milk. 'The kid dying?'

Vaughn shook his head. 'That's just the final straw. I've been feeling like this for a while now, and the only solution I can think of is to leave this place. I can't stay here forever. I just can't.'

Ditton cleared his throat. 'And where would you go?'

'Anywhere. Caribbean? I don't know. Anywhere.'

'And what are you going to get from that?' pressed Ditton.

The alcohol was beginning to affect Vaughn's reactions and facial expressions. If he had been sober his face wouldn't have expressed such horror at Ditton's question. He was also beginning to slur. 'What am I going to get from that? I'll be somewhere where I can get some respect and won't have to worry that the colour of my skin is going to affect the way people deal with me. That's what I'll get.'

Ditton nodded thoughtfully. 'But you know you'll go out there and they'll call you English, and they won't give you respect anyway. It's bad enough for someone born there to return and try to settle, let alone for someone like you who's only been there on holidays. Face it, you're English. This is your country.'

'I don't believe what I'm hearing,' exclaimed Vaughn. 'How can you say that? Especially you, with, you know, your past and everything.'

Ditton shrugged. 'That's just the way I feel. I'm not saying that this country's a great place to be or that our lives are brilliant, but it's where we are and what we've got. Anyway, you haven't done too badly out of it, have you? You've been to university, got a degree, a good job—'

'There's nothing good about my job,' interrupted

Vaughn. 'Nothing at all. And it's not as though it's what I ever saw myself doing.'

'OK, but it pays you enough money for you to have bought a flat, drive a car and maintain your lifestyle, true? Now, if you're honest, if you had been brought up in the Caribbean the chances are that you wouldn't have had any of that. And if you did, your parents would probably have killed themselves to send you to college in America or here, and then you would probably have tried to find some way to stay wherever it was that you studied. So, if you were to go there now with your qualifications and money, you'd just be taking the piss like any other colonial.'

'The way I look at it,' began Milk, ignoring the raised eyebrows of Vaughn and Ditton, 'is that I'm a Londoner. I wouldn't call myself English, British. None of that. If someone asks me where I'm from, I'd say London. And if they push and ask where I'm *really* from, I'd say Tulse Hill, you know what I mean? Now, if they actually asked me where my parents are from, which is what they're normally getting at, I'd say the Caribbean. But that's not me.'

The discussion raged for a while longer, during which Vaughn managed to knock back another two Iced Teas and request more. 'At the moment, this is the best thing about this country,' Vaughn declared holding up one of his newly arrived drinks.

Milk tried not to laugh and asked, 'But what about Courtney? Where is she in all these plans about fucking off somewhere?'

Before answering Vaughn reached into his jacket pocket and retrieved his phone. He glanced at the text message and snorted. In answer to Milk's question he replied, 'I never see her anyway. It wouldn't be much different to how things are now.'

Milk shot Ditton a questioning look. Ditton answered with a shrug. Milk sat up and forward. 'So how come you don't fuck about, then? I mean you sound as though you should be out there letting it off.' Milk paused and a smile spread across his face. 'You know, that's what I think you need to do. Go out there and be a man. Trust me, you'll feel better, get rid of some tension and stress.'

Ditton bit his lip in an attempt not to laugh. Failing to do so, he rose to get himself a beer.

Vaughn coughed. 'I'm satisfied with what I've got, thank you very much. Me and Courtney are all right, and I don't need to get rid of any tension or stress. I don't see how me saying that I could go and live in the Caribbean has led you to that conclusion.'

'Nah, it's got nothing to do with that. This is just Uncle Milk's diagnosis. Trust me. I'm never wrong.' Milk ignored Vaughn rolling his eyes. 'So haven't you ever slept with anyone else since you've been with Courtney?'

'No,' replied Vaughn indignantly. 'Why would I want to do that?'

Milk sat back, stunned. 'Why would you want to do that? Shit! You're serious, aren't you? You need straightening out quickly. Isn't there anyone you know that you could see yourself getting together with now and then for a sensible, adult relationship?'

'You mean to have an affair?'

'*You mean to have an affair*,' mimicked Milk. 'You could call it that.'

Vaughn hesitated. 'No. Nobody.'

Sharp Milk picked up on the hesitation. 'Who?'

'Nobody,' repeated Vaughn.

'Who?' persisted Milk.

'Nobody!'

'Who?'

Vaughn cracked. 'Some white girl at work keeps telling me she wants to know, but I'm not really interested.'

Milk grinned. 'Not *really* interested? Why's that? White girl's perfect for the first one, trust me. Everyone does it. Even Wrighty. How do you know that she wants to know?'

Vaughn frowned. 'Don't take the piss, man. Give me some credit. I know, OK?'

Milk raised his hands in apology and Vaughn continued: 'That was her that texted me. Wants me to call her.'

Milk sat forward. 'Well call her then, man. What are you waiting for?'

Vaughn frowned. 'I don't want to call her. What am I going to call her for?'

It was Milk's turn to frown. 'It looks like I'm going to have to spell this out for you. When you leave here in this moody, depressed state that you're in, you're going to go home, probably drink some more and pass out feeling no better than now. Courtney's not going to be there, is she?'

'No.'

'Does this girl at work know about Courtney?'

Vaughn nodded. 'Yes, and she still wants to know. Isn't that crazy?'

Milk thought to himself, someone's crazy but it's not her. All he said was, 'You could go round there, have a laugh, get your end away, forget all your troubles for a while and wake up tomorrow with a new outlook on everything. Trust me.'

Vaughn didn't appear convinced, so Milk asked 'Well what does she look like? Is she a dog, or what?' The vehemence of Vaughn's rebuttal made Milk grin. 'Listen to yourself,' he directed. 'You're gagging for it. Go and take a piece, man.'

Vaughn was having trouble holding his head straight so he slumped and supported it on the wall. 'But what about Courtney?'

'What about her? She's not going to know anything. What she doesn't know won't hurt her. Just think about that body the way you described it to me, all fit and ripe, and—'

Vaughn held up a hand. He didn't need to hear any more.

Ditton returned with more drinks and sat down. 'I just spoke to Earl. The fat git saw me when I was at the bar. Those three guys are sitting with him.'

Milk grinned. 'Business?'

'Yeah, business. Anyway, you planned this one's affair yet?' Ditton motioned towards Vaughn.

Milk winked. 'Almost.'

'Well, I'm not involved in any of this,' stated Ditton. 'Leave me right out. I'm going to make a phone call, see what Jonah's up to.' He rose again, squeezed past Vaughn and trotted up the stairs and out to street level.

Milk reached into his jacket and pulled out his phone. He punched a few keys then placed it squarely in front of Vaughn. 'Do the right thing,' he said. 'You know it's the right thing.' Vaughn looked at the phone. Milk persisted. 'Fuck it. I'll even dial it for you.'

CHAPTER TEN

It was cool and breezy on the street, a welcome relief from the heat and smoke in the bar. Ditton took a deep breath of fresh air and watched the constant stream of traffic making its noisy way along Streatham High Road as he dialled Jonah's number. Jonah answered immediately and sounded chirpy. Ditton wondered what he was on but was pleased, regardless. Jonah confirmed that he had been given the cash by Tyrone, fifty thousand pounds and was going to make the collection in an hour or so. Ditton told him to be careful and rang off.

While he was on the phone to Jonah, Earl's three business associates had filed out in exactly the same order that they had filed in. They bowled across the road and got into a green Golf that was parked just past the cinema. He speculated about what kind of business Earl would have been doing with a fucked-up crew like that, but gave up, as the possibilities were infinite. Ditton was about to turn to go back inside the bar, when an eight series BMW pulled up in front of him, beeped and managed to block three lanes of traffic while the driver parked, careful not to damage his alloy wheels. A muscular, smartly dressed black man stepped out and walked around the car to stand squarely in front of Ditton.

'Gary, how's it going?' the new arrival asked after peering at Ditton for a few moments.

'Not bad, Vincent. And you?'

Vincent Carty frowned and paused. He sighed dramatically and said, 'I'm OK, but I'd be a lot fucking better if people returned messages. Or didn't you get it?'

Ditton shrugged and smiled apologetically. 'Milk told me, last night. I just didn't get round to calling. Sorry.'

Vincent looked thoughtful for a second or so, then said, 'All right, forget it.'

'So what are you doing here, Vincent? This place is a bit below you, isn't it?'

Vincent scowled. 'Too fucking right it is. I came to find you, didn't I? Why else would I be at a shit hole like this?'

Ditton chuckled. 'But how did you know I was going to be here?'

Vincent folded his arms and winked. 'I've got my sources, haven't I? Essential they are.'

At that moment Ditton would have given his right leg to know who those sources were. 'What did you want to speak to me about?'

'What do you think? Jonah and the slag he's working

for. Now, the guy's supposed to be your cousin or something, which is the only reason he's still breathing, but that might not last for much longer. I hear he's saying things about my brother. Making threats about the both of us but claiming that he's going to start with Jonah. Now I don't like that at all, not one little bit.' He paused and seemed to be trying to look into Ditton's eyes and beyond at the back of his skull.

'Now, for his sake, you better tell him to leave before he gets seriously hurt. And make sure he knows that if anything happens to Jonah, anything at all, I'll shit down his throat before I gouge his eyes out and burn him alive. You make sure he understands that, all right?'

Ditton nodded. What was going on here? How had he got himself involved in this mess, and how did Vincent know so much about Tyrone's thoughts and actions? So much for his assurance to Tyrone that he would speak to Vincent and try to sort things out. He found himself saying something similar to Vincent. 'I'll speak to him, but I don't think there's anything to worry about. You've got him rattled and he's just talking, trying to make himself feel important. Don't worry about him, Vincent, it's not worth it, seriously. He's just in over his head.'

Vincent nodded vigorously. 'Too right he's in over his head. Way over. Now if I listen to what you say and leave him alone, what do I do if something happens to Jonah? Who's going to be held responsible? You?'

Ditton sincerely hoped not. 'Tyrone's not going to do anything to Jonah. It's just talk.' He hoped the

143

statement wouldn't be thrown back in his face as bullshit.

'Yeah, but talk has a funny way of becoming the truth, doesn't it? If I keep saying I'm going to kill Tyrone, Tyrone will be dead sooner or later. Know what I mean?'

Ditton understood. He heard the door behind him and stepped aside to let whoever it was pass and be on their way. It was a welcome break from Vincent's intensity, intrinsic violence and aggression. He wished it was a group of fifty pensioners walking at a snail's pace to give him a bit more time. Instead it was Earl, who stepped out grinning. He shook Ditton's hand, winked and said, 'Nice one, mate. See you about.' Earl then saw Vincent, nodded once, and was on his way without looking back.

The scene puzzled Ditton. The nod wasn't right coming from a friend of Tyrone's. It wasn't the fact that Earl had nodded; that was respect and Vincent was due a lot of that. But the nod itself seemed wrong, too assured, almost cocky. It tied in with the way Earl had been talking during the meeting at Tyrone's the day before. Was he as eager as Tyrone to get involved in a feud with Vincent? It seemed a crazy idea but Earl hadn't looked at all put out by Vincent.

Maybe the guy just had more balls than Ditton had realised.

'That was the fucker's friend,' stated Vincent, watching Earl step towards the traffic lights and then disappear around the side of Streatham Hill station.

He lanced Ditton with his gaze again and said, 'All right, I'm going to hold off for a while because of what you've said. But if anything happens I'm going to want blood, and I won't really care where I get it from. You understand?'

Ditton nodded.

Vincent slapped Ditton's cheek playfully and marched to his car. Before getting in he stopped, turned back to Ditton and said, 'Remember, I'm relying on you, *consigliere*, don't let me down.'

The situation was getting crazy, people everywhere wanted to kill each other and somehow he had found himself placed in the middle of the madness. Vincent had called him *consigliere*, the name the others teased him with, knowing that it wound him up, and he didn't understand how he knew or why he used it. Milk had started it by claiming that Ditton was Vincent's chief adviser, in Mafia terms his *consigliere*. It was nonsense as far as Ditton was concerned. Vincent was like an older brother. If he asked Ditton a question he got an honest answer, that was all, nothing more. If Vincent based his actions and operations on information and advice he received from Ditton, that was Vincent's business and nothing to do with Ditton.

True, he couldn't deny the fact that being linked to Vincent made things a whole lot easier out on the street, but Ditton didn't antagonise people, avoided conflict, and as such had never had to call on Vincent for assistance. But he knew it would be there if it was ever needed. For some reason, though, Vincent calling him *consigliere* was disconcerting. The whole thing was crazy.

The lunacy continued when he got back into the bar and found Milk and Vaughn laughing like demented children.

'D? You've got to take me somewhere,' announced Vaughn. 'I called that girl and she wants me to come round now. You going to drop me, or should I get a cab?'

Ditton looked at Milk and asked, 'Is this for real, or is it the drink talking?'

'It's for real,' said Milk, grinning. 'Tomorrow morning he won't be thinking about the Caribbean.' He got hold of Vaughn in a playful headlock, 'Will you, my son! Eh? Eh?'

Ditton shook his head and sighed. He had other things on his mind now, and the humour in this situation was lost on him. 'When do you want to go?'

'Right now,' Milk piped up. 'Don't you, tiger? You want to go now and be fed, don't you?'

Vaughn grinned and growled, 'Yeah, I want to go now. Go and get all that lovely flesh.' He wrapped his arms around an imaginary body and nuzzled.

Ditton shrugged and took a long swig from his beer bottle. 'All right, when you're ready.'

Milk put his arm on Vaughn's shoulder and tried to look serious for a change. 'Vaughn,' he said solemnly, 'whatever you do, don't let the side down. There's a myth going around – well, it's no myth in my case –

about the black man and what he can do. Don't fuck it up for the rest of us, OK?'

Vaughn nodded. 'OK, Uncle Milk.'

Milk frowned. 'Believe me, I'm serious about that one.'

When Ditton pulled up across the road from the flat in Tooting ten minutes later he turned to Vaughn and asked, 'Are you sure you want to do this? Maybe you should wait until you're sober and then see how you feel about it.'

Vaughn shook his head. 'If I was sober I wouldn't be doing it.' He grinned, grabbed Ditton's shoulder and directed, 'Wish me luck, then.'

'Good luck,' said Ditton without conviction. He watched Vaughn struggle out of his seat belt, almost fall out of the car, and proceed to walk unsteadily across the street, pausing while he tried to read door numbers. Finally he rang a bell. The door was opened almost immediately. One second Vaughn was a silhouette surrounded by light, the next he had been swallowed up by the light and the door closed behind him. Ditton was dismayed that he hadn't even managed to get a look at her, hadn't managed to see what all the fuss was about.

He sat there in the car for two or three minutes thinking about Vaughn and what he was doing. Milk's logic about Vaughn enjoying himself and feeling better in the morning was one thing when applied to the average guy, but Vaughn was an innocent romantic, always had been and always would be. He was likely to find himself deeply involved with this girl before he realised what was going on, and would then find it very difficult to extricate himself. Who knew? Maybe Vaughn had grown up. Maybe he knew what he was doing.

CHAPTER ELEVEN

Jonah swung into the flats and parked up, pleased with himself. Let Tyrone try and complain about what he had done tonight, he thought to himself. As directed he had gone to Bermondsey and collected the goods. He didn't like it round there; white people there were a dangerous set, so he had been armed and ready for any eventuality. Fortunately nothing had happened.

The guy Derek didn't look too pleased to see him and Jonah supposed that was because he had done his neighbour the last time, and the guy had called the police for Derek. Fuck that, Jonah thought. Shit happens and the guy needed to lighten up, but he didn't say anything to that effect when Derek opened the door and glared at him. Even when Derek said, 'If I knew it was you coming I would have told Tyrone to fuck off,' Jonah kept his cool. When Derek counted the money three times Jonah kept his cool. And even when Derek said, 'Tell Tyrone he shouldn't be sending boys to do his dirty work for him,' Jonah stayed calm. So OK, he had vowed to himself that he was going to damage the bastard at some point in the future, but there and then he had kept to his part of the bargain and behaved himself. He hoped Ditton was pleased.

Apparently Tyrone was going to be busy for the rest of the evening so he had told Jonah to take the gear home and look after it until the morning, when he could bring it round to the flat. That was no problem to Jonah. He wasn't fazed by having fifty grand in cash or gear. He whistled as he waited for the lift to get to the fourth floor, whistled in the lift, and whistled as he walked along the balcony. He was in a good mood, he had impressed himself tonight. Things were going OK.

Upon returning to the bar Ditton found Milk sitting with Zero and Star, two brothers, and friends of Milk, Ditton and Vaughn from school and the neighbourhood. They were also The Extremists, talented rappers taking the British hip-hop scene by storm. The brothers hadn't been sure they were going to be able to make it to Henrietta's; they were due to be rehearsing for a show they were doing the next night to launch their new album, and had expected to be occupied until the small hours.

'Look who's finally turned up,' said Milk displaying Zero and Star proudly. 'About time. *Extremely* late.'

Ditton sat, and they talked and joked for a while, Zero giving them details about the show, until Milk's eyes lit up and he said to Zero, 'I knew there was something special I wanted to tell you. Guess what happened to me yesterday? It's better than the twins story.'

Milk proceeded to relate his adventure of the previous morning to the astonished newcomers. Zero had to keep looking to Ditton for confirmation of the craziness he was being told. Ditton would nod whenever Zero looked at him.

'And then, to cap it all,' said Milk, 'I'm walking out the door and she says, "By the way, you keep calling me Nadine. My name's Nicole." '

The brothers fell about laughing. It was hard not to. Even Ditton, hearing the story for the second time, found himself laughing, although he didn't feel particularly joyful after his chat with Vincent.

Ditton had looked after Jonah from the age of eleven, and Vincent and Rodney went way back. As a result, immediately after Rodney's accident Vincent had plied Ditton and his father with money for months until Ditton had recovered from the shock of his brother's condition and started earning. Vincent had said it was the least he could do, that Rodney was like a brother to him and he had to help them to the best of his ability.

Ditton glanced up to see Milk, Star and Zero looking across the bar at another three guys that had come in and sat down. He couldn't understand why the others were so interested in the most recent newcomers, they looked normal enough and weren't causing any hassle. 'What's the big deal?' he asked raising a beer to his lips.

Milk frowned. 'Don't you know who that is?'

151

Ditton looked again and shook his head. 'No. Who is it?'

'Patrick – 'Pepper' – and his cousin, Kevin Hill. I don't know who the other one is.'

'Jester,' said Zero.

'I can't believe they've actually come into our bar looking for one of us. That's really taking the piss. Can you believe it?' asked Milk.

'You don't know that for sure, Milk,' said Ditton. 'They could be here for any reason.'

The others turned to look at him sadly. Milk stood up and said, 'Fuck it, there's one way to find out, isn't there?' He strode across the bar to the table where Kevin Hill, Patrick and Jester were sitting. The expression on their faces when they looked up and saw Milk with his hands resting on their table showed that they hadn't known he was in the bar. They looked surprised but not particularly put out.

'All right, man?' greeted Patrick, his gold left incisor glinting in the weak light and matching the gold around his neck, wrists and fingers.

Milk looked down at the short, ugly man and tried to understand how someone like Michelle could lie down with him. What was she thinking of?

'All right. How's it going?' Milk's gaze shifted from Patrick to his younger cousin Kevin Hill. They were as different as chalk and cheese. Kevin was tall, dark and athletic with a young but handsome face and a pencil-thin goatee framing a charming smile. Milk continued to look Kevin in the eye while talking to Patrick. 'So, what brings you here? It's a bit out of the way, isn't it?'

'We're having a drink, man,' answered Patrick. 'What's the big deal? There's no membership policy, is there?'

Milk was beginning to boil but he tried to keep it under control. He took a deep breath, aware of the undertaking he had given Ditton that as often as possible he would try to stay cool, be peaceful and be tolerant. Ditton had suggested the period of *glasnost* over the weekend when Milk had come too close to attacking a six-foot-five monster who had cut him up on the road. The idea was all well and good, although it had got off to a bad start with the creep in Nicole's pink room, but even Ditton had accepted that was self-defence. Now, though, Patrick and his cronies were really testing Milk's tolerance.

'Listen, Patrick,' began Milk through clenched teeth, 'me and you haven't got mixed up in anything yet, and we should try and keep it like that, so don't take the piss. Understand?' He didn't wait for an answer but turned to fix his gaze on Kevin while still addressing Patrick. 'Now, I know what happened between my boy Jonah and your cousin here. It was unfortunate, deeply regrettable. But I've also been hearing rumours about what your cousin is planning to do to Jonah. Fair enough, I have to admit that I understand him wanting to do some of those things, but let me explain something to you, I've watched that kid grow up. I've taught him a lot of what he knows.' Milk leaned closer to Kevin, still supposedly talking to Patrick. 'If your

153

cousin tries anything with Jonah when I'm not there, I'm going to be after him to do him something serious. If he thinks Jonah's bad, he hasn't seen me. If he tries to do something to Jonah when I'm around I'll do him something serious there and then, on the spot. And if he's come into this bar tonight, into my bar, in my manor, looking for Jonah, then even though Jonah's not here, I will have to deal with your cousin, properly. Right here, right now.'

Kevin didn't know Milk. He knew his face and knew that he got about, but he didn't know him properly. So being young and impetuous, he pushed his chair back, looked at Milk squarely, then at Patrick, and asked his cousin, 'Who is this pussy anyway? What makes him think he's so bad?'

Kevin looked Milk up and down and sneered so viciously that one corner of his mouth was almost hidden by the corresponding nostril. Ditton and Zero were at Milk's side and restraining him just as he was about to land the fifth punch on the hapless Kevin. Patrick and Jester hadn't moved, it had all happened too quickly for them to respond. By the time they were on their feet Milk had been pulled away and Zero was advising Patrick and Jester to 'Get him the fuck out of here! Quickly!'

The two of them were too deep in shock to argue and dragged the bloodied and bruised Kevin with them out of the bar. Ditton led Milk back to their table and assured him that Kevin and the others had left and wouldn't be coming back, then walked over to the bar and apologised to the staff for what had happened. George, one of the Greek barmen, shrugged and said, 'These things happen, I know. Too much to drink, too much of the hormones, and bang!'

Ditton apologised again and ordered another round of drinks, but he was beginning to feel very tired. He wanted to relax, get away from it all, have some peace. 'Drink up, you lot,' he said putting the beers on the table. 'I'm heading out when I've finished this.'

'I'm sorry, D,' said Milk. 'I was thinking tolerance and patience and all that, but the kid was too much. Did you hear what he was calling me? Now how often would I have let him get away with it the first time? It's a start, isn't it? I mean, you've got to do these things gradually, haven't you?'

'Yeah, man,' said a weary Ditton. 'It's a start.'

Patrick swung the car right, on to Morval Road, and again turned to look at Kevin. 'This isn't a joke thing, you know? Milk isn't a boy, he's a dangerous guy and you're lucky it didn't turn out a lot worse.'

Kevin was adamant. 'I ain't scared of him.'

Patrick laughed and Jester joined in from the back.

'What's so fucking funny?' snapped Kevin.

Patrick stopped laughing for long enough to say, 'You should be. After what he did to you just now, you should be very scared of him.' The laughter took hold of Patrick again and infected Jester, who began to howl from the back seat. Patrick was laughing so hard he was finding it difficult to drive and pulled up opposite

Brockwell Park Lido to compose himself. 'Listen,' he said wiping tears of laughter away, 'I'm sorry about what happened, but one day you'll have to admit that it was funny, because it was.'

Kevin couldn't see the joke. 'You're full of shit, you know that?'

Patrick's phone rang and he was still laughing so hard that he couldn't hear the caller properly when he answered it. 'Sorry, babe. What did you say? Say that again.'

Jester was busy trying to placate Kevin, who had started shouting again about what he was and wasn't going to do Milk. 'Shut up!' Patrick yelled, commanding immediate silence. He turned back and spoke into the phone. 'Now start again, babe. Slowly.'

Short and brown, with big eyes in a big head, Patrick Braithwaite had never left England, his longest journey being to Birmingham for a carnival. His parents were from Barbados and Patrick himself had been born in King's College Hospital south London. He had never lived further than ten minutes away from the notorious teaching hospital, but he had an annoying habit of speaking as though he had just landed at Gatwick from Kingston, Jamaica, with a fake British passport and a suitcase full of mangoes. Patrick was captivated by the Yardie image and lifestyle – big clothes, big colours, big talk, bandannas around his artistically barbered head, along with lots of crotch-grabbing, machismo and bravado. To give him credit, he carried it off well. To those who didn't know, he came across as a real, not-to-be-fucked-about-with bad boy. He walked the walk, talked the talk, leered and sneered, had this deal and that deal going, but not much else. So when he was approached by Dog Heart Devon, a real bad boy overstaying his welcome in Peckham, but originally from Kingston, Jamaica, on his seventh fake passport, Patrick thought he had it made.

Devon offered him a pile of cocaine on tick, allowing Patrick to sell it and repay Devon from the profits he made. Patrick was over the moon. Now he was mixing with the real movers and shakers and was due to make a pile of money too. When he closed his eyes all he could see was pound signs and pussy, and he loved them both. Of course, Devon wasn't the kind of guy to fuck about with, but Patrick had no intention of doing that. He was just going to break up the gear, sell it, make a big fucking profit, sort Devon out and hopefully repeat the process. Things were looking up, or had been until the call came through.

Kevin and Jester stared, eager to know what the caller could have told him that had made his jaw drop the way it had.

'What?' Patrick screamed. 'When? Why didn't you call me, for fuck's sake . . . I know the phone was off, but shit, shit, shit!'

Without saying a word Patrick slammed the car into first gear, did a U-turn at high speed, making the tyres squeal, and shot off back the way they had come. Over and over he muttered to himself, 'The bastard. The fucking bastard. I don't believe it.'

'What's up?' questioned Kevin. 'Where are we going? What's happened?'

Through clenched teeth Patrick answered, 'Back to the bar. And don't worry, this time I'll be right behind you. The bastard, I can't believe it. He forced his way into Donna's and took the bag with the gear. He robbed my fucking gear!'

Kevin was confused. 'Who did?'

Patrick looked across, his face clouded with anger. 'Milk.'

Kevin howled and slapped his thigh, laughing so hard his face hurt. He couldn't have cared less about the pain.

When they got back to Henrietta's none of the four remained. They had drunk up and gone about their business. Patrick was seething. He kicked out at a dustbin, then, not satisfied, picked it up and hurled it into the road, forcing a cruising Mercedes to swerve dangerously. Patrick paced up and down the pavement glaring at the drivers and pedestrians who skirted him warily. By now, Kevin was laughing so much that it was his turn to produce the tears. He laughed so hard that his face hurt terribly and he himself couldn't decide if the tears were tears of discomfort or amusement. Patrick couldn't see the joke.

WEDNESDAY

CHAPTER TWELVE

The Keeler case conference had been painful in a number of ways. Firstly it had begun at nine thirty and hadn't agreed with Vaughn's hangover. Secondly, throughout, while trying to stay awake, Vaughn's alcohol-affected memory had begun to kick in and snippets of the night before with Janine to return. Worse was the information Vaughn was hearing about Christopher Keeler being regularly picked up by the police at Victoria station. Martin Green had coughed and told the conference that he had received assurances from Christopher and was certain that there was no cause for concern. Vaughn was astounded and found himself remembering DS Rose's probing questions about Martin.

Vaughn had been in two minds about whether he should return to the office. More and more of the night before was coming back to him in all its sordid glory, and he wasn't sure he could face Janine. Every now and then he would remember something he had done to or with her and would groan and cringe at the thought of his mouth locked against hers, or the way he had clung to her. He had revealed his vulnerability to this woman that he hardly knew. At the first sign of stress he had cracked and gone to her like a child to its mother. The simile conjured up an image of him lying with his head on Janine's breast while she stroked his forehead and consoled him. At the memory he wanted to curl up and die, and he hoped she would be adult enough to go easy on him. He could do without losing Darryl and his manhood on successive days.

Fortunately Janine was not in the office when Vaughn arrived, and he spoke with Sue in the kitchen for a couple of minutes, recounting the events of the Keeler case conference and Martin's omissions and strange behaviour. Back at his desk the computerised schedules showed that Janine would not be in until the end of the day. Vaughn would be long gone by then. He breathed a sigh of relief and checked his in-tray, noticing a folded piece of lined paper with his name on it. He recognised the scrawl instantly as Janine's, and unfolded the note with apprehension bordering on trepidation. There was no need. In coded terminology she enthused about him and his performance, and expressed a desire to do the whole thing again as soon as possible, preferably later on that day. Vaughn sat down and heard himself chuckling, his confidence restored by one piece of paper and a few choice words.

So when Paul rang through from his office and asked Vaughn if he could pop in for a couple of minutes to discuss something rather delicate, Vaughn was still smiling. That wasn't the case when he stormed back to Sue and asked, 'Do you know what he's gone and asked me to provide? Only a report of everything I've ever had to do with Darryl.

Sue nodded. 'That doesn't surprise me. And I think that prat Councillor Goode may have had something to do with it. He was back on the phone to Paul after you left yesterday, and I know for certain that it was about the whole Darryl thing. He had Paul in a right flap, twitching all over the place he was.' She paused dramatically. 'I think you'll have to do it.'

Vaughn stood up, grabbed his coat from the rack next to the door, picked up his bag, said, 'We'll see about that,' and was out of the door.

The cage was a five-a-side football pitch and basketball court surrounded by wire mesh fencing. The local kids seemed to conduct all their business in and around it. It was a meeting place, a refuge and an arena. Vaughn parked the car as close to the cage as he could, and heard Marlon before he saw him. Although he was physically small Marlon had a big personality and an even bigger mouth, which he used to intimidate and terrorise kids twice his size. Aged only twelve, Marlon was the chief figure in a loose gang that were already well known to the local police. Darryl had been part of that group but Vaughn had got the impression that they had parted ways. Darryl hadn't spoken about Marlon and the others much recently, whereas previously they had been all he talked about.

Vaughn vaulted a low wall and walked down three steps to the door of the cage. He entered and walked over to where Marlon and his companion were sitting. Before he had a chance to speak Marlon said, 'I'm not going back there, *sir*. So don't even try and talk me into it.' He cut his eye and handed the white boy with him another cigarette.

Vaughn seated himself beside Marlon and said, 'Right now, I don't give a shit if you go to school or not. If you want to mess up your life the way you're doing, if you want to ensure that when you leave school you can't do anything but sign on, or get banged up, that's your business. I just want some information.'

Taken aback by Vaughn's tone, Marlon looked at the EWO closely and could see the passion in him; he could almost feel it seeping out and making its way along the wall. 'What about?' he asked civilly.

'Darryl. What happened. Why it happened. That sort of stuff.'

Marlon shrugged and spat at one of the butts in front of him. 'If I could I would. But I ain't really seen him for a while. Not properly anyway. A few months ago, well at the end of the summer holidays, really, he stopped moving around with us like he used to.'

'Do you know why? Who was he with?'

Marlon scratched his head and shrugged. 'Well, at the beginning we thought he was on his own because he's like that, ain't he? But then I find out that some of the time he's with that tramp Chris Keeler. None of us could understand what Darryl was doing with someone like him.'

Neither could Vaughn. 'Why do you think they were together?'

'I don't know, but they were up to something, because from then Darryl was always flush with money, and even Keeler was looking better.'

Vaughn was sceptical. 'And you never asked him what he was up to? Never tried to get a piece of the pie?'

Marlon's scornful look suggested that Vaughn had just asked to sleep with his mother. 'Yeah! Course I asked him, but he wouldn't tell me nothing. He went on all tight, and said that I wouldn't want to know anyway, that it was something that us lot wouldn't do. I just thought, listen to him going on like he's some big-time gangster, and left him to get on with it. He used to be one of us but I ain't begging no one for nothing.'

'Is that it?'

'Yeah, that's all I know.'

A group of four older boys, all white, came out of one of the blocks of flats and walked along the far end of the cage, rattling the fence and hurling abuse at the two boys with Vaughn. Two of them he recognised from school as occasional truants, the sort that he sent letters to as opposed to doing home visits. The other two boys he didn't know.

The kid with Marlon picked up a stone and hurled it at the older group. It fell short and they howled their derision, jumping up on to the fence, shaking it like chimps at the zoo.

'Who are they?' Vaughn asked Marlon.

Marlon spat and motioned at the boy beside him. 'His cousin and his friends,' he mumbled. 'Wankers.'

The group of boys disappeared into another block of flats and their hoots and hisses disappeared with them.

Vaughn motioned at the quiet white boy who was wearing a uniform he didn't recognise. 'What about your friend here?'

'Who? Rick?' Marlon shook his head. 'He don't know anything more than me. Do you, Rick?'

The white boy shook his head.

Vaughn asked, 'And what about what happened on Monday? What do you know about that?'

Marlon hesitated. 'I don't know nothing about that,' he admitted quietly, 'but I wish I did. Darryl wasn't going round with us any more, but he was still one of us, one of the originals.'

Vaughn nodded appreciatively and stood up. He couldn't help but lay a hand on Marlon's shoulder. The tough kid looked close to tears. 'Can you keep your eyes and ears open for me? See if you come across anything else. I need to know what happened.'

The two boys nodded and Vaughn reached into his jacket and brought out his box of cigarettes. There were about ten in the packet; he took two for himself and tossed the box to the grateful Marlon. I'll put that in the report too, Vaughn thought.

* * *

For a few years Ditton had been in a relationship with Jonah's elder sister, Esther. It had ended unsatisfactorily for Ditton, but that didn't stop him thinking about her, often.

It was ironic that Ditton's thoughts of Esther were interrupted by a phone call from Jonah. He regretted turning his phone on as he had been enjoying memories which still seemed so much better than all of the meaningless liaisons he had had since, all quick sex and no affection. Seeing Vaughn and Courtney's set-up had intensified the feeling for him; he had seen a working model of what he had been craving, and although he needed to sit down and talk to Vaughn about what was going on between him and Courtney, Vaughn's aberration the previous night hadn't spoilt the picture at all.

Ditton rubbed the sleep from his eyes, and coughed to clear his throat. 'What's up, Jonah? How did it go last night?'

'I was trying to ring you all evening, man,' said Jonah harshly. 'Your phone was off.'

'I was busy,' lied Ditton. 'What's up? How did it go?'

Halfway through Jonah's pause, Ditton began to have misgivings. If Jonah was asked a question he answered it, he didn't care if the answer offended or was inappropriate, but this pause boomed like thunder and lightning.

'I got stuck up and lost the gear,' said Jonah. 'On

my fucking doorstep. I was set up, and stuck up.'

Ditton sat up, fully awake now. 'Tell me what happened,' he commanded. 'And don't leave anything out.'

Jonah kissed his teeth in frustration and began: 'I've done the pick-up, yeah? No problems, everything's sweet. Nobody's followed me, I know that for definite. I get home, park up the car and go up to the flat—'

Ditton interrupted. 'You're sure there was no one around when you parked the car? No one in the car park waiting?'

'I didn't notice anybody, and that's my block, it's been my block for years, I would have known if something wasn't right.'

'All right, go on.'

'I've opened the front door, gone inside, and I'm just pushing it closed when the sky falls on my fucking head. Next thing I know, I'm on my back with the imprint of a Yale lock in my forehead, a shooter aimed at my face and two other fuckers going through my pockets.'

Ditton felt numb. 'What did they take?' he asked.

'This is the set-up. They didn't take anything but the gear. Nothing else. They didn't even go further than the passage, just took the gear off me and left. One of them even asked where the fucking gear was! Now if that's not a set-up, I don't know what is. There was no one on the balcony when I was outside my door. They must have been waiting up by the chute, waiting for me to come back.'

It sounded logical. 'Did you recognise any of them?'

'No. They was all black guys, though. All in leather, and gloves. Worked kind of professional. If I wasn't going to slay all of 'em I might consider working with them, they was that good.'

The million-dollar question. 'Have you told Tyrone?'

'Yeah, I told him last night once my head had cleared enough to remember what happened and how to use the phone.'

'How was he?'

'How do you think? Mad. Talking about how he's warned me already, and he ain't doing it any more, and I better get him his gear or his money and then make sure he never sees me again.'

Ditton rolled his eyes and asked, 'What did you say to him?'

'I said that I was going to do my best to find out who did it, and who told them to. And that if I didn't get the gear back, the least I'd do would be to kill some people.'

Ditton knew there was more. 'That was it?'

Jonah chuckled. 'I told him to get the fuck out my face with the threats unless he wanted to be looking over his shoulder all the time. I said this is my fucking town and no prick like him's gonna tell me to leave it. He said, "If that's the way you want it," and hung up.'

Ditton smiled to himself. The kid had balls, there was no denying that. How long he was going to keep them was a different matter.

'All right,' said Ditton, getting out of bed. 'I need

to think about this. In the mean time you stay clear of Tyrone, you hear me? Don't go looking for him. This is London. It's big enough for both of you.'

Jonah laughed. 'That ugly fuck doesn't think so.'

'He just needs a bit of convincing. Does Vincent know about this?'

'Not from me.'

'OK,' said Ditton, grateful. 'Let's keep it like that, for now at least.'

Jonah agreed. 'Yeah, mate, that's OK with me, but if you speak to that big ugly bastard Tyrone, just let him know not to fuck with me. I'm serious.'

Ditton scratched his stomach and yawned on the way to the bathroom. 'I know you are, Jonah. Believe me, I know you are.'

Despite the robbery Ditton was surprised to see that Jonah was now being careful and had checked the security screen before opening the door. He still held the pistol in his hand though, and he grinned and waved Ditton in with it.

'I've been on the phone to some of the guys,' said Jonah over the music, meaning his crew. 'They're keeping their ears open for any info about yesterday.'

Ditton stood by the window, arms akimbo, looking out at the skyline, trying to get his thoughts straight. The volume of Jonah's music didn't help. He turned sharply, reminding himself of Sherlock Holmes, and shouted the question, 'Who did you tell that you were going to collect for Tyrone yesterday?'

Jonah frowned as though thinking was painful. 'Nobody, well, except Cannibal, but he doesn't count.' Ditton raised an eyebrow but Jonah shook his head decisively. 'Uh-uh, not Cann. Definitely not.'

Ditton nodded. Cannibal to Jonah, was like Ditton to Milk. 'I can't see it myself either. But then who else?'

'That's what I've got to find out.'

Ditton turned back to the window. 'I knew, Tyrone obviously knew, Earl was there, and Cannibal knew. Could he have told anybody else, innocently?'

'Who? Cannibal?' Jonah shook his head emphatically. 'The most he would have said to anyone was that I was doing something for Tyrone. No more than that.'

'Well I'm at a loss then. That leaves only me, Tyrone and Earl.'

Jonah twirled the pistol around his finger like a Hollywood gunslinger and struck a pistoleer's pose in the mirror over the gas fire. 'I've never liked that skinny fool. He might have done it.'

Ditton had to laugh. 'Nah!' Whatever he thought of Earl, he couldn't see him ripping Tyrone off. Anybody else maybe, but not his long-time friend Tyrone. Surely not?

Jonah shrugged, accepting Ditton's scepticism. 'Well, if you're right about the people that knew, it only leaves you and Tyrone, doesn't it? And I can't really see Tyrone arranging this, why would he?'

'I don't know,' confessed Ditton. The idea was bizarre, ludicrous in fact, but the way Tyrone had been acting lately, many things were possible.

There was a knock at the door which Ditton didn't hear, but Jonah tensed and raised the gun as he stepped into the passage. Ditton was still worrying about the idea of Tyrone arranging the whole thing so that he could go after Jonah and ultimately Vincent. It was hard to accept, not least because it meant that Tyrone was playing Ditton for a fool, but the more he thought about it the less fantastic the idea seemed. Tyrone had always had mad-dog ideas and plans, but they always seemed to turn out OK, or at least to his advantage. He always joked that all of his plans went pear-shaped, but that he always seemed to get what he wanted out of them in the end. Like another bad dream Ditton's mind played a picture of Tyrone and Earl hunched over a plan of action and a battle-zone map, moving counters to represent divisions and battalions.

It was the draught and the billowing curtains that made Ditton turn around and realise that Jonah was not in the room. He walked out into the passage apprehensively; the front door was obviously open. It could have been the guys who'd robbed Jonah come back to finish the job. It could have been Tyrone. *Could* Tyrone have done it? Yes. *Would* he have done it? Ditton couldn't rule out the possibility, and that disturbed him deeply.

He turned the corner and saw Jonah standing with the front door open, the pistol still in his hand but hidden behind the door. He was talking to someone outside and he waved Ditton back and said, 'It's nothing. Only the bitch from next door come to complain about the music again.'

Ditton leaned against the wall and tried to hear what was being said. He couldn't hear much of what the bitch was saying, but he could tell she was annoyed and wanted the situation resolved. Ditton wanted to turn the music down himself. He would have done if the woman hadn't come to talk to Jonah, but he knew there was no way Jonah would allow that now. The bitch was going to have to suffer.

Suddenly, something she said provoked Jonah and his reply was quick and aggressive. 'Your old man? Where is he? Fucking bring him here! Go on, fucking get him!'

Jonah was winding himself up and Ditton could see something totally unnecessary taking place, something that shouldn't even have come close to occurring. He stepped forward but he was too late. Jonah brought his left arm from around the door and pointed the pistol at the woman on the balcony. 'Get your fucking man, and let's see what he does with this.'

Ditton grabbed Jonah's arm and manoeuvred him out of the way, coming face to face with the shocked neighbour in the process. She was a short white woman in her late twenties or early thirties wearing the uniform of Levi's, Reebok Classics and a flying jacket. She had dark hair in a shoulder-length bob and she seemed strangely familiar but Ditton couldn't understand why; he didn't know any white girls, leaving that sort of thing to Milk and, apparently now, Vaughn. He stopped trying to work out if he knew her, and still holding Jonah, who was behind the door finding the whole thing hysterical, tried to apologise. The woman was apparently too shocked to speak and elected to use the fact that Jonah was out of sight to make a quick getaway.

Ditton watched her enter her flat and slam the door. He heard it bolted and chained and turned to Jonah in disbelief and frustration, letting go of him so roughly that Jonah fell back against the wall.

Jonah grinned. 'Relax, man! I was just scaring her a little bit, that's all. It's cool, man. Don't worry.'

'I'm not worried,' Ditton stated. 'But you should be. What about her man?'

Jonah coughed, dragged up a lungful of phlegm, shook his head in response to Ditton's question, stepped into the adjacent toilet and deposited the mucus. Then he said confidently, 'I've never seen the guy, he don't exist. Trust me, she's just trying it on with her fucking phantom old man.'

Ditton sighed. 'Well that might be true, but as well as that, for all you know she's on the phone to the Old Bill right now. You put a gun in her face, for Christ's sake!'

That one seemed to sink in and Jonah thought for a second or two. Her boyfriend was one thing but the police were another, licensed bad boys with no restrictions. 'If she ever calls the police, if she ever does—'

'You'll deserve whatever happens,' finished Ditton. 'That was so stupid, I still can't believe it.'

They stared at each other in silence for a few seconds.

Jonah stuffed the gun into his waistband. Ditton was too pissed off to speak. He had too much to deal with. Tyrone and Jonah, Tyrone and Vincent, the robbery and Tyrone's role in it. Now this crap with Jonah's neighbour was another unwanted problem, and the stupidity of it made him wonder what Jonah was actually capable of doing. Maybe he was working with his brother.

Jonah leaned forward, stood on his toes and kissed Ditton on the forehead as though he were a Mafia don. He proceeded to effect what he thought was an Italian drawl. 'It is a good thing I love you, my child, for I forgive you for your harsh words and tone. Many men have died for less, but you, I owe you too much.'

'Get ready to get out of here,' snapped Ditton. 'Plod could be on their way up the stairs right now.'

Jonah bowed graciously and disappeared into the bedroom to make himself street-worthy. Ditton flushed the toilet.

CHAPTER THIRTEEN

'Trouble?' Milk called out affectionately to Shane when he stepped into his mother's flat. He ruffled his nephew's short spiky hair. 'What are you still doing here? Haven't you been home yet?'

The little boy shook his head.

Milk thought for a while, trying to calculate his time commitments. 'Look, I don't know if I'll have the time today, but if not, me and you can do something tomorrow. How about that?'

Instead of being polite and agreeing gratefully, Shane asked with typical childish innocence and curiosity, 'Something like what?'

'I don't know,' admitted Milk. He looked over Shane's shoulder and saw the child's Sony Play Station tucked away in the television corner of the living room. 'Maybe we could go and see if there's a game you want for the station. How about that?'

Shane beamed. 'Yeah, man! FIFA or Turismo.'

Milk patted Shane on the back and the boy trotted off to the living room to immerse himself in the much more fascinating daytime television.

'Whassamatter?' Milk asked his mother earnestly, while looking over her shoulder for signs of food.

Mrs Kerr folded the tea towel in her hand, threw it over her shoulder and stood with her hands on her hips, her bowed legs a shoulder width apart like a western gunfighter. 'Your sister is not well, I'm sure of it. She hasn't been to work since Monday, I phoned her there and they told me. She phones in the evenings and says that she'll come and get Shane the next day but she doesn't. Now she calls this morning and says that he should stay for the rest of the week. The Lord knows, I don't mind having the boy here. Under normal circumstances it would be a pleasure, but I don't think this is normal circumstances. Something is not right.'

'Did you say that to her?'

'I tried to, but she didn't give me a chance, just hung up once she said that Shane should stay for the week. It's not good.'

'Have Yvonne and Beverley been to see her?'

'Beverley tried to go yesterday. She called and told Sandra that she was coming down to see her, but Sandra stopped her, saying she was tired and about to go to sleep. Beverley says she knows it wasn't true, but what could she do?'

Milk thought for a moment. 'I'm busy today, but I might be able to get up there this afternoon. If not, definitely tomorrow.'

Mrs Kerr shook her head. 'No. I wasn't telling you

so you would say that. I don't think you're the right person to go up there anyway.'

Milk was put out. 'What do you mean? Why not?'

'Relax, child,' said Mrs Kerr softly. 'You know how she was last time when she accused you of telling tales.There's that, and we don't know who is in the house.'

Milk felt this temple begin to throb.'What do you mean? Keith?'

Mrs Kerr nodded. 'Uh-huh.'

'If he's there I'd just have to—'

Mrs Kerr folded her arms in rueful triumph as she interrupted her son. 'That's why I say you shouldn't be the one to go there. Your head is too hot and your hands too fast.'

Milk couldn't argue and lowered his head in thought. 'Why don't you call Vanessa and see if she'll go round there. It's her mum. If she's not well, she should be concerned, regardless of whatever disagreements they've had.'

Mrs Kerr sighed and shrugged.

'If it's him, I'll fucking kill him,' Milk mumbled.

Mrs Kerr frowned.

It was still dark when Michelle gave up trying to sleep, turned the television on and flicked through the early-morning dross. She felt as though she hadn't slept for a single minute throughout the whole night, tossing and turning thinking about the parcel hidden at the back of the boiler cupboard in the bathroom. She kept telling herself that there was no way Patrick could find out what she had done. If he had, he would have kicked her door down already, she was sure of that.

Michelle padded to the kitchen, in a masochistic way enjoying the feeling of the cold floor on the soles of her feet, thinking that her mother would have had a fit if she had seen her doing it. She could hear her: *Child, you want to catch cold? Put on your slippers!* She boiled the kettle for a cup of hot chocolate to take back to bed with her, then looked at the clock on the microwave – an hour and a half and she'd be waking Dale up to get him ready for school. She didn't feel particularly tired even though she hadn't slept, so she could spend the time thinking about what she was going to do. Maybe she should just give it back? Stupid and impossible. Throw it away? Even more stupid. She was already thinking about a mortgage, a car, a holiday for her and Dale; who knew,maybe Milk would want to tag along? She smiled. Where that thought had come from, she really didn't know. Milk wasn't the holidaying type, and she should remember that and expect no more than the amusement and entertainment she had got so far. Expecting anything more from someone with Milk's reputation was a recipe for disaster, and she had tasted that dish too recently for her liking. Before any of that she needed some luck with contacting someone to take the gear off her.

The only person she had left apart from Milk was Delroy, a guy she had known through ex-boyfriend Carl, which said a lot about him straight away. A couple of years ago she had heard that Delroy had fled the police and some serious vendettas and gone to ground in Birmingham. Apparently he was still dealing up there, and was doing better than he had in London. Even if that was the case, Michelle thought, Delroy would probably do her a favour and take it off her hands. The problems were how to find him, and what kind of conditions he would put on deal.

Delroy was a scary guy who had always looked one step away from throwing her down and violating her. Michelle shuddered at the memory but put it down to her bare feet. She didn't want to think about that side of Delroy. If she did she wouldn't make any effort to try to contact him, and she needed to; she had to.

Nash was seated in a booth in a small, dark pub in Catford with three other guys, one black and two white. The pub couldn't have been refurbished since the late sixties and smelled like it. It catered for a select clientele of like-minded people, and although the landlord was insistent that absolutely nothing went on on the premises, he welcomed every criminal, villain and ex-con that stepped through the door. On the wall behind the bar were numerous photographs of some of the pub's more notorious patrons, either in poses with the portly landlord or dedicated to him. There were even four or five where the subject of the photograph stood next to the landlord but with his back to the camera, presumably fearful of identification. These photographs took pride of place on the wall.

Nash sat at the table with an empty half-pint glass before him. He held it between both palms, rolling it gently and staring at the froth at the bottom as though he was trying to read tea leaves. His companions all slurped thirstily from their own pint glasses and tried to outdo each other with tales of bravado and debauchery. Nash could down his liquor with the best of them but he was not in a drinking mood. Although he would laugh occasionally at the wisecracks flying around the table and sporadically contribute with sharply delivered one-liners, he was in his own world. Even five years later it was hard to believe that Rodney could have done that to him, but facts were facts, and Rodney was the only person he had told about the job. Seeing the kid was like a sign confirming that he had to do something. How else could he live with himself?

'What's the matter with you, Jim?' someone asked him. 'Why ain't you drinking? You look like you've found out your missus is really a mister.'

Nash smiled. That would be easy, he'd just strangle the bitch and plead provocation. This thing with Rodney was different. It was still sickening to think that Rodney could have done that to him. It merited serious action. But in the state that Rodney was said to be in? Wasn't that punishment enough? Even Nash had to think twice about doing away with a former friend who was now a fucking retard. Once, twice, and the thinking was done and dusted. Nash knew what he was going to do – knew what had to be done. He just hoped the brother didn't get in the way. He had always been a good kid and still seemed like one, but that wouldn't affect anything if it came down to the nitty-gritty. He was expendable too.

Nash stood up quickly, taking his companions by surprise. They looked at him questioningly.

'My missus is a missus. Definitely. But she's got more balls than the lot of you put together, I promise you that.'

The three guys around the table shot quizzical glances at each other, wondering whether the wrong thing had been said. None of them were soft lads, but they all knew that when Jimmy flipped he did it big time, and like any good nutter there was often little warning of what was coming and no remorse after the event. But there was nothing to worry about. Nash was happy now that he'd made his decision, and he puffed out his chest and beamed, exposing his cracked teeth and causing his eyes to disappear beneath the considerable scar tissue he had accumulated on both brows.

'My round,' he said brightly. 'Same again, lads?'

'Lovely,' said three voices in unison.

CHAPTER FOURTEEN

There was a tangible expectancy and excitement in the air as they strolled up to the door with their complimentary tickets, making their way past pockets of people loitering outside. The posers' cars had already begun to line the street and in a few hours, when the show was over, they would be double-parked and it would be a nightmare trying to leave. But that was part of the experience, part of what it was all about, and all three of them, Ditton, Milk and Vaughn, could feel that this night was going to be special.

The club was a weird place, with the entrance at street level and stairs immediately leading down to a basement with wooden floors, wood panelling on the walls and a low wood-panelled ceiling. A circular bar in the middle enhanced the nautical feeling, and all it needed to complete the scene was the boom of cannons and Lord Nelson crumpled in a dark corner, probably next to the cloakroom, asking Hardy for his kiss. Beyond the bar the club extended way back into a large area with a sunken dance floor that had a raised stage at one end and a low balcony around the outside. A DJ was stationed in the control box nodding enthusiastically, lost in the hip-hop beats he was pumping out, one hand on his headphones, the other fiddling with his mixer and decks.

The place wasn't full yet, at most a third of the venue's capacity, so all three of them saw Jonah immediately. Jonah was having a red day. He wore a red jacket over a red shirt that matched the colour of his weeded, bloodshot eyes; black jeans and trainers, and a red baseball cap. He caught sight of them and bowled across with a bottle of champagne in one hand, a spliff in the other, and an I'm-buzzed-out-of-my-mind grin spread across his face. What Class A was swimming about in his system didn't bear thinking about. When Jonah was out on the town anything was possible. Ecstasy, cocaine, speed – he looked like he was on all three, and loving it.

For greetings he nudged Vaughn unsteadily and pinched Ditton's cheek, and would have laughed about it hysterically if he wasn't buzzing so hard. He put his arm around Milk's shoulders and slurred, 'Milk, man. D told me what you did to that lanky bastard Kevin last night. Nice one, man. Nice one!'

Once Jonah had disentangled himself and returned to his boys, Cannibal and some others, Milk turned to Ditton. 'He looks wild tonight. Capable of anything. You want to watch him, carefully.'

Ditton sighed. 'This is craziness. What am I doing in all this? I'm too old for this kind of bollocks now.'

'Sorry,' said Milk, 'but if you're in it you're in it. It doesn't matter how old you are. And as long as you're around people like Jonah, trouble's going to find you.'

Vaughn stood back a little way, slightly overwhelmed and intimidated by the amount of bravado and machismo on display. He looked around the club, which was slowly but surely beginning to fill. There were a lot of girls inside, and they looked good. There were the odd few wearing things they shouldn't even have bought, let alone put on. The mandatory ones who were nice and knew it. The coy ones playing up to their men, being clingy and dependent in public when ten-to-one they were real self-reliant sisters in private.

There were some who simply oozed sex from every pore in their bodies, and Vaughn had to concede that last night, or maybe just the way he had been feeling lately, was affecting him, because he desperately wanted to go and grab a few and offer them the time of their lives. He chuckled to himself. Who was he fooling? That was Milk's domain. Vaughn could offer enjoyable, pleasant evenings with stimulating conversation and whatever came afterwards. But at least it made his mind up for him and he decided that no matter what, he was going to Janine's again, sober, and was going to either enjoy himself tremendously or never do it again – or maybe both. Suddenly he felt a whole lot better and was determined that he wasn't going to spoil the mood by thinking about anything work-related. Darryl had to be put on the back burner, at least for one evening. He checked the other two's bottles and went to get another round of drinks in.

When Kevin came out of his bedroom with a pistol wrapped in a Kwik-Save bag, Patrick didn't say a thing. Twenty-four hours earlier he would have tried to dissuade his headstrong cousin from carrying the weapon. Guns generally seemed to generate more problems than they solved. Today, however, Patrick wasn't feeling so responsible or sensible, and instead he simply looked at the gun, looked at Kevin and led the way to the car. All he had thought about throughout the day was why did Milk do it? And then why did he behave in the bar as though nothing had happened? He couldn't find an answer that satisfied him, and it pissed him off something rotten. In addition to the loss of his gear he had Donna giving him grief about what happened to her and not speaking to him, and Michelle behaving as though she didn't want to know if he was alive either. She hadn't phoned in days. And on top of all that, he had Billy the Kid next to him looking for scalps but more likely to shoot himself in the fucking foot. Patrick was not in a good mood.

Kevin, on the other hand, was feeling fine despite his sore face. He liked carrying the gun, it made him feel good, made him feel mighty and powerful. When he was younger he had carried blades, walking the streets with ratchets, flick-knives, wooden-handled double-O's. Now he carried a Colt .32. Patrick had said that Jonah and his guys were likely to be at the show they were going to. All those Brixton, Stockwell, Tulse Hill and Norwood guys seemed to know each other, so it was likely that a fair number of them would be there. Kevin wanted to be prepared. Both of the encounters he had had with that group so far had ended in embarrassment. First Jonah and then Milk. He wasn't about to let anything like that happen again, no way. No way at all. He didn't care about their reputations or who their brothers were. And now that Patrick had differences with Milk, hopefully he wouldn't be so quick to play peacemaker. Things seemed to be shaping up nicely. All that was left was to link up with the other guys and then take the show by storm.

The club was almost full and the firm – Jonah and his boys, Ditton, Milk, Vaughn and their clique – had staked a claim to a section of the balcony in front of some recesses and cubby holes. Some of the Extremist firm, Nameless, Ronin and Solar had left Zero and Star backstage, and were scanning the club for girls. They had effectively cordoned off the spot for themselves and themselves alone. A short, stocky white guy in a blue puffa jacket squeezed past underneath Ditton's nose and he instantly thought of Nash. What was the guy after? Ditton was in two minds about whether to ring the nutter and tell him not to bother trying to make contact again, or ever. But something told him not to, that it was better to keep in contact and know what a psycho like Nash was up to. Ditton was sure that if he met with Nash the next day, as Nash had suggested, they wouldn't be talking pure business. There was bound to be more.

'You all right, D?' asked Vaughn. 'You're quiet.'

'Yeah, I'm all right. Just thinking about a few things, you know?' Ditton took a long swig of his beer and when he had swallowed the barely cool liquid asked, 'So what really happened last night?'

Vaughn was preparing to protest when he thought better of it and leaned forward conspiratorially. 'Guess what?'

Ditton made a 'What?' face.

For once, Vaughn grinned as though his mouth and eyes were made for it. 'I'm not really sure. I woke up this morning at home, couldn't remember how I got there, couldn't remember leaving her place. In fact, I couldn't remember anything after you dropped me there. Then, throughout the day, little bits kept coming back to me, but I still can't really remember anything juicy.'

Ditton shook his head then threw it back and laughed hard.

'I couldn't tell Milk, though,' Vaughn continued. 'He would have been giving me grief now. You know what he's like.'

They laughed and talked about Milk until Vaughn looked across the floor and saw the man himself, chatting and joking with a white guy and two white girls. They were much too far away to hear what was being said even if the DJ hadn't been pumping tunes at

Heathrow decibel levels, but it all looked friendly enough.

'So what's going on with you and Courtney?' asked Ditton. 'That thing last night wasn't like you, was it? Is everything OK?'

Vaughn paused before answering. 'Yeah, nothing that a bit more of what I got last night can't solve.' The answer sounded as false to Vaughn as it did to Ditton, compelling Vaughn to shrug apologetically and try again. 'Whatever's wrong, and I'm not sure what it is, is my problem and nothing to do with Courtney. She's just getting the backlash.'

Vaughn looked at Milk and the two girls and asked, 'Which one do you think Milk's going to take?'

'Both, probably,' said Ditton.

Jonah turned his back on the others, stepped into one of the recesses off the balcony, opened a little wrap of paper and took another toot. Yep, that was better. He was loving the buzz so much that he didn't want it to wear off, and he was going to do all he could to keep it. After all that rubbish with Tyrone he wasn't about to miss an opportunity as good as this for having a great time. All his friends were around to watch more of their friends on stage, drinks were flowing, there was gear everywhere and girls ga-fucking-lore! Heaven without a doubt, and he deserved it. It had been a long day. After Ditton had turfed him out he and Cannibal had tooled up and gone asking questions. It felt as though they had been on their feet or driving all day, knocking on doors and heads to get answers. Nobody had been able to tell them anything, even with a pistol levelled at each eye. He had even gone halfway to fulfilling his promise to himself regarding that fool Derek in Bermondsey, and had gone back and interrogated him. That was fun. Considering his tough talk the night before, Jonah had been mildly surprised to see the guy shit himself so messily when he opened the door to see Jonah backed by Cannibal, and neither of them smiling.

But all Jonah could do now was hope that the messages and demands they had left for people to get back to them would produce results and information. But that could wait, and so could Tyrone. For now, Jonah was just ready to have fun. He sniffed, wiped his nose with the back of his hand, blinked a couple of times and turned around to face the others, ready to party and feeling like the king of all he surveyed. Nobody had better fuck with Jonah Carty tonight, mate. Nobody.

Milk had gone for a little reconnaissance and was astounded to bump into Marty, of all people. 'This is black people's music,' Milk had said. 'What the fuck are you doing here?' Marty explained that it was 'music full stop, you bastard' and he liked it. That was why he was there. Then, with a wink, he graciously apologised for not introducing Milk to his two companions, two girls that Milk was having trouble deciding upon, they were both so hot.

'Don't worry,' said Milk loudly, 'you never had any fucking manners, did you?' The girls – Sarah, blonde, tall and shapely, Kimberley, brunette, slightly shorter with a kind of sleazy sexuality that Milk picked up on instantly and liked – smiled demurely. And then, the introductions made, Marty pulled Milk aside and asked if the bet was still on for Sunday.

Milk was puzzled, 'Course it is, unless you're getting cold feet. Are you?'

Marty smiled greedily and assured Milk that he was not, and that he was glad everything was still as they had arranged.

After a little more chat Marty put his arm around Milk and whispered, 'The blonde's mine, personal, so don't even think about it. The other one's her mate, she's free and willing.'

Milk's eyes said, 'Yeah?' Marty's said, 'Uh-huh,' and Milk was away and down to business. Both of them would have been good, but one would have to do, wouldn't it? Greed was a bad thing, his mother had always said, and mothers were usually right. Usually.

CHAPTER FIFTEEN

'Well, what do you think then? Was I wrong?'

'No way!' said Natalie forcefully, and then squealed again. 'Girl, I'm so proud of you! And you whacked her with the bat as well!' Finally, satisfied that she had heard all the details, Natalie said, 'So where's the drugs? Can I see it?'

'Sure,' said Michelle.

She rose, retrieved the package and dropped it gently into Natalie's lap.

'Mind the skirt, Mich,' Natalie shrieked. 'I've only just got it back from the cleaner's.' And then, hefting the packet, observed, 'But then I suppose this could pay the bill a few times over, couldn't it?'

Michelle was well aware of that fact. 'That's what I'm working on now, but it's proving to be more difficult than I thought. I can't find any of the old lot, and I'm trying to get Delroy's number but nobody seems to have it. I've been trying not to, but I think I'm just going to have to ask Milk and think of what I'll tell him if he asks why.'

A frown forced its way through the foundation caked on Natalie's forehead and she asked, 'Why are you going to have to think of what to say to him? What are you worrying about? He's nothing to you, is he? Just amusement and entertainment. That's what you said, wasn't it?'

Michelle smiled. 'Yeah, but I don't want him to think that I'm doing something with Delroy.'

Natalie spread her arms and nostrils and mimed, *Why not?*

'Because . . .' Michelle paused, thinking. 'Just because, I suppose.'

'Do you know what he's like, Mich? The guy's a . . .' Natalie scrabbled around for the right word. 'He's a slag, a whore, he's famous for it. And on top of that, people say he's mad, dangerous.'

'I know,' said Michelle, smiling sheepishly. She shrugged. 'But I suppose I do like him. I have to admit, I always have.'

'It'll be worse than Patrick,' Natalie predicted.

'No it won't,' said Michelle decisively. 'Because I am fully aware of what he's like. He's told me what he's like, you've told me what he's like, so I'm just making an informed decision to get my amusement and entertainment from one of the best. I'm not looking to marry him or anything. I'm not even looking to go out with him, just continue what we've got now.'

Natalie sat back and stared at her friend for a few seconds. 'You're serious, aren't you? You really meant that.'

'Sure.'

Natalie grinned. 'Good for you. In that case . . .' She reached for her handbag, extracted a well-worn address book and flicked through until she found what she was looking for. 'Have you got a pen?'

'What for?' quizzed Michelle, her hopes rising.

'Delroy's number. Do you want it or not?'

'Course I do,' said Michelle, sitting forward eagerly. 'Where did you get it?'

'I saw him at carnival last year.' Natalie raised an eyebrow and gave Michelle a sidelong glance. 'You weren't there because you were expecting Patrick later in the day, or something silly like that.'

Michelle hurled a cushion at her friend and skipped to get a pen and piece of paper. Things were definitely looking up again.

Natalie had encouraged Michelle to phone Delroy while she was there, but Michelle had refused and it even seemed silly to Michelle herself. She knew why, though. Because he scared her and she didn't want to call him, except that she was desperate and had to. She hadn't called while Natalie was there because she couldn't make herself, not because she wanted to keep Natalie out of it. Now, as she sat there alone, Dale asleep in his bed, she tried to collect herself enough to pick up the receiver and dial. She could see him in her mind. Delroy loved generating fear, he fed off it, thrived on it and she bet that somewhere in Birmingham, or wherever he was, he could smell her fear and was rubbing his hands together in glee. She picked up and dialled. It was only three rings, but it felt more like thirty, and when it was answered Michelle wasn't sure whether she should be pleased or petrified.

Zero tapped Milk on the shoulder. Milk looked across, saw Kevin, Patrick, Jester and a new face, a short, light-skinned guy with big red lips and flared nostrils, and grinned. What were these guys playing at? 'Hey, Ditton,' he called, 'we've got visitors.'

Ditton turned and saw the group making their way through the crowd on the other side of the hall. He turned to Zero. 'I bet Milk invited them. That's the kind of sick thing he would think was funny.'

'Well, I'm sorry,' apologised Milk with a look of chagrin on his face, 'but I didn't. It would have been a good idea though. Anyway, at least if shooting starts we'll be able to see Zero doing a bit of moving on stage, dancing and dodging bullets.' Milk did a little jig as though he was evading missiles hurled by the audience. 'Believe me,' he said, 'this performance could go down in history.'

Zero shook his head. 'You're a sick guy in truth, aren't you? Anyway, luckily I'm out of this for now. I've got to go backstage and get ready, but try and behave yourselves and get Jonah to do the same. I wouldn't want anything to happen before we've done our set, anything that could stop the show, you get me? This is supposed to be a night for Extremists, but the right ones.'

'Don't worry,' assured Ditton. 'It'll be cool.'

As Zero walked off, Milk lit a joint and said, 'That was a big promise you just made. Jonah's in another zone right now and anything's possible. Now, we could try and keep them apart, but if Kevin's in the same mood,' Milk spread his hands, 'kapow!'

Ditton had been aware of how volatile things could be from the moment he saw Kevin. Any situation involving Jonah on alcohol or drugs was volatile but this scenario was especially so. 'I know, that's why I'm relying on you to be sensible and not encourage anything. Don't go winding anybody up, all right?'

Grinning, Milk asked, 'Me? As if I'd ever do anything like that.'

It was unclear whether Kevin and his crew stayed over on the opposite wall because it was about as far as they could be from Jonah and his, or whether they hadn't seen Jonah and were just making themselves comfortable. Either way, returning from one of his trips to the bar, Milk bumped into Patrick and Jester and saluted as he was passing. Patrick beckoned for him to stop.

Milk immediately began to apologise. 'Sorry about yesterday, mate, but your cousin's out of order. I had to do something, didn't I? I couldn't let that pass.'

Patrick appeared taken aback and Milk noticed that his eyes were bulging, a vein in his neck pulsated at an alarming rate, and an arm from Jester looked as though it was there to support his friend. Patrick didn't say a word so Milk moved on, but looked over his shoulder and decided that Patrick was either buzzing hard, or he was ill. He didn't look good at all.

Putting Patrick out of his mind with ease, Milk decided to do another circuit of the venue and to look in those dark corners where all the best stuff happens. He couldn't stomach the idea that there could be a potential delight in the venue that he missed out on because he didn't see it, so sporadically he'd take flight, wheel, circle and land again, confident that he knew exactly what prey was in his immediate environment.

Milk had almost done his lap and was in the final straight when he found himself approaching a group of girls dressed like he wanted them to be dressed. Not all of them were scantily clad but they had their garments clinging and fitting in the right places, and an abundance of right places to be fitted. Milk strolled past slowly and had a look, nothing underhand or sneaky, all up-front. One girl had her back to him but she turned around and to his horror Milk found himself eye-to-eye with his niece, Vanessa, Sandra's estranged daughter, who said mischievously, 'Hello, *Uncle* Marcus,' and lit a spliff. Milk was too stunned to answer. When she offered him a puff he thought he must have fallen asleep somehow and found himself in a very bad dream.

But to his credit, Milk had the ability to be reasonably diplomatic at times, so he composed himself and asked Vanessa how she was getting home. She replied in proper gum-chewing, eye-rolling, strut-your-stuff south London style that some guy she knew was supposed to be turning up and she'd be going with him in his car. Milk bit his lip and nodded.

When she said, 'More time, I've just been staying with him for the last few months because my mum's going on all stupid again, and I can't be dealing with that right now. I've got too much on my plate already, you get me?' Milk considered dragging her around the corner by the ring in her nose and giving her a couple of slaps, but he didn't, he nodded. And when she said, 'You sure you don't want a puff, Uncle Marcus? You're not getting old, are you?' he took a sip of his beer and excused himself. If he could keep cool with Vanessa behaving like that, Kevin Hill would be a piece of piss. Jonah, on the other hand, was a different matter.

Jester's hand was partly on Patrick's arm for support but also for restraint. Patrick had said he was OK and that if he saw Milk he'd be calm and simply ask him what the fuck he thought he was doing breaking into his girl's flat and robbing his gear, then smiling and waving at her afterwards. But when he saw Milk coming back from the bar and the bastard had the barefaced cheek to stand in front of him and apologise for what he'd done to Kevin, with no mention of Donna, or more importantly the gear, Patrick thought he was going to have a fit and his head started to hurt. Donna had said that Milk saw her, he fucking smiled and waved at her, for Christ's sake, but he was here now, behaving like it hadn't happened. Twenty thousand loaned pounds taken away just like that, and the culprit smiling in his face like they were the best of chums. The guy had to be crazy. He wondered how many people Milk was with and if there was any scope in trying something there and then, so he decided to follow the route Milk had taken and spy on his camp. Shortly after setting off he bumped into a group of girls and one of them asked after Kevin and where he was. Impatiently Patrick pointed in the general direction behind him, and didn't wait for further questions; he was on a mission. Jester was trailing behind advising him to leave it alone, for now, but Patrick wasn't hearing that. All he could hear was the pounding in his ears, and all he wanted to hear was the sound of Milk's head breaking a bottle or preferably a bullet. And then, suddenly, he seemed to turn a corner, evade a body and find himself face to face with a mini army. He saw Jonah first, dressed in red and off his face; the big fat Cannibal was with him and about seven or eight of their boys.

Further on from them he saw Milk and his friend from the bar, Ditton he thought his name was, something like that. There were six or seven others with them and he could tell from body language that there were at least five other guys in close proximity that were known to them. Patrick regained his composure in an instant. He wasn't a betting man, but odds of twenty-something to one didn't seem too promising. Instead he walked up to Milk and said, 'We need to talk.' Milk looked at him strangely so Patrick coughed and said, 'Please?'

Milk looked at him even more strangely. 'Well talk then.'

'It's about yesterday,' Patrick began.

'Look,' Milk sighed, 'I already said sorry for yesterday. What did you want me to do? Just stand there while the arse sat in front of me and called me a pussy?'

'I'm not talking about that,' Patrick tried to say calmly, but instead produced a cross between a growl and a whimper. He cleared his throat. 'I'm talking about earlier.'

Milk appeared to close his eyes in thought but they weren't totally closed. You don't smack a guy's cousin and bed his girl one day, and stand in front of the same guy with your eyes closed the next. Stands to reason.

'Earlier? I don't know about anything earlier that would involve you,' Milk lied. He wasn't about to get into an argument about a girl now; he was too old for that, and he hoped he didn't have to bust Patrick's head over Michelle, nice as she was. If he'd done Kevin yesterday, Patrick today, who was it going to be tomorrow?

Patrick couldn't believe the front of this guy. The cheek of him was so galling, it was just too much. 'So you don't know anything, then?' he asked.

'That's what I said. Now is that all, or are you going to ask me again?'

Then, to compound Patrick's frustration, the lights went out, the MC cradled the microphone, and the show started. The audience cheered and moved forward en masse and Patrick found himself being buffeted like a pebble in the tow of a stream. He looked around frantically for Milk, again determined to get some answers, but he couldn't see him or any of the others. They had all been swallowed up by the crowd.

Zero and Star had torn the stage apart with lyrics and delivery, and produced a performance that had the crowd bawling for more. They had to return for three encores before they said their final farewells and ducked off-stage. A couple of minutes later the two brothers came out of a door alongside the stage and beckoned Ditton, Milk and Vaughn into their changing area, ignoring Jonah and his mob, who were preoccupied with a bunch of underdressed and game girls. The girls had allowed themselves to be met, and proceeded to alternate their tittering and strutting with admirable regularity and rhythm, uncannily resembling the mating ritual of some species of exotic bird.

Off-stage, congratulations were extended and accepted, and Zero directed the guys to a crate of beer on the floor. 'What are you lot doing afterwards?' he wanted to know. 'This place is going on for a little bit longer but I'm looking to go somewhere else. What are you lot up to? Ronin's cousin's got some rave going on up in Tottenham.'

Milk opened a bottle with the aid of the window ledge and once he had taken a long swig said, 'I'm going anywhere there's some action. What about you two?'

Vaughn declined with a shake of his head. 'Same as yesterday.'

Milk grinned, winked and performed a few exaggerated pelvic thrusts. 'D?' he asked.

'I've got to drop Vaughn, and then I'll probably go home, get some sleep.'

'Looks like it's just me, then,' Milk said to Zero. 'That doesn't mean anything, though, you wouldn't have noticed these two anyway. They both think that they've got the worries of the world on their shoulders. They just haven't realised that all it is is that they're black. The problems just follow on naturally.'

'Now he's the greatest philosopher of our age,' grumbled Vaughn. 'And all this time I thought he was just a dick with legs.'

Outside, amid the executive cars, the convertibles, the jeeps and the two-seaters acquired on hire purchase while their owners still had nowhere to call home, Kevin, Patrick and their group stood on the opposite side of the road from the entrance to the club, watching the other revellers come out. It was standard behaviour from people who weren't ready to go home and wouldn't have been able to sleep anyway, they were buzzing so hard. It was also an opportunity to observe any girls that had been overlooked inside. In the better lighting it would be easier to confirm that the beauties were indeed beauties, and the dogs dogs.

Kevin took a light from his cousin and as he handed it back asked, 'So what happened to you when the show started? Jester said he lost you in the crowd, and then I didn't see you again until halfway through.'

'I went to talk to that bastard Milk.'

'What did he say?'

'He didn't say shit. He was just talking about you and him yesterday. He's still going on like nothing happened and I'm just going to say, "Yeah, forget it." Now I know he's supposed to be crazy, but that's pushing it just a little bit too far.'

A wicked glint appeared in Kevin's eye and continued to twinkle mischievously as he said, 'Cous, you've got to deal with this now. The guy's taking the piss, he's probably there laughing about it with his boys now. You can't stand for that, man. For fuck's sake, tell me you're not going to.'

'What do you want me to do?' snapped Patrick. 'Walk up to him and say, "You took my fucking gear. I want it back now or I'm going to have to shoot you in the face"? Is that what you think I should do?'

Kevin shrugged. 'I wouldn't say I'd shoot him in the face, but basically, yeah.'

'You watch too many fucking gangster films,' Patrick concluded. 'This is real life, man, and although I intend to deal with him, I don't think this is the time or the place.'

'All right,' said Kevin, disdain smeared across his face. 'If you can live with yourself, go and be the pussy in the corner, but I'm surprised at you, let me tell you that. And I reckon Devon would be too.'

Patrick wheeled around and grabbed his cousin by the front of his jacket, slamming him against the shutters of a butcher's shop. 'I ain't no fucking pussy. You got that? I'm just not a fucking idiot ready to lose his life for a bag of fucking coke! All right?'

'Sure,' answered Kevin, without conviction. 'Are you going to let go of me sooner, or later?'

Patrick released Kevin, who thanked him, sarcastically. 'That's a bad temper you've got there, cous. Maybe you should try using it on the right people. You might get some results.'

And with that he turned and ambled over to Jester and the others, who were engrossed in a group of girls. Kevin slotted right in, on to a sure thing, while Patrick was left seething, gazing intently at the entrance, not sure whether he was angrier with Milk or himself.

Vaughn stepped out first, chilly but pleased to be in the fresh London air, away from the heat and smoke of the club. Ditton followed, buttoning up his jacket. He was in turn followed by Milk, who bowled out and to his surprise saw Desiree, a girl he had had a brief relationship with in the past, and a few other girls standing to one side. He walked over, said hello and proceeded to talk himself into a ride home and who knew what else? He excused himself for a second and stepped back to Ditton and the others, most of whom had exited the club by now.

'D, this girl, Desiree, she's going to drop me, so you're all right.'

Ditton smiled despairingly. 'I know I'm all right. Where's she going to drop you?'

Milk rolled his eyes ecstatically. 'Right on her chest if I'm lucky. Shit, man! Look at it. Isn't that something?'

Vaughn leaned into the conversation, winked and said, 'Milk, do it properly, for me, yeah?'

Desiree appeared by Milk's side, smiled radiantly causing Ditton and Vaughn a pang or two, and informed Milk that she had to drop two of her friends home first, and did he mind? Gracious to a fault, Milk answered in the negative and was just in the process of asking if they were ready when Patrick walked over, said, 'I need a word,' and didn't move.

Milk sighed and held his head in his hands for a second; he really was becoming tired of this family and their sorry saga of mishaps. He wanted them out of his face, but he tried to stay calm. So he reminded Patrick of what he had said earlier and informed him that he had nothing more to add, except that if Patrick had any sense, he'd get the fuck out of his face before something serious happened.

Kevin had riled Patrick so much that once he saw Milk come out of the club he knew that he was going to have to do something. He'd watched him talking to the short, fit girl, but once Milk had moved away from her, Patrick walked across the road, alone, determined to get some real answers. Now that he was there he felt his nerve beginning to go, and himself sinking deeper and deeper into something smelly. But to give him credit, he tried to see it through and asked gruffly, 'So what about Thornton Heath? What about my gear?'

Milk massaged his temple while excusing himself from Desiree and suggesting that she go back to her friends and wait for him to join her. He wouldn't be long.

Meanwhile, the other bystanders had noticed the face-off and were standing back slightly, Ditton knowing the signs and knowing better than to get involved just yet, Zero, Star and most of the others the same. Cannibal beckoned Jonah, who trotted over eagerly, grinning. Vaughn stepped back, amazed at what he was seeing and slightly disturbed too. He didn't like violence at the best of times and had always been strangely fascinated and repulsed by how easily it came to Milk. Fortunately he was rarely present when Milk went into action, normally hearing about it second hand, but he had the sinking feeling that he was going to witness something now.

If Patrick didn't know before, he knew now that he had bitten off more than he could chew, and unfortunately, he froze. If his legs could have taken him he would have turned and skulked back from whence he came, but right there and then, skulking was beyond him. All he was capable of was standing still so that his legs didn't give way. He wanted to look over his shoulder and see where the others were; they should have been looking, should have seen what he was involved in and been prepared to assist, even if that assistance was only to get him out of the way. But he heard nothing from them, just the blood rushing in his ears and the thudding of his heart. He continued to stand there, unable to do anything else.

'Look, fool,' snarled Milk, 'I don't know what you're talking about. Maybe you had one too many in there or something, but I don't know anything about Thornton Heath, and I don't know anything about your gear. You understand? I don't know anything about your shit. But I'll tell you something, though. A little while back another wanker stepped to me like this. I can't remember what it was about, but I reckon he had more of a reason than you do. Anyway, he was giving it the biggun and accusing me of some bollocks for about five minutes. I was with a girl at the time, so I was trying to play it cool and make sure that nothing happened to spoil her night, you know how it goes. Some girls like to see a bit of violence, some don't, and I was sure that this one didn't.'

Patrick stood there transfixed, as did everyone else that could hear Milk speaking, Milk was the kind of person that people listened to. Ditton was not as enthralled; he knew how the story went, he had been there.

'So, anyway, I'm keeping my cool and I'm trying to steer the girl out of the way and out of the club when the little shit hits me. Nothing major, just a little shot to the back of the head, fizzed for a second or two and then was all right. So I hand the girl over to my mate for safe keeping, beat this guy till he can't speak, leave him on the floor with his sorry friends trying to scrape him off it, and then leave myself, sure that I'm going to have to try and speech the girl to prove that I'm not a psycho she doesn't need to be scared of. That's if she'll talk to me at all.'

Ditton winced, remembering the occasion. For a while he had thought Milk was going to kill the guy, he went to town on him that much. And where were the bouncers? Conspicuously absent. They knew who Milk was, and had no intention of getting involved.

Those listening could have heard a pin drop as Milk continued: 'But when I get outside and to the car, what do I find? The girl's pissed off, sulking and giving out those you're-not-going-to-get-any signs. So I ask her what's the matter, and fuck me if she doesn't say that she wanted to watch me beat the idiot.

' "Is that all?" I say. "Easily solved." So I take her back in, find the guy sitting up on some chairs with his friends and say to the girl, "Watch this, then." And I beat him again, until I know that he's not going to be sitting up anywhere for a long, long time.'

Belatedly, Kevin appeared from across the street, followed by Jester and three others who looked as though they didn't really want to be involved, but didn't know how to stay out of it and still save face. Kevin said something to Patrick but didn't receive an answer.

Milk looked up at them contemptuously but eventually brought his gaze back to rest on Patrick. 'Now, like I said at the beginning, I can't remember what it was about, but that guy had more reason to be in my face than you do. So if you don't move your sorry arse,

211

quickly, I am really going to have some fun with you. Do you understand?'

Patrick hadn't managed to take in most of the tale; he had been floating in a zone he hadn't been to before, and hoped he wouldn't have to go to again. It might be a slight exaggeration to say that his life flashed before him, but it was something like that. His stomach threatened to splat its contents all over the floor and spectators, and he felt very, very hot and giddy. But when he heard Kevin's voice a load seemed to have been lifted from his shoulders. Not much, but enough for him to feel that he might not die there. So suddenly he realised that Milk had stopped speaking, and from the expression on his face was waiting for an answer or some type of action. Patrick didn't know what to say or do, but from somewhere the words 'Where's my gear?' came out. He didn't actually finish the question, because the left-hand side of his face lit up with pain, his head snapped back sickeningly and he was slammed into his insufficient supporters behind him.

A ruckus then ensued which threatened to suck any- and everybody into it. It was the type of brawl in which no one gets hurt badly unless there's a maniac with a knife present, or a Tyson imitator with a penchant for ears. Ditton, Zero and some others tried to extricate themselves first and then tried to separate the pro- tagonists. This led to a rolling maul which made its way towards, and eventually stabilised right outside the entrance to the club. The bouncers had been trying to ignore what was going on as it was yards away, but they couldn't any longer and used their bulk and expertise to separate the combatants. As so often happens, Milk was well away from the epicentre without a mark on him, while in contrast, Patrick had become the man with two faces, the right-hand side normal, the left already ballooning out like some hideous deformity. Patrick was not having a good day. He had mistakenly managed to have Jester in a headlock, and was aiming instinctive uppercuts at his friend's face. Meanwhile, Jonah was astride Kevin Hill, pummelling him relentlessly. The bouncers pulled them apart and when they realised the size of the mob that Jonah was with, sent him back and tried to occupy them while Kevin, Patrick, Jester and the others staggered off in the opposite direction.

Milk checked his clothes; then that everyone else was OK and no serious damage done. He looked around for Desiree and she waved as he walked over to her like Moses, bystanders parting before him like waves. Another chapter in the myth of Milk had nearly closed, but not just yet. The street outside was packed now. People had been coming out of the club throughout the encounter, but now it seemed as though everyone that had been inside was on the street, sweat drying like concrete on their dark faces. Those that had missed the fracas were being told about it by others whose noses should have been growing as they spoke. But that's how legends come about, a bit of spice from a romantic, and an already fantastic tale becomes fictitious.

Ditton was busy with Zero and Vaughn trying to restrain Jonah when Milk tapped him on the shoulder. He turned to see Milk looking apologetic but far from repentant.

'Oh, well done, Milk. Well fucking done!'

Milk grimaced. 'Sorry, D, but he really had it coming. I tried not to, but I had to. I couldn't take any more. Seriously, I couldn't.'

Glaring, Ditton observed, 'Well, it's done now, I just hope they're sensible enough to get out of here. I can't believe we got all the way to the end before this had to happen.'

Milk massaged his shoulder. 'Well, I'll hang around if you want. I can get a "lift home" any time.'

'Don't worry about it. It's probably better if you're not here anyway. One less to worry about.'

'You sure?'

'Yeah, I'm sure. Get out of here,' said Ditton, forcibly pushing Milk away.

Milk was doing as he was bid when he heard the sound of an engine screaming in protest at being thrashed in too low a gear. Immediately he knew there was something wrong and turned just in time to see a white car descend upon them from the King's Cross end of Camden High Street, main beam dazzling and engine roaring. Instinct made him dive behind a parked car whilst most of those on the pavement debated whether they needed to step back, scatter or scream.

The first shot rang out before the car was alongside the majority of people, and glass from a shop window behind them seemed to tinkle simultaneously. By the second shot the scatterers were scattering, the screamers screaming and the divers had disappeared behind cars or back into the club, trampling the doormen, who were desperate to lock up. Milk counted five shots over the screaming and cursed himself for not coming armed. It was a gesture to Ditton of his intention to behave, but it was looking as though it may have been a big mistake. Fortunately, as suddenly as the shooting had started, it stopped and the car roared off into the distance. Milk and the others stood up, dusted themselves off and looked around for injuries. There were none apart from a girl who had slipped and cut her hands on the broken glass strewn around. Milk looked at Ditton, Ditton looked at Zero, Zero looked at Cannibal, Cannibal looked at Jonah. Jonah glared down the road but the car was long gone and could no longer be seen or heard. He turned to the others and declared, 'I *have* to kill him. Mark my words. Look what he did to my fucking shirt!'

Investigating a dark smudge on the front of his own shirt, Milk caught sight of one of the girls that had been with Vanessa and asked where she was. He cringed when he was told that she had gone with her man, and sent the kid on her way.

Ditton found Vaughn face down under a blue Frontera, reluctant to move. He coaxed him out with a reminder that he couldn't be going to see a girl smelling of Camden streets. Vaughn slid out and raised himself to his feet.

'Is it over?' he asked, wide-eyed. 'That was madness. I can't believe it.'

Ditton shrugged. 'The whole world is mad, but it's over. Are you ready? I'll drop you now, if you want. I want to get out of here before the police come.'

Vaughn nodded and looked up in time to see Milk waving to attract Ditton's attention. He alerted Ditton, who looked up and across in the direction that Milk was pointing and saw Jonah sprinting to his car. The youth got in, wheelspun, and took off in the same direction as the drive-by vehicle, driving erratically and somehow managing to avoid hitting people and parked cars. Ditton swore and kicked the Frontera's wheel so hard that the alarm went off.

CHAPTER SIXTEEN

Vaughn eased himself out of the car, jogged across the street and rang the bell. Ditton put the car into gear and wondered what was going to become of his romantic friend. It was a chore having to look after the likes of Jonah and, to a lesser extent, Milk, but Vaughn was just as challenging in his own way. As the front door opened and Vaughn waved, Ditton pulled off, wondering not for the first time how he had landed himself the position of local guardian-cum-protector. Looking back, it seemed that Vincent had chosen him to look after Jonah because he must have had the capabilities, even then. It was no surprise really. After years of putting up with her husband's drinking, womanising and general abuse, his mother had packed a bag for each of her boys containing a change of clothes and bath stuff, and taken the kids to Mrs Gayle, where they had played contentedly with Tyrone and the others. Mrs Ditton had then walked out on to Brixton Hill and thrown herself under a number 109 bus, thus ending her nineteen years of misery and torment in cold, grey, flavourless England since arriving from Jamaica at the age of fourteen.

Afterwards, Mr Ditton's descent into full-scale alcoholism had been swift, almost as swift as Rodney's rise in the bad-boy leagues, but Ditton had tried to manage. Mr Ditton had a tiny shop in which he sold Caribbean foods and seasonings. When his father had lost his shop and his pride, his youngest son had attempted to manage the house, including the cooking and the cleaning, but it all became too much for him. When a kindly teacher happened to take him home one afternoon, wanting to speak to his father about why the boy was always tired in class, observed his home life – an alcoholic, incapable, single parent – and informed Social Services, things changed drastically.

Social Services in the early eighties were not what they are today, and that's saying something. The boys were placed with white foster parents who made no allowances for their dietary habits or the fact that the boys were used to bathing, creaming their skin and greasing their hair daily. So when Mrs Gayle came to visit one day and saw the situation there, she grabbed a Ditton boy with each hand and marched them out of the house past the speechless foster parents. She stopped to give them her address and telephone number, and asked them to call the social worker to inform her that the boys were going to be with her from now on. The social worker had arrived with the police but Mrs Gayle wasn't fazed and was adamant that it was only over her dead body that the boys would leave her house to go back to 'dem nasty people'. They came to an agreement, due in no small part to the size of Mrs Gayle and the magnitude of the dead body that would have had to be circumnavigated. As a result, the boys remained together with her until Rodney became old enough and bad enough to go back home, to live with the person he hated most in the world, his father.

The kids had been in Mrs Gayle's living room watching the television when Mr Ditton phoned and reported that his wife had died, and asked if Mrs Gayle could keep the boys there for a while. At bedtime Mrs Gayle had sent her kids upstairs and kept Gary and Rodney behind to break the news, Mr Ditton had had no intention of doing it himself; he couldn't.

After the news was broken, Ditton didn't cry for a week. He was sitting at Mrs Gayle's kitchen table with Rodney, Tyrone and his two younger brothers, eating soggy cornflakes with hot milk, when he felt a solitary tear roll down his left cheek. It hung from his chin for what seemed like an eternity, fell into his bowl and disappeared. His face trembled and was ready to crack, but Rodney had seen and he shook his head twice to say, 'No more.' That was that. Gary Ditton shed his last tear at the age of eight, and from then on had to become more adult than many adults ever are. Unlike Rodney, whose response to his troubles was to hit out at any- and everybody, Gary chose to do the opposite. He didn't try to please everyone because even at that age he knew it wasn't possible, but he did try to prevent conflict wherever possible: when Rodney pulled a knife on their father, Gary held on to his arm and pleaded him out of using it; when Rodney stole money from their father's wallet, Gary talked him into putting it back; when Mr Ditton brought one of his many women back to the house and she made the mistake of putting on Mrs Ditton's dressing gown, Gary grabbed Rodney's hands before they found their way around the poor woman's throat.

Now, at twenty-five, nothing seemed to have changed. From caring for his incapable father and restraining his wild brother, he had been required to move on to protecting Jonah from himself and, to a lesser extent, Milk from everyone, and everyone from Milk. Now the challenge was trying to prevent Jonah, Tyrone, Vincent, Kevin Hill, Milk and Patrick from killing each other and Vaughn from making a mistake he would regret forever. Ditton was tired of it all; it was about time someone looked out for him and his needs. However, the independence and self-sufficiency that he had been forced to acquire at such an early age now made it almost impossible for him to allow anybody to get close enough. Life was bollocks and he knew that, but carried on, hoping to gain some satisfaction from trying to make it easier for others.

Janine answered the door wearing a Chinese-style pale yellow gown that was so tempting Vaughn had to force himself to keep his hands off. The fabric looked so smooth and alluring around her body that he had the distinct impression she was wearing little or nothing underneath.

The flat was totally unfamiliar to Vaughn despite his visit the other evening, and he had no idea of the layout or what any of it would look like. She led him straight down the bare magnolia hall into a large, homely kitchen, and he sat as directed on a stool at the breakfast bar while she poured him a whisky and Coke, and a vodka and orange for herself. Vaughn looked at his glass with a quizzical expression and she informed him that it was what he had been drinking the night before. He cringed, and noticing, Janine laughed and shook her head, telling him that she should really be annoyed that he had come to her in that state the previous night. Was she so terrible that he had to be plastered in order to sleep with her?

Typically, Vaughn began to apologise, but she halted his embarrassed explanations with a very brief but very intense kiss that left him speechless but pleased.

'There,' she said. 'That's what I think about last night. What about you?'

Vaughn surprised himself this time by leaning forward instinctively and returning the gesture with a little more desire than he had expected. For one unwelcome second he noted that the kiss certainly held more passion than Courtney ever seemed to receive outside of two seconds before he was about to reach orgasm.

Vaughn took a sip of his drink, nodded his approval and then said, 'You know I don't remember much about last night, don't you?'

Janine smiled. 'I can believe that. What *do* you remember?'

Vaughn chuckled. 'Nothing really. Just some images, some snatches of conversation. Just enough to convince me that I was here.'

'You were here all right,' Janine said. She touched her lips and said, 'And here.' She touched her neck. 'And here.' Her hands moved to her breasts. 'And here.' She smiled and moved her hands down to her groin, bringing them to rest innocently between her legs like a primary school teacher sitting down to explain the day's tasks. 'And definitely here,' she said.

Vaughn stood promptly and took a step towards her. Before he reached her, she'd unbelted her gown just enough for him to see that she was indeed naked, and as trim and lithe as he had guessed she would be. He reached out but she skipped away, out of the kitchen, and disappeared down the passage as though she were some sort of mischievous nymph. Vaughn paused and made a little wish, hoping that the nymph wouldn't turn out to be a siren. It was too late to be thinking about things like that, so he took a deep breath and went after her. The adventure had begun in earnest and he still didn't know where he was going in his head, in his heart or even in the house. He was glad it wasn't a big flat; he had never enjoyed hide-and-seek.

The traffic lights changed and Ditton slowed the car and stopped. Had he been more alert and not so preoccupied he would have put his foot down and been through before there was a hint of red, but the news had distracted him. Real had won the European Cup, and the Saudi nurses were due to be freed in the morning. Ditton thought ruefully, well, if OJ can do it, why shouldn't they? He waited at the lights and looked across at the houses being built on the site of the old Tooting Bec hospital, and on the other side the eerie darkness of Tooting Bec Common, where he thought he might just be able to make out some goal posts skulking in the darkness. Briefly he thought about the weekend's match and the amount of money riding on it. He hoped Milk knew what he was doing.

Ditton picked up his phone just as the filter arrow shone green and had to drop it on to the seat to put the car into gear. It delayed him for half a second but that was half a second too long and some impatient guy tooted behind him. Two thirty on a Thursday morning and someone was beeping him at traffic lights: London.

Ditton looked in his rear-view mirror and allowed the Cavalier to overtake. It shot off down the road towards Streatham while Ditton turned left. Watching the car reminded Ditton of Jonah's exit from the club and he picked up the phone again to dial. Jonah's number rang and rang unanswered, which was strange. Jonah was usually good about answering, two, three rings at the most. Ditton dropped the phone intending to try again in a couple of minutes, and when he did he got the same result and began to feel slightly uncom-fortable. He couldn't put his finger on exactly why –

any innocent reason could have kept Jonah from answering – but Ditton was concerned. Cannibal's phone was off so Ditton left a message asking him to return the call, urgently. Then, not sure why, he headed for Jonah's

The car was there, which meant Jonah had to be also. Jonah was never without his car and he never took rides from anyone else if his car was working. Ditton pulled up alongside the Astra GTE and thought for a while about what he was doing there. It was almost three o'clock in the morning; for all he knew, Jonah was in bed asleep, or with a girl, but for some reason Ditton didn't think so. Jonah was more likely to be in the flat winding himself up and looking for a victim.

Ditton locked up and walked towards the stairs, looking up to see if there was any sign of light in Jonah's flat. The angle was too steep and he wasn't able to see over the balcony so he climbed the stairs, still unsure why he was there at that time of the morning. After all, Jonah hadn't been hurt outside the show; maybe his pride and his clothes, but nothing else. At Jonah's floor Ditton was touched by a definite bad feeling. There was no music. Jonah couldn't have been home for long, he was bound to be awake, so why was there no music?

Ditton raised his hand to rap on the door. He noticed a chink of light and was dismayed to see that the door was in fact open. He almost faltered for a moment but steeled himself and pushed the door gently. It swung open without a sound. The hallway looked normal, nothing out of place except the silence. Maybe Jonah had just seen someone out and forgotten to close the door properly, or maybe he had left in a hurry and not closed it behind him. But his car was there.

'Jonah?' called Ditton anxiously. 'You here?'

No answer. He carried on into the flat, headed for the living room. The first thing he saw through the open door was a speaker with a hole in the bass cone that looked as though it had been put there by a foot. That would explain the lack of music, but the presence of the hole itself now needed an explanation, and as Ditton turned into the living room the sight that met his eyes took a few stunned seconds to register. There appeared to have been some kind of struggle during which the stereo had been knocked down and lay smashed in the middle of the floor. Alongside it lay Jonah, on his back with his legs apart and arms spread. His face looked strange, relaxed and at peace, his eyes were closed but his mouth hung badly, and he would have looked like a drunk who had passed out if most of his chest and stomach hadn't been missing. A pool of blood so thick it almost looked black had pooled on the floor around him, while bright red dots were splattered on the sofa, the wall and the grubby net curtains. Jonah was dead, of that there was no doubt.

It seemed like an eternity but was probably only a matter of seconds that Ditton stood in the doorway and looked at the destroyed body of his charge, friend and acquired younger brother. The emotions threatened to hit him all at once and he felt giddy and weak, wanting to sit down and wake Jonah up, make him clean himself and stop pretending whatever he was pretending. Ditton knew that wouldn't happen and he quickly began to think of the practicalities. He couldn't touch anything, in fact he needed to get out of there as soon as possible and call the police. The idea irked him but he knew it had to be done, anonymously of course. There was no question of him phoning the bastards and waiting there for them to arrive and accuse him, or enquire into his affairs, or maybe even to take him somewhere and deal with him like they had dealt with Rodney.

Ditton wanted to bend down and touch a hand or cheek but he couldn't get too close. There was blood everywhere and he couldn't risk getting it on himself or his clothes, so he told himself aloud that Jonah's spirit had left his body and gone to a peaceful place. It helped, slightly, and the longer he looked, the less the body looked like Jonah. The glint in his eye couldn't be seen, and the silence and stillness of the corpse was the antithesis of the essence of Jonah. The soul had been wild, determined not to be restrained and pre- pared to watch others suffer as a result of its quest for rewards and payment. The body on the floor reflected none of that for Ditton, and although it was proof of Jonah's death, it wasn't Jonah lying there.

His detachment and objectivity began to falter in the passage and by the time he was at the front door he had shed his first tear since the cornflakes. Although the coast was clear, he tried to walk casually down to the car. It sounded as though the entire block was asleep and the only noise was traffic from Coldharbour Lane, but Ditton knew that all it would need was one other person to be returning home late and have enough of a memory to give the police a description or a car registration to go on. He was OK, there was no one around, at least not that he had seen, and he yanked the car door open, jumped in and tried to close it quietly behind him. He drove out of the estate with his lights off, not turning them on until he was well away and about to cross Coldharbour Lane headed for Herne Hill.

Ditton thought that he had steeled himself enough to be able to deal with most things, and that not much could affect him any more. He had been wrong, and suddenly he realised why he put so much time and effort into trying to ensure that the chances of this sort of thing happening to Jonah and Milk were reduced. He wasn't sure he could handle the situation; emotions were swimming around in him like a cocktail of drugs trying to outdo each other in their attempts to control him. One moment he felt angry, the next scared; one moment guilty, the next numb, unfeeling and unseeing. He screeched to a halt outside the Brockwell Park gates and walked all the way back to the crossing to get around the railings. Normally he would have vaulted them, but not tonight, he didn't think he could manage it.

He rested his head against the glass of the booth, as dirty as it was, squeezed his eyes shut tight and cradled the receiver to his ear. He squeezed his eyes tighter and butted the glass gently a couple of times, wanting to curl up on the floor and rock himself away somewhere. Then he took a deep breath and dialled nine-nine-nine.

THURSDAY

CHAPTER SEVENTEEN

Vaughn looked at the clock radio: eight twenty. Another ten minutes and he would call the office and leave a message on the answerphone to say that he was sick. He felt fine, better than fine, but on the way back from Janine's in the very early morning he had decided that he wouldn't be going in to work. He felt more relaxed and content than he had for a long time and wanted to enjoy it, admitting there was no doubt that in this instance Milk had been right. Vaughn felt invigorated, if not totally revitalised, and he stretched his arms to the ceiling and roared contentedly. Time for a cup of tea.

He padded to the kitchen whistling 'What a Wonderful World', and shuffled like James Brown as he put the kettle on. He made his drink, posed in front of the mirror for a while, then got back into bed, phoned in and left a message. Afterwards he yawned, switched the television on, plumped up the pillows and sat back sipping the nicest cup of PG he had ever had.

An hour later, when daytime television had begun in earnest, after the news had flogged the nurses story to death, and shown Sinatra's funeral over and over again, Vaughn got himself up and decided to take a luxurious bath instead of his usual shower. He put the answering machine on; bubble bath, bath salts, oil in the burner, and a jolly little joint for breakfast. Why not? He was feeling good.

Things were going so well that the phone didn't ring until he had got out of the bath, dried and creamed his skin and was posing in front of the mirror again. It was the same body he had had yesterday, but it had received so many compliments a few hours previously that it seemed different. He skipped to the front room to hear the message being left and admired himself in the mirror over the fireplace.

It was Janine. She was calling from her office in school, free to talk but still speaking in just over a whisper and prepared for a knock on the door at any moment. She hoped that he was OK, and that his exertions of the night before hadn't damaged him and enforced the day's sick leave. If they had and she had her way, he'd be sick all the time. She wanted to see him again, that night if possible. She was bursting with things she wanted to tell him and do to him, and announced that she would be in school for another couple of hours, and would he call her? She moaned erotically, blew him a kiss and rang off. Vaughn shook his head and returned to the bedroom. He would call her in a few minutes and arrange to see her later. He had things to tell her too, but he wasn't certain they would be the same as hers.

Vaughn lay back on his bed with his arms behind his head and looked at the ceiling. He had spoken to Janine and managed to prevent her gushing for long enough to arrange to meet for a drink in the Tadpole Bar, close to her home, straight after work. She was enthusiastic and had suggested that they go on from there to her flat. He hadn't said no, but he hadn't agreed either. There was no point in making things any more difficult than they needed to be.

He had phoned Courtney at work too, and the enthusiastic receptionist informed him brightly that Courtney had popped out, but would be back in a few minutes, and she'd get her to call just as soon as she returned.

When the call from Courtney finally came, Vaughn snatched up the receiver eagerly and told her that he wanted to see her later if it was possible. She would be out in the evening but there was a chance that she would be finished by nine thirty and could try to get to him for about ten. They agreed that she would call him if any circumstances changed. He told her that he missed her, she said, 'Likewise,' and that was that. He felt better still.

Even when Vaughn received an unexpected phone call from DS Rose wanting to clarify a few points, he wasn't flustered. She sounded OK, as though she really did just want information from him. He thought briefly about telling her what he had heard from Marlon, but decided against it. It was nothing to go on. But she offered him a mobile phone number, enquired whether he had had any contact with Martin since they last spoke, and gave permission for him to call at any time, day or night, if he had anything pertinent to the investigation. He wrote the number on the back of the card she had given him in the interview.

In fact Vaughn felt so good that instead of lazing about the house as he had expected to, he decided that he would go looking for Marlon and any of the other truants he could find. With luck he might pick up the tiniest scrap of information that could prove significant in ensuring that Darryl's murderer was apprehended. Shit, he thought, I'm sounding like a policeman now. But even that didn't upset him unduly or affect his new-found optimism, and he left the house, stepped out into the bright sunshine and concluded that even the weather reflected his frame of mind. It was as though someone or something up there had noted his change and sent the sun out to celebrate the fact.

Picking up the phone that morning was the hardest thing Ditton had ever had to do. But to his credit, he didn't stall. He thought about it for a second, and dialled. It rang once.

'I've been waiting,' answered Vincent quietly. 'You know what I want now, don't you? I want the bastard who did it, and I want him quickly. Who was it?'

Ditton hesitated before answering. 'I don't know,

but I've got some places to start.' He knew it sounded weak.

'Don't give me that!' Vincent roared. 'I don't want fucking starting places. I want the cunt's head on my table, and I want it quick. Do you get me?' He didn't expect an answer or wait for one. 'Now, that cousin of yours. Are you still saying he wouldn't have done this?'

Ditton took the plunge. 'I still don't think so.'

'Well, I'll take your word for it, for now. But I reckon the bastard is stupid enough to have done it, and I'm still going to be looking for him to ask him some questions. So if you speak to him, you tell him he can meet with me and we can sort all of this out. But he'd better have some fucking good answers ready. And you can go to your places to start and get started. But you'd better be quick. Do you understand? If you want to save your boy, that is.'

Ditton understood completely, just as he understood the information that Vincent would be at his mother's house in the afternoon to mean he was supposed to be there also. And not only was he supposed to be there to pay his respects to the family, he was expected to have, leads, preferably a name. It was just past nine o'clock now; he had better get up and started.

As he sat on the side of the bath and lost himself in the sound of the running water he went over Cannibal's revelation and tried to work it out. Cannibal had received Ditton's message and rung, correctly assuming that there was something wrong with Jonah. Ditton wasn't sure why he didn't tell Cannibal what had happened, but he didn't. Maybe it was to prevent the fat boy going on a killing spree that Jonah or Milk would have been hard pressed to match.

At the club Cannibal had bumped into a guy that he knew. This guy had said that he had overheard some others talking abut a job they had done in Brixton the night before. He didn't know them or their names, but he had heard them say that the whole caper had been thought up, arranged and put to them by some brother called Babbler.

The significance had been lost on Cannibal, but not on Jonah. Cannibal had only been able to relay the information to Jonah outside the club, after the shooting, and as soon as he had, Jonah had taken off like a bat out of hell. Cannibal had phoned half an hour later and been told by Jonah that he was at home waiting for a skinny cunt; Jonah had then hung up. Cannibal hadn't known who or what Jonah meant, but Ditton did.

He slipped into the bath and covered his head with the steaming hot flannel. Why would Earl have organised Jonah's robbery? Ditton had never been fond of the guy, but even he wouldn't have thought him capable of doing something like that. Why would he be stealing from Tyrone? Tyrone who always stuck up for him, defended him and vouched for him? It didn't make sense, but it tied in with Earl's business meeting at the bar on Tuesday night.

Ditton decided not to think about it until he actually saw Earl, and that if he managed to get hold of Tyrone before he had seen Earl, he wouldn't tell him either.

The next question was about the killing. Assuming that Jonah had gone off looking for Earl, which seemed likely, what then? Did it mean that Earl had killed him? Had he gone round to Jonah's, been confronted with Cannibal's information and felt forced to shoot? It was possible – Jonah had told Cannibal that Earl was on his way. The thoughts raged back and forth, one outdoing the other. Could Tyrone have got there before Earl? Could Kevin Hill have found out where Jonah lived and gone there from the club?

Michelle woke early, before the alarm was due. She hadn't slept well at all, tossing and turning, trying not to think about what was going on, and what she had done. The robbery wasn't the problem, neither was the fact that she had a large amount of cocaine in her possession. She was troubled by her contact with Delroy. He was evil, she'd known that before she called him but she had sensed it again while on the phone. She also knew that he had felt her fear, heard it, smelled it, and enjoyed her discomfort. As soon as she had identified herself she'd wanted to hang up, to drop the phone as though it was a forbidden key to a darker, even more horrible world.

But Michelle hadn't come this far to stop now; she was in it up to her neck, and she wanted to stay afloat. She would meet Delroy as arranged, and it would all go smoothly because she was going to be in control. She would be calm and composed, and nothing he would do or say would ruffle her. But his eyes, those cruel black eyes. With any luck he would be wearing shades and she wouldn't have to see them. Anyway, she could cope with those, she hoped.

As she got up and shuffled into the kitchen to prepare Dale's breakfast she kept telling herself that it was no big deal, Delroy was only coming to the flat to look at the gear. She would leave Dale at her mum's, Delroy would come around, they would make an exchange and he would be on his way. That would be that, simple and straightforward, nothing to it. She had to remember to ask Milk how much a kilo of cocaine should cost. She didn't know how to put the question to him, but she would manage. And if the worst came to the worst and she got cold feet, she might have to ask him for more than prices. But those decisions could wait for a while. Right now she had to be concerned with getting her son up, dressed and fed for school.

She smiled wryly and clicked the kettle on as she opened the kitchen curtains and looked out at the London skyline, imagining the people beginning to scurry to work on the streets below. No point getting hooked on Milk, she thought, but she couldn't help wondering where he was and who he was with.

Milk's phone rang and took his attention. He didn't recognise the number but sensed that it was important. When he ended the call and turned around to face. Desiree, the sleepy girl was compelled to sit up instantly, her breasts bare and her hair dishevelled. The expression on Milk's face seemed to paralyse her like a look from a gorgon. It was his face, but at the same time it wasn't. It seemed to be twisted but at the same time not, as though he was giving off energy that affected the air around him, making it shimmer and twist while inside it his soul blazed. She couldn't say or do anything but watch him dress, pick up the gun, change his mind and then place it carefully in a drawer before giving her a glance that literally sent shivers down her spine. He picked up his keys and wallet, put a jacket on, grabbed his phone and then leaned over and kissed her surprisingly tenderly considering the hostility on his face. 'Take the latch off when you let yourself out. I don't want to be burgled.'

Hearing his voice and being kissed assured Desiree that she was not the cause or the intended recipient of his rage, and she managed to ask, 'Where are you going? Is everything all right?'

Milk glowered. 'First I'm going to the hospital, then I don't know where.'

The door closed behind him and Desiree sat where she was for a few moments, still anaesthetised. She never wanted to see anybody look like that again; it was the most frightening thing she had ever experienced.

She shivered, and being a good Christian girl was touched by a moment of faith and a sex-spawned feeling of pleasurable, benevolent charity. She lowered her head and said a prayer for whoever had crossed the best fuck of her life.

* * *

When Mrs Barrett handed her husband the telephone and informed him that it sounded like the man that had called late on Sunday night, he glared at her and grabbed the phone from her hand. He covered the mouthpiece, told her to get out of the room and waited until she did. Finally he raised the mouthpiece and said, 'I meant to ask you the other day, where the hell did you get this number from?'

'I've got my sources,' the caller replied. 'But we've got more important things to talk about, don't you think?'

'I've been on him for a couple of days.' Barrett declared tersely. 'Got him sweating and running scared. It's obvious.'

'So when do I get to take a look?'

Barrett sighed as if about to explain something to a child. 'Look, I said I might be able to manage it, but that it would be difficult. I've thought about it and I think it's probably impossible. It can't happen again. It just can't.'

The caller didn't respond, but Barrett stood his ground and refused to break the silence. Eventually the caller spoke. 'I don't think you really understand what's going on here any more. I think you're getting old and you've lost the plot. I call the shots now. Don't you realise that? I've got enough to sink you, today, right now, without a trace, you nonce. Do you understand what I'm saying? Now, I've been polite so far, I've asked you to do things, requested that you do things, but that's just common courtesy, good upbringing. But if you continue with this rubbish about what you can or can't do, courtesy is going to have to end. Do you understand, nonce? Do you?'

Barrett didn't answer, choosing instead to scowl at his wife, who had poked her head around the door. She retreated swiftly.

'Good,' the caller said. 'Now, I'm going to be definite, OK? I want the delivery on Sunday down at the factory. We'll have to talk before then to arrange some of the finer details, so be prepared for a call. And next time I speak to you, don't even consider telling me anything about what you can and can't do. I've had enough. You are where you are because of me, and I can change all that instantly. I would have got here without you, and I will stay here without you. Remember that.'

Barrett lowered the receiver gently into its cradle, not because he was a gentle man, but because he was deep in thought. He was finally being forced to realise and accept that he had created a monster and it was threatening to destroy and devour him. He should have seen it coming, should have predicted that allowing so much power to be concentrated in one pair of hands could never be good, but he had been greedy. He looked around the drawing room of the mock-Tudor house that he wouldn't have owned if it wasn't for the voice on the other end of phone, and out of the window at the sleek black executive car in the driveway. He owed him a lot, he knew that, but it was supposed to be reciprocal, it was supposed to work both ways, but this guy just had him marked as a lackey now. Barrett knew that if he didn't do something soon it would get worse and eventually lead to his destruction. He locked the door and sat down to think harder than he had ever thought before.

Milk didn't recognise the feeling but he was scared of what he would see in the bed behind his family. His mother took one look at his face, rose from the bedside chair and intercepted him, physically placing herself between her son and Sandra, who he still hadn't seen.

Mrs Kerr held his hand and said, 'Don't say anything unless you're going to be calm. You hear? No badness in here.'

Milk clenched his jaw and nodded, apprehension increasing with every heartbeat. His mother stepped back to her chair without releasing his hand and Milk looked at Beverley and Yvonne before stepping around the end of the bed to lay his eyes on Sandra. The sight hit him like a hook to the solar plexus and he took an involuntary sharp breath, turned away from the bed, put his first into his mouth and bit his knuckles hard, hoping to regain some sense of reality before he turned to look again. His head felt like it was going to fall from his neck, roll away across the floor and explode, releasing a mushroom cloud that would wipe out London. For a second he seemed to lose his vision; even with his eyes open all he could see were shards of white light.

His vision returned slowly, the white light disappearing and finally he managed to focus on the bed opposite Sandra's. The old man in it was almost as grey as the sprinkling of hair on his head. He was amazingly thin and was propped up with pillows, and his mouth hung open loosely with his tongue lolling out of the left-hand side. His left eye was almost closed. The poor man had woken from a drug-induced sleep and happened to make eye contact with Milk. All he saw was a fearsome-looking black man staring at him with murder in his eyes and his fist in his mouth. The old man's chest began to hurt and his breathing became laboured – he needed assistance.

Milk removed his fist from his mouth, ignoring the teeth marks, and ran his hand from his forehead to the nape of his neck. He turned around slowly and glanced at his mother, who hadn't yet let go of his hand, then looked at Sandra. She lay in the bed almost totally horizontal, as though being propped up at even the slightest angle would have caused her immense pain. The sheets were up to her chest, and her arms and hands lay above the covers, unmoving. Her right hand was connected to a drip that stood at the side of the bed and machines above the bed flashed and beeped. Her face was almost unrecognisable, and if Milk's mother and sisters had not been present he would have had a hard time being definite that it was actually Sandra who lay there. Her face was so swollen that he couldn't see her eyes, and her lips were so bruised, blackened and distended that despite himself

Milk felt disgusted looking at them. He peered at her eyes and couldn't tell whether they were open or not.

'She's asleep,' his mother said. 'Drugs to put her to sleep.'

Milk massaged his shoulder. 'What happened?'

Mrs Kerr released her son's hand and sat back down in the chair. 'The doctors say that a cab brought her here early this morning. The cab driver got a call to collect from the house. When he rang the bell she managed to stagger out to the car, away from a man who was cursing from the doorstep.' Mrs Kerr shrugged. 'Until she wakes up and can talk, that's all we know.'

'Was it him?'

Mrs Kerr shook her head. 'I really don't know.'

Beverley stood up and looked down at Sandra's face. She turned to Milk. 'I went past the house yesterday evening. I was going to try to stop in and say hello, but I saw his car. The blue Cavalier, parked outside.'

Milk took a deep breath and bit his lip. He looked at his mother and sisters, and said, 'I'll see you all later. I've got some things to go and do now.'

'Marcus,' called Mrs Kerr, quietly but sternly. 'Come here.'

Milk did as he was bid, and stood before his mother. He raised an eyebrow questioningly.

'Marcus, what you going to do?'

'Mummy, you know me. Don't try to talk me out of this.'

'What you going to do?'

'What do you think?' snapped Milk. 'I'm not going to see him and say, "Well done," am I?'

From her chair Mrs Kerr reached up with both hands towards her son's face. He was forced to bend down so that she could reach and she clasped his face in both hands. She kissed him on the forehead and each cheek, the tears in her eyes shielding her somewhat from the fury emanating from her son. Milk was about to pull away, to stand up, eager to be on his way to find the father of his nephew and niece and to deal with him properly. Mrs Kerr held on tight and pulled his head towards her again.

'Marcus,' she said into his ear so that only he could hear, 'don't kill him. You hear? It's too easy for him, and silly for you. You understand? Do what you want, break what you want, but don't kill him.'

She released his head and leaned back slowly, almost regally. Milk stared at her for a moment in disbelief, wondering how it was that this woman never ceased to amaze him. On the reverse, he wondered how it was that someone as strong and resourceful as his mother could have allowed herself to be so badly treated and misused by his father. It baffled him and didn't occur to him that she might have sacrificed her happiness for what she saw as best for her children. But at least he was clear that his mother had given him permission to find Keith and beat him within an inch of his life. Milk knew that what she had said was true – it would be too easy for the scum if Milk killed him. No suffering for the bastard, while Milk would end up doing life, regretting his actions, but at the same time not.

Milk nodded curtly at his mother, took one last look at his three sisters, Sandra's deformed face meriting the longest gaze, and turned on his heel. He strode towards the door, stopped, turned again and said to his mother, 'You might want to call some help for that old geezer. He looks in bad shape.'

Mrs Kerr and her two healthy daughters looked across at the bed opposite Sandra's. They hadn't noticed until Milk pointed it out but the elderly occupant was having difficulty breathing and seemed to be suffering from some kind of fit. Mrs Kerr shuffled across to see if she could help or at least prevent him from hurting himself, while Beverley sprang up and ran out of the room to get help.

CHAPTER EIGHTEEN

A cluster of bubbles spun madly in the centre of the coffee as Ditton set the mug down in front of Milk. Milk snorted and looked at Ditton over the cup. 'My mum told me that I can't kill him, so I won't. But I'll do everything except that.' He looked at his watch. 'I want to get up there before I hurt someone innocent. You coming?'

Ditton nodded. He would go because of what had been done to Sandra, but he was also going to make sure that Milk didn't kill. He knew Milk understood what his mother had said and the logic behind it, but if the killing rage took hold, logic and reason were likely to be the last things Milk called upon. 'And depending on what time you finish with him we might go to Jonah's mum's from there.'

Milk took another sip. 'Yeah, what was that stuff you were saying on the phone about Jonah? What's he gone and done now?'

It was Ditton's turn to snort. 'He's dead. I found him last night.'

Milk wasn't one to waste words on exclamations of grief and disbelief, and Ditton didn't want a drawn-out retelling of what he had found. They understood each other.

'Where?' asked Milk.

'His flat. Straight after I dropped Vaughn.'

'How?'

'Shot a few times, house messed up a bit, but I don't think it was robbery.'

Milk flexed his shoulder and sighed. 'You found out why he took off last night?'

'I think so. It's a long story, I'll tell you later. But I'm sure he found out that it was Earl who set up the robbery on Tuesday night. Jonah must have got hold of him on the phone and arranged for Earl to come round and see him. The next thing is me finding him lying in a pool of blood with holes in his chest.'

Milk didn't say anything straight away, but after a while he asked, 'That stuff about Earl. You know that for sure?'

Ditton turned around, unfolded his arms and sat down. He nodded. 'Cannibal told me. He didn't know the importance of what he was saying but it all fits and makes sense. Believe me.'

'I believe you. So what do we do now?'

'We go and see Keith, and then Earl.'

'Where's Earl going to be?'

'I spoke to him just after I spoke to you earlier. I told him that we had to meet up sooner rather than later, and that I'd call him again when I was ready. He said he'd make the time.'

Milk frowned. 'Why didn't you just meet up with him?'

'I was waiting for you.'

'Thank you,' said Milk

The annoying recorded message informed Ditton that the mobile phone he was trying to call had been switched off, and that he should try again later. Not only was he becoming fed up that he couldn't get hold of Tyrone, but the longer he was unable to speak to him the harder it would be to look Vincent in the eye and claim that Tyrone wasn't responsible. But then a horrible thought entered his mind and he turned to face Milk.

'What if they were both involved together?'

Milk looked in the rear-view mirror, indicated, manoeuvred, showed a finger to a car behind that had the audacity to beep, and asked, 'Who?'

'What if Tyrone and Earl planned the whole thing together to get at Vincent using Jonah?'

Milk shrugged and said, 'Yeah?' unsure.

Ditton closed his eyes to think aloud. 'Tyrone's getting too big for his boots and wants Vincent out of the way, or at least to give him some breathing space. Right?'

Milk nodded. 'Uh-huh. So if they decided that they were going to get at Vincent, what have they done? The robbery. What did that do?'

Ditton pinched his bottom lip and tried to think of an answer. He couldn't. 'I don't know, I just don't understand any of it. Why would Earl organise a robbery to clean out Tyrone? If they were in it together, it wouldn't have hurt Tyrone, but it would have discredited Jonah.'

Milk nodded. 'True, but what would that have done to Vincent? If Jonah gets blamed by Tyrone for losing his gear, Vincent just laughs and rubs his hands together. Unless Tyrone does something to Jonah which means that Vincent will become involved, like now. And who is it that you can't find? Tyrone. If they were in it together, it doesn't look to me as though anything could be working out the way Tyrone wanted it to.'

'I suppose you're right,' agreed Ditton. 'None of it makes sense. It's all crazy.'

Milk shrugged and said, 'Just wait until you speak to Earl. That'll clear a few things up at least. Tyrone's a different matter. The longer he stays out of touch, the guiltier he's looking.'

Keith Boyce owned an old-fashioned hi-fi shop on the London Road, Norbury, the kind of small, privately owned shop that tends to go out of business in the face of competition from the leading high-street electrical retailers selling goods from clock radios to computers. The shop seemed to have been there forever, and was one of those establishments that had given black people a sense of pride in the late seventies and early eighties, showing that they too could run a business and succeed. As a result the community had supported it whole-heartedly and made Keith, now in his mid-fifties, a wealthy man. It didn't matter that he was a thoroughly nasty person who had fathered countless children, most of whom he refused to acknowledge, and it didn't matter that he beat his women mercilessly and any of their children who spoke out of turn, which usually meant speaking at all. Keith Boyce was an upstanding member of the black community, he was a successful businessman that many aspired to emulate, and in a lot of people's eyes that was all that mattered.

Keith was leaning on the counter poring over a new retailer's price guide that he had acquired, checking the feasibility of ordering a new range of speakers and amplifiers before he had managed to off-load the current batch. He thought he would give it a try; you had to take risks to succeed. The phone rang in the back and he forced himself to move and answer it. Business calls were all right, he could take those all day long, they normally meant capital. What he didn't want was any of those damn-fool women calling up for his time or money. He had never once told any of the idiots to get themselves pregnant, yet they continued to turn up on his doorstep expecting him to finance their children. And as for that fool Sandra, if it was her ringing to apologise for making him mad last night he was going to tell her about herself and her blasted children. He didn't care if he was their biological father, fuck that. Crazy woman, saying that he was making her unwell again, damn cheek. She was lucky she called that cab when she did, because he was ready to finish that bottle and bust her arse some more.

Keith ducked through the doorway to the back, made his way past boxes of stereo equipment and snatched up the phone. 'Who is this?' he snapped.

No answer.

'Who is this?'

Again there was no answer, so he kissed his teeth long and loud and slammed the receiver down. 'Damn-fool women,' he growled.

Keith wasn't a tall man, but he was broad and powerful. He was so used to people being deferential because of his money and position that he thought of himself as bigger than he was. Also, being in his fifties with a full head of hair, regardless of the fact that he dyed it religiously, gave him immense pleasure and confidence. He saw himself as a ladies' man, and to a certain extent the evidence was there: kids and women all over the place, in most Caribbean communities from London to Leeds.

He walked back to the counter grumbling, his head down looking at the catalogue. It wasn't until he had been back in the shop for a few seconds that he realised it seemed to have got darker. He looked up to see that the blind covering the glass door had been pulled down, and that some of the lights in the small shop had been turned off. Next he looked to his right in the amplifier section and saw a tall, slim, strangely familiar dark-skinned young man sitting on one of the most expensive Kenwood speakers. Who the hell did he think he was? And what the hell did he think he was doing?

The young man didn't say or do anything except doff his baseball cap, raise his eyebrows and show Keith a mobile phone. Keith didn't speak, but he guessed that it was this bastard that had just phoned and not spoken. He grabbed a piece of pipe that he kept under the counter for situations like this, and showed it to the young man.

'Hey, you fuck,' growled the foul-tempered shop-keeper. 'What you think you're playing at? Why did you pull the blind down? Eh? And get off that damn speaker, now!'

Ditton shrugged and did as he was told, raising himself slowly and putting his phone away. He stayed where he was, holding his ground, even though Keith had lifted the bar-flap and was now on the shop side of the counter, still brandishing the metal pipe menacingly.

'What do you want?' Keith demanded. 'Tell me now, before I bust your head with this here piece of pipe.'

Ditton shrugged and raised his hands in a peaceful gesture. 'It's not me that wants anything,' he explained. 'It's him.'

Keith followed Ditton's gaze cautiously, aware that the youth might be trying to trick him, but out of the corner of his eye he detected movement behind him, and turned to see another young man, slightly shorter than the first but still far taller than the shop owner, appear from behind a stack of tuners and tape decks. Now Keith realised why the first man had looked familiar. He was a friend of this one, Marcus, Sandra's brother.

Keith had never given any time to getting to know Sandra's family. He had had two children with her but hadn't spoken to any of her family for over eight years. Admittedly, they all loathed him so much that he would have been hard pressed to get a response from any of them if he had tried. But because he didn't know the family, although he recognised Milk as Sandra's brother, he didn't know what Milk was like, didn't know what he was capable of, and certainly didn't know that Milk was standing there deciding whether to kill him or not.

'It's you,' Keith observed. 'Well, what do you want?'

Milk was beginning to feel that his mother's plea was going to be ignored. This guy was amazing, he really was something else, and Milk felt that he was about to carry out a public service.

'What do you want?' repeated Keith. 'If it's about that sister of yours, I don't want to hear it. Damn-fool—'

'Fool' happened to be the last word that Keith said for approximately six weeks. Ditton gave Milk some space and watched him carefully, and when he felt that Keith was unconscious and making no attempt to defend himself, or even shield himself from the blows, he stepped over and eased Milk off. That was the first step, getting him away from the body lying prone on the floor. But once he had stepped back, Milk pulled out his pistol and Ditton had to talk him out of using it on the inanimate body on the floor. Milk had worked himself up into a frenzy and he had that insane light in his eyes that Ditton hadn't seen for years. At one point he thought he had failed as Milk stepped forward and took aim, but finally he relented, stuck the gun in the back of his waistband, aimed a final kick at Keith's head, and left the shop feeling somewhat satiated. Ditton sighed, said, 'Phew!' under his breath and followed Milk out.

Vaughn waited at the cage for five minutes and was eventually rewarded by the sight of Marlon arriving with two cronies wearing the distinctive maroon blazers of another local school. Vaughn hailed him and saw Marlon roll his eyes and drag himself across to the car. He stooped in front of Vaughn's open window and said, 'Yeah?'

'Have you heard anything since yesterday? Anything to do with Darryl?'

'I haven't heard anything. Honest. Sorry, man.'

'All right,' said Vaughn turning the key in the ignition. 'Nice one anyway.'

Marlon spat. 'Yeah. Nice one, sir.'

Vaughn put the car into gear and had just released the handbrake when Marlon asked, 'Sir? How can you drive a car that dirty? That needs a wash *now*.'

Vaughn chuckled and shrugged. 'I know, I've been meaning to do it for ages but I just haven't managed to get around to it. You know how it goes?'

Marlon's expression suggested that he didn't.

'You know,' continued Vaughn, 'that was one of the

last things that Darryl said to me before—' He broke off in mid-sentence and said, 'Well, you know.'

This time Marlon answered, and asked, 'What was?'

Vaughn paused. 'About how dirty my car was. How I needed to clean it inside and out, because it was disgusting. You can imagine how Darryl would have said it too.'

Marlon grinned, showing that his imagination was working well, and then spat as though it was a waste product of the thought manufacturing process. 'Yeah, I can imagine.'

Patrick woke up sore – his body, but mostly his face – and didn't need to get out of bed to know that his left jaw and cheek were swollen. When he did finally look in the mirror he couldn't help but exclaim in surprise. And then the pain set in as the alcohol and drugs from the night before finally wore off. Milk had got away with his gear, and then done him properly too.

When Patrick had gone to sleep he had been in a bit of a state, although he did his best not to let Kevin and the others see it. He was excited, yes, but his body was still suffering from the number of emotions it had contained in the last few hours – excitement, anger, fear and regret. Patrick regretted the fight outside the club because it made it that much more difficult to sort things out. There could be no more talking between him and Milk now, that was out of the question. As far as Milk was concerned Patrick had shot at him and tried to kill him. He wouldn't listen to Patrick's protestations that it was Kevin that had done the shooting, that Patrick didn't want anything to do with it and had tried to stop it. Milk wouldn't hear that, and what was worse was that Patrick wouldn't be able to say it either. As far as Kevin was concerned, they were in it together. He would seriously believe that what he had done he had done for himself *and* Patrick. Patrick knew that he would have to suffer for Kevin's actions as though they were his own, unless he was able to do something about it first. But what? He could get a gun, find Milk and shoot him in the back of the head, but what would that solve? Patrick wanted his gear returned, that was all he cared about at that moment, and his face hurt too much to think about fighting; that he could leave to Kevin. Patrick would just have been satisfied with a small parcel that he had hidden in a brown leather holdall.

The leather bag made him think fleetingly of Michelle but he put her out of his mind, he couldn't afford to be distracted by things like that at the moment. He walked out to the toilet, passing Kevin's room on the way. Hearing his cousin snoring like a volcano he peered in through the open door. Kevin was lying on his back with his girl's arm draped over his chest. It seemed like the spoilt bitch was always there nowadays, spending the whole day on her back in bed and getting up at nine or ten in the evening to get ready to go out. Again Michelle popped into his head and he forced her out again. She wasn't important, he thought, just another ungrateful girl who couldn't make her mind up about what she wanted or where she was going. He couldn't be bothered with a girl like that, especially after all he had done for her too.

Patrick pulled his shorts down and sat on the toilet. He had to think, but it was difficult because his face hurt so much. Ah, Milk, he thought, if you only knew what I'd like to do to you.

When they got back to the car Milk asked Ditton if he was going to call Earl or whether they were going to head straight for Jonah's parents' house. Ditton thought for a second and said, 'As we're this far, let's try Tyrone's, see if he's there, and then call Earl.'

They drove straight up the London Road, which hadn't become too busy yet; a few hours later and it would be almost impassable, seeming as though everyone in the world lived in Croydon and was returning there after a day's work. Ditton looked out of the window at the pedestrians hurrying by and the workers toiling in shops, wondering how many of them had things to do like he did. How many of them had found their friend murdered and had set out to find his killer to prevent someone else being killed mistakenly? He wondered how many of them lived with alcoholic fathers and brain-damaged brothers, how many of them sold drugs and couldn't stop because the money was too good and there was no other realistic way of earning anything similar. He smiled ruefully, knowing that there would be very few people whose circumstances were exactly the same, but there would be a considerable number out there who could claim similar hardships and dilemmas.

Ditton glanced at Milk. This thing with Sandra really seemed to have got to and affected him. Milk would have been young the last time Keith had beaten Sandra badly, just after Shane was born. In fact Ditton remembered that Milk hadn't seen her until more than a week had passed as he had been caught up in one of his feuds, and had been lying low until he was totally sure who was after him and who he should go after. It had ended satisfactorily for Milk. He had found the guy and with Ditton's assistance hung him by his legs from a fifth-floor balcony until he had given the assurances Milk wanted to hear. There had nearly been an accident, though. Milk's instinctive reaction to the smells produced by the guy's fear-induced bowel movements was to let go. For a couple of seconds Ditton had been holding on alone while Milk covered his nose and accused the guy of having no balls and no shame.

Ditton shook his head. Looking back, it had been a funny day, but at the time it had been intense; a real roller-coaster ride behind Milk at his most uncontrollable.

Tyrone's flat was situated in an awkward place to get to by car, underneath a flyover and off a dual carriageway. To be able to park the car right in the flats meant navigating a series of roundabouts and slip roads when it was just as easy to park and cut through a pedestrian area. Following Ditton's directions Milk parked the car and switched off the engine.

'I want to see if his car's there,' said Ditton. 'He's not answering the phone or the pager.'

'And if it is, then what?'

'Ring the bell. Find out if he knows about Jonah.'

'He shouldn't, should he?' said Milk, looking at his watch. 'It's too early for him to have found out yet. And if he does know, you should be questioning how.'

Ditton was about to open the door to step out but he stopped and turned to face Milk. 'You think he could have done it, don't you?'

Milk nodded vigorously. 'Yeah, why not? It's only you that thinks Tyrone is some sort of decent guy that wouldn't stoop to certain lows. He's all right and everything, but he's just like everyone else.'

'How's that?'

'Greedy, selfish. You know how it goes.'

Ditton shook his head.

'Look,' directed Milk, 'he didn't have to do it himself. Tyrone's a wealthy guy, there's no disputing that. Money to pay someone would have been peanuts for him. And if he's serious about going up against Vincent, which to all intents and purposes means killing him, he'd have to do Jonah at some point anyway. He couldn't get rid of Vincent and have Jonah running around loose. Jonah would kill him, bury him, and dig him up to do it again.'

Ditton sighed. 'I can't get my head around all this killing talk, and so-and-so taking so-and-so out. Tyrone's a boy to Vincent.'

'Times are changing,' said Milk. 'There's always a new guy on the block who's ambitious and looking to take someone else's crown. I don't see why it can't be Tyrone. Do you?'

Ditton didn't answer. Milk's logic was undeniable but frightening, and he didn't want to accept it. Not yet, anyway. He opened the car door and was again about to step out when Milk put his arm on his shoulder and hissed, 'Earl.'

'What about him?' asked Ditton, not understanding.

'He's over there,' said Milk, pointing towards the steps leading up to the pedestrianised shopping centre. 'Up by the side of Debenhams.'

Fortunately it wasn't Saturday and the pavements weren't too crowded with shoppers. They set off after Earl, jogging to catch up, but hanging back so that they could come alongside him somewhere secluded. He was oblivious to them behind him, weaving in and out of people, and he didn't turn around once. Up the street at the side of Allders an alleyway ran between a building society and a butcher's. Ditton drew up alongside Earl just as he was passing the opening and said, 'All right, Babbler. How's it going?'

Earl froze.

Milk shepherded him down the alley, not all the way down, but far enough for people on the street to not be able to hear what was being said.

Earl was grinning nervously and licking his lips. 'What's up, guys?' He turned to Ditton. 'I thought you were going to call?'

'I was,' said Ditton. 'But we just happened to see you down by the market.'

'That was lucky then,' said Earl, jamming his hands into his pockets.

Milk frowned. 'I hope you haven't got anything naughty in those pockets. Nothing that could hurt me. Have you?'

Earl shook his head decisively. 'No.'

Milk smiled a charming smile. 'Good. Nice one.'

'So what's up?' repeated Earl, looking from one face to the other for a sign of what was to come.

Neither answered the question, but Milk asked, 'When you saw us just now I had the feeling that you were going to run. Why would that be?'

Earl licked his lips. 'Nah, it's just that I'm not used to people calling me Babbler any more. People that call me that are usually from the old days, and there's a lot of history there.'

Ditton nodded. 'But you are Babbler, though?'

'I guess so,' Earl answered.

Ditton nodded again. 'So if I hear that some guy from Junction says a piece of shit called Babbler organised the heist on Jonah on Tuesday, would I be right in thinking that was you?'

Earl's eyes shot from one to the other and he swallowed. 'What?' he exclaimed. 'What do you mean?'

Ditton's hand shot out and slapped Earl's cheek. It was back at his side before the *Crack* of the contact had finished echoing off the walls.

'I don't know what you mean,' mumbled Earl

through the hand on his face. 'I don't know what you're talking about.'

Milk nudged Ditton gently out of the way and placed one hand on the wall next to Earl's head, effectively imprisoning him. 'You've got to be nice to him,' he said to Ditton. 'He's our friend. Let me be nice to him.'

Ditton shrugged. 'Whatever.'

The punch caught Earl just above the navel. It would have been a sickening blow to anybody, but for someone as thin as Earl it was even worse, and Milk could have sworn that he felt his knuckles touch Earl's spine. Earl would have crumpled to his knees and curled into a ball but Milk denied him the pleasure and propped him up so that the full effect of the blow would be felt.

'Well done,' said Ditton without humour. 'Now he can't speak.'

It was true. Earl was fighting to find breath; speaking would be out of the question for a few moments at least.

Milk grinned and pinched Earl's cheek. 'It's a good thing I'm being nice, isn't it? Can you imagine if I was being a cunt? You'd really be in trouble then, wouldn't you, eh?'

Earl was in no state to agree or disagree, and finally Milk allowed him to bend with his hands on his knees to get his breath back. After a few seconds Ditton slapped him again and said, 'Don't waste my time. Why did you do it?'

Earl raised a hand and nodded to show that he would

answer but that he needed a little more time. Then two middle-aged white men, one with a child in a pushchair, crossed the entrance to the alley, glanced up instinctively and stopped. The one with the pushchair was the bigger of the two and it was him that spoke.

'Oi! You two, leave him alone. Look at the size of him.'

Milk and Ditton looked at each other and in that instant Earl regained his breath and the use of his legs. He shot down the alley, hurdled the pushchair and was off around the corner. Ditton groaned, Milk cursed.

As Milk walked past the pushchair he gave the man a look of such malevolence and bad intent that the guy flinched and took a step backwards. The toddler began to wail.

CHAPTER NINETEEN

Ditton didn't know the woman that opened the door. He didn't recognise her as a relative of Jonah's but she might well have been. He guessed she was probably one of the congregation from Mrs Carty's church who had come to be of support. She stepped aside to let them in. The house was the same as it had always been, red shag-pile carpet in the passage and up the stairs, and the protective plastic strip running along the middle of the carpet straight from the front door through to the dining room and kitchen at the back of the house. It smelled the same too, of frying, old oil and beans soaking overnight. Mrs Carty saw it as sacrilege to use kidney beans from a tin; they had to be soaked and done properly.

Ditton took a deep breath and walked in, glancing into the cluttered front room as he did so. It was full of shiny metals and cabinets displaying crystal and the best crockery. A garish combination of doilies, ornaments, plastic settee covers, souvenirs from seaside resorts and Jamaica, a picture of the Last Supper on the wall over the fireplace and a sculpture of Christ on the cross on the wall opposite. It was the first time he could remember seeing anybody use the room. As in many homes, the front room was reserved for special occasions and all family business was carried out in the kitchen or dining room.

Milk nudged him in the back and Ditton squeezed past an elderly man in the passage and entered the back room. There were eight or nine people that Ditton knew were all family of some kind or another. He saw Mrs Carty first, at the head of the table. A small, attractive woman who had put on weight since he had last seen her. That was no bad thing; it had softened her face and prevented her fine, angular features becoming harsh and severe with age. Her eyes were red from crying and there were dark semicircles below them. Mr Carty sat next to her, a plate of food untouched in front of him. He looked weary. He had always been a quiet, thoughtful, sensitive man that Ditton had admired. He was nothing extraordinary, your typical Caribbean immigrant that had settled in London, got his head down and worked hard to make something for his children.

Ditton had always been impressed by the man's quiet strength and composure, but as he looked at him now he was horrified by how small and downtrodden Mr Carty looked. He had taken the news very badly. Ditton walked over and kissed and hugged Mrs Carty. Mr Carty held his hand for what seemed an age. The fingers felt bony and old, and Ditton was forced to accept that it was too long since he had last seen the couple.

Mrs Carty directed a great-nephew to get beers for Ditton and Milk and the two young men sat down at the table. The boy, Jamal, returned with the bottles and placed them in front of the two newcomers. The conversations resumed, most of them about Jonah as a child and the antics he had got up to, and how the country had changed so much from when his parents had first arrived penniless but optimistic so many years ago. After about ten minutes Mrs Carty took Ditton's hand and asked quietly, 'You seen Esther?'

Ditton shook his head hoping that would be the end of it.

'She's upstairs in her room. You can go and talk to her, you know. I'm sure she would like to see you.'

Ditton frowned and shrugged. 'I don't know,' he said. 'Maybe I should just wait until she comes down.'

Mrs Carty issued a knowing look, a motherly glance that he could only gratefully accept from the likes of her or Mrs Kerr. 'Have it your way,' she said, squeezing his hand. 'I can never work out you young people.'

'Neither can I,' said Ditton smiling. 'Neither can I.'

He sat there for the next half-hour drinking beer and chatting, and wished Vincent would arrive, wanted to get it over with so he could leave and do what he had to do, but Vincent didn't show.

The more Ditton drank, the more he wanted to use the toilet, but the toilet was upstairs and he had to admit to himself that he would rather stay down here and rupture his bladder than have Esther think he had gone upstairs to see her. In all truth she was probably up there with her door locked and he could have exploded a bomb without her coming out. But he didn't want to risk it. Stubbornness was not a fault that was usually associated with Ditton, but every man has his moments and he asked Milk for the car keys, claiming that he had to get something from the car, excused himself and went outside. He found a convenient spot, relieved himself and walked back to the house feeling a new man.

Milk was outside smoking with a puzzled expression on his face that grew as Ditton got closer. 'Where the fuck did you go, man? You didn't go to the car.'

Ditton mimed opening and closing his fly and Milk's confusion continued. 'What was wrong with the fucking house?'

Ditton shook his head and waved Milk away, but Milk was beginning to put the pieces together, slowly. 'It's Esther, isn't it?' Slightly shamefaced, Ditton shrugged.

Milk was horrified. 'You wouldn't go upstairs to the toilet because she was there? You're crazier than me, man. I can't believe that one.'

'Shut up and give me a puff of that.'

Milk shook his head and began to laugh. He sat down on the front wall of the house and handed Ditton the joint. 'You should talk to her, man. Say hello at least. What harm can that do?'

'The harm's been done already. She made sure of that when she did what she did.'

'But that was years ago,' said Milk, springing up and standing in front of Ditton. 'Look how many things have changed since then.'

Ditton frowned. 'Changed? Like what? Rodney's the same, my dad's the same . . . and I'm the same. That's what she said she couldn't handle. We've got nothing to say to each other.'

He looked up to see Milk with a strange childlike expression on his face, his eyebrows raised and his lips pursed. Every now and then he would squint and incline his head slightly, but Ditton failed to read him.

'The more I think about it, the less I want to know. It pisses me off too much.'

Milk stamped his feet and grimaced. Baffled, Ditton turned around slowly to see Esther standing on the doorstep leaning against the door frame with her arms folded across her chest. Ditton turned back and mouthed, 'Why didn't you say?' Milk's pained expression said, 'I tried.'

'You're still smoking, then,' Esther observed as she glided along the path and out of the gate to stand alongside Milk. 'That was another thing I couldn't handle, wasn't it?'

'I suppose so,' answered Ditton flatly.

There were a few seconds of silence, which Milk took it upon himself to break. He commiserated and asked Esther the things that his friend should have. Ditton smoked in silence and appeared disinterested, but he took in enough of Esther to be angry and disappointed that she still did the same things to him.

She wasn't wearing anything special – black trousers, boots and a dark grey V-necked jumper that exposed her collarbone. Ditton felt a twinge. He used to joke about her collarbone, she called it her clavicle. He just called it sharp and dangerous.

Although she was talking to Milk he could feel her watching him but he couldn't look up and meet her gaze, worried about what he would see in her eyes and terrified of what she would see in his.

'I'm going to get another drink,' declared Milk. 'You want one, D?'

Ditton glared, knowing that Milk was trying to leave them alone. He told himself that it was the last thing he wanted. 'Don't worry, I'll come back in with you.'

'I've got a message for you,' Esther cut in. 'Vincent called a while ago but I didn't know you were here.' She paused and Milk shot Ditton an I-told-you-so look. 'He says he's not going to make it up here this afternoon but you should go and meet him at the gym.'

'Thanks,' said Ditton. 'I'll do that.'

There was silence for a few moments except for a car that passed by with its music pumping and windows vibrating. Ditton steeled himself, stood up and asked, 'Was that it?'

He might as well have slapped her. Her eyes opened wide and her lower lip trembled. She looked as though she wanted to speak but instead wheeled sharply and went back into the house.

Ditton groaned inwardly and eventually glanced

at Milk, whose expression showed that he was not impressed, not impressed at all.

'All right,' pleaded Ditton, 'I know. I know. It wasn't meant to come out like that. I don't know why it did.'

Milk gestured towards the open front door. 'After you, sir. I think you know what you need to do.'

Ditton sighed and nodded. 'I guess I do.'

They found her in the passage talking to the po-faced woman that had opened the door to them. Esther had obviously been waylaid and hadn't had a chance to retreat upstairs to her room. Ditton hovered trying to make eye contact but the woman seemed intent on keeping Esther talking for the rest of the day. He could tell that although he had upset her and he wasn't currently her favourite person, she was in need of rescuing. He linked arms with her, said, 'Excuse us, please,' and led Esther away and back out of the front door. She didn't resist and Milk winked as they passed.

'I'm sorry,' said Ditton once they were outside. 'I was rude. I'm not sure why but I was wrong and I apologise.'

Esther was silent for a moment as if gauging the sincerity of his words, but finally she took a deep breath and said, 'It's OK. I suppose you've got reason to be angry with me.'

She was about to speak when a car pulled up outside the house and offloaded four or five people that Ditton recognised as family members. Esther frowned, said, 'Wait here. Don't go anywhere.' She greeted the new arrivals and led them into the house. A couple of minutes later she floated out again looking tired, and asked, 'Where were we?'

'Nowhere, really,' replied Ditton.

Again Esther stared at him as if trying to read his mind. He wanted to close it off to her, deny her access, but he couldn't and had to admit to himself that whatever he might say, however brusque and off-hand he might be with her, she would always have him around her little finger. Not that she would manipulate him or take advantage, he didn't expect that, which was why her actions those years ago were so hard to understand.

He returned her gaze until he felt that she was hypnotising him and that he might say something he would regret later, something soppy that he would call another guy a wanker for exposing.

She spared him and asked, 'Have you got a pen?'

'Why?'

'To take my number.'

Ditton was taken aback. 'Don't you live here any more?'

'No. I moved out a couple of months ago. I've got a little flat in Norwood now.'

He bit his lip. 'Alone?'

She smiled a beautiful smile and nodded.

'I can put your number straight into the phone,' he suggested, reaching for the back pocket of his jeans.

Esther grimaced and shook her head. 'No. You can do that afterwards. I can't stand seeing guys do that on the street. It makes the girl look so cheap.'

Fortunately Ditton had a pen. That was fate, he hoped. As he scribbled the number on a receipt he felt a surge of emotion rise from his stomach and travel the length of his right arm, making writing difficult, but he managed. Nothing was going to stop him.

'Why have you given me this?' he asked seriously.

Esther ran a hand over her hair. 'So we can talk. That's what you want, isn't it?'

He wanted more, much more, but only managed to say, 'Yeah. Sure.'

She nodded. 'Are you going to phone me tonight?'

'Should I?'

She shrugged. 'Yeah. Quite late, though. I'll probably be here for most of the day.'

'Helping your mum?'

She frowned again, the cutest little wrinkling of her nose and brow that hit Ditton bang in the centre of his chest and upset the rhythm of his breathing. 'From what I've seen, my dad's taking it the worst. His youngest boy gone and all that. Mummy seems quite together, I don't think it's surprised her too much.'

Ditton lowered his head and sighed.

'They're really grateful to you, though. They know what you've been trying to do for him, and they know what a handful he is.' She shrugged sadly. 'Was.'

Ditton led her into the house.

'I suppose you're going to meet Vincent now?' Esther asked once they were in the passage at the bottom of the stairs.

Ditton looked at his watch. 'Yeah, I'd better get

moving, actually. I don't want this stuff to take all day.'
He smiled. 'I've got to phone you later haven't I?'

She returned the smile but it faded when she said,
'Yes, you run along and see Vincent. That was something else I couldn't handle. Did you remember that
one?'

He nodded reluctantly, and flinched as she
unexpectedly kissed him on the cheek.

'I'll speak to you later then,' she said, and walked up
the stairs.

Ditton almost skipped to find Milk.

Because he had promised to take Shane to get a game
for the Play Station, and because for some reason he
was feeling guilty about the whole Sandra and Keith
situation, Milk dropped Ditton at home and then went
to his mother's to collect his nephew.

Maybe he felt that he had nearly killed the boy's
turd of a father and could make some amends for it by
buying him a game. Whatever the thinking, he arrived
to find that his mother had also returned from the
hospital and was pottering about in the kitchen.

'Did you see him?' she asked immediately.

Milk nodded and squeezed past to get to the fridge.
'Ditton was there,' he told her, and saw the worries
drain away and gurgle like an emptying bath. She knew
Ditton's calming effect on him and was grateful for it,
grateful that he had Ditton there to guide him and save
him from himself. Where he would be without that
boy she would never know, and Ditton, so sad himself

with all his tragedies and pain, it was a wonder he could help anybody else.

'How is she?' asked Milk with his head in the cavernous fridge. 'How come you're back already?'

Mrs Kerr busied herself tidying the already cluttered but spotless kitchen. 'I didn't want to stay there any longer, not after the old man opposite had a heart attack. I think he died, you know. They drew the curtains and didn't open them again.' Milk raised an eyebrow. 'And your father needed to go out so I had to get back here for Shane.'

'Does he know?'

'No. I've just got back, I haven't told him yet.'

'I've come to take him shopping. Are you going to tell him before we go?'

Mrs Kerr frowned, sighed and shook her head. 'That poor, poor boy. I don't know how to tell him that the mother who has abandoned him has nearly been killed by his father, who abandoned all of them.'

'Just tell him,' said Milk flatly. 'It's the truth.'

'Are you offering?'

Milk looked up from the drink he was pouring, grimaced and said, 'No I'm not.' He replaced the carton, looked at his mother and shrugged. 'But I suppose I could.'

Mrs Kerr draped a tea towel over her shoulder and met her son's gaze. 'That would be good, if you could. I'm tired of all of this.'

Milk downed his drink, looked closely and saw that his mother did indeed look very tired, more so than usual. He rubbed her back, more of a pat than a rub, said, 'OK, leave it to me,' and strode down the dark passage.

Mrs Kerr watched the two of them leave the house and thought to herself that these things always happened to nice people. Shane didn't deserve any of this, he was only a child, but then Marcus hadn't deserved his treatment at the hands of his father. He was no older than Shane when it had started. Maybe, she thought, maybe Marcus was the right person to talk to the boy. If not, she would have some consoling and grannying to do when they returned.

Milk came out of an electrical goods store in Streatham with Shane, who had become the proud owner of his own copy of FIFA. It's now or never, thought Milk as they walked back towards the car. He asked Shane if he knew where his mother was. The boy shrugged as if he didn't care, and said that he didn't know.

'I'm sorry to have to tell you,' Milk began, 'but she's in the hospital.'

'Oh,' was all Shane said.

'Are you upset?'

The boy shrugged. 'What's wrong with her?'

Milk lost his bottle, badly. 'She had an accident in the house. Fell down the stairs, I think.'

'Oh,' said Shane quietly.

'I don't think it's a good idea that you go to see her yet. It might upset you.'

'All right,' the boy agreed without any arm-twisting.

'What do you think about your dad?' Milk asked quickly.

The boy shrugged again and kicked an empty crisp packet on the floor. 'I don't know.'

'Do you ever spend time with him?'

The little boy shrugged and wiped his nose with the back of his hand. He looked up at his uncle and shook his head, not sadly or angrily, but like a wise man who knows things for the way they actually are. 'No. When he first started coming Mummy said I should be nice to him, but he just shouted at me and hit me.'

Milk winced and asked, 'Well, what did your mum do?'

'She would tell him to stop hitting me because it wasn't fair and I hadn't done anything.'

'What would he do then?' asked Milk, trying to keep the gate shut on his own too vivid memories.

Shane shrugged uncomfortably. 'Sometimes he stopped, sometimes he didn't.'

They were walking side by side and Milk suddenly felt Shane move closer. Instinctively he put his arm around the boy's shoulder. It felt strange. It wasn't like him at all, but it didn't feel wrong.

Shane looked up at his uncle. 'And sometimes he would hit my mum too. But not like he hit me. Really hard. And he would shout at her and tell her that she was stupid and that he didn't know why he was there.'

Milk tried to pull him closer still and Shane was forced to contort himself to accommodate the gesture.

'He won't be doing that again for a while,' Milk informed the youngster.

'Who won't?' asked the boy.

'Your dad. He won't be hitting anybody for a while. Maybe not ever again.'

Shane smiled a sad smile. Too sad for someone so young. Milk recognised it; he had learnt it himself at an earlier age. 'I don't know about that. Mummy says that he can't help it. That some people are just like that, that they're born to be like that and they don't know how to be nice to people.'

'That's true,' admitted Milk, 'but some people can be helped and I think your dad might have got some help.'

Shane nodded like a nine-year-old who either doesn't understand or is trying to humour an adult. But then he asked, 'Did my dad push my mum?'

Milk was again impressed by Shane's intelligence and perception. He didn't know what to say so he tried to be as honest as possible. 'We don't know yet, mate. He might have done but we really don't know.' It was true-ish. In fact he hadn't given himself time to ask Keith for his version of events. The fool had just opened his mouth and dug his own grave.

'Was that why you had the fight at school?' he asked Shane. 'Did the boy say something about what was going on at home?'

Shane bit his lip and nodded, tears filling his eyes. He wiped one away just as it threatened to meander its way down his cheek. Milk stroked his nephew's face as they waited to cross the main road and continued to pet him while they crossed and passed the library. They talked some more as they walked down the quiet street, and eventually Shane's tears no longer threatened to pour. As they came to a crossroads about fifty metres from Milk's car they stopped to let a red Astra turn right, looked both ways and stepped out into the road. From nowhere a metallic-blue XR2 shot across the junction at a furious pace, directly towards them. Milk was alert and instinctively fell back and rolled, taking Shane with him so that as he hit the ground he managed to hurl the boy on to the pavement and roll himself out of the way. He was up in a flash and on his feet, glancing briefly to make sure that Shane was OK. Assured that he was only shaken, Milk stared after the XR2 and saw it whack a parked car as it swerved wildly around a corner and headed for the cinema. In that instant when it hit the other car with a loud bang and the rear end was thrown out, Milk's mind snapped a picture of the registration number, as vivid as a photograph – C152 OWL.

He checked on Shane more thoroughly this time, becoming angrier by the second at the thought of what could have happened to his nephew, and swearing to himself that one day he would come across that car again. When he did there was going to be merry fucking hell to pay. He was so angry that for the first time ever even he was unsure whether he was fit to drive, until Shane said, 'I've had a good day today, Uncle Marcus.'

'Why?' asked Milk.

Shane smiled and shrugged. 'I got my game, we talked and then we had an adventure with that car.'

Milk shook his head at how sometimes, only sometimes, it could be so easy to be young. He started the car and drove back to his mum's at the slowest pace he could remember since his driving test.

Shane blurted out the whole story as soon as he saw his grandmother and she looked at her son for confirmation. He nodded and explained what had happened, but the story hardly differed from Shane's. Once the boy was safely ensconced on the Play Station Mrs Kerr beckoned her son into the kitchen.

'Did you manage to tell him?' she asked.

Milk made a face. 'Sort of. He kind of did it for me.'

Mrs Kerr looked puzzled and Milk was forced to recount the conversation as exactly as he could manage.

'I'm impressed, boy,' Mrs Kerr said. 'You seem to have learnt at least a few skills that are legal.'

'Don't go there, Mummy,' Milk warned. 'It's not worth it. Believe me.'

Mrs Kerr held back. She was beginning to agree that it wasn't, but would never admit that to him.

CHAPTER TWENTY

The gym was located in a railway arch off Coldharbour Lane. Vincent had occupied it for years, and it had been used for scores of nefarious activities in that time.

When Rodney was in hospital, and just afterwards, Ditton used to frequent the gym regularly. He would spend time there trying to press and curl his frustration and anger away, but only seemed to succeed in giving himself sore muscles and headaches.

It was Vincent who had suggested to Ditton that he come down to work out, and promised that he would find him some odd jobs to do occasionally. The jobs turned out to be very odd, and Ditton soon learned not to ask what was in the packages he was delivering or collecting. Vincent would pay him generously, too generously, and that was in addition to the sizeable lump sum he had given Ditton for the family as soon as it was diagnosed that Rodney would not be the same again. Ditton couldn't argue with anyone's perception of Vincent, but he had to admit that as far as his family was concerned, the guy had been a lifesaver and a saint.

Ditton skirted the guys working out. Some of them
he knew and nodded to. As he approached the massive
two-way mirror he doffed his cap. He always did it,
convinced that nine times out of ten Vincent would be
looking and see him coming. He reached the security
door leading to the private part of the building and
was buzzed in. He was always impressed by how cool
and fresh it was in the back as opposed to the heat and
humidity of the gym itself. It was a welcome relief.

He knocked twice on Vincent's door and entered.
The office was a fair size, and L-shaped. The walls were
brickwork painted white, there was a large desk immediately opposite the door, a drinks cabinet behind it to
the side and around a corner a couple of sofas and a
coffee table. There was nothing extravagant about it,
but nothing shabby either. Being an arch, the far wall
of the office sloped away and there were a couple of
up-lighters against it that threw weird shadows around
the windowless room. Vincent sat behind the desk
framed by the two lights.

'Drink?' Vincent offered.

'No thanks,' Ditton declined. 'I've had enough at
your mum's.'

Vincent insisted that Ditton have a beer, at least.

'How are they?' he asked. 'My parents? All talking
about the Lord and what he taketh away?'

Ditton smiled. 'Something like that.'

Vincent stood, walked over to the cabinet and
poured himself a vodka and orange. He returned to
the desk and placed a beer in front of Ditton. He took

a sip of the vodka, smacked his lips and said, 'It's a tart's drink, I know. But what the fuck? Here's to Jonah.'

'To Jonah,' Ditton toasted.

Vincent's mood seemed to have changed so much from the conversation in the morning that Ditton was perplexed and wary. He was expecting something out of the ordinary.

'So what have you got for me, then?' asked Vincent.

Ditton sighed and grimaced. 'Nothing yet.'

Vincent raised an eyebrow, spread his hands and inclined his head like some sort of guru. 'Now, have you spoken to Tyrone yet?'

'No, I still can't get hold of him. I've tried his phone, his pager, his flat, even his mum's.'

Vincent smiled. 'Suggestive, don't you think? I mean, where is he? He should be out and about, making sure his name's clean. But no, even you can't find him. Now I think I'm going to have to set a limit of the end of the week. I want to talk to him and straighten this thing out, but if it doesn't happen by Sunday I'm going to have to assume that he's guilty. After that . . .' He spread his hands even further and shrugged. 'So where are you going to go now?'

Ditton stood up. 'I'll have to try Kevin Hill next. The Peckham guy Jonah had something with.'

Vincent stayed him with a motion of his hand. 'Before you go,' he said quietly, 'three things.'

What now? Ditton thought.

'Firstly, I must stress that I'm not expecting this, but

I might as well get it out in the open, eh?'

Ditton nodded.

'If I find out that you knew Tyrone was behind this and didn't tell me,' Vincent suddenly looked pained, 'I don't know what I'd do.'

Ditton didn't want to imagine but he knew it wouldn't be nice.

'And secondly,' Vincent continued, 'I might have a proposition for you later in the week. Remind me if I forget to bring it up.'

Ditton nodded, slightly confused. 'Thirdly?'

'Thirdly,' said Vincent, sipping his drink, 'be nice to my sister.' He waved Ditton out, Ditton thinking that Vincent always knew too much.

Ditton sat on the swings listening to the cars, sirens and shouts from Brixton. He looked skyward, suddenly trying to remember the last time he had heard birds.

Nash had called and asked if they could meet. Ditton had wanted to put it off but had agreed. He hadn't thought twice when Nash suggested that they meet in the playground, but once he drove into the flats, as he had done so many times before with the intention of meeting Jonah, memories of the night before flooded back. He still couldn't believe it. Jonah was gone and would not be returning.

Ditton was still deep in thought when Nash bowled over in the same jacket, jeans and trainers as on Monday and settled his thick frame into the adjoining swing.

'Sorry about that,' he said smiling and showing off

his cracked front tooth. 'I had a phone call I couldn't get rid of.'

'S'all right,' said Ditton, with an accommodating gesture. 'Gave me time to think about a few things.'

Nash looked at him.

Ditton sighed and motioned over his shoulder at the block of flats. 'Did you hear all the commotion last night?'

Nash looked blank. 'No. What commotion?' he asked.

'You haven't heard about the shooting?'

Nash sat up, interested. 'No. I was out of town last night, come back this morning. The missus has gone out to work so I haven't spoken to her yet. What? Who was it? A mate of yours?'

Ditton nodded. 'Yeah. The guy I came to see on Monday when I saw you. Got shot in his living room last night.'

'I'm sorry to hear that,' said Nash. 'Really sorry.'

Ditton waved away Nash's sympathy and said, 'Anyway, I'm here. What's up?'

Nash's face changed instantly. It wasn't dramatic, but Ditton noticed it. It suddenly became serious and severe, and his eyes seemed to lose their sparkle and began to burn fiercely. Nash planted his feet on the floor and used them to turn himself in the swing so that he faced Ditton. Ditton tried not to be concerned but felt that he should be. Nash was the kind of guy it was sensible to be concerned about.

'I don't want to talk about business,' Nash declared.

'At least not your kind of business.'

Nash paused and Ditton nodded encouragingly. 'So what then?'

Nash pinched his nose and cocked his head to one side like a bird, complete with a vicious stare. 'I want to talk about me, your brother and five years' jail I've just done. Do you know what I'm talking about?' Nash asked.

Ditton shook his head. 'No, I don't.'

'No, I don't think you do,' said Nash after another pause. 'But that's beside the point.' He cracked his knuckles and jammed his hands into his jeans pockets. 'I can do my time as well as anyone, that's not the problem. But when I know I've been grassed, then there is a problem, a serious one.'

Ditton nodded. 'I can understand that. But what's that got to do with me? Who are you talking about?'

'Your fucking brother! Who else?' roared Nash.

'What's it got do with Rodney?' asked Ditton, taken aback. 'What are you saying?'

'I'll spell it out for you,' Nash said, calmly this time. 'Just so you understand properly. The only person who knew about the job I was doing was your brother. He was the only person I told. The *only* person. Do you understand? The police came and got me within an hour of the job. No forensic evidence, no witnesses. How the fuck did they know? There's only one way they could have known. If someone told them. And there was only one person that could have done that: your brother Rodney.'

Ditton began to protest but Nash whipped his hands out of his pockets and pointed aggressively. 'Don't say a fucking word! I don't want to hear it! Now, I want to talk to Rodney. I want to find out what happened, and how I got banged up. If you get in touch with me before the end of the week and take me to Rodney, or bring him to me, then we can discuss it sensibly.'

Nash paused again, for effect. Ditton thought he knew what was coming next.

'If you don't,' Nash continued, 'I'm going to come looking for both of you, and believe me, that won't be nice.'

He thrust his hands back into his pockets and stood up, too close to Ditton. He concluded, 'The choice is yours. You know how to get hold of me. You've got until Sunday.' And with that he bowled out of the playground, weaved his way through the parked cars, and disappeared into the flats.

Ditton followed Nash with his eyes until the block swallowed him up. He sighed and pinched the bridge of his nose between finger and thumb. He really didn't need this now. He slapped his thigh. 'Shit,' he said aloud. 'Shit, shit, shit!'

Vaughn pushed his chair back noisily and stood up. 'Would you like another drink?'

Janine blew him a kiss. 'Same again, please.'

Vaughn stood at the bar feeling uncomfortable. Things were not supposed to go like this. She was making it difficult and he hadn't wanted that. He had hoped she'd be cool and reserved, not over the top like this. Things were not going to plan.

Standing at the bar he looked at his watch. Two burly white guys stood at the bar beside him, drinking, and as he reached across to pay, his elbow caught one of their drinking arms. Although nothing was spilled and Vaughn apologised profusely, the man glared down at him with eyes full of bad intentions. Vaughn was annoyed; it was an accident and absolutely no harm had been done. He took a last surreptitious glance at the man – tall, big, mid to late thirties, with longish hair, slightly greying. Not one to mess with. He returned to the table and sat down.

'What took you so long? I missed you.' Janine raised his hand from the table, pulled it towards her and nuzzled it too publicly for his liking.

Vaughn glanced around to see if anyone was paying attention, and saw no one looking except the guy from the bar, still scowling. He released his hand and said, 'Don't look now, but there's a guy that looks like he wants to kick my head in. I don't know why.'

Immediately Janine swung her head around. Vaughn groaned. 'I said "Don't look now"!'

'Oh, don't worry about Terry,' she said. 'He's harmless.'

'You know him?'

'We've gone out a couple of times, but he's not my type. He understands.'

'Don't be so sure. He looks like he wants to understand my face on the end of his fist.'

'Forget about him,' directed Janine. 'Concentrate on me. I'm much nicer, don't you think?'

'Of course,' said Vaughn. 'Much nicer.'

She told him that the office had been busy in his absence; Darryl's death seemed to have sparked a frenzy of efficiency and apparent professionalism. Everybody had been writing copious notes in their files and had been on the phone to Social Services reporting the smallest details and concerns.

With a bitter smile Vaughn asked, 'And I'm still supposed to write my report?'

Just as Vaughn was about to raise his bottle of beer to his mouth Janine said, 'Let's not dwell on things like that now, eh? Let's go back to mine, and be nice to each other. What do you say?'

Vaughn took a swig of beer, swallowed and braced himself. 'I can't. I'm afraid I have to go and meet someone for a drink in half an hour,' he lied.

'Oh,' said Janine coolly. 'I hadn't realised.' She took a sip of her drink. 'Well, what about after that?'

Vaughn tried not to squirm. 'I don't know. I don't think it's such a good idea.'

Janine sat up, and then back, and he could see that she was unsure of how to take his refusal. He decided that he had started and might as well finish. 'I've been thinking,' he said slowly, 'and I'm not sure whether we should continue with this – us, I mean. At least not how it's been going.'

Janine stayed as she was, impassive and silent, refusing to give him any help.

'I mean, it's been great and everything, but where do we go from here?'

'What are you saying?' she asked quietly, almost without moving her lips. 'That you want to fuck me silly and then say "That's it"? Is that what you're saying?'

Vaughn could feel that things were moving slightly too fast, and in the wrong direction. 'No, I'm not saying that, but you know my situation. You know that I'm with Courtney. What do you want me to do?'

Janine fixed him with a gaze that threatened to raze him. She stayed as she was for a moment or two. Although she kept her poise he could tell from the tightness of her mouth, the rise and fall of her chest and the occasional swell of her jaw line as she clenched her teeth that she was fuming.

'I actually thought you were different,' she announced finally, her voice trembling with emotion. 'But you're not, are you? You're just like all the rest. Just another one who wants a piece of game for his trophy cabinet. You make me sick!'

'Look,' he said, 'why don't we let this blow over and talk about it some other time? We're both getting emotional and likely to say things we don't mean. What do you think?'

When she called him a bastard an alarm bell rang somewhere in his mind and he knew there was something else on the way.

'You bastard,' she repeated, and then enunciated every syllable as she said, 'You bloody black bastard.

You make me sick,' and stood up.

Vaughn bit his lip and asked her to sit down. She refused. She was getting louder and Vaughn was aware that people were beginning to cast more obvious glances at them, as though the worse she got, the more right they had to stare. 'Janine, sit down,' he pleaded. 'Don't do this, please.'

'Just piss off!' she screamed this time. And before he realised what she was doing, she had picked up what remained of her drink and covered him with it.

Vaughn shot up out of his seat, more from surprise and indignation than anything else, sending his chair flying and a glass crashing to the floor. He reached to grab her arm in case she tried anything else. She was totally out of control now and screamed, squirmed and writhed as he tried to pin her arms to her side. Just when he thought he had managed to subdue her he felt a blow to the back of the head. Still reeling from it, he felt himself lifted bodily off the ground and steered towards the door. He tried to put up a struggle but his head was fuzzy and he only managed a token resistance; he hadn't even seen who was carrying him.

He was bundled through the door and out on to the High Road – banging his head again in the process – propelled around the corner on to a side street, propped up against a door which looked like a delivery entrance to the bar, and came face to face with a snarling Terry. Terry said, 'Leave,' and hooked him to the ribs, 'our,' and hooked him again, 'girls,' and buried his fist into Vaughn's stomach, 'alone,' and slammed him so hard against the door that his head made a sickening noise as it made contact. He saw nothing, bit his tongue with the force of the impact and slumped to the ground. Fortunately he saw the foot coming and was aware enough to curl up and turn away from it, catching it on his shoulder and arm.

'Black bastard!' was Terry's imaginative valediction, but Vaughn didn't even hear it.

The message from Courtney came through on the pager as Vaughn was getting out of the car at his flat. She wouldn't be able to make it, but he could call her on the mobile and she'd be able to explain and apologise. On the one hand he was disappointed but on the other he saw it as a blessing; he wasn't feeling particularly sociable after the evening he had had, and wanted to have a soothing bath and a healing sleep. He saw the wood splinters on the ground in front of his door and immediately got that sinking feeling. He walked across and pushed the door with his foot. It swung open and he walked inside, sure that whoever had broken in was long gone. He headed for the living room first as it was the most likely to have suffered the largest loss, and was amazed to see that the television, video, stereo and Play Station were just as he had left them. The room had been turned upside down, drawers open or on the floor, videos strewn about, cushions from the sofa scattered around and cabinets and cupboards open. The rest of the flat was in the same ransacked state but to his surprise he was sure nothing had been taken.

He didn't call the police, and instead spent twenty minutes tidying things up before he went downstairs to inform the neighbours. They were horrified and commiserated, but hadn't heard a thing. He thanked them anyway, went back upstairs, flicked through the *Thomson Local*, and dialled a twenty-four-hour lock-smith. He poured himself a stiff drink and laid himself down gingerly on his bed to wait. He ached all over from the incident at the bar and his castle had been invaded. The new-found mood of optimism and confidence was evaporating fast.

The phone was answered on the second ring before Ditton had a chance to get nervous or consider changing his mind about making the call. Half an hour later he was still on the line and speaking more freely and easily than he could ever have expected. A further hour later he and Esther reluctantly but sensibly decided that they had talked for long enough. There was nothing more to say that couldn't wait until tomorrow, and they both had more than enough to think about for one night.

Ditton lay on his bed and closed his eyes. It had been a long, horrible day, and he hoped he never had another like it. Fortunately he had been so busy that there hadn't been time for grief or sorrow. It was quiet in the house and he hadn't heard any sign of the neighbours for almost an hour; the chances of getting some rest were looking good. An hour and a half later he still tossed and turned, hearing Jonah's voice, picturing his walk and his smile, and when Ditton finally managed to remove Jonah from his thoughts his sister would jump in to replace him.

He sat up as a crash resounded through the house, but lay back as he heard the thud, thud of feet on stairs. He gritted his teeth and covered his head with the pillow as the sounds of laughter, plates and cutlery and then the dreaded music flooded his room from next door.

At the same time, in another corner of south London, a girl raised her head briefly to check what effect her efforts were having. She wiped her mouth, licked her lips, lowered her head and went back to work.

Marty McGinty was doing some thinking. He lay on his back, hands behind his head, smoking a little joint laced with a line of Charlie, staring at the ceiling. His brain ticked over, searching for something, an idea, inspiration. As the girl gobbled and slurped tirelessly, a thought suddenly came to him and he reached for his phone and dialled. Noticing, the girl raised her head, unimpressed and more than slightly offended that her hard work was apparently going unnoticed. Her jaw aching, and her wrist and forearm stiff, she downed tools dramatically. Marty winced, grimaced, explained, 'It's the coke,' and gestured that she should continue. She didn't. He shrugged and made his call. The girl listened briefly before pouting and saying with extreme sarcasm, 'I really love it when you get excited about football. It makes you so sexy.' Marty covered the phone for a second, said, 'I love it when you pay me lip service,' and guided her back to work.

FRIDAY

CHAPTER TWENTY-ONE

The new locks were stiff and Vaughn jiggled the key noisily in the Yale, trying to achieve a gratifying click. Finally, as satisfied as he could be, he set off for the office. He still ached and his ribs felt worse than they had yesterday. When he woke he had sneezed and pain seared through his sides bringing tears to his eyes. The painkillers had been helpful to an extent, but they had replaced a sharp pain with a heavy, nagging ache. He could cope with that, but the serious damage had been done to his pride and the state of mind that had just begun to bowl along nicely. The thought of seeing Janine in the office after what had happened troubled him deeply.

Janine wasn't in, Paul was, and after enquiring whether Vaughn was feeling better, he politely and diffidently asked how the report was coming along.

'Fine,' answered Vaughn, removing his jacket and switching his computer on.

'Good,' said Paul, visibly loosening. 'Is there any chance I could have it by Monday?'

'Sure,' said Vaughn in an even flatter tone. 'Monday.'

The dream woke Ditton for the second time that week and it disturbed him. Even if he had wanted to go back to sleep it would have been impossible; Kiss FM was being provided courtesy of next door. He groaned, yawned and rubbed his eyes. Maybe the dream was for a reason – he had intended to speak to Clive following his meeting with Nash but had put it off. He wasn't going to put if off any longer.

He rose and made his way to the bathroom, making sure that he washed the sink and bath carefully before using them. He had heard his dad stumbling around the house one night, and in a rare moment of compassion had followed him to the bathroom to see if he was all right. He had seen his father urinate in the sink, turn around unseeing, and walk past his son as though he wasn't there.

On the way out Ditton glanced up at next door's first-floor window, catching sight of the girlfriend of one of the guys who lived up there looking at him. She turned away quickly, leaving the net curtain askew, and for a second he contemplated ringing the bell to complain about the noise. Their answer would be that it was the girls downstairs, not them. He decided against it. It would have to be done, but not now; he had more important things to deal with.

Ditton had told Clive about the meeting with Nash while Clive neatened his hair. The barber had been more serious this time and after some thought remembered seeing Rodney the day after Nash was arrested. Rodney had been mad, according to Clive, who remembered that he had been with someone, a guy called Sean, also known as Cut Throat. It was possible that he knew something. Clive promised to find out Sean's whereabouts, if he wasn't in prison.

Although Clive had offered a ray of hope with his revelation about Cut Throat, he had also made sure Ditton understood that Nash's threat was serious and had to be treated as such. Ditton had understood, but hearing Clive's concern really forced the threat home, and he left the barber's with a haircut, some hope of a solution, and the intention to do something he had promised himself he would never do – buy a gun. If he couldn't convince Nash that Rodney hadn't informed on him, he had to be prepared to defend his brother, and with someone like Nash the only chance he had of achieving that aim was with real firepower.

From the car he phoned Milk and asked if he would be able to get hold of a gun or take him to someone who could. Milk had said, 'Yeah, course,' and had sounded excited about something. He had also sounded as though he was running, but had said he would talk about it when they linked up later. Feeling hungry, Ditton drove home intending to make himself something to eat. At his front gate he looked up at next door, nodded to himself and rang their bell to complain, sensibly and diplomatically. He rang three times; there was nobody in. Typical, he thought.

* * *

Shane was kicking a football tamely around the living room when Milk stepped in. He whipped the ball away from Shane, flicked it up, bent at the waist and caught it cradled between his head and shoulder blades. He stood up straight letting the ball fall, spun one hundred and eighty degrees, and caught it on his instep before it had a chance to hit the floor.

'Can you play football, Uncle?' asked Shane innocently.

'What?' Milk exclaimed. 'I'm the best player you'll ever see,' and he flicked the ball up and juggled it on his head a few times before walking around the room with it balanced on his forehead.

Shane smiled and rolled his eyes at his grandmother. She kept quiet.

Milk wasn't happy with the scepticism shown by his nephew, so he said, 'Get your trainers on. We're going to the park.'

Shane jumped up and retrieved his trainers from the passage. As he put them on hurriedly he asked, 'What for, Uncle Marcus?'

'To prove what I just said to you, of course.'

Milk was put out to see Shane smirk and roll his eyes again.

'Well, bring the ball, you twit,' directed Milk. 'Even I can't play without a ball.'

They didn't reach the park, even though it was visible from the flat. Milk started his tricks as soon as they got down to the forecourt. There was no need to cross the road to the park gates. After two minutes Shane was a believer and was in awe of his uncle. He would never disbelieve anything he said ever again.

Shane wasn't into football as much as some of the boys at his school, but he liked to play and watch. He had just seen his uncle do some things that he couldn't believe and was prepared to bet that David Beckham couldn't do. Milk had made a favourable impression on his nephew the day before when they had spent time together and bought the all-important game for the Play Station, but by spending a few minutes juggling a ball Milk had Shane for life.

Milk's phone trilled and he answered; it was Ditton. While speaking Shane threw the ball at him, hard, and with the phone to his ear Milk bent his legs and took the ball on his chest, arching his back and straightening his legs so that it flew straight up and high into the air. Still speaking he watched it come down from a distance and blasted it straight back where it came from, vertically up into the air as high as the second-floor balcony. Shane was squealing with delight and shouting, 'Third floor, third floor!' so Milk obliged and did it again, sending the ball up to the third-floor balcony. From the time Shane threw the ball to him it hadn't yet touched the ground, and as the ball came down again Shane was squealing, 'Nanny's, Nanny's!' Milk had a quick glance up at the fourth-floor balcony, the angle being so steep that he couldn't actually see the front door, said, 'Hold on, D,' into the phone, and then connected with the ball so sweetly that it flew up, and up, and disappeared over the balcony to clatter against his mother's front door. He winked at the speechless Shane, said, 'Whenever you're ready,' to Ditton and rang off.

Shane gushed about Milk's skills all the way up the stairs; Milk didn't say anything, just took the praise. But he did think about the match on Sunday, and knew that it was going to be a doddle. Fuck Marty and his team, Milk was going to piss on them from a great height and they were going to be grateful. He was simply the best.

CHAPTER TWENTY-TWO

It was Friday lunchtime and the cage was teeming with kids, many of whom had no intention of returning to lessons in the afternoon. Vaughn knew all of Marlon's group and greeted them warmly, relieved that they were all familiar faces. Marlon's friend Rick was there too, grinning broadly and sucking hard on a 'Twenty-five per cent extra free!' carton of Ribena.

Marlon stood, spat, and motioned for Vaughn to follow him as he walked a few feet from the rest of the group. Vaughn followed, interested. The boy gestured over his shoulder and said, 'Chris Keeler's over there, why don't you ask him what he knows?'

Vaughn wanted to, but he had never met the boy and didn't know what he looked like. 'Which one is he?' he asked.

Marlon peered at the group of boys in the far corner. 'The little one with the long blond hair. You see him? In the green jacket.'

'I see him.'

'I'll call him,' offered Marlon.

Vaughn watched Marlon strut past his group and hail Christopher Keeler, loudly and harshly. He saw the blond boy raise his head, note who was calling and drag himself from his perch, his body language suggesting that he didn't particularly want to respond to the summons but felt he had no choice. He walked across as though he was full of dread. Marlon made no attempt to allay his fears; he was enjoying himself.

Keeler skirted Marlon and walked up to Vaughn like one of life's victims. He was short for his age, very slim, with pale skin, almost white hair, and the bluest eyes – real choirboy material and obviously Kevin's brother. Vaughn tried not to smile as he remembered that this was the brother who had informed Kevin that black people were like monkeys and that dreadlocks were dead worms.

Christopher Keeler gazed dolefully up at Vaughn for a second before looking at his feet and waiting to be addressed. 'Do you want to step over here and have a chat?' suggested Vaughn. The boy didn't answer, but he followed.

A short distance away from Marlon and the others, who were trying to look as though they weren't interested, Vaughn stopped and introduced himself as an education welfare officer. He saw the boy miss a breath and something like alarm flit across his face for a fraction of a second.

'I visited your mum on Monday and met Kevin as well; did she tell you?' The boy shook his head. Successful visit, thought Vaughn.

Christopher bent to tie the laces on his trainers and Vaughn turned away and aimed a kick at a cigarette butt on the floor. There was a rustle of clothing, he saw a flash of colour out of the corner of his eye, and turned around to see Keeler streak towards a hole in the chain-link fence, slip through, shoot off across the grass and disappear into the flats. Vaughn spread his arms and mouthed, 'What?' to Marlon.

Marlon shrugged and spat.

The swelling on Patrick's face was still as large, but by now it wasn't as tender, and he could speak without dribbling. Thursday had been a bad day for him, painful in more ways than one. He had got into his car in the morning and found that he'd knackered the engine in that stupidness outside the club. If his estimate was right he'd be shelling out a small fortune to repair it – more than the car was worth. And, he was down financially anyway because of that bastard Milk. He still couldn't believe it. All his hard work and savings taken away just like that by a mad Brixton bastard who attempted to break his jaw when he had tried to talk about the matter sensibly. Patrick's problem was that he had the talk and he looked the part, but he had never actually been tested. Now that something had come up, he wasn't sure he could deal with it. However, he had been so insanely angry that dangerous thoughts and plans had come into his mind. One he had even acted upon. He had been in the right place at the right time and reacted instinctively.

On Friday Patrick woke up mad, and determined that something had to be done to sort the situation out. He had seen Devon in the street and hid from him, unable to smile in his face and say that everything was cool, and definitely unable to tell him the truth. Kevin had made it clear in no uncertain terms what he thought of his cousin's apparent inability to take care of business, and Patrick had to admit to himself that he was behaving like a pussy. So when he woke up on Friday morning and heard Kevin with his girl in the next room, he felt mad. He didn't even have a girl to console him. Donna had told him to fuck off on the phone, and he hadn't heard from her since. Michelle had made it obvious that she wasn't interested, but he still didn't know why. His world seemed to have fallen apart in the space of a few days, and Milk was at the centre of most of it.

He got up, dressed and knocked on Kevin's door. Eventually Kevin opened it, scowling, and not pleased at being interrupted. Eager to get back to the business at hand, he threw Patrick his car keys. 'Try to be careful today, OK?' he advised.

Patrick nodded and left the flat, *his* flat, and jumped into Kevin's car. He wasn't sure why, but he was going to Donna's. He wanted to see her, needed to see her to sort out the situation, and knew she was bound to be there because she always went out on Thursday nights and slept in on Friday mornings. In fact, the lazy cow slept in most mornings. He considered pointing that out to her as a reason for why she got robbed, but recognised that it might not go down too well.

Patrick pulled up outside Donna's and noted that the curtains were still drawn. He pictured her warm body in the bed that he had bought, her face and lips puffy with sleep, and felt a pang deep in his chest. He got out of the car, rang the bell and waited. He rang the bell again and waited again. He rang the bell for the third time, impatiently keeping his finger on the button for long enough to wake the dead. He heard a knock on the window above his head, removed his finger, stepped back and looked up.

A big, topless black guy stood at the window gesticulating wildly, and for a moment Patrick thought he must have come to the wrong house. But he knew he hadn't, and something snapped inside him, forcing him to gesticulate just as wildly. The thought of some half-naked guy in the flat incensed him. It was only a couple of days ago they had argued, and here she was with another man already. Patrick was fuming; he had furnished most of the flat, albeit with a lot of stuff from Michelle's place, but that wasn't the point. And here was this ungrateful girl picking up with the first ruffian she met.

The guy inside threw up the sash window and asked Patrick who the fuck he thought he was. Patrick asked the guy exactly the same thing, and told him to get Donna. The guy warned Patrick not to tell him to do anything, and that if Donna had wanted to speak to anyone she would have answered the door. Patrick repeated his demand that Donna come out and called the guy a mother-fucking bastard pussy. Stunned, the guy stared agape at the gold-toothed runt below him, deciding whether to run down the stairs and smash his head in or just jump out of the window and land on him.

He had decided to take the stairs when Donna herself appeared, leaned out of the window, called Patrick an idiot and told him to get lost, he was making a fool of himself. Totally beside himself now, Patrick told Donna to fuck off, then asked her to come down to speak to him – common sense had gone out of the window. So much so that when a couple of neighbours came out on to their doorsteps he asked them what the fuck they thought they were looking at. A fucking show? And then informed them that this wasn't an episode from the fucking *Bill*.

But to give him his due, as wild as he was feeling, as enraged and hurt, his innate survival instincts must have been in working order. When Donna's front door opened and the big guy came out wearing nothing but his shorts and a baseball bat (Patrick's bat), Patrick took action. The guy had looked big when he was at the window, but downstairs in the flesh he was a black man mountain, and in his boxer shorts he looked like some kind of super-model. Patrick was back in the car and trying to start it when the bat came through the driver's door window and showered him with glass. He put the car into first gear and burnt rubber, but was too late to avoid the rear passenger door suffering the same fate, and the back of the car taking a whack in the area of the number plate and boot. Patrick didn't look back.

Kevin was on the balcony playing big-shot, talking to one of the local youngsters who aspired to be like him, when Patrick returned and limped the car into a parking space. Patrick looked up to see Kevin hold his head in his hands, and through the broken windows heard him wail, 'Nooooo!' Kevin ran frantically down the stairs, his eyes staring wildly at the car in disbelief. 'What the fuck happened this time?' he demanded. 'Yesterday you borrow the car to go to Streatham and tell me that someone hit it while it was parked and scraped up the whole fucking wing. Now this? What the fuck happened this time?'

Patrick sighed and scratched his head.

CHAPTER TWENTY-THREE

'We'll go to Peckham first,' explained Milk as he cut through the traffic like a stunt driver. 'Find out Kevin Hill's address, and on the way back go and sort out the gun.'

After Peckham the next stop wasn't far away, off the Old Kent Road, in a red-brick thirties council estate, much like Milk's mother's flat. Milk dialled a number and told someone at the other end that he was downstairs.

'You'll need to come too this time,' said Milk. 'If you still want it, that is.'

Ditton answered by getting out and following Milk to the second floor. A couple of old folk gossiping, probably on their way to or from the post office, followed them with their eyes, then, not having peripheral vision, turned their torsos stiffly to continue the observation. On the stairs Ditton could hear a mother and child laughing and playing as they descended from the floor above. When they hit the same landing as the two black guys all hilarity ended and the woman grabbed the toddler's hand and pulled her close. Ditton shook his head, disappointed but not surprised; after all this was British National Party heartland. Milk didn't seem to notice.

They stopped at a door in the middle of the balcony and Milk rang the bell. After what seemed like ages the door was opened by a burly, clean-shaven white guy in his early thirties. He was average height, wore jeans, trainers and a sweatshirt, and sported a blond crew-cut above an open, friendly face. He waved them in smiling at Milk and studying Ditton. Once the door was closed Milk made the introductions.

'Ditton, this is Jerry. Jerry, Ditton.' He turned to Ditton. 'Me and Jerry used to play non-league together. He's a chopper. Likes breaking legs.'

Jerry said in a gravelly coarse cockney, 'I know who he is, or at least I know the name.' He put an arm around Milk and said to Ditton, 'He was always going on about me and Ditton did this, and me and Ditton did that. I tell you, it got so fucking boring after a while that every time I heard your name I wanted to smack him in the mouth.'

Jerry directed them into a living room that was small and simple but showed that he made enough money to live comfortably. There was a television, a classy music system, a coffee table and a terracotta-coloured leather sofa and armchair. One wall of the room was covered from ceiling to floor with LPs that were obviously cherished.

'What can I do for you gents?'

'Ditton here's in a bit of a sticky situation,' Milk began. 'He needs something small, quick. Self-defence kind of thing.'

Jerry addressed Ditton. 'So you don't want something big and impressive. Nothing intimidating. Just functional?'

'No,' said Ditton laughing. 'Definitely not big and intimidating.'

'Do you actually want to use it?' Jerry asked.

'No,' said Ditton, not laughing this time.

'But you think you might have to? If the worst comes to the worst?'

'Only if the worst comes to the worst. And then I'll probably be scared shitless, freeze and not be able to.'

Jerry nodded. 'I understand, and I think I know what you need.'

He stood up and left the room, returning a couple of minutes later with two objects wrapped in bubble-wrap and brown tape. He unwrapped them and placed them on the coffee table in front of Ditton.

'This,' said Jerry, holding up a small black revolver, 'is a .22. "Saturday-night special" they call it in the States.' He looked at Milk, who was investigating some of the records, sighed, and said, 'I can let you have that with six rounds for two hundred.' He held up the other pistol, a small semi-automatic. 'And this,' he said, gazing at it fondly, 'is a Beretta, as made famous by Mr James Bond himself, although Q forced him to use the Walther PPK.' He grinned and said conspiratorially, 'And I don't care what that fucking Q says, I've never heard of one of these jamming yet.'

He sat back and gestured for Ditton to hold them and have a feel. Ditton lowered his hand to the .22 as though he expected it to rear and bite him.

Jerry winked at Milk and said to Ditton, 'Come on, you better get used to it before you need to use it, or you'll be in serious trouble.'

Ditton reached for the small pistol, picked it up and hefted it in his hand, surprised at how heavy it was. 'What am I looking for?' he asked Jerry.

'For it to feel right.'

Ditton put the .22 back and reached for the Beretta. As he did so Jerry winked at Milk and the two of them struck up the James Bond theme tune, standing and assuming Bond's characteristic pistol-levelling pose.

'All I need now is Pussy Galore to walk in,' Milk said.

'And I'll have Bambi and Thumper, for starters,' Jerry replied instantly.

Ditton looked at them, amazed at how infantile and normal people could be when their vocations would have suggested differently. He picked up the Beretta and understood what Jerry meant about it feeling right. The gun fitted his hand perfectly, and it took him back to his childhood where anything and everything even slightly L-shaped had become a gun. He looked at Jerry and nodded.

'I can give you that and two clips for four hundred,' said Jerry.

Milk coughed quietly and Jerry grimaced, sighed and said, 'All right. Three fifty.'

Ditton was silent while he looked from one gun to the other, prompting Jerry to say, 'Seriously, mate, I can't do you no better than that.'

Ditton looked up and nodded. 'I tell you what. I'll take both of them off you for five.'

Milk's face showed that he thought Ditton had lost his mind. First he didn't want a gun, now he wanted two?

Rodney was curled up on the end of Ditton's bed when he got back home, and next door they seemed to be returning from work in dribs and drabs and preparing themselves with loud music and raucous laughter to go out again. Ditton thought once, twice, and phoned Esther.

Half an hour later Ditton rolled a joint for the drive, trotted downstairs to the kitchen and left Rodney a note and some money in case he wanted to buy food.

He checked his wallet, returned it to his back pocket and patted it contentedly. He checked his keys, his appearance in the hall mirror and, unable to stall any, longer let himself out of his house and headed for his car. One of the African girls from next door sat chatting to her boyfriend in his BMW. They both looked at Ditton as if daring him to say something, but this was going to be a good evening for him and he wouldn't bother with them now. He got to the car, put the key in the lock and was about to slide in when he heard his name hissed and felt a hand on his shoulder. He whipped himself around, prepared for the worst.

CHAPTER TWENTY-FOUR

'Where have you been, Ty?' asked Ditton tersely. 'People have been looking for you.'

Tyrone sighed and nodded. 'I've been staying at my cousin's in Thornton Heath since Wednesday night. I didn't even hear about Jonah until today.'

Ditton tossed him a sceptical glance but didn't speak.

'It's the truth,' Tyrone insisted. 'I caught the end of something on the news on Thursday, but I didn't know who it was until today when my cousin told me.'

'And that's why you're here now?' asked Ditton.

Tyrone puffed out his cheeks and shook his head.

'So who are you running from?'

'I don't know, that's the problem. White guys. Sometimes two, sometimes three. They've been following me for a while, I was sure of that. I told you on Monday, didn't I?'

Ditton lit the joint he had rolled for the drive. 'I don't remember.'

Tyrone shrugged. Maybe not. I thought so, though. 'Well, on Wednesday they stopped trying not to be seen, and just kept pulling up alongside me at traffic lights and staring. Wherever I was I'd look out of the window and the car would be there. I'd be in the flat, the car would be there. I went to see a girl, I looked out of the window and the car was there. It was too much, man.'

'What did you do?'

'I took a bag, jumped out of my back window and got a cab down to my mum's. I stayed there on Wednesday night, made some business calls and left in the morning to go and stop at my cousin's for a while.'

Ditton looked up sharply. 'You were at your mum's all Wednesday night? She'll swear to that?'

'Yeah, I got there about nine, and left early Thursday morning, about eight.'

Ditton sighed, took a puff and offered the joint to Tyrone. 'It would have been a lot easier if you had just phoned and said all that instead of giving people reason to think you were in hiding because you did Jonah,' he said. 'You've gone and made yourself look a lot guiltier than you needed to.'

'I can see that,' said Tyrone. 'But like I said, I didn't even know about Jonah until today so I had no reason to phone, did I? And I was a bit paranoid about using the mobile. I was having thoughts about them being able to trace me when I used the phone. That's if they are police.'

'Who else would they be?'

Tyrone shrugged. 'I don't know. Some nutters Vincent's paying?'

It was possible, but Ditton didn't think so. If that was the case they would have closed in and done him before he had any idea he was being followed. That was what Milk, Jonah or even Tyrone himself would have done. He didn't point it out. 'So what are you doing here now?' he asked.

'I need some help,' Tyrone stated after a pregnant pause. 'I need you to help me.'

'What's wrong with the cousin you're staying with?' Ditton asked, wary.

'I would have asked her but there was an argument this morning and I went after her boyfriend. I ended up smashing his car a little bit, the neighbours came out and I thought it made sense to disappear before someone called the police. I could tell that she wanted to call her man and make up with him too.'

'Who is this cousin anyway?' Ditton asked, still sceptical and wanting confirmation that Tyrone was telling the truth.

'Aunt Joyce's daughter, Donna. You remember her? Big eyes and lips to match. Aunt Joyce always used to give her those big plaits that stuck out all over her head, and put her in those funky polkadot dresses.'

Ditton nodded; he remembered, but he stayed silent. It was up to Tyrone to make his request. After another pause he did. 'I need some money from the flat. I need you to go in there and get it for me. If they're police they'll be looking for me and I wouldn't trust anyone else to go in.'

Ditton snorted and his lip curled in disdain. 'What about Earl?'

Shamefaced, Tyrone admitted that he had tried Earl a few times and got no answer. Ditton wasn't surprised.

'So what is it that you want me to do?'

'Just go in, get some cash from where I keep it, come out and drive me to Mitcham, that's it.'

'That's it? Risk arrest or a bullet in the head and you say, "That's it?" and I'm just supposed to go skipping along and do it?'

'Look, I'm in trouble,' snapped Tyrone. 'I need help and I've got no one else to turn to. Can you help? Will you help?'

'All right,' said Ditton. 'But on one condition. You come with me now and we go to Vincent. Sort this thing out once and for all. What do you say?'

Tyrone kissed his teeth and grimaced, but eventually he nodded.

Ditton dialled Esther and apologised; he was going to be late, something had come up. After all those years, she had said, 'As usual.' Ditton felt like scum, but at least she seemed satisfied with his assurance that it wouldn't take too long. If Tyrone messed this night up for him Ditton would never, ever forgive him. Next he dialled Vincent. He explained the situation, where he was, and that Tyrone had agreed to talk to him. Vincent had said that he was on the road and he would try to come to them. If he hadn't made it in half an hour Ditton was to bring Tyrone down to the gym.

'These guys,' Ditton asked Tyrone, 'what do they look like?'

Tyrone sighed and rubbed his neck. 'What can I say? White guys, suited, driving a black Rover.'

'Come on,' encouraged Ditton. 'You can do better than that.'

Tyrone shrugged. 'What can I say? The driver's always the same, dark hair, burly, gold on his wrists. I'm not sure how tall. The second one looks tall, shortish black hair and a little goatee. The third one is the one that worries me. I've only seen him once, but I won't forget him. He was in the passenger seat when they pulled alongside me at the lights and they'd never done that before. It was like he was the daddy, running the show.'

'What did he look like?' asked Ditton, interested despite his annoyance.

'Tall, I could tell that, and big. Decent age, late forties to mid fifties. Short dark hair, going grey, a fucked-off hooked nose and a scar on his chin. But it was his eyes. When they pulled up alongside and he looked at me. Trust me, D. The guy looked fucking mean. He had these staring black eyes that looked like he could see into your soul.'

Ditton turned and peered at Tyrone through narrowed eyes of his own.

Taken aback, Tyrone asked, 'What's the matter, man? What is it?'

'That description,' said Ditton, remembering a Saturday afternoon many years previously. Remembering being with Rodney when an old Rover pulled up and a big man with jet-black hair, a hooked nose and terrible eyes had doffed his hat and sneered. 'It sounds like someone I've seen before.'

The young Asian waitress forced a smile which came across as a constipated grimace, picked up the menus and hurried away. 'What's wrong with her?' grumbled Milk.

'Why? She looked all right to me,' observed Michelle.

'She took off like she thought I was going to bite her or something. Is that what I look like? Like I'm going to bite?'

Michelle creased her face in over-exaggerated thought. 'Sort of. But I like the idea, so it's not a problem.'

Milk sneered to show that he wasn't thrilled. He took a sip of his beer and wondered what the fuck he was doing sitting in a restaurant with a girl on a Friday night. It was the sort of thing that Vaughn did, and what made it worse was that Milk had suggested it himself. Shameful, but true. If he was honest he would have admitted that this was what annoyed him most.

He fingered his glass, perturbed, and looked at his watch. He wanted to get Michelle somewhere and research her like a PhD, extensively and thoroughly, making copious notes and revisions. To his dismay, throughout the meal he found himself observing her when she wasn't aware and having to brazen it out when she looked up and found him gazing at her. And worse, she would give a little knowing smile and look away again, leaving him to continue. Milk talked a lot normally, but he found himself talking ten to the dozen just so that he had an excuse to stare at her. Fuck, she was yummy. Even when the food was brought out he would have got up and left it untouched if she had said she was ready to take him to bed. And that was another thing, he was even finding it hard to be direct about sex with her now, as though she had become too precious for that sort of thing. He thought he could tell that she was still as up for it as ever, but something within him was changing his behaviour and he wondered if this was what it felt like to be a smitten schoolboy He didn't know because he had never been one. Surely it couldn't happen now?

Milk was still ruminating on this when Michelle asked him a question that he heard from somewhere in the distance. He apologised, another new action, and asked her to repeat it.

He had heard correctly the first time. 'If I had a bag of Charlie this big,' she said with her hands spread in front of her, 'about a kilo, how much would it be worth?'

Milk stopped slouching and sat up.

Vaughn had emitted an involuntary squeak when Courtney suggested that they go to the Tadpole Bar for a drink and something light to eat. He had protested vehemently about his dislike for the place, which was in his opinion cramped, uncomfortable, expensive and full of noisy, trendy white middle-class kids with too much money and too few responsibilities.

'Oh,' was all a surprised Courtney could say, 'I thought you quite liked it there, but never mind. We can go somewhere else.'

Vaughn wanted to stay at home in his own little space where no one could jostle him, abuse him, spill drinks on him, look him up and down however innocently, or slap him or aim kicks at him. If he could have found a way to leave his soul at home and send his body out with Courtney he would have done it.

They settled on a little place up by Wandsworth Common that was just as cramped, more expensive and still full of noisy, trendy white middle-class kids with too much money and too few responsibilities, but Vaughn felt slightly more at ease. The Tadpole had too many unwelcome memories and he balked at the thought of showing his face there. The possibility of Janine showing up while he and Courtney were being the intimate and secure couple made him cringe, and the thought of Terry turning up on the scene made his stomach churn and threatened to shatter his mood like a plate-glass window in a riot.

Courtney worked in fashion PR, and handled press coverage for five or six foreign designers. Over the general hubbub she chattered on about the foibles and occasional merits of her colleagues at work, her successes over the past week, pleased clients, stroppy clients, lovely clothes, tasteless clothes, ludicrous clothes – the lot.

Courtney touched Vaughn's hand and he jumped like a startled rabbit. 'Where were you? What were you thinking about?' she asked.

'Nothing much,' said Vaughn with a shrug, trying to keep his elbows out of the way of the riotous bunch that had just come in the door doing the conga. 'Just work.'

'Well, it's Friday evening and you're with me. Try to switch off from work for a while. OK?'

He nodded and tried to concentrate on her and what she was saying, but once again her monologues gave him the opportunity to immerse himself in his own concerns as opposed to those of the fashion industry.

Vaughn was about to speak when Courtney said, 'Oh yeah! Guess what?'

Vaughn shrugged and picked up his beer glass.

'I had a dream the other night,' said Courtney with a rueful smile, 'that I heard you were sleeping with some white hussy. Blonde as well, and I rushed into her flat and found you two together in bed.'

In an attempt not to spray Courtney with his Belgian beer, Vaughn ended up choking himself and having his back banged by a hale and hearty, ruddy-cheeked rugger type from the table behind who possessed hands like rudders on the *Titanic* and had been swilling pints like there was no tomorrow. To his annoyance, after nearly having his spine broken, Vaughn had to thank the guy.

* * *

Patrick got a call from Donna to say that if he wanted to come round and talk, she was in. He was almost dialling for a cab before she'd hung up, and when he got there she began to rebuke him for his performance in the morning, asking him who the hell he thought he was coming around to her house like that and embarrassing her in front of her neighbours and her cousin.

Patrick took it all on the chin. He had taken a lot worse recently and this was tame in comparison. He explained that he hadn't known the guy was her cousin; he'd just seen some half-naked guy in the flat and seen red. On top of everything else that had happened that was the final straw and he'd just snapped.

Donna was slightly mollified and asked how Kevin had taken the damage to his car. Patrick shrugged. She asked what had happened to his face and he shrugged again, mumbling something about walking into a door. She asked him whether he had found that guy Milk and sorted him out. He shook his head and said, 'Nah, he must be laying low.'

Ditton got out of the car after circling the block twice on Tyrone's insistence. They hadn't seen anything suspicious, no signs of surveillance or an ambush. 'If there's any trouble, just get out of there,' advised Tyrone from the passenger seat. If it was that simple, Ditton thought, why couldn't Tyrone do it himself?

He had parked the car near the shops, in the same place as when he and Milk had seen Earl. It allowed him a short walk to the flat during which he would be able to scout some more. As he cut across the grass and walked up to the main intercom door, Ditton wondered again what the hell he was doing and how he had got into it. There was no black Rover in sight, and no one who looked out of place, but that didn't mean a thing. If the guys harassing Tyrone were police they could have been manning a camera and microphones from miles away, sipping tea and telling racist jokes.

He opened the heavy door, trying to look as though he did it all the time, trotted up the stairs to the first floor and stopped at Tyrone's door. Ditton inspected the door opposite Tyrone's for any signs of obvious surveillance. He gave up, accepting that he wouldn't know what he was looking for anyway, and that if they were thorough they had probably already been inside Tyrone's flat and rigged up their equipment.

He turned the key in the lock, aware that he was trying to be quiet for no real reason. If they were watching, they were watching, and no amount of stealth would make him less visible. The flat felt cold after two days unoccupied, and the smell of stale smoke still hung in the air, trapped, unable to escape and resentful. He made his way to the kitchen as instructed, opened the cupboard over the kettle, found the protruding screw in the bottom corner and pulled it outwards gently. The back of the cupboard swung forward, a squeezy bottle of ketchup fell on to the work surface and then on to the floor. Ditton gasped and held his breath, telling himself that he was being ridiculous, the noise wasn't loud, no one would have heard, and most importantly he wasn't doing anything illegal. Who was he fooling? He had let himself into the home of a known major drug dealer who hadn't been seen for days. He didn't work either, but looked far from destitute – the police would have a field day.

Behind the back of the cupboard was a cavity roughly eight inches in height, by eight inches across, and maybe another eight inches deep, covered by a wire-mesh grille. Ditton pulled at the grille as instructed and it came away from the wall despite the appearance of being screwed on. He felt inside. Tyrone had said that the money was stacked in bundles of ten thousand and he wanted Ditton to get five bundles. Pocket money, Ditton joked to himself as he removed the fifty thousand, hardly making an impression on the remaining stack of cash. Ditton knew he shouldn't have been surprised – Tyrone's operation and turnover was obviously huge – but he found himself impressed nevertheless. Tyrone had almost two hundred thousand in cash in the house. It was silly to have the money there, but impressive nonetheless.

Ditton let himself out of the flat as quietly as he could, jogged down the stairs and exited through the main door. Nothing happened, no one pounced or challenged him. In fact there was no one to be seen, and no noise to be heard apart from the cars whizzing along the flyover ahead. Tyrone would be pleased to learn that he seemed to have lost his followers, for the time being at least. Hopefully it would give him time to sort out his affairs, and for the whole Jonah business to be settled once and for all. That reminded Ditton that he needed to call Milk to see if there was news on Kevin Hill's address.

Ditton stepped over the low railings that bordered the grass around the block of flats and set off on a casual walk towards the car. Out of nowhere sirens began to wail in the distance and his heart sank, but he kept on walking; it was all he could do. The sirens grew louder and louder until he was sure they were almost on top of him and he was surprised that he couldn't see the blue lights. He expected an Astra to skid up alongside him at any moment, tyres screeching, and for it to spew uniformed louts with more energy than brains. He kept on walking, looking straight ahead. Nothing happened, the cars raced past on the flyover headed for some emergency. He kept on walking.

Ditton had opened the door and thrown himself into the driver's seat before he realised that Tyrone wasn't in the car. He looked in the back as though Tyrone could have been hiding in there and then peered out in bewilderment. There was no reason for Tyrone to have left the car; where could he have gone? Ditton dialled his number and banged the steering wheel with the heel of his hand as Tyrone's phone rang, and rang. Where the hell had the boy got to now? Five minutes later Ditton dialled again with the same result; the phone continued to ring unanswered and increased Ditton's frustration and agitation. He had somewhere to be, and what was he supposed to say to Vincent now?

Tyrone's phone still rang unanswered as Ditton drove sedately along Beulah Hill with fifty thousand pounds in his car and no way of explaining it.

He was thinking about this as he pulled up at the traffic lights, thirty seconds from Esther's road. He yawned and stretched, wondering when the lights were going to change. He was about to turn to his right, to gaze idly at the grim-faced people at the bus stop, when something crossed his vision. He felt something jabbed forcefully into his neck and a restraining hand on his head that kept him looking straight ahead. A voice said, 'You see how easy it would be. No one would know.'

The hand moved, and after a fearful moment Ditton turned to see Jimmy Nash bowling across the road towards a parked BMW containing a couple of white guys. As he got to the car he turned, formed a gun with his index finger and thumb, and showed it to Ditton before placing it to his head and letting the hammer fall. He slid into the back seat of the car and winked as it started up and moved off, the other two occupants staring deadpan at Ditton. The lights changed but Ditton didn't notice until a chorus of car horns started blaring behind him. He crunched the car into gear and pulled off like a learner driver in need of many more lessons. There was too much going on, too many points, too many angles, and he was tired, tired of it all.

On Esther's road he removed his seat-belt, switched the engine off, closed his eyes and groaned. He felt

physically sick. His legs were like jelly and his breath
came in short, ineffective gasps. For a few seconds he
wanted to curl up and scream that he needed to be left
alone, that he didn't need all this, all he had ever done
was try to help people. But he didn't give in. He
composed himself and accepted that he still had people
to help and look out for, one of them being himself. If
Nash was determined to do his worst there was nothing
that Ditton could do, except be prepared for it, and be
prepared to deal with it.

'What are you doing on Sunday?' asked Michelle when
they got back to her flat and were standing in the
kitchen.

'Playing football,' answered Milk, leaning against the
door frame, playing with his phone and ignoring a call
coming through from Nicole. The girl didn't seem
able to take a hint. 'You know that,' he said to Michelle.

She had thought about this moment for a long time.
'What about afterwards? What time do you finish?'

'About quarter to twelve. Why?'

She was desperate to avoid making him suspicious,
making him put her on the spot and force her to tell
him what was going on. She opened the fridge and
extracted a carton of orange juice.

'What are you doing afterwards?'

Milk smiled and she could see his mind working,
trying to come up with answers. 'Nothing planned, at
the moment,' he said, not wanting to commit himself.
'Why?'

Michelle made a dismissive no-reason face, and asked, 'Can you come here?'

Milk grinned, looked her up and down, and up again. 'Course I can come here. What's up? What's on offer?'

'What time are you going to come?'

'You tell me,' answered Milk.

Michelle took a beer from the fridge, reached up to a cupboard for a glass and handed it to him. 'No, you tell me,' she said. 'Because whatever time you say, you have to stick to. It's important, you can't be early, you can't be late.'

'What's this all about?'

'You'll see.'

Milk sighed and thought for a second. 'All right, two thirty?'

Michelle nodded. 'Two thirty. Good.' It was around the time she had been hoping for. Not too early, not too late.

Michelle walked out of the kitchen and over to a basket on a little table by the front door. She picked up a set of keys which she held out towards Milk.

'What are these for?' he asked, not taking them.

'Don't worry,' Michelle soothed. 'I'm not trying to get you to move in, but I want you to take these for Sunday. You can give them back straight afterwards if you want, but you have to use them. Add them to your bunch now.'

She led the way into the living room, sat down on the sofa and folded her legs while Milk pocketed the keys and watched her. She had done nothing out of the ordinary, she would have sat down exactly the same way if it had been Natalie in front of her and not Milk, but she had seen his nostrils flare and his intake of breath. He probably didn't recognise them himself, but she did, more signs. She smiled, she couldn't help it; she was pleased. She patted the cushion next to her and winked. Milk was seated in a second.

Later, as they lay in bed in total darkness, Milk steeled himself and propped himself up on an elbow. He looked in the general direction of Michelle's face.

'Mich,' he began, 'if I was to say that I thought I wanted us to become more serious, more sort of . . . exclusive, what would you say?'

For a moment he thought she must have been asleep, she took so long to answer. But just as he was about to lie down and close his eyes she said, 'I'd say that you were too nasty to ever be able to stick to something like that. And that I, knowing that's the case, would be a fool to think it could ever be different.'

Milk was thrown. 'Even if I said I was prepared to not see anyone else?'

'Even if you said you wouldn't see anyone else.'

'Oh,' said Milk quietly. 'All right then.' He lay down. If that was how she thought about him he'd make sure he didn't make a fool of himself and bring the subject up in the future. He shut his eyes, resolving to never mention the subject again, but he couldn't sleep. Didn't she realise what he was getting at? Didn't she realise that was the closest he had come to making a commitment to anyone, ever? He huffed and sighed, and tossed and turned.

Beside him Michelle tried to lie perfectly still, hoping that he would think she was asleep. If he didn't stop fidgeting soon she was going to have a giggling fit, and he wouldn't like that. She wasn't being horrible, she was looking out for herself, that was all. She grinned, and it was only when she eventually fell asleep that the smile slid slowly, reluctantly off her face.

SATURDAY

CHAPTER TWENTY-FIVE

Ditton woke on the sofa. When he had found his bearings and worked out what was going on he tried to move Esther enough for him to be able to swing his legs out and straighten them. He gave up and lifted her bodily, and even then she didn't wake. He grimaced as he moved his cramped legs and rubbed them furiously, trying to restore some kind of circulation. It was eight in the morning, and after a strange evening of initially tentative conversation which had become a cathartic occasion for both of them, they had been asleep on the sofa for just over four hours. When his legs were functioning well enough for him to walk, Ditton limped to the bathroom and relieved himself. It felt glorious.

Upon his return to the sitting room Esther was sitting up, rubbing her eyes and yawning. They said sleepy good mornings and Ditton slumped back groggily on to the sofa beside her.

'My neck's stiff,' declared Esther, wincing and kneading her shoulder. 'Rub it for me?'

Ditton did so without hesitation, and a few minutes

later Esther stood, rolled her head and smiled appreciatively.

'For that,' she said, 'I'm going to make you breakfast. It's the least I can do.'

For a moment it all felt good, being in Esther's flat on a Saturday morning. Kids' television, having breakfast cooked and waiting to see what the day would bring. The thought reminded him of the reality of what was actually going on and it brought him back down to earth with a bump. If all the contacts worked out they would be finding and questioning Kevin Hill and Clive would come through with the whereabouts of Cut Throat. He sighed and closed his eyes, suddenly feeling very tired again.

Just before nine thirty Ditton's phone rang and he looked at Esther as he spoke. He hung up, sighed and shrugged apologetically.

'That was Milk. I've got to go and meet him now. I'm sorry.'

Esther sighed too and shook her head. 'You see? Nothing's changed, has it? Milk calls and you jump, just like it always was when I used to worry myself sick about what you were getting into, whether you were going to be arrested or killed. After all we talked about last night, you jump straight up and throw it all out of the window.'

They had spoken exhaustively the previous evening about the options open to him if he really wanted to get out of the game. Esther had been pleased with his willingness to talk and listen to suggestions, sensing that he was serious about making changes. But this was different and Ditton wanted to make her understand the importance of what they had to do. He wanted her to know that he would rather be with her than any-where else in the world, but all he managed to say was 'It's not like that now, honestly. It's about Jonah.'

'Leave it!' she cried. 'Leave it alone or let others deal with it, Vincent for example. Don't let yourself get dragged in.'

'But this is important.'

Esther gazed at him sadly. 'It always is,' she said.

Milk was woken by a gentle but insistent prodding in his ribs. His hand slid automatically under the pillow before his eyes had opened, but returned empty. He had forgotten where he was and that he felt strangely comfortable in Michelle's home. He closed his eyes again and mumbled, 'What?' sleepily.

Just as he was settling down to close his eyes again he felt a hand on his shoulder and something cold and hard pressed against his head, behind his left ear. Milk thought, gun! He took a deep breath and somehow managed to get enough purchase with his legs and one arm, to hurl himself over the side of the bed and on to the floor. He scrabbled along the floor to the end of the bed and came up on one knee wearing his war face, his pistol aimed in a double-handed grip. He was face to face with a small boy, no more than six or seven years old, holding an Action Man and rocket launcher accessory. The boy looked at him in obvious awe, wide-eyed and mouth all set to catch flies.

Milk stayed in the pose for a while longer, enjoying it, buck naked and the pistol levelled at the boy's head, just giving himself time to make sure there would be no further surprises.

'Are you Dale?' asked Milk.

The boy nodded as though he had lost the art of speech.

Milk lowered the gun and stood. 'I'm Milk, sorry about that, mate. Just a little misunderstanding. No hard feelings, eh?'

Milk extended his hand for Dale to shake, and the little boy instantly dropped his rocket launcher to accept it.

'Not the best way for us to meet for the first time, was it?' Milk observed.

Dale shook his head, still gazing up at Milk as though he was a deity, until his gaze shifted to the pistol and stayed there.

'Sorry about this,' said Milk, 'but I know a few people that aren't too nice and sometimes it pays to have this around, do you know what I mean?'

Dale nodded. Milk sat on the edge of the bed and slid the gun under the pillow.

'When did you get back?' Milk asked the boy. 'You were at your gran's, weren't you?'

Dale nodded.

'You don't say much, do you?'

Dale shook his head.

'Come on,' encouraged Milk. 'Say something, let

me hear your voice. Let me hear if you can really speak.'

Milk raised an eyebrow and waited, wondering what the boy was going to come out with. For some reason he felt that the first words Dale said would shape their future relationship. Not that the relationship was likely to be anything major after what Michelle had said before going to sleep. But whatever happened, if Dale was a spoilt brat they would have problems. If he was a cry-baby they would have problems too. And even though Milk continued to remind himself that it didn't matter how he got on with the boy, because his relationship with the child's mother was apparently just about fun, he was still interested in what Dale would say. Would it be football? Clothes? What?

Dale looked at Milk and then towards the door his mother had walked out of a minute or so earlier. He's a baby, thought Milk. Needs his mum in the room so he can speak. Dale looked at the door again, looked at Milk and licked his lips. Definitely a pampered baby, thought Milk. Michelle's gone and ruined him already, fucked him up, made him soft and incapable of looking after himself.

Dale swallowed and flashed another look at the door before saying, 'That was wicked, man. Let me look at the gun. Go on, let me see it.'

Milk vowed that when Michelle came back into the room he would apologise just for the sake of it.

Ditton heard the beep, pulled back the curtain, and let himself out of the front door. Milk pulled off. 'The guy called me last night,' he explained. 'I rang you but the phone was off, from early. What were you doing?'

Ditton gave Milk a sidelong glance and asked, 'So what? I'm not allowed to have my phone off?'

Milk's curiosity increased the longer Ditton refused to tell him where he had been. 'Stop fucking about, D, man. Where were you? Fucking?'

Ditton groaned in despair. 'No. Is that the only thing you do when your phone's off?'

Milk thought for a moment. 'Yeah, I guess so,' he answered honestly. 'So what's the secret?'

Ditton laughed and slapped Milk on the back. 'Why're you so touchy, boy? Did you miss out last night?'

'I don't miss out,' Milk stated.

'I was with Esther,' admitted Ditton. 'Satisfied?'

Milk couldn't conceal his surprise. 'Yeah? I didn't think she would have given it up already. I thought she was too stuck-up for that.'

Ditton sighed. 'Firstly she didn't give it up, and secondly she's not stuck-up. What made you think that?'

Milk grinned. 'No reason. Just an impression I had.'

Ditton wasn't going to press the point. 'I saw Tyrone yesterday,' he revealed. 'Last night. He came to my house.'

'Now we're getting somewhere,' said Milk. 'I like it, I like it. What happened? What did he say?'

Five minutes later, Milk whistled during a daring overtaking manoeuvre, did a move in the bus lane outside King's College Hospital, and pulled up at the lights. 'So what do you think happened to him?'

'I haven't got a clue, but I don't understand it at all. If he'd taken the money from me and then disappeared, I would have stood back and let Vincent have him. But it seemed as though he needed the money. So for him to shoot off without taking it seems odd.'

'What did you do with the money?'

'Stashed it at home. What else could I do?'

'You believe him about Jonah?'

'I suppose so. Well, I did. I'm not sure how his disappearance affects it. He said he was at his mum's, and that I could ask her. I can't imagine that she would lie to me if I did.'

'My mum would.'

'I know.'

'That just leaves Kevin Hill.'

'I know.'

Just as Milk was about to turn left on to Peckham Hill Street he touched the brakes a bit too hard, looked across and asked Ditton if he had brought his gun. Ditton hesitated before answering then nodded curtly. Milk grinned and said, 'Good, because I just remembered the guy told me that Patrick and Kevin live in the same flat. We're probably going to have at least the two of them to deal with.'

Ditton yawned. 'I don't know why you're asking if I've got the gun, because if I wasn't around, you would have come on your own anyway, wouldn't you?'

Milk grinned and increased his speed. 'Nearly there,' he said.

Almost immediately they turned right, and then Milk swung left into a small council estate, and stopped.

'This is the block, according to the guy. Number forty-four – top floor. I used to fuck a girl at number eighteen. You ready?'

Ditton was looking out of the window and he turned back slowly to address Milk. 'Yeah, I'm ready, but I think you better have a look over there. You might find it interesting.'

Milk tried to peer out of the window past Ditton but didn't see anything that interested him. 'What are you on about now?' he said as he got out and walked around the bonnet to Ditton's side. 'What is it?'

Ditton nodded towards a blue XR2 – C152 OWL. Milk clutched his temple. 'The little bastard!' Milk exclaimed. 'I don't believe it. The little *bastard*!' And with that he turned and stalked towards the stairs and a meeting with Kevin Hill.

Kevin didn't stand a chance, but then he didn't really give himself one. There was no peephole in the door and when he called out, 'Who is it?' and Milk answered, 'Me!' Kevin opened the door in a vest, a pair of football shorts, and trainers. His eyes were still encrusted with mucus, his face was dry and his hair untidy. Milk yanked him out on to the balcony, sank his fist into his stomach, raised him up and sank it again, each time forcing an expulsion of air from Kevin's mouth that sounded like a tyre being deflated. Milk stepped back and made a face that suggested Kevin needed to bathe quickly; the joke was lost on Kevin, who was still fighting to find his breath.

'Where's Patrick?' hissed Milk.

Kevin shook his head, struggling to get the words out. 'He's not here,' he croaked.

'Where is he?'

'At his girl's.'

'Who else is in the house?'

'No one,' said Kevin quickly. 'No one, just me.'

And with that, Milk yanked Kevin along the balcony and with a combination of pushing and dragging took him downstairs to the parked cars. When they finally stood in front of the XR2 Milk hit Kevin again. Kevin sank to his knees and Milk was about to aim a kick at his head when Ditton intervened and said, 'Hey, Milk, tolerance, remember? We want him to talk.'

Milk nodded and adjusted his T-shirt on his shoulders. 'Whose car's this?' he asked politely.

'Mine,' admitted Kevin, and took a slap on the left cheek that echoed around the flats.

'Is that it?' asked Milk.

'What else is there?' Kevin asked petulantly, and took a back-handed slap to the right cheek.

Milk looked at Ditton with an expression that suggested Kevin was mad. 'What else is there?' he mimicked. 'How the fuck did it get into that state?'

Kevin breathed deeply, gasping and wincing from the pain around his stomach and ribs. 'What the fuck's it got to do with you? You offering to repair it?' he asked, regretting it as soon as Milk's knee rebounded off his jaw and laid him out on the tarmac.

Ditton stepped in between Milk and Kevin again. 'Easy, Milk,' he said. 'Hold on.' He crouched down in front of Kevin and spoke quietly. 'If I walk away from here you could be dead very quickly, and if you don't die you're going to be left with some reminder of this day for the rest of your life. It might be a limp, a crippled hand, anything. But there will be something, and you might end up wishing you had died. Do you understand me?'

From the ground Kevin glanced at the prowling Milk and nodded.

'Good,' said Ditton. 'Now what happened to the car?'

Kevin swallowed, and keeping an eye on Milk, explained that Patrick had borrowed it twice and each time returned it in a worse state.

'That wasn't too fucking hard, was it?' asked Milk. 'Was one of those times Thursday morning?'

Kevin nodded.

'Where does Patrick's girl live?'

'Thornton Heath.'

'Right, you're going to show us where.'

Kevin screwed up his face like a child presented with his least favourite food. Milk glared like the child's overworked and underpaid parent who equates disagreement with ungratefulness. Kevin's face straightened out as though it had been ironed on steam.

'Get up and get into the car,' Milk directed, grabbing Kevin by the collar.

Kevin coughed and held his ribs. 'I need to change my clothes and get my keys, man.'

'Get in the fucking car,' repeated Milk, advancing with menace.

Ditton put a hand on Milk's arm as he moved towards Kevin. 'Let him get the keys at least, Milk.'

Milk sighed, rolled his eyes and nodded impatiently. 'You take him then, I might do something to him up there.'

Ditton escorted Kevin back upstairs to the flat and watched him collect a bunch of keys from a small shelf underneath a cracked mirror just inside the front door. Ditton felt strange covering Kevin with the Beretta and questioned whether he would actually be able to use it, but after what had happened at the club it had to be done. Kevin was foolish enough to be dangerous. He prodded Kevin in the back and walked behind him further into the flat. On the floor outside the bathroom was a pile of clothes including a pair of jogging bottoms and a long sleeved T-shirt. Ditton dragged them out with his foot. 'Put them on,' he directed.

'They're not even mine,' complained Kevin. 'They're Patrick's.'

'It's them or nothing.'

Kevin glared and picked the clothes up, sliding his legs into the short bottoms and pulling the T-shirt over his head. 'They fucking stink,' he grumbled.

'You don't smell much better yourself, mate,' Ditton pointed out.

Suddenly the front door swung open and Ditton

tensed. Milk stood framed in the doorway, gun in hand and ready for use. 'What's the fucking problem?' he demanded brusquely, glaring at Kevin. 'What's taking so fucking long?'

Milk was simmering, close to boiling over, and needed turning down to prevent someone being scalded. Ditton explained, 'I was letting him get some clothes. Relax, man.'

Milk lowered the gun. 'I thought something was wrong and I realised that we only had his word for it that Patrick wasn't here.'

'You have a point,' admitted Ditton.

'There's no one else here, I told you that already,' protested Kevin.

'Well, I'll just have a little look for myself, if that's OK with you,' replied Milk. He looked Kevin up and down and said, 'You're stupid enough to try and lie to me. While I'm at it I'll try and find you some clothes too. You look like Wurzel fucking Gummidge.'

Kevin stepped forward to intercept Milk and found himself with a pistol at his chest.

'Be careful, boy,' said Milk. 'Don't tempt me. For the time being you might be off the hook about the car, at least until we see Patrick, but we've still got to discuss Jonah and that little incident outside the show. You understand?'

Kevin nodded.

Milk looked in all the rooms before throwing the remaining door open to expose a dark, drab room with some type of soiled cloth tacked over a large window as a permanently drawn curtain. A large double bed took up most of one wall and the only other furniture was a small, ancient wardrobe and matching chest of drawers with more gold-coloured handles missing than not. The floor was littered with clothes, and in the corner were a couple of dumbbells. Milk was about to close the door on the messy, musty room and comment on how Kevin had the style and the chat on the street but a home that looked like shit when he heard a groan from the bed. He swivelled, crouched and took aim.

'You all right, Milk?' asked Ditton, nudging Kevin forward so that he could get a look inside the room.

'Someone in the bed,' said Milk, holding up a warning hand. 'Sleeping like a baby.'

Ditton peered into the room. 'Patrick?'

'I don't know, but I'm about to find out.'

Milk stepped forward briskly, kicking clothes and shoes before him, the gun still levelled at the bed. The room smelt so funky Milk considered tearing down the curtain and throwing the window open, but was reluctant to touch anything. He reached the bed and bent over it trying to get a look at the occupant. He glanced at Kevin and Ditton before pulling the quilt back sharply. The sight caused Milk to gasp like a small child. Ditton winced and turned away. Kevin looked so fearful it was embarrassing.

CHAPTER TWENTY-SIX

Milk dropped the duvet back on to the startled Vanessa, wheeled and leapt at Kevin. He was just about to smash Kevin's head against the wall for the third time when Ditton managed to insert himself between them. He forced Kevin into the bedroom while he kept Milk outside. Milk was almost foaming at the mouth, and his eyes glowed with a dangerous rage that was very different from his normal day-to-day level of instinctive violence. Kevin's future depended heavily on how he carried himself from now on, and Vanessa's behaviour was going to play an important role in Kevin's survival also.

Milk turned his back on the room, put his fist into his mouth and bit hard. After a second or so he took a deep breath and turned.

'You cool?' asked Ditton.

Milk nodded. He strode into the room and walked up to the bed. Vanessa was sitting up naked but covered by the duvet and Kevin sat on the edge of the bed beside her, seemingly fully aware of what kind of trouble he was in.

'This your man?' Milk asked Vanessa.

'Yeah,' she answered churlishly, her top lip threatening to curl in contempt. She thought better of it.

Still looking at Vanessa, Milk addressed Kevin, as though he couldn't bring himself to look at the guy. 'You're stupid enough to fuck my niece but you've got enough sense to lie about it. I suppose that's a start, isn't it?'

Kevin's lips parted slightly, his posture changed, and for a terrible moment Ditton thought he was actually going to attempt to answer. It all happened in slow motion for Ditton, who could see Milk itching for the slightest provocation. Milk didn't get his wish, but if a fly had farted in the room at that moment Milk would probably have shot Kevin Hill.

Milk asked Kevin, 'Were you with her on Wednesday night? All night?'

Kevin nodded.

Milk asked Vanessa, 'When did you link up with him on Wednesday?'

Vanessa cut her eye at her uncle and asked, 'Why?'

Kevin's head snapped back as Milk backhanded him, almost knocking him off the bed.

Vanessa squealed. 'What did you do that for? He didn't do anything.'

'When did you link up with him?' Milk asked again.

'You've got no right to ask me anything,' Vanessa pointed out.

Milk reached across to Kevin, put one hand on the back of his head and the other on the scruff of his neck, and slammed him into the wall. Vanessa squealed again, dropped the duvet, exposing her breasts, and clawed at her uncle. Milk palmed her off and continued to slam Kevin into the wall.

'OK, OK!' wailed Vanessa. 'It was at the show. We left the show together!'

Kevin groaned and heaved himself back on to the bed where he flopped like a doll and didn't move. When Vanessa had made herself more presentable she looked up at Milk, full of hostility. When he turned to look at her and she got an idea of the fury within him she suddenly realised that this was not a time for late-teen petulance and attitude.

Ditton stepped up to the bed and peered down at Kevin, relieved to see that his eyes were open and that he was breathing. He wasn't hurt badly, more dazed than anything else. Ditton glanced at Vanessa, trying to remember the little girl that he and Milk used to collect from school years ago when she was as skinny as a rake, wore pink National Health glasses and sported big disorganised plaits all over her head. She sure had changed.

'Vanessa,' said Ditton, trying to maintain calm, 'that means you were in the car when they were shooting at us?'

Vanessa looked at the bed, the wall, her hands, then flicked the briefest of glances at Ditton and nodded. Ditton placed a restraining hand on Milk's chest.

'Allow it, Milk. He's got to take us to Patrick,

remember? And I reckon we'll have to take Vanessa with us too.'

When Kevin had revealed that they would be going to Thornton Heath, Milk hadn't thought twice. Even when they turned on to the same road that he had taken Michelle to he didn't become suspicious. He noted that it was the same road, but that was all. So when Kevin pointed at the same house Milk had waved at a few days earlier, and slurred through a sore mouth, 'Thash it,' Milk was understandably puzzled, and decided that if Michelle's friend lived there and Patrick was fucking her as well as Michelle, he had to have more going for him than Milk had realised.

They all piled out of the car and crossed the road to the flat. Ditton held Kevin out of sight while Milk stepped back and told Vanessa to ring the doorbell. An age later there was a sharp rap at the window above and Vanessa stepped out into view and waved up at the window.

A few seconds later footsteps could be heard slapping down the stairs, followed by the sound of an internal door being opened. Finally the front door opened to reveal Patrick in his underpants and a pair of girl's slippers.

'Vanessa,' he said. 'What are you doing here? What's going on?'

Milk stepped out from around the corner. 'I'm here. I'm what's going on,'

He grabbed Patrick by the throat and forced him inside and up the stairs. Ditton brought up the rear like a sheep dog, herding Kevin and Vanessa before him.

The hardest thing for Patrick was going to be to have to admit to Donna that Milk was back to take liberties again. He had promised her that he would take care of it and that the guy would suffer for what he had done to them. Now he was back, and from the look on his face and the state of Kevin and Vanessa obviously upset about something. Patrick began to panic as he was shoved roughly towards the flat. Roughing someone up on the street was one thing, but kidnapping and false imprisonment, which was effectively what Milk was embarking on, was a different level. For him to be doing it he must have thought he had a good reason. But then by all accounts the guy was a nutter, capable of anything, and Patrick silently prayed that Milk didn't know about the car incident; it had been just a rush of blood to the head and he hadn't seen the boy. By the time he had, all he could do was swerve and hope, the result being the damage to Kevin's car. Patrick hoped that the whole visit was just about what had happened at the club and that Kevin's injuries were a result of Milk taking exception to finding his niece in Kevin's bed.

Patrick was shoved roughly through the front door of the flat and into the living room. Donna called from the bedroom but a sign from Milk told Patrick not to answer. As Ditton shepherded Kevin and Vanessa in, Milk followed the sound of Donna's voice to the bedroom. She was sitting up in the bed wearing nothing but a stocking on her head to protect her waves. Her face dropped a mile as she saw Milk, and even more when she saw the gun, but she didn't get scared, she got angry and threw back the covers to confront Milk in her birthday suit.

Milk was Milk, and regardless of the situation he had to take stock of what was in front of him and make an assessment. She was shapely and moved well, not particularly good-looking but not a dog, and she obviously had a bit of spirit. That was evident from the way she walked past him to the door, put on her robe, issued him a withering look and flounced out towards the bathroom. Milk grabbed her arm firmly but not roughly, and guided her to where the others were assembled.

'You've got a fucking nerve,' hissed Donna as she threw herself on to the armchair beside Patrick.

'You can talk,' said Milk. 'You're fucking your friend's man and you tell me I've got a nerve?'

'What are you talking about?' snapped Donna, aware that Patrick had turned his head sharply to scrutinise her reaction. 'What friend? What man? And what the fuck are you doing in my house anyway?'

Milk pointed the pistol at Patrick. 'I came to see this piece of shit, to ask him some questions that he better have good answers for.'

Patrick squirmed.

Milk continued: 'For example, why he tried to run me and my nephew down the other day. I'd like to hear what he's got to say about that.'

Patrick's throat had suddenly become so dry it was painful, and he swallowed furiously trying to lubricate it in order to say something in his defence. Nothing emerged except a pitiful croak.

Milk walked over to the window, flung the curtains open and said, 'Let there be light.' He frowned. 'On second thoughts, we don't need any nosy neighbours, do we? This is a private affair.' He drew the curtains again.

Milk walked slowly back from the window to stand in front of Donna and Patrick who was trying his best to disappear into the sofa. Milk stared at him while placing the pistol carefully in the back of his waistband. He removed his jacket and folded it carefully, retrieved the gun, pulled the coffee table towards him, and stepped around and sat on it so that he was about three inches from Patrick's trembling knee.

Donna glared at Patrick and crossed her legs, sending a waft of stale sex and sweat towards Milk. He frowned and shifted position slightly.

'You lied about everything, didn't you?' Donna asked Patrick. 'You haven't sorted anything out, have you? You're just as rubbish as ever. Go on, tell him why, then. Go on, tell him!'

Milk told Donna in no uncertain terms to keep quiet unless she wanted to remove herself to the bathroom and do them all a favour. She snarled with rage but a restraining arm from Patrick prevented her doing anything rash.

'You know why I did it,' Patrick managed to blurt

out, finding his voice from somewhere behind his fear. 'You know why I did it, man.'

Milk didn't, but an idea had begun to nag at the back of his mind, started by Donna's apparent failure to understand his reference to her friend's man. He was beginning to wonder whether Michelle was in fact central to Patrick's behaviour. If so, he wanted to hear him say it in front of Donna.

'Well? Why?'

Patrick looked at his knuckles. 'You know why, man.'

Milk sighed and inspected the pistol. He turned to Ditton and said, 'Look, I'm being tolerant and he's just taking the piss. How much fucking longer do I have to do this?'

'Tell him, for fuck's sake, man!' urged Donna.

'Yeah, just fucking tell him, you've told me enough times,' Kevin piped up, and received a knock on the back of the head from Ditton for his pains. Vanessa shot Ditton a reproachful look. He returned it with interest.

'Well, I'll tell him if you won't,' stated Donna. 'It's because you and your partner come in here, knock me about and make off with the bag he's stashed his gear in. That's what he's upset about, and it's what I'm mad about. Does that answer your question?'

She uncrossed and re-crossed her legs, and sat back haughtily. Milk moved as soon as he saw the legs shift, keen to avoid another scent-sample of Donna's wares.

Ditton looked across and raised an eyebrow. Milk gave him the slightest, most imperceptible of head shakes, stood and sauntered for a few paces, deep in thought. He turned to Patrick and asked, 'That brown leather bag? That's what she's talking about?'

Patrick could only stare at Milk, it was all too painful for him, but Donna was on a roll. She stood up brazenly and stepped towards Milk. 'Of course it was the brown fucking bag, you know that. And this is the face that got punched, and the head that got whacked with your friend's bat! So don't be asking any more stupid fucking questions!'

By now Donna was up in Milk's face and he wasn't happy about that, or the way she was speaking to him, so he told her to sit herself the fuck down and to shut the fuck up. She delayed so he placed a palm over her mouth and shoved heartily. She shot backwards, stumbled and landed on Patrick with her legs spread and up in the air. Purely on grounds of nasal offence Milk regretted his actions. Vanessa rose to go to Donna's aid but Milk's look of astonishment that she could have the nerve to make herself conspicuous after what she had done put her back down on the sofa quicker than an elephant gun.

Milk turned to Patrick and asked, 'How much gear was in the bag?'

'You know how much.'

'How much?'

'A kilo.'

Milk nodded and turned away, but he suddenly spun and was about to land a hook on Patrick's jaw when he pulled out and turned to Ditton. 'You satisfied with their alibis for Wednesday night?'

Ditton shrugged. 'For now I'll have to be. It all depends on whether your niece is telling the truth, doesn't it?'

Vanessa looked down at the floor shamefaced and gave a slight nod. 'It's true,' she said. 'It couldn't have been them that killed Jonah. I was with them all the time.'

Ditton turned to Donna and asked her what time Tyrone had arrived on Thursday morning. Donna was confused and peered at Ditton before asking, 'What's it to you?'

'You don't remember me? Gary Ditton, Tyrone's friend. Used to stay with Mrs Gayle a lot in the old days. I know your mum, Aunt Joyce.'

Recognition passed across Donna's face and she nodded. 'He came early Thursday morning, and left yesterday afternoon.'

Ditton shrugged and said, 'Well that's that then. But if I find out that any of you lot were involved somehow, anyhow, I'll get wicked on you like you've never seen. I'll unleash some madness that you'll never forget. Do you understand? Any of you.' The last statement was directed at Vanessa, and she noted it and nodded. The other three remained impassive.

'You ready?' asked Milk.

Ditton looked at him curiously, finding it hard to believe that Kevin and Patrick weren't going to receive more punishment. He said, 'Yeah, if you are. You sure you're finished here?'

Milk nodded and picked up his jacket. 'Well, thanks

for having us,' he said with a huge grin. 'We must do it again soon.' And with that he stepped across, slapped Kevin once more for luck, tried to put the barrel of the pistol into one of Patrick's nostrils, and informed him that this was the luckiest escape of his life and he had better be thankful. Ditton backed out of the room and Milk followed, grinning broadly.

Milk continued to grin all the way to the car and even once they had started driving, but he waved away all Ditton's attempts to find out why he looked like the cat with the cream. Finally, when Milk began to chuckle, Ditton demanded to know what the hell was going on. Milk's answer was even more confusing; it didn't make sense at all.

'I think I'm in love,' declared Milk. 'I think I've found the girl I hadn't even begun to dream about yet.'

'All this over sex?' asked Ditton in astonishment. 'All that grinning and shit was over sex? What's the matter with you, man?'

Milk shook his head. 'This isn't about sex. Can't you hear what I'm telling you? I think I'm in *love*,' and with that he proceeded to explain his understanding of events.

'I know she did it, because yesterday in the restaurant she asked me how much a kilo of Charlie would go for. That's not your normal dinner conversation, is it? And on Monday when I asked her what made her call me and what had happened to Patrick, she told me that he'd thrown away his chance, and didn't want to say any more about it. I could tell she was angry. So my guess is that she found out about him and putrid pussy back there, and wanted revenge.'

'Which she roped you into, used you? And you're all right with that?'

Milk shrugged, still grinning. 'She did it with style, though.'

'Let me get this right. You took a girl out to a restaurant last night, where she asks you the price of a kilo of Charlie. True?'

Milk grinned. 'True.'

'Then today you find out that she robbed her ex-man, smacked his other girl, and made off with a kilo of his gear, while you were the unwitting getaway driver and the only one who's been identified? True?'

Milk nodded. 'True. And today I woke up and pulled a gun on her six-year-old son.'

Ditton's mouth dropped. 'Her six-year-old son? So you're telling me that this girl has got a six-year-old son, used to go out with Patrick but stopped that, beat his girl, stole his gear, has him chasing you because you were seen, still hasn't told you anything about the robbery, but you're in love with her?' Ditton scratched his head. 'Milk, mate, I always knew you were strange, but this really is the icing on the cake.'

Milk was still grinning; he couldn't stop himself.

Clive revealed that he had found Cut Throat's address, and that the guy that had given it to him had been drinking with Nash on Wednesday night at a pub in Catford. Nash had been talking about taking action against a grass, so Ditton knew that speed was vital.

When Ditton came out of the barber's Milk took a look at his face, grinned and shrugged an apology to the guys he had been talking to out on the street. As he got into the car he called out to the guys, 'Remember, Sunday, Herne Hill stadium, ten o'clock.'

'Coldharbour Lane,' Ditton directed.

'Yes, sir!' Milk replied, putting the car into gear and wheel-spinning away.

CHAPTER TWENTY-SEVEN

As he drove, Vaughn asked himself over and over again why he was going to Janine's. He shouldn't have wanted to hear her name again, let alone go out of his way to see her. Milk would have parked her off instantly, and banished her with a threat about what would happen if she ever showed her face again. But Milk was Milk and girls didn't do that kind of thing to him. After he had parked the car, though, and was approaching her gate Vaughn knew why he was there. As he fixed his jacket and brushed a couple of stray locks from his face, he knew that he still wanted her to want him. He had enjoyed himself and hadn't denied that; in fact he had volunteered the information and expressed a desire for the relationship to continue, albeit in a watered-down form.

He rang the bell and stood back trying to look casual, although he had to admit that the prospect of the encounter excited him. He saw her form approaching through the glass in the door and he waited, wanting to see remorse, repentance and, importantly, longing in her eyes.

She opened the door, lowered her eyes momentarily and gave a weak smile, stepping back for him to enter.

'The kitchen?' he asked.

She nodded and Vaughn strode along the passage to seat himself at the table by the kitchen window.

Janine trailed in behind and offered him a drink. He asked for a beer. She produced a bottle, opened it and placed it on the table before him. He thanked her but remained silent while she busied herself pouring a glass of wine and lighting a cigarette. Eventually she sat down, tossed her hair back and attempted to look at him coolly. She was flustered and he was pleased to see it.

'I'd like to apologise about the other day,' she said taking a sip of her drink. 'I'm sorry it happened. It shouldn't have.'

Vaughn had no desire to make things easy. As far as he was concerned he was due an apology, and she deserved to carry a lifetime of guilt around with her.

'You've got every right to be upset with me,' she continued. 'I don't know what happened in there. It was out of order.'

Vaughn snorted lightly, put out that her apology was so forthright and well delivered, almost putting him on the back foot. He had wanted to see her squirm and beg for forgiveness, his innermost keen for her to offer herself up as a sign of her atonement, but she hadn't done that. He was disappointed but impressed.

'I was having such a good time,' she said, 'I don't

suppose I was thinking properly. Everything you said made sense, I just didn't want to hear it. I knew it and I had already accepted it for myself, but I didn't need you to say it as well. It made it worse.'

'And that justifies what you and your minder did?'

She shook her head decisively. 'It's no justification for what I did. I'm sorry. But Terry was nothing to do with me, I promise you that. There's no way I would have encouraged him to do something like that.' She sat back with an offended frown and took a long drag on her cigarette.

He knew she was telling the truth, and she had scored another point. If he had really thought that she had encouraged Terry he wouldn't have been sitting in her kitchen listening to her now. But one other point about Thursday night still bugged him, and he had to ask.

'Why didn't you come out afterwards? Your mate roughs me up on the street on account of you and you don't even come out to check that I'm alive?'

She shrugged and sighed again. 'The state I was in I wasn't thinking about you and him outside. Once you went out of the door it was as though you had never been there, and I couldn't understand why everyone was staring at me. It only really hit home when Terry came back in looking chuffed. And at that point I was certain that you wouldn't have wanted me to come out. I thought that I would have been the last person you wanted to see right then.'

He couldn't fault any of her logic, unfortunately, so

he nodded stoically and sipped his beer. 'What did you do afterwards?' he asked.

'I had another drink and then Terry took me home.'

'Perfect.'

'It wasn't like that, honestly. I just wanted to get home as quickly as possible, and he offered to drive. That was it.'

They sat in silence for a while before Janine apologised again and offered Vaughn another beer.

They talked for a while longer. Eventually Vaughn stretched and yawned, placing his hands on the table as though he was about to stand up. Janine stood in anticipation and said, 'I can understand that you never want to see me again after everything that's happened. At work I'll be strictly professional and stay out of your way as much as possible. I've been looking for jobs anyway.' She smiled. 'I'll just have to look a bit harder now.'

She offered her hand and asked, 'Friends?'

Vaughn took it and asked, 'When did I say I never wanted to see you again?'

Kelvin House had started life just after the first riots in '81 as an inexplicable construction and an immediate eyesore. Before its completion it had come to be known locally as the prison, and passers-by looking up at the higher levels swore that nothing short of incarceration would get them to live there. The single block of flats took up approximately one American block, and loomed over all the surrounding buildings like a fortress of doom and despair, waiting patiently to house all the worst excesses of poverty-stricken inner-city life. Within a couple of years the predictions had been borne out, the block became run-down and crime-ridden, and it was virtually impossible to house anyone there. So much so that Ditton had never stepped foot in the flats, had never known anyone who lived there, and hoped for their sakes that he never would.

The corridors were so wide they could have taken cars, and had recessed doors to the flats on one side and a balcony and drop on the other. Wire-mesh fencing stretched the whole length of the balcony on each floor and prevented objects or people falling into the desolate courtyard below. They were punctuated every twenty feet by massive square pillars daubed in graffiti as far up as the artists could reach. As one looked into the distance along the length of the corridor, the wire-mesh rippled gently in the wind and created an eerie visual effect.

Cut Throat's flat was on the sixth floor and they trudged up the dark stairs, their footsteps and words echoing throughout the stairwell. Milk let a globule of spit fall between the banisters and closed one eye to watch it descend. He lost sight of it at the first floor but heard it hit something, man, beast or banister he didn't know.

'Reminds you of school, doesn't it?' he grinned.

Ditton smiled at the memory. 'All you need now is some mad fifth-year to come chasing you up the stairs. Remember?'

Milk grinned.

As they walked along the sixth floor looking for the number Clive had given them, Milk ducked behind pillars and took imaginary aim at the Empire's storm-troopers serving Lord Vader. His mouth emitted laser noises and explosions, and when he sprang from behind a pillar to confront Ditton they both drew their light sabres and took guard. Milk circled and took a few swings, the imaginary sabre crackling and buzzing through the air to be blocked by Ditton's, until eventually they thrust and parried as though the destruction of the Empire was a real possibility.

Junkies never open their doors quickly to unexpected knocks, that is if they open them at all. So Ditton knocked again and was prepared to wait.

He knocked once more while Milk aimed imaginary balls high into the top right-hand corner of an equally imaginary goal, accepting the adulation of his team mates and the crowd.

'What makes you so sure he's there?' asked Milk. 'He's probably out snatching a handbag or burgling a house.'

'He has to be here,' answered Ditton. 'I need him to be here.'

'Those are two different things,' Milk pointed out.

Ditton knocked again and wheeled away from the door in frustration, but then he thought he heard sounds of life from inside the flat. He stiffened and leaned towards the door, listening intently. Milk noticed and stopped in mid-shot, standing on one leg, the other cocked ready to drive the ball hard and low. He raised his head. Ditton remained frozen, listening.

'Cut Throat? Sean, is that you? It's Gary Ditton, Rodney's younger brother. You remember me?'

Milk looked puzzled until Ditton pointed at the door. 'I heard him,' he mouthed.

'Sean? Can you open the door, I need to speak to you. I'm hoping you can tell me something.'

'Tell you what?' a voice answered from the other side of the thick, imposing door.

'Can you open the door so we can talk about it? I just want to ask you a few questions, that's all, honestly. Can you open the door?'

There was a pause, and then the sound of lock mechanisms and the scraping of a chain. Milk grinned, controlled the ball on his chest and fired an unstoppable shot past the despairing keeper.

The door opened wide enough for them to enter and Ditton stepped in, followed by Milk. The flat was one of those weird ones where you entered a small, cramped hall containing nothing but a space under the stairs for junk, and had to walk up two flights of stairs before you came to any rooms or any kind of light. There was no bulb in the hall and they stood there in the darkness and watched a figure poke its head out of the front door, look left then right, and eventually lock the heavy door with a disconcerting finality and purpose. The figure squeezed past them and made its way up the stairs mumbling for them to follow.

At the top of the stairs it disappeared into a room on the right and they followed, noting as much of the bare, shabby flat as they could. Milk hung back and poked his head into the one bedroom to satisfy himself that there would be no surprises.

The flat was oppressively hot but Cut Throat made his way straight to the radiator under the window and stood there, his hands behind his back, swaying gently from side to side. The only light in the room came from chinks that found their way past the grimy curtain, and from the kitchen window across the passage which was bare except for grime. Once Milk was in the room Cut Throat rubbed his arms briskly for warmth, and motioned for him to shut the door. Apart from a grimy, broken two-seater sofa, there was no furniture in the room, and the carpet had lost the right to be so called. Milk stood by the door, looked at Ditton and shook his head in obvious contempt. Ditton stayed standing also.

In the old days Cut Throat had cut an impressive figure. He had been tall and athletic, always immaculately dressed, and flush with money and a bevy of girls on his arm. He would have had them without the money; he was a good-looking guy. Light-skinned, straight nose and 'good' hair, a Coolie with a black and Asian racial mix somewhere along the line that seemed to attract the girls like flies to shit. But what Ditton was faced with now was totally different. Cut Throat seemed to have wasted away. He was gaunt and obviously undernourished, his face was drawn and he had dark rings around his haunted eyes. His hair was long, bushy and unkempt, as was the wispy beard growing on his face like an unwanted garden weed. He wore a sweatshirt and torn jeans that both looked within seconds of falling off him, and his white socks were grimy and in need of throwing away, never mind darning. There was no way Ditton would have recognised him on the street as the guy that used to be with his brother. It saddened him. He glanced at Milk, whose look of disdain spoke volumes.

Ditton outlined the reason for the visit: he wanted Cut Throat to think back to the day after Nash was arrested, and try to remember where Rodney was going and why. It was important. Ditton didn't want to reveal any more than that; there was no reason for Cut Throat to know, and anyway, junkies have notoriously loose mouths.

By now Cut Throat had sunk cross-legged to the ground and sat hugging himself with his back against the radiator like a strung-out Buddha. A strange look entered his eyes and he flashed a pale, desperate imitation of the smile that used to charm the girls senseless.

'Have you got anything for me?' he mumbled.

'Like what?'

'Come on, man,' Cut Throat whined. 'I know what you two do. Have you got anything?'

Ditton had foreseen this eventuality, with Clive's help, and had brought Cut Throat a foil-wrapped incentive. The addict sat forward eagerly, reaching out a bony hand with stained fingers. Ditton withdrew his and Cut Throat leaned back, yearning and resentful, but ready to co-operate.

'Afterwards,' said Ditton.

'If at all,' added Milk.

Ditton folded his arms. 'Can you remember anything? About that day? And tell the truth, yes or no?'

Cut Throat shrugged. 'Yeah, man, but it depends what you want to know.'

Ditton shook the wrap in his hand as though it were a dice. 'You were in the car with him when the police stopped him?'

Cut Throat nodded and proceeded to recount what he remembered of the day.

'I remember it because it was the day after Jimmy Nash got nicked for that post office in Mitcham. I asked Rodney what he knew about it, but he was tight-lipped and I could tell he wasn't happy. And then when we got where we were going and met up with the guy we were meeting, he said something about it too. Rodney nearly bit his head off. He was in a bad mood when the police stopped the car, he got up their noses straight away.'

Ditton wanted to be spared the details so he cut him short and asked, 'Where were you going when you got stopped? Did Rodney say he had anything to do? Anyone to see?'

Cut Throat shrugged. 'Your brother always had things to do, people to see.'

'Anyone in particular? Did he mention anything about having to see anyone in connection with Nash?'

Cut Throat shook his head. 'Not that I remember.'

Milk snorted and said, 'He's going to have to do better than that if he wants the wrap.'

Ditton raised an eyebrow, Cut Throat wrung his hands miserably and closed his eyes in a desperate attempt to remember something. He rocked back and forth, the tempo increasing and decreasing erratically.

Suddenly he stopped and looked up like a wretched biblical character just blessed with a touch from Jesus. 'He phoned Vincent Carty from the guy's house.'

'And what?'

'I remember that he was insistent that he had to see him right away.'

'You're sure about that?'

'Positive. After some arguing they arranged for Vincent to come to the guy's flat, park outside and beep. He was supposed to be there in ten, fifteen minutes, something like that. After half an hour, Rodney said he was going to take me home and then go looking for him.'

Ditton crouched down. 'What happened then?'

'We got in the car and almost straight away they came from nowhere and swarmed. They had Rodney out of the car before I knew what was going on and were bundling him into the back of one of theirs.' Ditton was about to interrupt and protect himself from the memories, but Cut Throat sounded like a man seeking absolution, so he held back.

'The thing that I remember the most was the big pig. I'd seen him before. Big guy, tall. Not young, probably forties, because he was going a bit grey. And I remember that he had a nose that looked like a beak. The guy looked mean.'

'Did he have a scar on his chin?' Ditton asked before the question or the reason for asking it had fully lodged in his mind.

Cut Throat frowned as he remembered, but confirmed the presence of the scar. 'It was what the two of them said that was strange,' he continued. 'Rodney told the guy to give him a break. The policeman said that he'd tried, but Rodney hadn't wanted to take it, and that he was foolish. Rodney said yeah, but he still had his pride. Then the guy said there's more to life than pride and that some of Rodney's mates knew that. The guy just grinned, and I remember Rodney got really mad then, and started struggling. Next thing he was cuffed and in the back of the car.'

Ditton had more than enough to think about, disturbing things that didn't make sense. A planned meeting with Vincent that didn't happen, an arrest by a policeman that had to be the same one described by Tyrone, and probably the same man he had seen all those years ago with Rodney. None of it made sense, at least not as he saw it. He withdrew the wrap of heroin from his pocket and was about to toss it to Cut Throat, who had risen to his knees, almost panting like a dog. Milk stepped forward, so close to Cut Throat that he was forced to lower himself again.

'All of that better be true, you know?' said Milk. 'No fantasies or illusions. Understand?'

Cut Throat nodded and Milk stood aside while Ditton tossed him the wrap like a zoo-keeper at feeding time.

'Let's go,' said Ditton.

'Gladly,' Milk replied.

CHAPTER TWENTY-EIGHT

Ditton waved at the mirror and Vincent buzzed him into the back of the building. Vincent was speaking on the phone and he nodded towards the seat on the other side of the big desk. Ditton sat.

Finished with his call, Vincent steepled his hands in front of his face and leaned back in his plush chair. 'So what happened?' he asked. 'I was expecting you last night.'

Ditton spread his hands and explained Tyrone's disappearance. 'I called, but your phone was off.'

'I had some business of my own to attend to. What did he say about Jonah?'

'He said it wasn't him, and that he only found out about it yesterday.'

Vincent's face twisted in a derisive grimace.

'I'm just saying that's what he said,' explained Ditton. 'He sounded genuine enough, said that he was being followed all over the place, and that he went to ground on Wednesday night. He stayed at his mum's before moving to his cousin's in Thornton Heath. He had to leave there yesterday because her man came and caused a commotion.'

'You believe that?'

'I've got no real reason not to. Believe me, he was only worried about who was following him, not you, as though he didn't expect you to be after him. Do you know what I mean?'

'I know he's a fool. I know that.'

Ditton sat back while Vincent explained that if Tyrone wasn't able to convince him by Sunday that he hadn't killed Jonah, the man-hunt would begin, and he would be found and dealt with.

Ditton nodded his understanding and said, 'We caught up with Kevin Hill and his cousin this morning. I hate to say it, but it looks like they're off the hook. They did the shooting outside the club, but they didn't go to Jonah's afterwards.'

'So that brings us back to Tyrone.'

Ditton shrugged. 'Well, there's still Earl to find. It seems as though it was him that organised the robbery on Tuesday night. I don't understand it but it looks that way.'

Vincent lowered his head for a moment before raising it slowly to look at Ditton. 'I know,' he said.

Ditton thought Vincent must have misunderstood until he saw him lean back in his chair and peer around the corner into the lounge area. 'Oi!' he growled. 'Come here.'

Ditton heard the sound of someone being released by leather-clad cushions and waited, intrigued. He could tell this person was being brought out for him to see, and when the figure emerged Ditton couldn't believe his eyes, but he tried to conceal some of his astonishment. He looked at Vincent and asked, 'What is this? What the fuck's going on here? Is this some kind of joke?'

'No,' said Vincent with a rare twinkle in his eyes. 'But you have to admit, it's kind of funny.'

Ditton couldn't see the funny side of it. He stared at Earl. Earl stared back.

Perplexed, Ditton exclaimed, 'But he's the one who robbed Jonah! Or at least organised it.'

Vincent nodded. 'I know, I asked him to. Jonah didn't get hurt.'

Ditton thought back to the night at the bar, and the nod from Earl to Vincent that hadn't seemed quite right in the circumstances. He turned contemptuously towards Earl. 'So all this time you've been stringing Ty along and working for Vincent? You're full of shit! You know that? You're full of fucking shit!'

Earl opened his mouth to speak but didn't get a chance to protest, or whatever it was he wanted to say. Ditton stood and told him to fuck off in no uncertain terms. Earl shrugged, unconcerned.

Vincent smiled grimly. 'Sorry to have wasted your time, Gary. But you couldn't have found out any earlier. I had to make sure that fool cousin of yours didn't get to know about it.'

Ditton didn't speak. He was still too stunned and angry.

Vincent tutted and rolled his eyes. 'Don't look like that. At least I didn't do him, just messed up his show, slowed him down a bit. I could have got rid of him before it came to this, but I didn't.'

Ditton stabbed a finger in Earl's direction. 'So all the hits on Tyrone were done with his help? He told you everything?' Ditton could remember few occasions when he had been prepared to really hurt someone. This was definitely one of them.

Earl looked down and cleaned his nails. He didn't appear to be put out by the scene; there didn't seem to be any fear, remorse or contrition. If anything, he seemed quite content to stay and listen.

'Did you know that Jonah was waiting for him the night he died? That he spoke to him after leaving the club, and was waiting for him to turn up at the flat?'

Vincent's eyes narrowed ever so slightly. 'You didn't tell me that,' he directed at Earl.

Earl shrugged again. 'I didn't go there. He rang me, I told him that if I didn't see him in half an hour or so I'd see him the next day. I had no intention of getting out of bed, and I was with a girl, anyway. The bitch can tell you that I was with her from eleven.'

Vincent was quiet for a moment, before nodding and saying, 'That may well be the case. But the fact of the matter is you didn't tell me. Now what the fuck's that all about? You're the last person known to have spoken to my brother. Not only that, but you may or may not have told him that you were on the way round there, and you didn't think to tell me about that?'

Vincent was standing by now, and at last, to Ditton's rather petty satisfaction, Earl was not looking so confident about his position.

'Sorry,' mumbled Earl. 'I didn't want to complicate things.'

Vincent fixed Earl with a stare that came close to making Ditton wince, and said, 'Get out. I'll call you when I need you.'

As soon as Earl closed the door behind him Vincent said. 'Right, that's that option out of the way. Narrows the field down a bit, doesn't it? He hasn't seen Tyrone since Tuesday, and now he can't get hold of him. Neither can you. What does that tell you?'

'That he's busy?' answered Ditton, not sure why he had said it.

Vincent steepled his hands and touched the tip of his nose with his fingers, as if contemplating something of immense importance. He clenched his jaw, trying to keep his calm. 'Gary,' he said, 'I'll ignore that, but only because I can understand how you must feel seeing that piece of shit selling out your cousin. It must be hard. But don't get fucking cheeky with me now. History or no history, Rodney or no Rodney. Not now. You hear?'

The phone rang, and Vincent talked business for a few minutes while Ditton used the time to sit back and think through what he had learnt from Cut Throat. Firstly, Rodney had indeed been upset by the news of Nash's arrest and had snapped at anyone that wanted to talk about it. The only person that Cut Throat could remember Rodney arranging to meet was Vincent, but that happened all the time and didn't mean a thing. Vincent didn't turn up, Rodney left the flat in frustration and was pounced on immediately by police, who seemed to have been waiting for him. The description of the one in charge sounded remarkably similar to the man following Tyrone now. That same policeman had claimed that he had tried to give Rodney a break, but that he had refused it foolishly, and suggested that maybe some of Rodney's friends hadn't?

Vincent put the receiver down and stretched, noted Ditton deep in thought and asked what was on his mind. Ditton hesitated, unsure of how to phrase the question, but feeling that he needed to ask it. He blurted out, 'Rodney was waiting for you when the police took him. Where were you?'

Vincent's tone didn't change. 'What made you ask that?' he said smiling. 'Do you think I'm to blame for what happened to Rodney?'

Ditton sighed and told Vincent about bumping into Nash at Jonah's, the meeting in the playground and the idea to try and speak to Cut Throat. When he had finished he sipped his beer and shrugged. 'That's about it. I was hoping that you'd tell me you and Rodney were meeting up to deal with the guy that did grass, or something like that.'

'Why didn't you tell me about all of this?' asked Vincent with an air of disappointment.

'I can't keep coming to you every time there's a problem. People will have me up like a pussy.' Ditton shrugged, 'And besides, I'm supposed to fix things for other people, I should be able to do it for myself now and then, shouldn't I?'

'Everyone needs help sometimes,' said Vincent. 'Everyone.'

They talked about the situation for a while longer, Vincent confirming that Rodney had not and would not have informed on anyone, let alone Nash. 'I'll ask some questions, see what I can find out. In the mean time, if Nash gets back in contact, tell him I'm dealing with it, and he can come talk to me here.'

Ditton thanked him, and then wondered why Vincent was staring at him so intently. The answer became clear when Vincent took a deep breath and spoke. '*Consigliere*,' he said. 'I like the name. It suits you.'

Ditton frowned and snorted. He didn't think it suited him and didn't want to hear it.

'*Consigliere*,' repeated Vincent. 'How would you like it to be official?'

Ditton shrugged, unsure what Vincent meant. 'What's that? What's official?'

'I need a rest, to take a back seat and have someone else run things for me. I've been at it for too long, since I was younger than you. And it wasn't supposed to last this long, or to be me on my own. It was supposed to be Rodney and myself, for a certain amount of time. Neither of those ideas have gone as planned.'

Vincent reached to his back pocket and produced a bunch of keys. He held one up before Ditton, a long key that was almost black, with a red handle that attached it to the bunch. 'This,' he said, 'is the key to the safe over there. Inside that safe is all you'll need to take over, with a few pointers from me of course. It's got information on everything and everyone. Spend an afternoon reading the contents, and you'll be set. What do you say?'

Ditton was speechless.

'I'll be around,' said Vincent, 'if that's what you're worrying about. I wouldn't drop you in at the deep end straight away. I'll make sure you're comfortable before I pull out completely. And anyway, I'm not giving you the operation, just asking you to run it, keep it ticking over as it is now. You'll get a very good wage, and you'll have the opportunity to set up whatever you and maybe Milk want to run. With my backing and protection.'

Ditton sat there dumbfounded. The offer was astounding. The power and money involved would be stupendous. It was the offer of a lifetime, and he couldn't quite believe it had been made. As it finally began to sink in Esther's face appeared before him, and he groaned inwardly. There was absolutely no way he could tell her about this, even if he turned it down. In her eyes, even the offer would bury him.

'Think about it,' said Vincent graciously. 'Let me know, soon.'

As Ditton nodded and stood to leave, his phone rang. He looked at the number, mouthed, 'Tyrone' to Vincent and spoke briefly. He didn't attempt to establish what had happened to Tyrone the previous night; he was just pleased the guy had got in touch. 'Where are you?' he asked.

Tyrone replied that he was standing outside Ditton's house. Ditton promised that he would be there soon and rang off.

'Remember,' Vincent said, 'it'll be a lot better for him if he comes and talks to me.'

Ditton left the gym feeling relieved. Tyrone had got in touch, which suggested that maybe he wasn't as guilty as he was looking. And then there was Nash. He should have told Vincent earlier, he knew that. But now that the matter was in Vincent's hands he suddenly felt more relaxed. For a moment or two he allowed himself not to care about who had killed Jonah or who was after Tyrone. It felt good.

Vincent rose and stood before the two-way mirror. He watched Gary step lightly through the gym and engage in some banter with Lenny at the door before disappearing out on to the street. Vincent walked over to the bar and poured himself another drink.

He stood at the mirror, watching the sweating, pumped-up bodies working out, drained the glass and turned, hurling it at the wall and smashing it into a hundred pieces. He stalked back to the desk, picked up the phone and pressed a button to dial one of the preset numbers. After a few seconds the phone was answered and Vincent barked for 'Barrett!' When asked who was calling he replied, 'Don't worry, he'll want to speak to me,' and waited. Moments later a voice responded from the other end.

'Apparently he's outside the Ditton boy's house now,' reported Vincent. 'Don't mess up this time.'

CHAPTER TWENTY-NINE

Driving along a busy Tooting High Street, Milk looked left and right trying not to miss anything that might take his fancy on either side of the road. There was a lot for him to take in, colours and shapes, hair and attitudes, but he managed it. He linked it with his footballing ability to read the game, to see everything that was going on, and to know what everyone around him was doing at any given time. It started him thinking about the match, and he decided that he would try to get an early night, and not be deflected by anything. He hoped Michelle wouldn't phone, because that would mess things up straight away.

He was due to see her after the match, and for some reason he felt that it had something to do with the gear she had taken from Patrick. Was it just that she was going to tell him about it? Strangely, part of him wished that she had told him and involved him, but he also wanted to see how far she would go. He wanted her to impress him, and keep impressing him.

He had just inched his way past the busiest section

of the main road, the shopping area with all the bus stops, when he saw it on the left-hand side of the road, walking ahead of him. Black leather mini-skirt with a slit up one side, black high-heeled sandals. On top, she wore a sheer black blouse beneath a tiny green suede waistcoat, and her thick golden hair had been piled up into a black suede cap. Milk slowed and crawled up behind her, trying to assess her racial origin, which in these days of processed hair and processed skin had become increasingly more difficult. Convinced that he couldn't tell what she was, he sped up, pulled in front of her and looked in his mirror. Now he could tell that she was white, but that didn't bother Milk. He didn't give a fuck what colour the girl was, he just wanted to give a fuck. She stepped closer to the car, turning heads as she came, and Milk removed his seat belt and wound down the passenger window.

She must have been aware, because as soon as she came level with the car and Milk called out to her she turned and leaned in.

She seemed as surprised to realise that it was him as he was to realise that it was her. He asked her where she was going and threw the door open, and she slid herself in, filling the car with an impressive frame and the scents of a thousand different cosmetic products.

'You in a hurry?' Milk asked with his customary grin.

'Not really, why?'

'You fancy making a detour, by way of my place? I've got something there you might like.'

She smiled and fluttered her eyelashes coquettishly, asking, 'What could you possibly have for me?'

Ditton was still thinking about Esther when he pulled up outside his house, intending to call her as soon as he'd met with Tyrone, handed over the cash and tried to get him to speak to Vincent. He wanted to plan his Saturday night. If she didn't want to, or wasn't able to see him, he would try to arrange something else. But at least if he determined her part in the equation first, he might be able to fit in some sleep.

He couldn't see Tyrone anywhere, not standing on the street and not in a car. He threw his hands up in frustration and let himself into the house. He tried calling Tyrone; his phone was switched off. He didn't try again. Tyrone was playing games and Ditton didn't want to play with him. He was getting to a point where he felt that whatever happened to Tyrone was of his own making; he seemed to have made his bed, so it was for him to lie in it. Right then Ditton wanted to lie in his.

He spoke to Esther, arranged to see her later, and lay down, feeling better than he had for most of the week. Tyrone was working to his own hidden agenda, the Nash situation was a lot more stable now that Vincent was involved, and Vaughn hadn't been in touch, which suggested that he was OK. Ditton was going to be seeing Esther later on, and had a feeling it was likely to become physical. He wouldn't have been bothered if it didn't, but he had a feeling it would, and for the first time in ages he almost felt good. *Consigliere?* he wondered and closed his eyes.

Patrick had told himself that he would call Devon at four and tell him what had happened. That had been put off until five, then six, and now seven. He had to do it this time.

At five to seven he heard Kevin enter the flat. Their relationship had been strained after what had happened in the bar on Tuesday, but the events of the morning had made Kevin *mad*. In fact they hadn't spoken since Milk and Ditton had left and Vanessa and Donna had had to release Patrick from Kevin's headlock.

He should have told Kevin the truth about the car, he'd known it at the time and he knew it as he stood by the window, but that was done now. The present was Devon, and Patrick sighed and reached for the phone. But before he had a chance to dial, his door was thrown open. Kevin stood in the doorway, still mad.

'Have you decided what you're going to do?' asked Kevin. 'Have you?'

Patrick nodded. 'I'm going to tell Devon. I have to.'

Kevin started at him for a moment, snorted and turned to walk away.

'Hold on,' cried Patrick. 'Why'd you ask?'

Kevin turned, almost reluctantly, to face his cousin. 'Because I know where Milk's going to be tomorrow if you wanted to sort this thing out once and for all.'

Patrick looked at his phone and at the time. One minute past seven – too late to phone Devon he lied to himself. 'Well, thanks for that,' he said. 'Though I don't know if I can be bothered with any of this any more. But, regardless, I appreciate that you were looking out for me and trying to help.'

Kevin's face twisted in disdain. 'Fuck you,' he spat. 'This is about me. Firstly, I still want the bastard for myself, and secondly, unfortunately, you're my cousin. Everybody knows what he's done to you. That reflects badly on me.'

Patrick remained silent.

'Now,' Kevin continued, 'if Devon doesn't know already, he's going to know very soon. You know that, don't you?'

Patrick nearly dropped the phone.

Kevin sneered. 'Milk's playing in a match tomorrow up at Herne Hill. If you're anything, if you're anybody, you'll be going there to get what's yours.' And with that he left the room, slamming the door shut behind him.

Patrick turned and stared out of the window once more.

As Michelle lay beside her son and read him his bedtime story, she wondered what she would be doing at the same time the next evening. She tried to tell herself that she was being ridiculous in worrying about Delroy, he was just like anyone else. And anyway, the last time she had seen him had been years ago; he had probably changed a lot, grown up like the rest of them. Tomorrow was just going to be about business, and he

would come, look at the stuff, and take it or leave it. That would be it, done and dusted. Nothing to it, it was that simple. So why was she still worrying about it?

Dale pointed out that she had read the same page twice, and she snapped and said he should read it himself, then. He was old enough, wasn't he? She apologised, and explained that she wasn't feeling herself, that she had things on her mind that were making her slightly ratty. By the time he returned from Grandma's tomorrow evening, everything would be fine. Dale had nodded, too smart for his own good, assuming that his mother was suffering from her period.

He didn't know what it meant, except that she bled and wasn't herself. Michelle knew what he was thinking, and although on the one hand she wanted to correct him and make sure her son didn't become one of those men who blamed everything on monthly cycles, on this occasion she preferred him to think that was indeed the problem.

When she had finished the story, and leaned forward to give Dale his customary hug-before-the-light-goes-off, she let out a little sob and hugged him as though she would never let go. 'Hey, Mum,' said Dale. 'Easy!'

Easy, Michelle thought. That's what it was going to be. Easy. Milk just had to do his part. He couldn't let her down.

Meanwhile, Milk's plans for an early night had been dashed by a phone call. The girl Marty had furnished him with at the show had phoned to say she was local, and was he interested in seeing her? He had just put the other one in a cab, and had just enough time to change the sheets and wash his body before she rang the bell. He trotted down the stairs, hoping that she was going to ring the same bells for him that she had on Wednesday night. She did.

Upstairs in his room she produced a bottle of Jack Daniels and a bottle of lemonade, which she insisted that he share with her. At that moment drink was the last thing Milk had on his mind. He was trying to be responsible and ensure that alcohol didn't impair his performance the next day, although he wasn't counting sex as a possible impediment. Milk was a warrior, but he would never have made a boxer. However, Milk poured himself a drink, knocked back half in one go, and got down to business.

Milk fitted her into the bed as though it had her name on it, and did her justice. At about nine thirty she was making I-need-to-go noises, but Milk was persuasive and she was obviously easily persuaded. After the next coupling, the comment was, 'I really *must* go.' The next produced, 'Please . . . I've got to go,' and after that Milk looked at his watch, took pity, and called her a cab.

He had to help her down the stairs and out of the front door. He returned to his room, positive that even though it was early he'd be able to sleep now. Then he saw the remainder of the drink she had poured for him and finished it in one go, before pouring himself another, which he dealt with the same way. He looked in the mirror, blew himself a kiss and said, 'See you in the morning, gorgeous.'

SUNDAY

CHAPTER THIRTY

Esther woke early and turned to look at the clock beside the bed. It was six fifty, and she had slept poorly, not used to having a real, live body beside her. She had woken continually during the night, and each time panicked momentarily before realising who was next to her. On each occasion the realisation filled her with a warm feeling, and she would look in his direction in the darkness, see the outline of his shoulder and smile. Ditton, on the other hand, slept as though he hadn't slept for weeks.

Esther raised herself on to an elbow and leaned over to peer at his face. She traced an eyebrow with a finger, followed his cheek bone, nose and lips. He didn't move. She kissed his mouth, lay back and sighed heavily, unsure if either of them was ready for this yet, unsure that it was wise. They had both gone through too much in the last few days, and had been thrown together.

She had felt it necessary to end their last relationship because she thought she could see where he was heading, and she didn't want to be a part of it. Always involved in something at Milk's side, or running errands for her brother. The only future she could see for her Gary was prison or death, and she didn't want to be with him when either happened.

Although on the surface his situation hadn't changed, she had sensed a change within him. It told her it was only a matter of time before he did what he knew he had to do. She hadn't found anything comparable to him out there; they were either too full of themselves, full of nothing, or too needy to be attractive. She touched his cheek gently, knowing she could wait for him to make the right decisions, accepting with a sigh that she wanted to.

When Esther got up to bathe and make something to eat, he didn't stir. At eight o'clock she shook him softly, and he snuffled and blinked a few times before settling down to sleep again. She shook again, more insistent this time, and he sat up, gripping her arm so tightly that she had to prise his fingers away. It saddened her to see him wake like that, tortured and anxious, but the expression on his face when he realised who she was and where he was made up for it. She saw him relax, smile more with his eyes than his mouth, stroke her cheek and fall back to the bed.

'Gary,' said Esther softly. 'Time to get up. You're supposed to go to Milk's.'

Ditton grunted, but no more.

'It's Sunday, the day of the match. Remember.'

Ditton sat up like a balloon pumped full of air at

high pressure and rubbed his eyes.

Esther smiled and pushed him back, proceeding to talk him awake until she was sure that he wasn't going to sleep again. When she was convinced, she excused herself and produced food.

When he had eaten, dragged himself to the bathroom and dressed, Ditton called Milk. It was eight forty-five, and there was no answer.

Michelle was fully awake by six o'clock; washed, dressed and in the kitchen by half past. It was the first Sunday she could remember being up before Dale for a long, long time, and needing something to do with her hands and to occupy her mind, she cleaned the small but pristine kitchen from top to bottom, before starting on the rest of the flat. By now Dale had woken up, and she steered him away from the cartoons and into the bathroom.

When he finally emerged, having accidentally emptied half a bottle of bubble bath into the tub, she directed him to his clothes, gave him his breakfast and checked that he had packed a bag to amuse himself while at Granny's.

At nine o'clock they left the flat, Dale lugging a rucksack full of toys, Michelle, absent-minded, forgetting to lock the door and having to be reminded by her son, who feigned despair when it was revealed that his mother had also left the car keys in the house. Michelle advised him not to be so cheeky, but even that was done on half-speed. Her mind was far, far away, cruising south down the M1.

Her mother asked her why she looked as though someone was walking over her grave. Michelle could only shrug, and her mother, thinking she must be unwell, threatened to concoct some kind of cure-all medicinal brew. Michelle insisted that she had never felt better; the last thing she needed when she met Delroy was a stomach full of one of her mother's bitter herb teas. Her mother wasn't convinced, but she didn't press the point.

As she was leaving, Michelle picked Dale up and hugged him. Eventually he rolled his eyes and went limp. She took the hint and lowered him to the ground, tears forming in her eyes, and trying to control a quivering bottom lip.

Driving back from her mother's her mood lifted considerably. The pale sun washed over her with a comfortable warmth, and as though for the first time that year she noticed birds singing and instantly knew that things were going to go well. The deal would be done and she would be thousands of pounds better off, able to set herself and Dale on the road to something better.

When the buzzer made its farting sound in his room, Milk grimaced, looked heavenward and tried to hold on, hoping it was Ditton. He grabbed his keys, flew to the front room window, hauled it up with an effort, peered out and threw the keys down to his bewildered partner. Then he took a deep breath, ran out of the room, jumped down the six or so stairs to the next landing and kicked the toilet door open. He didn't reach across to lock it until he was safely seated.

Ditton let himself in and trudged up the stairs, wondering what he was about to encounter. It wasn't unusual for Milk to throw keys down, but no greeting or acknowledgement was strange. As he got to the first landing he couldn't help pausing to listen for signs of life from behind Jackie's door. From what Milk said, if she was in the house she was giving it to somebody, but he didn't hear anything until a tinny voice called out from the toilet, 'D? That you?'

'Yeah, what's going on?'

'I'm fucking dying,' wailed Milk. 'That's what's going on.'

Ditton rolled his eyes and made his way up to Milk's room. The bed was unmade, unusual for Milk, and a half-empty bottle of Jack Daniels stood on the floor beside it. Ditton fell into the armchair and switched on the television. A few minutes later Milk threw the door open and collapsed on to the bed, pulling himself into a foetal position, clutching his stomach. He lay there with his eyes closed for a few seconds while Ditton tried to work out the joke. He gave up.

'What's the matter with you?'

'I said I was dying.'

'Of what?'

'My stomach.'

'What did you eat?'

'Nothing out of the ordinary. I didn't have much

time yesterday. I don't know what the fuck this is all about.'

Ditton glanced at the bottle of bourbon. 'Maybe it's the liquor.'

Milk grimaced and shook his head. 'I only had one or two. Believe me, it's not that.'

'So who drank the rest?'

Milk winced. 'Some girl I smashed last night.' Despite his condition he managed to open his eyes, wink and grin. It became a grimace. 'She was all right too.'

'So who was she?' Ditton enquired, curious.

Milk squeezed his eyes shut, clutched his stomach like it was the most precious thing in the world, winced, and revealed, 'Some girl Marty introduced me to at the show. She called up last night and asked if she could come round.'

Ditton swung his leg over the arm of the chair so that he could look at Milk squarely, incredulously.

'Considering what you know about Marty, one of his girls calls you up the night before the match, comes round with liquor, and the next morning you're laid up in bed, and you're wondering what it's all about? Give me a break. She slipped you something.'

Milk stopped his writhing and sat up with considerable effort, his face contorted in pain. He glanced at the bottle, and then at the glass sitting innocently on the chest of drawers on the other side of the room.

'I think you might be right. She was egging me on to drink, but I didn't until just before she left.'

Ditton raised his hand as though he was in school. 'Or to put it another way, she didn't leave until you'd drunk it.'

The twenty minutes it took Ditton to drive to Streatham, seek consultation from the pharmacist and return with a bottle of some disgusting pink liquid and a set of tablets had to be the longest twenty minutes of Milk's life. When he heard himself cry out he knew that Marty was going to have to pay.

The sun came out in earnest as they approached the ground, forcing Ditton to shield his eyes and squint. Milk didn't bother; his eyes were closed anyway.

Ditton swung in through the gates. Ahead of them to the left was the pitch, encircled by a running track with a grandstand on one side. Small figures were visible on the field, and although the crowd couldn't be seen, from the number of cars strewn across the grass it had to be sizeable. Ditton drove slowly, peering over the wheel for somewhere to park, while Milk opened his eyes at the sound of a shrill whistle from the pitch and cheers from the stands – the match had started.

Ditton was amazed that even in this condition, Milk's body language screamed that he had to be out there on that pitch.

Ditton finally found a parking space directly behind the stand, from where the feet of the spectators could be seen between the slatted pews. As he applied the handbrake a roar went up, accompanied by rhythmic stamping that sent a shiver down Ditton's spine and caused Milk's stomach to churn even more violently. Ditton paused to wait for Milk, who was retrieving his bag from the boot of the car, and whipped out his phone, in two minds about attempting to call either Tyrone or Vincent. He decided not to; it was time to enjoy the match and deal with anything else afterwards. He had a feeling that this contest would be eventful, probably even unforgettable.

Looking over his shoulder to see what was keeping Milk, Ditton saw him trotting away from the pitch in the direction of a row of trees that bordered a school playing field.

'Where are you going?' Ditton called out. 'I thought you wanted the toilet.'

Milk beckoned for Ditton to follow him to where he had stopped beside a soft-top white XR3 with the roof down. 'Stand there and turn around,' Milk directed. 'This is Marty's car.'

'What are you going to do?'

'Just stand there and turn around.'

Ditton sighed, shrugged, and did as he was told. Standing with his arms folded, facing the back of the stands and able to see one corner of the pitch, he was sure he caught a sight of Puppy, the fat goalkeeper of Milk's team, ambling around on his goal line. Then Ditton felt the car move behind him, as though someone had got in or out. He chanced a look over his shoulder and couldn't believe what he was seeing. Milk's bare behind was perched over the car door and a puddle of liquid, reminiscent of school mince, nestled comfortably in the well of the driver's seat.'

Ditton swung away in revulsion. 'Oh my God! That's so disgusting. That's so disgusting. Oh my God!'

Milk pulled a roll of toilet paper from his bag and sorted himself out. He stood up, grinning. 'You know what? I feel better already. Not perfect, but definitely better.'

They skirted the far end of the stand and turned left towards the pitch. Ditton looked up at the crowd and saw the Extremist contingent immediately – Zero lounging in a white vest, dark glasses and cap, Star joking with Nameless in the row in front, and the others grouped around gazing at the pitch and laughing about something. Vaughn stood, spread his hands and mouthed, 'What?' Ditton raised a hand and nodded, as if to say, 'Hold on, I'll tell you in a minute.'

It was obvious that the crowd of around three hundred was predominantly there to support the All Stars, Milk's team. Ditton had a quick look at Marty's team. There was one player that looked mixed-race. What the mix was, Ditton didn't know, but every other player on the team was white, while the crowd was very black in the best possible sense. Ditton could have sworn that he knew ninety per cent of them, and those that he didn't were there with people he did know.

Ditton scoured the stands for Esther and her parents. He didn't see them, but he noticed a flash of yellow over the entrance to the changing rooms at the bottom of the stands. Jonah's shirt had been hung there in his honour, a painful but pleasing reminder for Ditton.

'You all right?' he asked Milk.

Milk didn't need to answer; it was obvious. His face lit up when he walked on grass, but when he stepped on to a pitch to play, he glowed.

'I'm good,' replied Milk. 'Considering. Go on, get yourself a seat, and tell them lot to be ready for something special.'

Zero and Vaughn each moved along a seat to make space for Ditton, who sat down, removed his jacket and rubbed a hand across his head. Vaughn, Zero, Star, Nameless and Ronin all stared at him, waiting for an explanation.

'It's a long, long story,' Ditton began.

They kept staring.

'Are you coming, or not, dear?' Jean Barrett called out to her husband from the hall. 'You know we want to get there early.'

George Barrett frowned behind his newspaper. 'No, I'm not coming. I've got some things to do, and I might have to go down to the station.'

Mrs Barrett fussed for a few moments, clucking her disappointment. He had said he would accompany her and their daughter to the antiques fair, and she had given him plenty of warning and numerous opportunities to change his mind. But of course, he didn't think to tell her until she was putting her coat on and heading out of the door. He had been like that all week.

'You've been a nightmare to live with recently. Do you know that?' she asked as she entered the living room, slipping on a jacket.

Barrett snapped the newspaper, folded and lowered it. The sound made his wife jump and she faltered and gasped. He glared at her, knowing the effect his eyes had on her, holding her there, captive.

'I have changed my mind,' he said slowly and deliberately. 'And I will not be going with you and Margaret to your antiques fair.'

Mrs Barrett nodded meekly.

'Do you have a problem with that?'

'No, dear.'

'Good.'

He watched his wife bustle down the drive to her little car, and throw a nervous glance back at the house before getting in. She was upset, he could see it, and she was right, it had been a bad week. It wasn't her fault, she didn't know what was going on. He wasn't really sure he did either, or at least not how it had come to this.

It had begun routinely enough, just after he made detective inspector and knew he was on the way to making it in the force. He was good at his job, he nabbed villains and made things better for the honest citizen, but he wasn't born yesterday, wasn't wet behind the ears or just out of college. He wasn't a blind, romantic fool looking at the world through rose-coloured glasses. He saw things in black and white, he knew how things went, the way of the world, that nothing came easy or cut-and-dried. He knew that rules had to be bent now and then, that paperwork and procedures didn't always have to be completed or followed, especially if the results came rolling in. And they did come rolling in, arrest after arrest, and conviction after conviction.

Much of it was down to good, solid police work, but he had to admit that many if not most of his successes were provided by informants he had cultivated himself, developed relationships with, and sometimes engaged in further business dealings. That was the way the job went nowadays. Detection was a myth, a fantasy propagated by the television. In reality informants solved crimes.

Barrett was not averse to making on the side, either. Most of the people he encountered through his job were scum. Why should they be living life while he didn't? He was working for the right side; it was only just and proper that he received some perks from the job.

Then there were others who did things properly – professionals. Those were men he could really work with because they were men he could respect. It panned out as mutual back-scratching, and he was always on the lookout for opportunities of that type.

So when he began to hear reports about two partners, young, ambitious and talented, he took note and monitored their progress. It was prolific, terrifyingly swift, but timing was everything and he waited patiently, and while he waited he calculated their operations and their earning power. It was phenomenal, and he knew that if they were making that kind of money in his manor, donations had to be made. It was only common courtesy that they extend the hand of friendship and reward him for what he had allowed so far. They could get around to discussing the future later.

He picked his moment to introduce himself and what he knew about them. It was a lot – dates, places, times – and he made sure they were aware. They knew he was serious and they were hostile, but he sensed the differences between the two of them early on. One was more ambitious than the other, greedier for wealth and power, knew exactly what he wanted and was prepared to do anything to get it. Barrett could smell it on him; it was the same smell he had worn himself for years.

The other was more restrained and, in a sense, more honourable. No less vicious or volatile but it was obvious that he lived according to some kind of code that told him particular actions were out of the question. He would be worked on afterwards. If Barrett could manage to get the other partner on board, he thought, that one would eventually be able to convince his associate that it was wise to co-operate.

Barrett had been sure of that, so he made his play. The pitch had to show that he was in control. It wasn't always that way, but he recognised that this target was different and had to be suppressed. He had to be made to understand that Barrett had the power to decide his fate.

He had watched Vincent Carty sit there as cool as a cucumber and deny everything. That was customary, but he was so composed it was disconcerting. And then, just as calmly, Carty had declared that he would come on board and was flattered by the shabby, frankly quite amateur attempt Barrett had made. Barrett was disturbed, and for the briefest moment considered withdrawing the offer, but he couldn't; Vincent had called his bluff. Even then he had the feeling that although Vincent had the potential to make him financially very comfortable, there was just as much potential to cause trouble. Initially he had thought Vincent Carty was wild, but the more time he spent with him the clearer it became. The man was calculated and evil.

It had gone well for a number of months: secret meetings in out-of-the-way places, Vincent providing information on crimes that had happened or were about to happen, putting names to faces and scenes described by Barrett. Barrett would claim that he was overlooking the activities of Carty and his partner, but the truth was they were too good. Barrett knew it and didn't like it. He wanted to reassert his authority and not feel as though Vincent was doing him favours, so he asked Vincent for money, told him the trial period was over and it was time to contribute regular, healthy amounts. Vincent had smirked and reported that he had to discuss the situation with his partner. It would have to be a joint decision. Of course, he was willing to do everything he could to co-operate with the servants of the law, but he wasn't so sure about his associate.

At the next meeting Vincent reported that unfortunately the answer was an emphatic no. He added that any action Barrett wanted to take against the hindrance would not meet with opposition from him, and could even receive a reasonable degree of support. Barrett took the hint and began a campaign to wear Rodney Ditton down, to break him. He didn't want him totally crushed, just weakened enough to agree to the contributions that would benefit everyone. Barrett was on the streets then and he tracked Rodney Ditton tirelessly, making sure Rodney knew he was around, and more importantly, making sure that the people Rodney dealt with knew he was around. But the boy was stubborn and refused to back down, effectively sticking up two fingers, saying 'catch me if you can'.

Vincent on the other hand seemed to have accepted that he had to play ball. Although he was conveniently unable to pay his dues, he more than made up for it with information that got better and better. And then, the day after Vincent had given him the name of the villain who'd robbed a post office in Mitcham, Jimmy Nash, he'd phoned again and made a suggestion:

'Why don't you do it? Pick him up right now, put him in a cell for a while and let him stew. Let him out, offer him a lift he can't refuse, and bring him to me. Then we'll all be able to talk about it, sensibly. But you'll have to hurry, you'll have to do it right now. I can tell you where he is.'

It had sounded so persuasive that Barrett had done

just that. He'd swooped mob-handed, picked Rodney up on some trumped-up charge and let him sit in the cells for a few hours. Then he'd given the order for him to be released, claimed that he was going home and waited around the corner in his car. Rodney had stalked out and Barrett had offered him a lift, which he had accepted reluctantly. The rest was painful history and he had paid for it ever since.

Barrett picked up the telephone and dialled. He stroked his chin while waiting for the call to be answered, tracing the jagged scar acquired from the end of a villain's broken bottle. He took a deep breath as the call was connected and gritted his teeth, the muscles of his jaw and above his temple flexing.

'It's me,' he said. 'I've got him. What do you want to do?'

The answer was short, curt.

Barrett nodded once. 'OK, I'll be there – *we'll* be there.'

He replaced the handset, folded his arms and closed his eyes, deep in thought. He sat there for a few minutes, immobile. Then he opened his eyes, sat forward and again reached for the phone. He dialled and waited once more.

'It's me, Barrett.'

The person on the other end began to babble, alarm evident. 'What's happening? You were supposed to call yesterday. I've been sitting about like an arse, waiting for you to call.'

The complaints were set to continue, but Barrett wasn't in the mood to listen. 'OK,' he said. 'I hear you, but this is about something else. The matter we discussed a few days ago? It's on for today. Are you ready?'

There was silence.

'Good. I'll meet you at the usual place at quarter to two,' said Barrett and replaced the receiver, his mind elsewhere. He stroked his chin with a distant look in his eyes, before sitting forward and heaving himself to his feet with an effort. He smiled ruefully. If he was struggling to raise himself from an armchair, he needed to treat that as a sign that things were coming to an end. It was time to get out, and if everything went to plan, it would happen today. The only problem was that he had to rely on someone else. He hated having to do that, but he could take some insurance measures of his own.

He strode to the kitchen, pausing to retrieve a set of keys from an ornate box on the wall. He unlocked the back door and made his way purposefully down the flagstone path to the shed at the end of the garden. He delayed to nod good morning to next-door, pruning roses on the other side of the fence.

'Doing a spot of gardening, George?' his neighbour enquired.

'Not today, Jim. Just looking for something in the shed.'

Barrett yanked the door of the shed and stepped in, reaching to his right for the light switch. It contained the usual garden paraphernalia – lawnmower, shears and assorted tools, an old bicycle frame, bags of peat and other varied junk. Barrett skirted it all and headed for the far corner, for a small trunk covered in an old travel blanket and a box containing decorating fluids.

He placed the box on the floor, pulled off the blanket and unlocked a padlock on the trunk with one of the keys he had taken from the kitchen. He then removed a black velvet cloth to reveal a fitted tray containing intricately detailed and painted miniature military figurines in their own individual compartments. He removed this tray to reveal another identical one below, removed the second tray and extracted an oilskin pouch.

Barrett opened the pouch and produced two revolvers and ammunition. Deftly he released the chambers, spun them and loaded the guns. Then he reconstructed the trunk, locked it and placed the rug and box back on top. He was as ready as he would ever be.

CHAPTER THIRTY-ONE

Marty's team scored first with a dubious goal. Up in the stands the crowd were becoming restless. Some of them knew Milk was class, others who didn't know his football history could see it from his passes and touches, but he wasn't producing much, and they wanted more. Some of them weren't happy that he had turned up late in the first place.

'Don't worry,' said Zero to no one in particular. 'Milk'll come through. Just watch.'

No one answered; it looked as though it could go either way.

'You're right,' stated Vaughn. 'My money's on Milk.'

Beside him, Ditton felt a big hand on his shoulder, and as he was turning to confront the owner, a voice asked, 'What's wrong with your boy? He's not playing like himself.'

It was Leon, a good-natured but hopeless gossip-and rumour-monger that Ditton had known for years. Ditton explained that Milk was sick, it was amazing that he was playing at all.

True to form, Leon nodded and lied, 'Yeah, I
knew it had to be something like that.' He turned
to a group of guys a few rows behind him and
shouted, 'He's sick! You're lucky he's playing!' The
guys stood up and roared their approval and began
to stamp their feet, encouraging other people to
join in. Quickly, the noise became deafening, and
Ditton couldn't hear Leon properly when he asked,
'What's the matter with that cousin of yours, Tyrone,
man? I was chatting to him on Friday and all of a
sudden he just went mad and ran off up the road like
a nutter.'

Ditton smiled, humouring Leon, hearing 'Tyrone'
and 'nutter', but failing to fully comprehend.

'He said he was waiting for you,' reported Leon.
'Then all of a sudden this black Rover comes round the
corner, slows down and then stops next to your car.
Next thing I know, Tyrone darts off without saying a
word.'

Now Ditton wheeled around, ready to give Leon his
full attention. 'When was this? Where?'

'Croydon. On Friday evening. He said he was
waiting for you in your car, then he saw me and came
out to chat. We were there for a couple of minutes, the
Rover came and he was off, without saying a word.
Trust me, it was weird.'

Ditton nodded.

'Didn't you know?' Leon asked, prying like a tabloid
journalist after a tasty story.

'Yeah,' lied Ditton, reluctant to open up to someone

like Leon. 'I just didn't know exactly how it went. Thanks, man.'

Leon hung around for a while longer hoping to receive some juicy titbits of information, but Ditton was noncommittal, so he gave up and returned to his crew. Ditton sat forward with his elbows on his knees and began to think. At least he now knew why Tyrone had disappeared, but surely he was cracking up if he went running off in a state every time he saw a black Rover. But then Leon had said that the Rover had stopped beside Ditton's car. He had to admit that was likely to be more than coincidence. It was also worrying. If it was the police in the Rover, it meant they were aware of Ditton too. Why else would they have stopped beside his car? But if that was the case they must have followed him and Tyrone. The only possibility was that they had followed Tyrone to Ditton's, and then followed both of them from there. But then why hadn't they grabbed Tyrone as soon as Ditton left the car? For that matter why hadn't they just grabbed Tyrone as soon as they had found him? If they had wanted proof that Tyrone was going back to the flat they could have swooped and nabbed Ditton in there, and then made a case that Tyrone had asked Ditton to enter it for him. It wouldn't have been hard to prove. None of it made sense. He was sure he would have spotted the Rover if it had been following, and if he didn't, he was sure Tyrone would have. But if they hadn't been followed, how on earth had the Rover known where they were? It scared him to think about it.

The score stayed the same until just before half-time when an off-side Marty ran on to a through ball and side-footed past Puppy for his first goal. The crowd groaned collectively.

On the way back from the bar Vaughn pointed and asked, 'Isn't that Jonah's sister over there?'

Ditton spun around and followed Vaughn's finger to find himself smiling as he answered Vaughn in the affirmative.

'Take these to Zero and the others for me,' he said, passing an armful of crisps and soft drinks. 'I need to say hello.'

Esther walked slowly along the area between the stands and the touchline, arm in arm with her mother. Mr Carty followed a few paces behind. He had looked old and tired at the house on Thursday, but he had aged even more since then and Ditton found it hard to look at him. Esther returned Ditton's long-distance smile, smothering it appropriately as they drew nearer.

'Mr C.' Ditton shook the old man's hand.

'Mrs C.' he stooped to kiss her, and she winked as he straightened and inclined her head towards her daughter. 'Not before time,' she said.

For some bizarre reason, it occurred to Ditton that if he had been white, his cheeks would have been as red as a bus.

'Mum!' Esther remonstrated.

'Mum what?' snapped Mrs Carty. 'Allow me a little something to smile about. What's wrong with you?'

'I agree,' Ditton declared, and promptly took Esther's hand and kissed it.

Mrs Carty nodded haughtily. 'Yes, man. Good stuff.'

'Now, where are you going to sit?' Ditton asked the trio.

Esther raised her hand to shield her eyes from the sun and scoured the terraces. 'Up there.'

'OK, I'll join you in a minute. I'm just going to tell the others.'

'No,' she said, surprisingly forcefully. Then, softer, 'No. You go back to your friends and remember Jonah how you want to. How you knew him. You can't do that with us there. Go and laugh and joke. You don't want to be inhibited by his old parents and square sister.' She pushed him playfully. 'Go on. I'll talk to you later.'

Ditton made his way back to the others, reflecting that if it hadn't been for Milk's admonition outside the Carty house a few days earlier, the joy he now felt deep in his chest would still have been the painful pang of longing. He made a note to try and remember to thank Milk without making his head swell any further, or provoking any unwanted comments or observations.

When he got back to his seat and explained that Jonah's parents had turned up, he was forced to point them out. The Extremists rose, led by Zero, and set off to pay their respects.

'Guess who's here?' Zero said upon returning.

'Who?' Ditton asked, routinely.

'That Yardie guy, Devon.'

'Who?' Ditton was blank. The only Devon he knew was in south-west England.

Zero pointed to a group of three gaudily dressed, gold-laden men who were just settling into their seats. The one in the middle was big enough to be a heavy-weight boxer, but in no shape to even put on a pair of gloves. He wore a full beard, and navy-blue dungarees that struggled to contain his stomach, over a long-sleeved T-shirt composed of horizontal navy and white stripes. With the huge gold ring in his ear all he needed to complete the pirate outfit was a sword.

Ditton watched him sit back smugly, like a visiting dignitary used to the pomp, ceremony and hospitality of the most prestigious social occasions. Gold glittered everywhere, and aware that people had noted his entrance, Devon removed a fat wad of notes from his back pocket, peeled off a large red one and handed it to one of his companions, who went trotting off to the bar.

'Who is he?' Ditton was curious now.

'Supposed to be a bad boy. A real one. I hear he's been about a bit, New York, Toronto. Now, here. I also heard that Patrick sells for him.'

'So what's he doing here?'

'Maybe Patrick? Milk?'

'I'd better tell Milk, then.'

Zero shook his head. 'I just told him. He's all right about it.'

'What did he say?'

Zero began to chuckle, and leaned forward. 'He

said, "Yardie? Fuck the Yardie. This is London, my town, and I haven't got his gear." '

Ditton shook his head and sighed, looked at Zero for a second, then shook his head again and sighed even deeper.

'But guess who else is here?' Zero urged.

'Who?'

Zero pointed them out. Earl sat with two of the guys he had met at Henrietta's on the night of the robbery.

'He's got some fucking nerve,' said Ditton. 'Coming with the guys who robbed Jonah, too.'

When Milk came out of the toilet at half-time he felt like a new man, and told his team mates so. They agreed that it was a good thing because he had played the first half like a pensioner and had to sort it out, especially if he was expecting to win this bet he had going on the match.

Milk raised an eyebrow. 'You've heard about that, then?'

With sour expressions a few of them declared, 'We've heard about it. Thanks for letting us know that you're making money off our backs.'

Milk scowled. 'Well, it's not a personal bet any more. This match is in Jonah's honour. If I win the bet, I'm going to donate the money to the family. So if any of you were feeling half-hearted about getting stuck into some of those tackles, there's your incentive.' And with that, Milk strode out of the changing room and up into the stands, where he shook hands with the crew.

The first half had been physical but not particularly rough, and the players came out tossing grudgingly respectful looks at each other. Marty made his way to the centre circle with his striking partner, their heads together. The referee put the ball on the centre spot and looked around to see if everyone was ready to start. Marty looked around too and locked eyes with Milk. Marty grinned and nodded. Milk returned the nod.

'It starts now, Marty,' Milk called out.

Marty grinned and gave Milk the thumbs up.

'Don't say I didn't warn you, Marty.'

'So how is your stomach? Still gippy?'

'Not as good as my dick,' Milk explained. 'You see, I was in Tooting yesterday afternoon and I met a friend of yours. She had me going until just before you sent the other one around.'

Marty's eyes narrowed in confusion, but he laughed as he said, 'What are you talking about, man? You must have had too much Jack Daniels last night. You're still pissed.'

Milk walked up to the edge of the centre circle. 'Yesterday afternoon when you phoned your bitch and she told you that she couldn't talk because her battery needed charging, what do you think was really going on.'

'Fuck off!' Marty exclaimed, throwing up an arm in disbelief.

' "Sorry, babe. But you know this battery was low

from this morning, don't you? I'll call you as soon as I get to a phone." Wasn't that how it went?'

Marty scowled but Milk could still see that there was some doubt in his mind. 'Black leather mini-skirt with a slit up one side, black high-heeled sandals, black blouse and a green suede waistcoat with a black suede cap. And that little teddy bear tattoo in that hollow bit at the top of her thigh.' Milk licked his lips and then proceeded to lick each finger on his right hand, lingering on the middle one. Marty's jaw dropped and he looked ill. His striking partner looked as though he wanted a hole to appear in the ground and swallow him up.

'Come on, Gints,' the big number nine advised. 'Ignore the black bastard and bang some goals in. Don't let him wind you up.'

Marty couldn't reply. He hadn't really needed the tattoo as final confirmation; the word-for-word re-counting of his brief conversation on the phone with his girlfriend was enough.

Just as the referee placed his whistle in his mouth to blow for the start of the second half, Milk slid his hand down his shorts and added, 'But you can't blame her, can you?'

Marty's bellowed reply was drowned out by the whistle. Milk grinned and followed the ball.

The second half started like a different match. Milk and his team came out fired up and for the first five minutes the only touches of the ball Marty and his team got were from goal-kicks. Milk ran the show, drifting all over the pitch, from the centre to both wings, up into attack and even dropping back in front of his back four to collect the ball for distribution, which he did with a class and talent that was plain to see. Marty's team were being run ragged, and even though they were still two goals up they were losing their composure and team spirit, arguing with each other and ignoring their team plan.

At fifty-three minutes into the match Milk collected the ball, dummied a defender and slid an exquisite pass in to Michael, the roving striker, who had been steaming down the left with his hand raised. The pass cut out the keeper, and if he had wanted to Michael could have rolled a joint before slotting the ball into the back of the net.

The air was filled with cheers, whistles, fog horns and a rhythmic stamping of feet that could have graced KwaZulu land. Body language suggested that Marty's team had lost the match, but he wasn't about to allow that to happen. As Milk and the others celebrated, Marty paced around the field, exhorting and encouraging his team to keep pressing. They didn't have his confidence.

Ten minutes later Milk latched on to a loose ball from a corner, the defence having failed to clear properly, and blasted it as hard as he could. The shot was unstoppable, and the keeper, unsighted, took it squarely on the forehead, knocking him down and allowing the ball to rebound into the goal. The celebrations began again in the crowd and Zero said smugly, 'I told you so, Milk's the man.'

After the restart the match continued as it had before the goal, with Milk pulling the strings and slotting balls through for his team mates to latch on to. Michael hit the post, and from a corner won and taken by Milk, Clinton, the hard man in midfield, aimed a powerful header goal-bound, producing a brilliant save from the goalkeeper. Then one of Marty's defenders almost put the ball into his own net trying to pass to the goalkeeper but finding a divot.

A little later the ball came to Milk on the left wing. He beat one man and saw another heading for him but he was way too fast and knew he was away and free, until he felt his legs taken and saw the ground rushing to meet him. He rolled and sprang up to take the free kick, and then couldn't believe that play was still continuing. The tackle had been diabolical but the referee had apparently been unsighted and the linesman, who was no more than ten metres away, hadn't seen fit to raise his flag. Milk was astounded and confronted the linesman, telling him exactly what he thought of his lack of a decision. The ball had gone out of play on the other side of the pitch and the players gravitated towards the touchline, where an unsightly rolling maul had developed. The linesman was in the middle of lots of pushing and shoving from the two teams, and the referee struggled to sort it out. It ended with Milk receiving a yellow card and a warning that another outburst would see him ejected from the game.

Milk took his censure tight-lipped, with his arms behind his back. But as soon as the referee began to jog away, he turned to Ditton and Zero in the stands, raised his head, ran his forefinger across his neck and pointed at the linesman.

Three minutes later Marty collected a long ball from his defence and set off for goal. Milk looked at the linesman in horror, as Marty had been at least five metres offside, but he didn't approach the official even after Marty poked the ball past Puppy and punched the air in celebration of his second goal. The crowd rose as one and bayed for the linesman's blood, and a few missiles sailed through the air, sending him scurrying on to the pitch out of harm's way. Over the tannoy the announcer appealed for calm, reminding everyone that there were children present. Reluctantly the crowd lowered themselves back into their seats.

A couple of minutes later Marty was again blatantly offside but failed to score, scuffing his shot and sending it well wide of the furious Puppy in goal. In the stands Zero shook his head, looked at Ditton, handed his phone to Star, rose from his seat and wandered down to the pitch. Milk looked across to see Zero sauntering towards the linesman, and continued with the game. From the stands Ditton saw Zero come to a halt about six feet behind the linesman, who turned around sharply as though responding to something Zero had said. The linesman turned back to face the game and then swivelled even more sharply, turning his whole body to face Zero this time. Ditton read the pot-bellied linesman's body language and the dropped jaw that followed Zero as he strolled back along the touchline, and knew the linesman had been taken care of. He didn't know what unrefusable offer Zero had made him, but the linesman had accepted. So much so that less than a minute later, before Zero had even retaken his seat, Marty was flagged offside when he had been level. He glared and approached the linesman, who looked over his shoulder as though trying to locate Zero in the stands before shrugging apologetically at Marty. Marty stormed over to hurl abuse and after lots of finger-pointing and arm-waving was dragged away by his team mates. The linesman looked for Zero again before shrugging and explaining to one of Marty's team why Marty's investment was no longer valid.

With seven minutes left of the match Milk was becoming slightly frustrated. He had evaded so many flying tackles, embarrassed so many of the opposing team and laid on so many chances that they should have been 10–3 up. His forwards had missed so many opportunities that he was beginning to feel the match might be beyond them, and that after everything Marty could possibly come out on top. But then Clinton charged through the middle of the pitch sending two opposing midfielders sprawling and sprayed the ball wide on the left for Milk. Milk looked up, saw that Clinton wasn't open for a return pass, saw no one heading for the box and raced down the touchline to wait for support. He beat one man and looked up, wanting to cross the ball for Clinton to use his heading ability, but saw him on the ground on the edge of the box remonstrating with the referee. Nathan was marked and David, a full-back, was courageously trying to support from deep but had no chance of making it into the box before the defence swarmed the area and the initiative was lost. Milk used them as decoys, beat the same defender again, flicked the ball over his out-stretched leg, collected it on his laces and scooped it over the head of the centre back, who had lost his discipline and rushed out to confront him. As the centre back floundered and the ball fell to earth Milk considered controlling it and taking it closer to goal. The goalkeeper seemed to read his mind and screamed for one of his defenders to intercept the wizard. Milk saw him coming, set himself and looped a volley over the despairing keeper's outstretched arm and into the far top corner of the net.

As the noise died down, Ditton realised his phone was ringing. He sat down, put a hand over one ear, and the phone to the other.

'Yeah?'

'Ditton? That you?'

'Yeah. Who's this?'

'Trevor. Tyrone's brother.'

Trevor was a good kid, and Ditton had always liked him. He wasn't square, just your average nineteen-year-old college student, still idealistic about working in the music industry for a few years before making it big as a producer himself. It was a nice dream, the sort that Ditton could never remember having. He wished the kid well.

'Course I know who you are. What's up?'

'Have you seen Ty? He said he was going to see you yesterday.'

'He was supposed to, but he didn't show up or phone or anything. It's not the first time he's done it recently, so I didn't pay it any mind.'

There was a pause before Trevor asked, 'Is he in trouble? Real trouble?'

What could Ditton say that wouldn't alarm the kid? 'What makes you ask that?'

'He's been acting strange for a while now. And when he was here on Wednesday, he seemed nervous and agitated, you know? But then he calmed down when Earl got here, and he was still OK when Earl dropped him back. But yesterday when I spoke to him, he sounded funny again.'

Ditton's jaws were clenched so tightly he had to make a conscious effort to loosen them in order to speak. 'Between what times was he out with Earl on Wednesday?'

'What? Exactly?'

Ditton was still on the other end of the phone, being buffeted by the celebrations around him while Trevor paused and thought.

'From about eleven to maybe four in the morning?'

'Thanks,' said Ditton. 'If I speak to him, I'll tell him to call you.'

'So, is he in trouble?'

'He might be . . . now.'

Ditton ended the call and looked across at where Earl was sitting, roughly thirty metres away. The skinny schemer failed to turn his head this time, apparently intent on what was happening on the pitch. Ditton was tiring of the lies and deception, and was tempted to drag Earl out of his seat and beat the truth out of him behind the stands. He decided against it; he wasn't the beating type, although there would have been a stand full of volunteers had he asked. It would have made too much of a scene, and he couldn't be involved in that with Jonah's parents, and more importantly Esther present. Besides, Milk would be distraught if he missed out.

CHAPTER THIRTY-TWO

'You ready?' asked Patrick, checking his gun and turning around in the car to look at Kevin.

'Ready,' his cousin answered with a quick nod.

Patrick turned to the driver of the car and patted him on the leg. 'Ronnie, you can stay here if you don't want to be seen, but you'll have to keep the car running.'

Ronnie shook his head and frowned as he swung the car through the gates of the stadium and scoured the grass with his eyes for somewhere to park. 'I'm coming,' he said. 'I want to see this.'

Patrick shrugged, inserting the pistol carefully into an inside pocket of his long, shapeless jacket. 'Have it your way.'

'How you going to do it?' asked Jester. 'Just walk up and do him?'

'What would you suggest, then?' snapped Patrick.

'Easy, man,' protested Jester. 'I'm only asking. I just want to know what to expect. What's the matter with you?'

'Sorry,' said Patrick, peering out of the car for a face he recognised. 'Yeah, I can't think of any other way to do it.'

'You should do it when he's still on the pitch,' suggested Kevin. 'That way everybody will see it and know he fucked up, big time.'

For several seconds Kevin's idea appealed to Patrick and he visualised walking on to the pitch while the ball was still in play and blasting Milk away. 'Too many witnesses,' he said finally. 'It needs to be after the match.'

'I know,' said Kevin, a hint of annoyance in his voice. 'It was just an idea that came into my head. I wasn't actually telling you to do it.'

'There he is!' remarked Jester, pointing out of the window at a group of players in yellow shirts celebrating on the pitch. 'He must have just scored or something. I wonder what the score is?'

Kevin turned to face him with a look of incredulity stuck to his face. 'Fuck the score, man,' he said. 'We didn't come here to watch football, we came to deal with a prick who's overstepped the mark one time too many. A bastard who dragged me out of my house and kicked me about and then tried to kill me in my own bedroom.'

Jester shrugged. 'But what do you expect if he finds his niece in your bed, man? Look at it from his point of view.'

'What?' Kevin roared. 'Do you want to go and sit over there and watch the match? Because if you do, you better fuck off now, you get me?'

'Easy,' said Jester for the second time. 'I was only pointing it out.'

'Well don't,' said Kevin, gingerly feeling his swollen face behind his sunglasses. 'I don't need it pointed out. All I have to do is look in the mirror, OK?'

'Cool it, Kevin, man,' snapped Patrick. 'You panicky or what? You want to stay here and wait?'

Coming from Patrick the comment stung. But Kevin bit his tongue, threw the car door open and strode out, stuffing his pistol into the back of his trousers. Jester stepped out behind him, squinting because of the sun and bending to rub the circulation back into his long legs. 'Don't lock the doors,' he said to Ronnie. 'We might have to get back in in a hurry.'

'Fuck the doors,' snarled Patrick. 'I'm strolling back to the car.'

All three turned to look at him as he drew his black wrap-arounds from his pocket, placed them on his face and ran a hand over his head. He withdrew a bandanna from the back pocket of his baggy jeans and tied it around his neck, threw his jacket open, jammed his hands into the front pockets of his jeans and strutted towards the back of the stands with a stiff-legged, lop-sided gait that suggested Patrick 'Pepper' Braithwaite had found himself. He was a man on a mission, a mission that would decide his future and shape the course of history. It was a mission that he couldn't afford to mess up, but Pepper felt hot, and he knew that he was going to succeed.

* * *

The tension and excitement doubled after the goal, so much so that the crowd remained on their feet cheering like punters at a racetrack. The referee checked his watch, signalled two minutes remaining in the game and pointed to the centre circle. Marty was almost foaming at the mouth as he stormed around the pitch screaming at his team to give one last effort.

Eventually Milk won the ball and waved his team forward for one last attack before the end of regulation time. He burst to the right, slid the ball to Colin, who was hugging the right touchline just inside his own half, and rocketed infield to receive the return pass. Clinton came across and took it instead, frantically waving Milk forward into the box.

Milk smelled a goal, looked around for cover and knowing what a good crosser of the ball Clinton was, charged towards the box.

Clinton's pace and power took him past the only defender that had a chance of stopping him. He looked up and hurled a delightful cross towards the six-yard box. The crowd went silent as the ball seemed to arrow towards Milk in slow motion and he set himself to deal with it. But at the last minute the cross faded and almost as one the crowd groaned as they saw the ball curl so that when it did reach Milk it would be behind him. Milk noted the trajectory and shifted his feet, turning one hundred and eighty degrees to cope with the deviation. He sprang, eyes on the ball, everything else unimportant, and threw himself into the air, pivoting on an invisible axis to execute a bicycle kick.

Zero dropped his phone; Ronin and Star stopped in mid-sentence, the words hanging from their lips; Ditton felt Vaughn's fingers digging into his arm; Nameless could have caught birds the way his mouth hung open, and Solar, who had been retying his locks, stopped, unable even to move his hair from his face, and stood there like Samson.

Everyone in the stands expected Milk to send the ball hurtling into the back of the net. He missed it, landed on his back, jumped to his feet and appealed to the referee for a foul. Having back-tracked and made the challenge, Marty stood beside Milk with his hands on his hips, looking anxiously at the referee and berating the rest of his team for their inept defending. The linesman raised his flag and the referee blew his whistle and pointed to the spot.

Zero grinned and took a seated bow.

'What did you say to him?' his brother asked.

'I just told him that I knew he'd taken money from Marty to tip the balance,' Zero answered. 'And that if he didn't sort things out it was unlikely that he'd leave here in one piece. He took a look at the crowd and seemed to agree.'

'Look at that!' exclaimed Vaughn, pointing at Marty, who was being hauled off the linesman by the rest of his team. 'He's gone mad.' It certainly looked that way as Marty threw out-of-range punches and kicks at the beleaguered linesman, who hadn't bargained for anything he had encountered that morning. And then the referee dismissed Marty and was subjected to a torrent of abuse that was clearly audible from the stands and elicited unsympathetic cheering and jeering. Milk stood beside the penalty spot with the ball under his arm, grinning broadly and orchestrating the cheers of the crowd.

Once Marty was off the pitch Milk placed the ball on the spot and measured his run-up. There was no doubt in his mind that he was going to score; it was a formality even though it was a four-thousand-pound kick. But being Milk he decided to entertain, and walked back to the spot, re-placed the ball and watched the keeper sweat. He returned to the start of his run-up, waved to the crowd and to Marty, who was brooding on the touchline, and began to run.

If the situation had been slightly less tense Ditton would probably have had the presence of mind to ignore his phone when it began to ring, but he answered it instinctively, at the same time that Milk dummied the keeper and scooped the ball over his head as he dived to the ground. The crowd roared, surpassing any noise levels they had reached previously, and Ditton was unable to hear who he was supposed to be talking to.

'Who is this?' he shouted, clamping his hand over his free ear. 'Who?' His heart sank as he heard Nash's voice, and it hit rock bottom when Nash said, 'You've run out of time,' and hung up.

The next five minutes were amazing and it would have been easy to think that the All Stars had won the World

Cup. The crowd made their way on to the pitch to mob the players, Milk sank to his knees exhausted and dehydrated but found himself hoisted on a pair of shoulders and carried for a mini lap of honour. He milked it, waving to the crowd, but then his exertions caught up with him and every step his carrier took shook his insides to the core. He beat the guy on the head to be let down so he could run and throw up. The guy eventually got the message and sank like a camel to allow Milk to dismount. Milk staggered blindly, waving his arms to clear space for himself as he headed retching for the changing rooms, hoping against hope that he could keep it down until he got out of sight. To his dismay he bumped into someone and screamed at them to get out of the way, but they didn't move and Milk couldn't summon the energy or willpower to go any further.

Tears stung his eyes as he bent at the waist and threw up. From somewhere in the distance he heard the roar of a wounded animal and almost instantly his vision cleared, his hearing returned and he stood up straight, ready to celebrate.

Patrick stood there, paralysed, staring agape at Milk. For a second the group that had witnessed the incident, had seen the collision and the spew, seemed to be caught in their own bubble of silence, while elsewhere the noise was riotous, the crowd cheering and whooping and the announcer tying to make himself heard over the public announcement system.

Milk looked at Patrick, who proceeded to look

repeatedly down at his shirt, then up at Milk, his arms spread in a 'Why? Why me?' gesture.

Kevin had wheeled away at the moment of impact in a combination of disgust and evasive action. Now he turned, stood beside his cousin, but not too close, and said, 'Remember what you were saying? Don't fuck up now. There's too much riding on this. Your head for starters.'

Patrick was still unable to speak, incapable of anything but blinking and raising and lowering his head, reminiscent of a grazing animal.

'Come on!' Kevin hissed. 'What are you going to do?'

'Shut your mouth,' advised Milk. 'This is between me and him. You can stay the fuck out of it.'

Kevin was frustrated; he wanted to rush Milk himself, but Patrick had to do it if he wanted to be able to show his face anywhere again. 'Well?' he urged. Patrick didn't move.

'I told you to shut up,' Milk reminded Kevin.

'Fuck you!' Kevin replied, less than graciously.

Milk was feeling fine now and he hit Kevin on the point of the jaw before anybody realised he had moved. Kevin's knees gave way and he was on the floor like a bewildered puppet, legs straight out in front of him, wide-eyed. But to give him credit, the speed with which he returned to his feet was also reminiscent of a puppet. He came up with a gun in his hand and it was pointed straight at Milk.

Milk raised an eyebrow, but nobody moved.

Normally, when a gun appears, people scatter – but nobody moved. Those next to Milk stayed where they were and stared at Kevin. Those behind Milk stayed where they were and stared at Kevin. Patrick still hadn't spoken or moved. People were ready to take bullets, and Kevin would not have got away.

'Well?' asked Milk.

Kevin was psyching himself up for his moment of glory. As far as he was concerned, shooting Milk, even though he was unarmed and in his football kit, would make him forever. His finger tightened on the trigger but then a big hand appeared from nowhere and grabbed his forearm and wrist, twisting, forcing him to drop the gun. His face contorted and a strangled cry forced its way from between his lips. It stopped when Devon's other hand found its way to the back of Kevin's neck and tossed him away like a chocolate wrapper. He skidded for a few feet and came to a halt against Jester.

Devon stood over him, scowling, and in a thick Jamaican accent said, 'You a fool or what? You want to shoot a hero? You expect to shoot a hero, so? And get away with it?' He glanced at Patrick and then back at Kevin. 'Get yourself out of here, and take your cousin with you. I'll have words with him later.'

Kevin got to his feet, pure hatred in his eyes, directed solely at Milk, and didn't look at anyone or anything else. Jester shoved him away gently and was about to do the same to Patrick when he remembered the state of his shirt and jacket and thought better of it.

'You better take that off,' Jester mumbled.

Patrick tried to walk off towards the car without heeding Jester' advice, but the condition of his clothing made it so uncomfortable that he began to cry. Before he got to the car, he was wearing nothing but his boxer shorts and trainers.

The atmosphere relaxed and the rest of the team went off to sort themselves out, get drinks and wait for the presentation. Milk told Ditton to keep an eye on Marty and prevent him sloping off without coughing up the cash.

Ditton winked. 'Star's been under his bonnet. He won't be going anywhere until you want him to.'

Devon folded his arms and regarded Milk closely.

Milk placed his hands in the top of his shorts and regarded Devon. He knew what this was about. Zero had told him the word was that Patrick sold for this guy, but he couldn't believe that Patrick would have run crying to Devon.

'Me and you need to have words,' explained Devon. 'I think we might have a little problem somewhere.'

'What kind of problem?'

'Can't we go somewhere else and talk?'

'Right here's fine with me.'

Devon's companions had sauntered over and taken their places flanking their man. One of them, as black as the silky T-shirt he was wearing, and as skinny as Devon was big, with a bandanna in the Jamaican colours on his egg-shaped head and another in the back pocket of his jeans, said with a mouth full of gold, 'The man say he want to go somewhere and talk.'

Milk looked the newcomer up and down and said, 'Now I don't know who the fuck you are, but I haven't got any business with you. So keep your fucking mouth shut and your ugly face out of my sight. OK?'

Devon's boy snarled, again exposing his golden incisors, and reached for his back pocket. Devon placed a restraining hand on his chest.

Milk regarded the guy distastefully before turning to Devon. 'You should talk to your boy and tell him that this isn't Kingston now. This is London. This is our town, born and bred, homegrown. He can't come here on the run from Miami or wherever and try to take over here. We're not having it, y'understand? You can find your corner and do your thing, but don't think that because you can't speak English without screwing up your face you can just step on everybody. Your accent don't mean fuck. I can go home, say "Hello, Mummy" and hear Jamaican till I'm blue in the face, so that doesn't impress me.'

A round of applause broke out from the people assembled and Devon threw the dirtiest of looks at his hot-headed companion.

Milk said, 'So, you wanted to talk?'

CHAPTER THIRTY-THREE

There was no one at home when Ditton returned from dropping Milk.

Earl had tried to use the confrontation with Patrick, Kevin and Devon to make a getaway, but Zero had grabbed him and forced him to wait until Ditton came across and questioned him about Trevor's phone call. Earl spilled the beans, revealing that he had been with Tyrone on Wednesday night after all, but that they hadn't gone near Jonah's. He also revealed that he had been working with Tyrone all along, feeding him information on Vincent's actions and intentions. Ditton didn't care – Rodney took precedence, all he could do was tell Vincent that Earl had lied to him.

He had been calling home constantly from the minute he had received Nash's call, but with no luck. So it was with some trepidation that he let himself into the house and called Rodney's name, a real come-down after the euphoria of the match and the subsequent presentation of the cup containing four thousand pounds in cash to Mr and Mrs Carty. It had been over an hour since Nash called; plenty of time to do whatever he wanted to do and be long gone.

Ditton peered into the living room and saw his father's foot extended over the arm of the sofa. He was about to leave him there to check upstairs when it occurred to him that this might be the one time he wasn't drunk. As he rolled him over on to his back, the smell of alcohol suggested that this wasn't the case, and then the old man began to snore. Ditton left him in disgust and ran upstairs to Rodney's room – he wasn't there. He ran back down and tried to wake his father to question him, see if he knew anything, but the old man was dead to the world and couldn't be woken. He would open one glassy eye, stare blindly and let it fall closed again.

Ditton was beginning to feel panic rising in his chest. He felt helpless, trapped, a hostage to the madness of a psychotic runt who had the wrong end of the stick. Nash had him running around, frantic, chasing shadows, when for all he knew Rodney had gone on one of his usual aimless walks. But with Nash's threat still ringing in his ears Ditton couldn't allow himself to accept that it could be so simple. He tore his phone from his pocket, retrieved Nash's number from the memory and dialled. It rang but there was no answer and he almost hurled the phone away in frustration, managing to restrain himself just in time. But what could he do? Nothing but wait.

He lay on his bed hoping to nap and wake up more positive, or even better to find Rodney at the end of his bed. Maybe some ideas would come to him while he lay there, and if not, all he could do was tell Vincent again and hope that he would intervene immediately. Ditton lay there for five minutes, trying to calm his mind, trying to think about anything other than Jimmy Nash. It was difficult but he tried to think about the match, Milk and Marty, Milk and Patrick, the presentation. Nothing seemed to work because through all of them Nash's face would appear, and behind him loomed Vincent holding a bunch of keys with a label inscribed *CONSIGLIERE* attached. It was Esther that saved him. He could focus on that face forever. He felt himself falling asleep, floating off when the noise began from next door.

Ditton jumped up and proceeded to pound on the wall. The music stopped for a moment and he began to shout and curse that they were driving him mad, that he couldn't get a moment's peace in his own house. And then, as if they had heard his protest, noted it and deemed it unworthy, the music started again. He couldn't believe it, couldn't believe that they could be so disrespectful, inconsiderate and selfish. He *really* couldn't believe it and for a moment he stood there facing the wall. Then he flipped, completely, and in a moment of hysteria asked himself what someone like Milk would do in the same situation – go next door and raise hell. He asked himself what someone like Nash would do – go next door, gun blazing, and with that thought Ditton reached into the back of the wardrobe and extracted the pistol. He was about to knock next door and show them that he was no longer joking when he stopped and sat down. There was a thought trying to get through his muddled head but he couldn't quite put his finger on it; his head was too full of other things, anger and fear and resentment. It was something he had thought about Nash, something about going next door, that being what Nash would have done if his neighbours were noisy and ignored pleas for quiet.

Ditton stood up. Was it possible? Could it have been that simple? Something Nash had said about his neighbours on Monday came back to Ditton and his eyes widened with the realisation.

He grabbed a jacket, hung it on his arm over the pistol and headed out of the door. Ten minutes later he swung into Jonah's block and parked up. He took the lift and emerged on the third floor, walked past Jonah's door to the next flat and knocked hard, twice. He fingered the gun in his pocket and waited. Seconds later he heard sounds of movement from inside and the door was opened by the same woman Jonah had pulled the gun on. It made sense now why she had looked familiar, though he hadn't understood why then.

'Yeah?' she asked, obviously not recognising him as the person that had been with her neighbour when she had run terrified back into her house.

For a second Ditton was unable to speak but he composed himself, took a deep breath and sought the final proof.

'Is Jimmy in?' he asked.

'You've missed him,' she said flatly. 'Left about an hour ago.'

'Thanks,' said Ditton. 'I'll try him another time.'

She nodded and closed the door. Ditton stood staring at it until he made himself head for the stairs.

He couldn't believe it. All that time Jonah had been living next door to Nash's girl. Ditton had never thought to ask Nash what number he lived at; it would have saved a lot of time if he had, or if Nash had told him to come up to the flat instead of meeting at the swings.

Nash had killed Jonah. All that time he had been the boyfriend Jonah was being threatened with, but he was away at Her Majesty's Pleasure, unable to act. The woman had looked familiar to Ditton but he hadn't understood why, hadn't realised that she was the same girl Nash had been with for years.

And then there was the alibi that Nash had used when Ditton asked him about the shooting. He claimed that he hadn't known about it because he had been out of town, but Clive had said that Nash had been seen in Catford on Wednesday night, the night of Jonah's death. It wouldn't have stood up in court, but Ditton knew he was right, and knew that Vincent had to be told as soon as possible.

He strode to his car and set off for the gym, dialling Vincent as he drove, totally unaware of the red Fiesta that set off after him, that had been following him since he left his own house.

* * *

It seemed to Vaughn that he had been queuing for ten minutes to pay for the car-wash. In fact it was only five, but that was bad enough.

Twenty minutes later, having tried to occupy his mind with the radio, the match and thoughts of Courtney, Vaughn finally drove his car through the wash. For some reason, as the dryer came on he remembered the report for Paul and felt a brief stab of panic. But then thought, why should I? He tried to forget about it.

After another five minutes of queuing at the vacuum cleaner he stepped out and began to tidy the inside of the car as much as he could, bagging any large litter, sweet wrappers and the like, putting cassettes in cases and jackets in the boot and banging floor mats to remove excess dust and dirt.

When it was his turn he moved the car forward so it was adjacent to the machine, inserted his token and began to vacuum. He had been at it for a while when he poked the nozzle as far as he could underneath the passenger seat and met an obstruction. He kneeled down to peer under the seat, pushing his hand underneath and pulling out a video cassette, frowning as he remembered Darryl off-loading the tape on him. His heart missed a beat as he asked himself, without much real doubt, whether this was what all the fuss was about. Could this video cassette be the reason Darryl was dead?

He tossed the cassette on to the passenger seat and,

to the surprise of the other drivers, drove off leaving the vacuum running, the hose on the ground and his car half done. But they didn't feel what he felt – that answers were close.

With a sense of trepidation Vaughn inserted the cassette into the VCR and sat back on the floor, legs crossed. He retrieved a half-smoked joint from a cigarette box and lit it, sucking in smoke and feeling himself relax slightly. The tape started with the fuzzy, grainy blank portion and then almost immediately cut to a home-video picture of a fair-sized bedroom with a large bed as the focal point.

The camera had obviously been located high up and with care because it managed to cover the vast majority of the room, failing only to pick up the area directly beneath it. On the left wall was a window and a dressing-table-cum-wardrobe unit. Directly opposite the camera was the bed, immaculately made. To the right of the bed in the same wall was a door which Vaughn watched open.

Two men stepped into the room. One walked straight forward and disappeared beneath the camera. He had been quick but Vaughn saw that he was a large man with jet-black hair, piercing black eyes and a hooked nose. The other man looked around, apparently appraising the room. He seemed satisfied, noticing, looking straight at and pointing up at the camera. It was Martin Green.

Martin reached out to accept a drink from the other

man, who was still out of the picture; all that could be seen was his arm extended as he passed a tumbler over. That was the first time Vaughn heard any sound. He could hear that they were speaking but it was too muffled for him to understand anything of what they said. They appeared to chat amiably for a minute or so until Martin downed his drink in a greedy, head-thrown-back gulp and returned the glass to the faceless, bodiless hand.

Vaughn re-lit his joint and continued to watch, engrossed, feeling almost voyeuristic and with no doubts that the tape was the cause of everything. What the hell was Darryl doing with it? How had he got hold of a tape of Martin Green and this man? And furthermore, what was the tape showing?

The hand reappeared from the bottom of the screen, extended once more. Vaughn only realised that it contained a wad of notes when he saw Martin begin to count them. He did so twice, looked up, nodded and winked, before stepping over to the window, moving the net curtain and making a beckoning gesture to someone outside.

Martin began a conversation with the faceless guy who had taken a step forward and was revealing the back of his head and a shoulder. Everything seemed a lot more jovial now that money had been passed over and Martin could be seen laughing and extending a hand to shake the one offered by the other man. But then Vaughn's world was turned upside down when Martin left the room and reappeared with a small boy in tow – Darryl, in his school uniform, complete with sports bag.

There was a brief discussion during which it looked as it though Darryl was being introduced to the big man with his back to the camera. Martin looked at his watch and pointed something out. Vaughn could see the man look at his own timepiece and nod a response. Martin left the room, closing the door behind them.

Vaughn's eyes began to smart the minute the door closed, and he thought his heart was going to burst. He fumbled around for his joint, realised he had finished it and opted for a cigarette, struggling with the lighter and eventually inhaling deeply. Although he was reluctant to admit it to himself, he knew he was about to see a nightmare on tape.

Darryl sat on the end of the bed looking like an angel, his knees together and his hands clasped in his lap. He gazed up at the big man before him, anxiously licking his lips and scratching his ear, appearing to answer questions the man was throwing at him. Every now and then, Darryl would smile weakly as though acknowledging a feeble attempt the man had made at a joke. The man disappeared and the extended arm came into view again, holding a drink which he offered to Darryl. The small amount in the glass made it clear that it was not something Darryl should have been drinking, and this was confirmed by his response. He sniffed it cautiously, flicked a glance at the man, who had stepped forward gesturing encouragement. Darryl tried to knock back whatever the drink was but only succeeded in choking, and clawed at his throat while he coughed and wheezed.

The tears were waiting to roll down Vaughn's cheeks. If he had moved his head they would have. He was horrified and mesmerised at the same time. At the big man's direction Darryl removed his blazer and looked around for somewhere to hang it up. He sat there until the man's head inclined sharply to the right as a pointer which Darryl followed, tossing his jacket on to the floor. Next he removed his tie, and by the time he had got to the top button of his shirt, Vaughn found himself biting his lip and blinking hard and fast.

Darryl leaned forward and removed his shoes and socks, looked up for instructions and then removed his trousers, also tossing them on to the floor beside his blazer. He did a pirouette as instructed and sat back down. He looked so young, so frail and so vulnerable, there was no big talk there, no rudeness, no flippant, infuriating remarks, just a small, obviously frightened twelve-year-old boy. Vaughn's face was set, jaws clenched. The tears rolled down remorselessly. He made no effort to wipe them away.

And then, as Darryl sat there with his hands in his lap, his toes curled, one foot atop the other, the man stepped forward so that he was directly in front of the boy and fully in the picture, although his back was still turned. He reached down, took Darryl's hand and placed it somewhere that Vaughn couldn't see and didn't want to, even though the man was still dressed. Then he sat down beside Darryl on the bed and

Vaughn's face crumpled like a Fiat Panda in a head-on collision. He began to sob uncontrollably.

Vaughn could not believe his eyes as he watched the man take off his shirt and direct Darryl to touch him while he removed the rest of his clothes. Vaughn noticed that a jagged scar ran across the man's chin.

The next fifteen minutes were the worst of Vaughn's life, and he was sure he stopped the tape before the worst scenes of depravity were displayed. But he had needed to see, and had seen more than enough to last him a lifetime. He had heard about men and young boys, knew it went on across the world, but he had never stopped to imagine what it actually meant, the gruesome reality, the abuse, the violation and the injury. When he finally stopped the tape he was glad that Darryl was dead, that he had gone somewhere better and wouldn't be subjected to any more harm. Glad that he would never be defiled again.

Vaughn fumbled for his wallet and retrieved the card given to him by DS Rose. He reached for the telephone and dialled.

In his office Vincent ended the call and tossed his mobile phone on to the desk before him with a sigh. Clenching his jaw he swivelled in his chair and glared through the two-way mirror out into the main hall of the gym at the body-beautiful enthusiasts sweating, straining and preening. Vincent wasn't seeing them; his mind was elsewhere. He sat perfectly still for a few seconds, his nimble brain weighing up the options open to him, annoyed that one unexpected new factor could change things so quickly and completely. Gary Ditton had done all that could be expected of him and more. He had identified Jonah's killer, and now he was on his way to reveal his identity. But the timing was wrong. Vincent had things to do, business to conclude; how was he supposed to tell Ditton that he was busy and would speak to him later? They were talking about the killer of his brother.

Vincent stood and walked over to the safe, bending down before it and removing the bunch of keys from his pocket, isolating the key he had shown Ditton roughly twenty-four hours earlier. He inserted it into the lock and opened the safe, reaching way to the back and withdrawing a small, gleaming silver pistol which he checked cursorily and dropped into the inside pocket of his jacket. He closed the safe, stood and zipped up his jacket, rolling his shoulders to ensure that it felt comfortable and to lessen the bulge below his heart.

He walked back to the desk and sat down to await the *consigliere*, having decided that Ditton would have to come along. He could drive and wait in the car, the whole thing wouldn't take five minutes, and then Vincent would be able to give the kid his undivided attention and find out if he had made a decision about the proposition.

Slouching, Vincent closed his eyes and rested his head against the high-backed leather executive chair. Gary Ditton had the potential, of that there was no doubt, and if he was half the man his brother was, he would have no problems at all. There were so many similarities between them it was frightening.

It had been good in those days, so good that because they were still young it had never occurred to them that it could end, it was supposed to go on forever. But then Detective Inspector George Barrett had reared his ugly head with his pathetic attempt at entrapment and changed all that.

The mistake had been giving up Nash. Nobody else had known about Nash doing the job, *nobody*. Rodney had called him in a rage wanting to meet.

Vincent looked at his watch before closing his eyes again and pinching the bridge of his nose between finger and thumb. He had called Barrett and told him what had happened, that Rodney suspected his involvement and wasn't likely to believe his denials. 'What am I supposed to do?' Barrett had asked mischievously. He could remember the look in Rodney's eyes when Barrett had brought him in and he'd seen Vincent waiting there. Vincent had known that his name would be dirt if Rodney left the factory alive; he would be branded a grass and become an outcast. He couldn't allow it to happen. He'd picked up a piece of rubble and attacked his unsuspecting partner savagely, leaving him for dead. Barrett had watched the whole thing, making no attempt to intervene; to him, one was as good as if not better than two.

They'd left the factory together and sat in Barrett's car discussing arrangements for the future now that Rodney was out of the way. Barrett had spoken candidly about the attempted murder of Rodney Ditton, implicating himself, as well as outlining his normal modus operandi for collecting money. They'd shaken hands and parted, and it wasn't until almost two years later, when Barrett's greed made him ask for larger contributions, that Vincent played him the damning audio tapes he had wisely made of their conversation, and of subsequent meetings.

The relationship had changed immediately, Vincent calling the shots and making the demands, Barrett providing information and services. And then Vincent had discovered that Barrett had a weakness for young boys. A sordid, nasty weakness that he couldn't control. Vincent turned the screw.

He had known that it couldn't continue forever, that Barrett's resentment or fear would boil up until he had to take some action to extricate himself from the situation. That time had come. Vincent could feel it and knew he had to make a pre-emptive strike, kick before he was punched, kill before he was kicked. Gary could wait in the car.

A tap on the glass behind his head made him turn around and look up. Ditton was on the other side of the two-way mirror. Vincent reached for the entry-phone on the wall and buzzed Ditton in, again adjusting the position of the gun in his jacket pocket and standing up.

'*Consigliere*,' he said with a smile as Ditton walked in looking pensive. 'Let's go.'

* * *

The doorbell chimed and Michelle was roused from a doze she hadn't intended to take. She glanced at the clock – half an hour early, but she knew it was him. She stood up groggily, straightened her jeans and sweater and checked that all her protective measures were in place – under the cushion on the sofa, and behind the television – telling herself she was being silly but that it was better to be safe than sorry. She walked out to the passage, glanced at herself in the mirror, and opened the front door with a flourish.

Delroy was taller than she remembered, and much bigger. Life in Birmingham seemed to be treating him well. He wore a black fine-gauge V-neck jumper, black jeans and black loafers, had a black leather pouch on his shoulder and carried a black casual jacket slung over his arm. Michelle stepped aside with a smile and waved him in.

'I'm early,' he said apologetically. 'Is that all right?'

Michelle assured him it was fine and directed him to the living room, walking behind him and noting the width of his shoulders and the size of his arms. He sauntered into the room, raised a questioning eyebrow and sat in the armchair when Michelle nodded. 'Is it all right if I skin up?' he asked.

'Of course,' said Michelle, declining the cigarette papers he offered her, but noting his pectoral muscles flexing as if they had a life of their own. They chatted amiably about names and faces from the past. He offered her his joint and she waved it away explaining dishonestly that it was too early in the day for her to be

461

smoking. He smiled and stared at her for what she considered to be just a little too long, and for a moment the doubts and fears she had felt throughout the week returned, but she banished them, telling herself she was being foolish.

'Would you like a drink? Tea? Coffee? Juice?' she offered.

'Nothing stronger?'

Nothing,' she lied and then felt slightly guilty but reminded herself that safety was a must.

Delroy shrugged. 'Juice then.'

Michelle rose and went to the kitchen, returning with Delroy's orange juice. She was about to place it on the coffee table in front of him but he raised his hand and reached for the glass, managing to cover her hand with his. She ignored it. It was nothing, she told herself.

He took a sip, held the glass with both hands and regarded her silently for a few seconds. She realised that the effect of the weed she had smoked earlier was wearing off and she no longer felt as relaxed as she had done.

Delroy sat forward and placed the glass on the table. 'So, why did you ask me to come here?'

'I told you,' said Michelle with a look of puzzlement. 'I've got some gear that I want to get rid of and I don't want people knowing that I'm doing it. I made that clear.'

The corners of Delroy's mouth moved ever so slightly, a hint of a playful smile. 'OK,' he said quietly.

'I thought there might have been another reason.'

'No other reason,' said Michelle, hoping that would be the end of it.

Delroy hadn't finished. 'I was thinking that maybe it was just your way of getting me round here to start what we never managed in the past.'

Michelle looked at him but didn't answer. Her face suggested that she didn't understand his point, and as such was not flustered by his words. Inside, her stomach churned and her brain was working overtime, producing fear and then trying to counteract it.

'Have you seen Carl lately?' asked Delroy, smirking openly now. 'He doesn't look good at all. But then I never understood what you saw in him.'

'I thought he was your best friend.'

'What's that got to do with anything? I'm talking about him and you. I could never understand it. You know I used to watch the two of you together and know that I could do things for you that he couldn't.'

Michelle raised an eyebrow like a schoolteacher listening to a poor excuse. Inside she was trying to figure out how Delroy had managed to turn the conversation so quickly, and was dismayed to find that it deteriorated even more rapidly until five minutes later he rose and sat beside her on the sofa. It was then that she knew she had made a terrible mistake.

CHAPTER THIRTY-FOUR

Ditton sat in the car at the industrial park wondering why he was there. He looked at his watch impatiently and called home again, but there was no answer, and he fidgeted, restless, flicking from station to station on the radio, dissatisfied with what he heard and eager to establish Rodney's whereabouts and safety. Ditton was worried, frightened for his brother. He had expected the revelation about Nash to send Vincent scrambling to find him, ordering his hirelings to scour the area until they had tracked down the diminutive killer. Vincent hadn't done that. He had taken note, obviously, but he hadn't even made a call, just asked if Ditton could drive him somewhere. He had to be doing something important.

A couple of minutes later Ditton could take no more and left the car to peer around the corner of the last unit. There was still nothing to see. He phoned home again without success, and kicked a piece of wood in frustration. For all he knew, Nash had already found Rodney, and here he was being Vincent's driver and sitting like a plum in an industrial estate on a Sunday afternoon waiting for him. He couldn't wait any longer, so he locked up and set off to find Vincent. He hadn't seen the red Fiesta parked on the other side of the railings separating the estate from the road. And as a result, he didn't see the driver get out, lock up, and set out after him.

The front units had looked tatty and run-down, but the back looked like something from a cheap eighties sci-fi film. It was obviously where the local joy-riders and car thieves destroyed and stripped their cars, and he didn't doubt that more than a few junkies jacked up there as well.

There were four or five car shells scattered around and piles of rubble and rubbish waiting to be set alight. Ditton felt uncomfortable, due in no small part to the menacing presence of the old factory on the other side of the chain-link fence. He was puzzled – there was no sign of Vincent and the units all seemed to be closed and locked up. He tried the doors of the first three and guessed that the others were also locked. Unless Vincent had been spirited away he could only be on the other side of the fence, on the factory site, but what would he be doing in there? If he was meeting someone it was a strange place to choose, slightly dramatic, but definitely private if Vincent was OK with the idea of condemned one-hundred-and-fifty-year-old bricks above his head.

About ten feet beyond the chain-link fence was a

brick wall, originally eight feet high but so dilapidated there were very few sections left where it was more than three feet in height. Between the wall and the fence was an expanse of weeds followed by an incline of about four or five feet. Ditton thought he heard something behind him and looked around. Nothing. He hoped he wasn't embarking on a futile and ridiculous trek, and that Vincent wasn't in one of the units. He could hear Vincent's incredulous question: 'What the fuck made you think I'd be in that place?'

He turned, again responding to a noise he thought he had heard, but saw nothing. He clambered over the wall at one of the low points, made his way down the steep incline on the other side and found himself dwarfed by the massive old factory building. There was no sign of an entrance facing him so he turned to his left and walked roughly thirty metres to the corner of the building and turned right, surprised at how big the structure actually was. Most of that wing was composed of massive aircraft-hangar-like doorways, many of which had long lost their doors, and Ditton was able to walk along the outside looking in at the vast amount of unused space and old machinery. He was just about to turn back, convinced that he had made a mistake and that Vincent couldn't possibly be anywhere close by when he heard voices and followed them into the factory and around a corner. When he saw them, he couldn't believe his eyes – Vincent, Tyrone and a big white guy with dark hair, a hooked nose and piercing eyes. From his position, Ditton couldn't see a scar on the man's chin, but he knew it was there.

He approached quietly, Jimmy Nash now forced from his mind. 'Vincent, what's going on? Ty? You all right?'

Tyrone looked up and nodded, pensively. 'Could be worse.'

Ditton tore his eyes away from the white man in the blue raincoat and turned to Vincent. 'Is that—' He couldn't find the words to describe the man before him: *Is that the man that destroyed my brother's life, my life? The man I've hated for so many years? The man that has caused so much pain and suffering?*

'That's him,' confirmed Vincent, saving Ditton the trouble. 'The bastard that did Rodney.'

'Now hold on, sunshine,' Barrett interrupted with a shake of the head. 'We both know that's not true, don't we?'

Ditton felt his head lighten and his stomach begin to churn. He wasn't ready for this. He had spent so many years hating a faceless man for destroying his brother, had found a face twenty-four hours previously, and now that very man stood before him.

He glanced at Vincent, reluctant to take his eyes off Barrett. 'What's he talking about, Vince?'

Vincent kept his eyes on Barrett as he answered. 'Don't mind him. He's a liar, they all are. He's just a scared paedophile trying to squirm his way out of a predicament. Ask him about your friend's kid getting killed. Go on.'

Barrett licked his lips and shifted the gun in his

pocket. He kept his eyes on Vincent as he addressed Ditton.

'What I meant was that I was involved in your brother's unfortunate accident, sure. But I wasn't the major player. Ask Vincent, he can explain, he knows all about it.'

Ditton's head began to throb as though someone were trying to hammer a rusty bolt between his eyebrows. He had to keep calm, he told himself, but he was feeling the panic rising, and again appealed to Vincent, an emotional tremor in his voice. 'What's he talking about, Vincent?'

Barrett smirked. 'What's the matter, Vincent? Lost your tongue?'

'Vincent?' Ditton pleaded, desperate to understand Barrett's point but equally adamant that he wasn't going to ask the scum to spell it out. 'Explain, man. What's he talking about?'

Barrett took it upon himself. 'Look, son—' He raised a hand in apology, acknowledging Ditton's flinch at the word 'son'. 'Look at this situation, here. What do you think it's all about? It's the same as your brother's; in fact it's even worse this time. Back then I didn't have a clue what this madman wanted to do to your brother. The arrangement then was that I bring him here so that we could all talk. I had him released and I brought him here, just like I've done with Tyrone today, but I didn't know how far he was prepared to go.' He gestured with his head towards Vincent. 'I didn't know he was going to try to kill your brother.'

Barrett sighed and glanced at Tyrone, his eyes immediately flicking back to Vincent. 'This time I knew what he wanted to do, and I couldn't be a part of it.'

For what seemed like forever, Ditton was unable to hear over the roar of the blood rushing in his ears. His head hurt, his legs felt barely able to take his weight, and he was having trouble focusing on anyone or anything.

Barrett smiled, almost fondly, as though he was about to explain something to a cute, confused toddler. 'How do you think it is that he's never been touched? I'll tell you how, because he had me over a barrel because of your brother. He did your brother and then held me to ransom over it.'

'No,' snarled Ditton. 'No way. I don't believe it.' He spun on Vincent, breathing deeply, struggling to suck in precious oxygen. 'Vincent?' The throbbing in his head was so loud that he almost screamed his appeal. 'Defend yourself, then!'

Vincent shook his head. 'I've never worked with this guy. True, I know him, he's an opponent, an enemy, it pays to know them. But I've never worked with him, as such. He's trying to fool up your head. Don't let him do it.'

Barrett smiled and shook his head.

Ditton wanted to believe Vincent, and in any other situation he would have done, unequivocally. But things had changed in the last few days and he had learned that Vincent was capable of much more than he had thought. But trying to kill Rodney? That was too much to accept.

Then Tyrone piped up. 'Ditton, think about it,' he urged. 'How do you think they managed to find me all the time? Every time I was supposed to meet you, they found me. How do you think that was possible? Think, man! He was the only other person that always knew where I was going to be. It was him that told them where I was going to meet you. He used you, he uses everybody.'

Ditton stepped back and searched Vincent's eyes for the truth. They were cold and didn't inspire confidence. For the first time in years he had no idea what to do, no idea how to react.

Suddenly Ditton saw Tyrone's head shoot up and he tensed, staring at something beyond Ditton. Barrett did the same and Ditton turned, aware that Vincent refused to take his eyes off Barrett, and for the first time noticing the menacing bulge in the pocket of the policeman's raincoat.

When Ditton turned he came face to face with Jimmy Nash and a sawn-off shotgun. It was all the situation needed.

Seeing Ditton move, Vincent turned his head, and catching sight of Nash he took a wary step backwards, making sure he could still see Barrett.

Nash grinned and motioned with the shotgun for Vincent to step back even further. 'Well, this is a pretty party,' he said. 'A right old knees-up. I bet you're wondering what I'm doing here, aren't you?'

No one answered.

'I followed our Gary here. He didn't notice me, of course, that would have spoilt everything, wouldn't it? I wasn't sure what I was expecting to find, but this is better than I could have dreamed of. I've got all the answers I need, and all the victims I could want.'

Ditton had stopped laughing. 'Where's my brother?' he asked quietly.

Nash shrugged. 'I haven't got a clue, and frankly I don't care any more. I've heard all I need to know from these two.' He winked. 'Sorry about all those threats. No hard feelings, eh?'

'If you've done anything to him . . .'

Nash tutted loudly and rolled his eyes. He grinned again and it was hard to accept that he was a psycho with a shotgun. He came across as a kid with a high-powered water pistol.

'I haven't seen your brother. True, if I hadn't got any joy this afternoon I would have come looking for both of you, but there's no need now.' He nodded towards Barrett and then Vincent. 'They're right, they're both bastards, but as far as your brother's concerned, my money's on Vincent.'

Ditton glanced at Vincent, then returned his gaze to Nash.

Nash grinned again and said, 'You see, I followed you yesterday too, spoke to Sean, though not as nicely as you, I'm sure. I couldn't really imagine Rodney being a grass, but then who would think that about this cunt either? But what that junkie said happened the day that Rodney got done proved that *someone* was a grass. How else would that wanker over there have known where to pick him up?'

Barrett shifted uncomfortably, his attention divided between Vincent and Nash. Vincent kept his eyes on Barrett and his ears on Nash. Tyrone stood beside Barrett with an expression that suggested he couldn't understand where he was, or how he had got there.

'So the question is who grassed, if not Rodney. Now, if I was nicked because someone grassed on me, and I'm standing here with the policeman that nicked me and he's saying that Vincent's been his grass for years . . . I'm going to have to take his word for it even if he is Old Bill. I reckon you should too.'

Ditton glanced at Vincent again. Vincent stared back. But then he turned to face Nash head on, apparently forgetting Barrett. He peered at Nash as if contemplating what to say, and then asked calmly, 'Is that what you killed my brother with?'

Nash's grin faded to be replaced by a bemused frown. 'What the fuck are you talking about, grass?'

'Wooley House. That's where my brother lived. Number thirty-two. Next door to a bitch who complained about noise, and threatened him with her boyfriend. A bitch who had a gun waved under her nose and ran into her house like the sorry tart she is.'

Nash flinched at every 'bitch', 'tart', 'whore' and 'slag' that Vincent produced, and as he carried on Nash's frown grew deeper.

Ditton watched the confrontation horrified but fascinated. Before Nash had arrived the scene had been tense; he hadn't been quite sure what he had walked into, but the atmosphere had been charged, explosive. With Nash's arrival and Vincent's accusation it had become far, far worse. He knew he was right about Nash and Jonah, he had to be, but it had never occurred to him that Nash wouldn't have known Jonah was Vincent's brother. He watched Nash's face, his eyes and mouth, and realised that this was the case, he hadn't known. But Ditton could see that Nash was himself slowly coming to the realisation that the person he had come to kill had a greater reason, if not desire, to kill him. And there was Barrett too. If Nash had followed Ditton there was no way he could have known Barrett was going to be present. He would have to kill Barrett too. He couldn't kill Vincent and leave the policeman alive, and would in fact probably relish the opportunity to take out the man that had arrested him and had him sent down.

Ditton looked over his shoulder and saw Tyrone backing off; he had read the situation too. Ditton's eyes flicked briefly to Barrett; what was his position in all this? If what he had said about Vincent was true, they had obviously fallen out, big time. That meant a pile of problems to be resolved. If the policeman had spoken the truth – and Ditton hoped to God that he hadn't – there was no way that Vincent or Barrett could allow the other to live. That meant the

474

policeman couldn't allow Nash to live either.

For some reason unknown to him, Ditton raised his hands and stepped forward. He looked at Nash. The baby-faced killer had changed position. Vincent had moved too, and the three of them – Nash, Vincent and Barrett – had formed a triangle. Ditton had placed himself in the centre of it.

He turned a full circle, his arms spread, appealing for peace, though nothing came from his mouth. Tyrone beckoned to him but Ditton kept turning, his arms spread. They were three of a kind and weren't about to listen to appeals for common sense. He had seen the policeman's hand in his pocket and knew he was carrying a pistol, obviously brought for Vincent. Vincent nearly always carried a weapon and Ditton doubted that today would be any different, and Nash was standing there with a sawn-off shotgun so casually that one could have been forgiven for thinking it was a rolled-up newspaper.

Ditton stepped out of the triangle and left them to it. None of them moved to intercept him or said a word to stop him; they only had eyes for each other. Tyrone beckoned him with more urgency and hissed, 'We've got to get out of here quickly! Can't you see what's going to happen?'

Ditton raised a hand to halt him. Vincent was speaking.

'So, Nash. How is that bitch of yours? Did she miss you while you were away, getting it up the arse?'

Nash flinched, but re-found his grin quickly. 'The

missus is a lot better than your fucking brother, wouldn't you say?'

Vincent shrugged, conceding Nash's point. 'So who are you going to go for first, Nash? How many shells you got in that thing? Three? Four?'

Nash continued to grin. 'That's for me to know, grass. But I will tell you that it's two less than I had before I met your brother.'

Vincent shrugged again, once more conceding Nash's point. 'You know he's carrying too, don't you?' he said, gesturing at the policeman. 'And you know he's going to go for you as well, don't you? Who're you going to go after first, Nash? Think about it.'

At Tyrone's insistence, Ditton followed him away from the pallets to a small flight of steps that led up to a chest-high platform that had probably once been a loading bay. From there they mounted a few more steps to a landing leading to a storage area and had a view of the proceedings without being in any firing line. Ditton felt sick, but knew he had to watch. Barrett was down there and he had made Rodney what he was. Jimmy Nash was down there and he had killed Jonah. And then there was Vincent, who hadn't convinced him that Barrett was lying, but was still Vincent.

The dialogue between Vincent and Nash continued, Vincent shrugging seemingly deeper every time Nash countered his arguments. Barrett stood as he was, hand in pocket, eyes but not head moving to follow the two younger men. Up above, Ditton and Tyrone knew it would come soon.

Vincent said something else to Nash, and Nash answered. Vincent shrugged again, but it was different this time, longer, as though it was a shrug of resignation. It wasn't. He flipped his jacket open and went to his waist, diving to the floor as he did so and rolling behind a large wooden trolley.

Nash realised what was happening just a bit too late, and from his vantage point Ditton was amazed to see that he hadn't yet sent a cartridge to the breech, but he did so quickly as he too sprang from where he had been standing and slid behind a pillar.

Barrett skipped to his left, pulling his pistol from his pocket, peering around and under obstacles. Unfortunately for him he assumed that Vincent had moved from behind the trolley, and as he approached it cautiously two shots rang out from the other side. Barrett was sent flying as though he had been hit in the chest by a charging bull. He screamed, landed on his back and skidded for a few feet before coming to a halt against a pillar.

Up above, Ditton noticed a frown on Tyrone's face but he didn't have time to dwell on it because a massive *boom!* filled the factory and reverberated off the walls and machinery. Nash had fired one round, but in looking at Tyrone Ditton had lost track of both Nash and Vincent.

He found Vincent first, crouched behind two packing crates stacked one atop the other, his right shoulder against the crates, listening for any signs of a five-foot-nothing white guy carrying a sawn-off pump-action shotgun.

Ditton couldn't believe he was watching it, couldn't believe he had seen one man killed and two others hunting each other determined to kill. It was lunacy, but he was transfixed, almost scared to breathe. And then he saw Nash squirming along the ground, commando style, to Vincent's right, his blind side. How he had got there, or how he had known where Vincent was, Ditton was unable to work out. But Nash was bearing down on Vincent.

Again Ditton glanced at Tyrone, whose eyes flicked from Vincent to the advancing Nash. Ditton could guess what outcome Tyrone was hoping for, that Nash would end all his worries and blow Vincent away just like he had done to Jonah. It would be so convenient for him, he could walk away knowing that both Vincent and the policeman that had been on his tail were history. Tyrone's eyes seemed to light up more the closer Nash got to Vincent. It was unbearable.

Ditton felt the train before he heard it, the vibrations travelling up through his body. Then the whole building began to vibrate and puffs of cement and plaster were dislodged to waft around, caught in the rays of sunlight forcing their way through the broken glass like a laser show. Nash was about twenty feet away from Vincent and had increased his speed, trying to take advantage of the noise cover provided by the train, which was still some way away and would get louder.

Ditton felt Tyrone stiffen beside him with expectation and excitement. He glanced again. The look on Tyrone's face was one of glee.

The train was upon them now and the noise was deafening. Everything rattled and shook, including Ditton. Debris fell from the roof, and on the far side of the factory, beyond Nash, a few small panes of glass escaped from ancient putty to destroy themselves on the floor.

Nash leapt to his feet and sprang towards the crates Vincent was crouched behind. Tyrone gasped. The roar of the train was rising to a climax with the falling wood and plaster cascading down like rain. Without thought or consideration Ditton stood and roared, 'Vincent! To your right!'

Tyrone scowled and grabbed his arm.

Over the noise Vincent somehow heard the warning and heaved against the crates with all his might, at the same time diving straight ahead and away from them. The top crate fell just in front of Nash, who tried to hurdle it but caught his trailing leg on the inside lip. He cartwheeled and landed on his back with what seemed like sickening finality, but he quickly rolled to his left, reaching for the shotgun that had flown from his hands. He had just reached it and pulled it towards him, sitting up with his legs spread as though he was building sandcastles on the beach, when Vincent rose from behind the lower crate and spotted him.

Ditton didn't hear either of them fire, the blasts were drowned out by the roar of the train, but he saw the belch of flame and smoke from the shotgun, saw Vincent wheel and fall to the ground and saw Nash slump backwards as though he was lying down to sleep. The train passed on into the distance and as suddenly as it had been upon them, it was past and the factory became silent again.

CHAPTER THIRTY-FIVE

Milk got out of the car, walked briskly to the entrance
to the flats and cast a glance over his shoulder. He
thought about taking the lift, imagined the state it was
likely to be in and turned for the stairs.

At the second floor he began to feel the burn in his
legs and loved it. He thought about the cause – the
match – and grinned. It had been a good day so far, if
he ignored the early morning.

He looked at his watch and increased his pace up the
stairs.

As he stood on the balcony outside her door he was
tempted to knock. Why on earth was he supposed to
be using a key if she was there? Being Milk it crossed
his mind that maybe Michelle had set up a little love
nest, and that he was letting himself in to fight his way
through linen veils and incense to find her in a Bedouin
tent, lying elegantly on a bed of cushions wearing
nothing but a veil, gold discs on her nipples and a
camel-hair whip covering her groin.

He inserted the key into the lock, tentatively, unused

to the mechanism, but it opened easily and quietly and the door swung open.

Instantly he knew that something was wrong, or at least that something was going on that he wasn't supposed to have found. Muffled sounds came from the living room to his right, sounds of exertion.

For a second he contemplated closing the door and leaving. He wavered, physically leaning away from the noises and towards the front door, but then his indecision surprised and spurred him on. The day before he had told Ditton this was the girl for him; if he thought she had someone else there he owed it to himself to find out, not go mad – he had no right, just find out. Milk closed the front door quietly and moved towards the living room, the source of the noises. As he got closer he became convinced that something was definitely not right and pushed the door with his left hand while reaching for the pistol at the back of his waist with the right. It never occurred to him to call out.

The sight that confronted Milk was horrific. Michelle's arms were pinned beneath her torso on the coffee table in the middle of the room. Her knees were on the floor, and above and behind her a man stood, his knees bent, left hand exerting pressure on her upper back and head, one foot on her calves to keep her legs in place. His right hand tugged viciously at her jeans.

Milk took it all in in an instant – the kitchen knife on the floor, the red welts across Michelle's lower back caused by the waistband of her jeans, the man's belt hanging undone. But what struck him most vividly was Michelle's face. She was so calm and focused despite the fact that she was struggling to avoid being raped, that, along with the red mist that had descended over him, was a feeling of immense admiration and pride.

In a bucking effort to dislodge her assailant Michelle turned towards the door, grimacing as she strained every muscle in her body. Milk noted her eyes as she saw him standing there, the way she closed them in an extended blink, the way she appeared to relax and her face seemed to become serene and a semblance of a smile flashed briefly across her lips.

Even though she had stopped struggling the man carried on just as viciously in his attempt to remove her jeans, almost yanking her off the table on to the floor. Milk stepped forward at pace, lowered his right shoulder and swung a kick at the man's head. If he had connected with a football as sweetly it would have burst the net and taken the goalkeeper with it. Instead he caught the man on the back of his shaven head, raised him a few inches and sent him sprawling. Michelle rolled off the table on to the floor and lay there.

Milk had carried on moving and aimed another kick at the head on the carpet, but it moved and his foot caught the man's collar bone, causing Milk to gasp as pain travelled from his toes to his hip. The man yelped and rolled on to his back, and it was then that Milk saw his face and really lost it.

He had come across Delroy in the past. They had people in common, which had always prevented a full-scale confrontation, but there was still no love lost between them. He had read Delroy like a book, sensed that he was scum and that no one was safe around him, especially women. That incensed Milk, who had longed for the day when he could really go to town on Delroy and beat it into his thick head that women had to be respected, at least until they gave you reason not to. Didn't everyone come from a woman after all?

And then he had met Dawn, a cutie from Streatham, and had become intoxicated with her, determined that he was going to chase her until she caught him, charm her until she seduced him. He had worked at it and knew he was making progress until one day she disappeared. At the time he hadn't linked her disappearance with Delroy heading out to Birmingham or wherever it was. Why should he? He rang Dawn and was told that he had the wrong number. He went to her house, there was no answer. The next time he tried, new people had moved in. He was baffled and needed answers.

They'd come from his sister Sandra, of all people. She knew Dawn's elder sister and revealed in hushed tones that Dawn had been viciously attacked by someone she knew and had been so traumatised she had kept it to herself and not gone to the police. Her family had known something was wrong but she hadn't told them what had actually happened until weeks afterwards. By then Dawn was adamant she wasn't going to report the attack despite concerted efforts to convince her. Sandra whispered that the attacker's name was

Delroy, and that he hadn't been seen since the incident.

Milk and the others had hunted high and low for him, but hadn't found a trace. It wasn't until almost a year later that someone came back from Birmingham carnival and reported that he was based up there. Milk had sworn to himself that one day he would catch up with Delroy. Now that day had come.

If Milk had had any doubts that Michelle was a willing participant in what he had just witnessed, they were dispelled when he identified Delroy as the assailant. He aimed kick after kick at Delroy, who attempted to curl up and protect himself, grunting every time a blow hit him. And then Milk went for the gun at his waist and bent his back to pistol-whip the bastard within an inch of his life. He was going to break every bone in Delroy's hands and arms until he dropped them, giving Milk access to his face.

But from somewhere deep inside the swirling dark mists that clouded his mind and drove him on, Milk heard his name being called. He felt something touch his shoulder but ignored it, intent on his work, until he felt himself being dragged away and found himself on his back, Michelle beneath him, her legs wrapped around his and her arms trying to clamp his behind his back.

His head was thudding and his brow ached from his war face, but slowly he calmed enough for Michelle to release his legs.

'You all right?' she whispered.

Here she was, he thought, the victim of an attempted

rape, and she wanted to know if he was all right. Amazing.

'I'm all right. How about you?'

She insisted that she was fine and he rolled off her, checked that Delroy was no danger and lay beside her on the floor, his breathing as heavy as hers. He appraised her torn blouse, dishevelled hair, the red marks on her arms and her undone and twisted jeans, and he wanted to go for Delroy again. He would have done if she hadn't reached up, pulled his head gently down to her breast and asked quietly, 'How was the match? Did you win?'

Milk heard himself whimper and hugged her as tightly as he could.

One thing Milk remembered about Delroy was that he always kept his cash close. If he had come with any intention of doing a deal the money would be on him; the car was too far away for Delroy to feel comfortable. He rolled him over, ignoring his groans, and patted him down – nothing. He spied a black jacket slung over the arm of the sofa and raised an eyebrow. Michelle nodded but Milk didn't even get as far as checking the jacket because he saw the leather pouch beneath it. Inside was roughly twenty-five thousand pounds.

'Why didn't you tell me what you were doing?' asked Milk as he zipped up the pouch and handed the cash to Michelle. She looked puzzled and hesitant but took it between finger and thumb and dropped it on to the windowsill.

'I didn't want you to know what I was doing. I didn't want you to know what I'd done.'

'Patrick's girl?'

Michelle nodded.

'But why not? I love the idea, except this bit. I could have stayed in the bedroom or something. You could still have done it on your own, but I would have been there. Imagine if I hadn't got here—'

Michelle held up a hand to stop him. She didn't want to imagine and he understood.

Milk kicked Delroy, who groaned and opened his eyes fearfully, expecting another savage attack. Milk ordered him to his feet and had to help him up. He led him down to the street, asking him what his car was and then placing him in it. He informed him that he had relieved him of his cash as compensation, and that if he wanted to dispute the matter when he was better, he needed to take it up with Milk and not Michelle. If he ever approached her again, he would be killed. 'If she turns up in your house, you better get the fuck out,' Milk told him.

Ditton couldn't help looking at Nash as he passed. Vincent must have fired at least twice. Nash lay with his jacket open displaying a wound where the '10' would be on a target practice figure. Ditton could see a dark red stain slowly spreading as he watched. Nash's stomach was bathed in red too, from a lower wound. Nash wasn't grinning now.

Ditton moved towards Vincent, not sure how he

would feel about seeing him lying there, dead. If Barrett was to be believed, Vincent had beaten Rodney senseless, but he couldn't be sure the policeman's evidence was trustworthy. He felt that Vincent's denial should have convinced him, but it hadn't, and he felt guilty about not believing him. After all, Vincent had taken Ditton under his wing and protected him. He couldn't have done what Barrett said he had.

Tyrone noticed Ditton's movements. 'What are you checking on him for? After what he did?'

'You don't know if that was true,' said Ditton, trying to sort things out in his mind, not prepared to try to get Tyrone to understand his difficulties. He kneeled beside Vincent's prone form, lifted his jacket, noting the hole blown in it, the splatters of blood on the front of his shirt and Vincent's right hand still covering the pistol. He gazed with mixed emotions at the man that had meant so much to him, and didn't feel sad, or elated; in fact he felt nothing, numb, and he struggled to understand it.

'Come on,' Tyrone urged from behind him. 'We've got to get the fuck out.'

Ditton heard but continued to gaze.

And then Vincent moved, a twitch of his hand, a slight flaring of the nostrils, a flutter of his eyelashes. Ditton gasped and jumped. He bent down to listen to Vincent's breathing and it was then that Vincent spoke, so quietly that Ditton could barely hear him. 'I'm sorry. About Rodney.'

Ditton nodded and clasped Vincent's hand, telling

him to hold on. He turned to Tyrone who was on his way outside but had stopped and turned having heard Ditton speak.

'Ty!' Ditton called. 'He's alive.'

He saw Tyrone pause and begin to walk back towards him, silhouetted against the light streaming into the factory. Ditton turned his attention to Vincent, who was still struggling to speak, and for the briefest moment asked himself whether Vincent's words a few moments earlier were an attempt at admission and an apology over what had happened to Rodney. If so, what was he doing holding his hand and trying to comfort him? He should be leaving him there to die with the others.

Ditton held on but lowered his head to ask, 'What did you mean, Vincent, when you said sorry about Rodney, what did you mean?'

Vincent's mouth moved as he struggled to speak but no sounds were emitted. Ditton became aware that Tyrone had returned to stand beside him, his thigh touching Ditton's shoulder. He turned to look up at Tyrone and ask what he thought they should do, but Tyrone already knew what he was going to do. Ditton saw as well as he felt Tyrone's thick thigh knock him to the ground so that he had to release Vincent's hand and fall awkwardly to avoid crushing Vincent's legs. As he looked up to see why Tyrone had knocked him down, two shots went off close to his head and he screamed and clamped a hand over his ear in shock and pain. When he was finally able to open his eyes Tyrone stood over Vincent with a smoking pistol and glanced at Ditton before turning and striding for the door. Vincent was definitely dead now.

Ditton raced out of the warehouse, shielding his eyes from the light. 'Oi!' he shouted, as he clambered over the brick wall in pursuit of Tyrone. 'What the fuck did you think you were doing?'

Tyrone continued to make his way towards the car as though he was on a Sunday stroll.

Ditton caught up with him amid the litter and wrecks at the rear of the units and placed a hand squarely on his shoulder.

'What the fuck was that?' he repeated.

'Keep your voice down,' hissed Tyrone. 'There are three dead guys in there, one of them a senior police-man, and I don't want to be linked with any of them.'

Ditton stared in anger and disbelief. 'There would only have been two if it wasn't for you!'

'He was going to die anyway. I just speeded it up, that's all.'

Ditton stepped right up to Tyrone so that they were toe to toe and cap peak to cap peak. 'Who gave you the right to speed anything up? Who do you think you are?'

Tyrone shrugged. 'What do you want me to say? I'm sorry?'

Ditton shook his head and sneered in disgust. 'No, I know you couldn't or wouldn't do that. I want to know what the hell you thought you were doing. Who are you to be going round shooting people?'

Without answering Tyrone again set off towards the car. Ditton walked behind him and admitted, 'You know, this week I've been defending you like only your mother or your bitch would do. I've been telling people that you're not capable of doing certain things, or that you've only done certain things because you were under pressure, or panicked. But now I've seen that all those people were right. You are a stupid, ignorant bastard after all.'

Tyrone stopped in his tracks and waited for Ditton to draw level. 'There's nothing stupid about what I've done, or what I do. I saw an opportunity and I took it. Vincent would have done exactly the same if the roles were reversed. You know that's true. Not only that, but I witnessed Vincent kill Nash and a policeman. Do you think he would have let me live after that? Considering he wanted me gone anyway?'

'He said all along that he didn't want you dead, I tried to tell you that.'

It was Tyrone's turn to stare in disbelief. 'What do you think I'm doing here? I'm here because Vincent told Barrett to bring me here so he could wipe me the fuck out! What's the matter with you, man?'

Ditton was silent until he sighed and looked into the distance over Tyrone's shoulder. 'You're right. I wasn't thinking. But there must have been some other way, man. There's no need for all this killing.'

Tyrone shrugged. 'I don't know about other stuff, but in this instance there was no other way. It's the business, it's what it does to you if you want to progress. And believe me, I'm going right to the top. I will do what I have to do, and nobody is going to stop me.'

Until the next Tyrone comes along, thought Ditton. And he would come.

Ditton started the car and was about to pull off out of the estate when he paused, lowered his head in thought, swung the car around and drove towards the warehouse, stopping as close as he could to the chain-link fence. He told Tyrone to hold on and said he was going back inside. Tyrone thought he was joking, but he turned and watched Ditton retrace his steps through the fence and over the wall. Ditton returned almost instantly and explained that he had dropped something inside. Tyrone was curious, but all he said was 'OK, can we get out of here now?'

Five minutes later Ditton turned to Tyrone. His mind had begun to whirl, just as it had when he realised it was Nash who had killed Jonah. His thoughts shot off at tangents so quickly that he wasn't able to pursue them, or trace them back to their source. Finally he worked out what it was that was bothering him. He sighed, gritted his teeth and asked, 'Where did you get the gun, Ty?'

Tyrone hesitated before answering: 'I just picked it up off the floor.'

Ditton sighed again, deeper this time. 'Nash had the shotgun, Vincent's pistol was by his side when you shot him and you didn't go anywhere near Barrett. So where did you get the gun?'

Tyrone was about to repeat the lie when he stopped, shrugged and admitted, 'Barrett.'

Ditton shook his head, misunderstanding. 'What a bastard. He must have really thought he was Caesar or something. Throwing two slaves into the arena to kill each other.'

Tyrone stayed silent and looked out of the window.

'When did he tell you what he was planning? In the cell?'

Tyrone continued to look out of the window in silence.

'Well?'

Tyrone chuckled. 'I told you no one would get in my way, didn't I? And that I would do what I had to do, right?'

Ditton nodded.

'Well, there was no cell, because I wasn't locked up.'

Ditton frowned at Tyrone for clarification. 'But it was supposed to be the same as Rodney—'

'It wasn't. He called me and we met up. I wasn't in custody.' He glanced at Ditton. 'Don't look at me like that, man. I haven't done anything your beloved Vincent didn't do. The guy approached me a while back and confronted me with so much information about my operation that I didn't have any choice but to do what he asked. It's the same thing he did to Vincent, and probably tried to do to Rodney.'

'But Rodney wouldn't have it; why did you have to? Who have you sold out? How many people have you given up?'

'Get real, Ditton, man. This is a game for survivors, and I will do what I have to do to survive. I don't know how to do anything else. This is my chosen career, and I'm going to get well ahead in it. Now if you want to play by your honourable but outdated rules, go ahead, but I'm not about to cut off my nose to spite my face and end up like your brother.'

Ditton checked the rear-view mirror once, slammed on the brakes and skidded the car to a halt at the side of the road. Other drivers who had heard the squeal of tyres were as startled as the pedestrians that had witnessed the manoeuvre.

Tyrone stared before raising his hands and nodding several times. 'OK,' he conceded. 'That might have been a bit out of order.'

Ditton leaned across Tyrone and opened his door. 'Get out,' he ordered, and repeated the instruction more forcefully when Tyrone sat there looking wide-eyed and confused.

'But what? What did I do?'

'Just get out. I've had enough of you today. Enough of you and your business and your ambitions. Just get the fuck out of my car.'

Tyrone rolled his eyes and folded his arms. 'Stop being silly,' he said. 'Start the car up and let's go.'

Ditton reached under the seat and produced the Beretta. 'I wouldn't trust you with anything any more, do you understand? You cannot be trusted. Earl blabbed today about you and him and Vincent – you played me there. Now you tell me that all that panic shit was a load of bollocks, all that hiding from the police and disappearing was a load of crap – you played me again, and I'm sick of it.'

Tyrone attempted to explain his reasons, but Ditton simply raised the gun to Tyrone's neck, repeated his demand and added, 'Quickly, my finger's beginning to itch.'

Tyrone did as he was told, slamming the car door behind him. Ditton drove off in search of his real friends.

HENRIETTA'S

Draining the last of his Iced Tea with his straw, Vaughn asked. 'So what about you, D? You spoken to Tyrone?'

'No. And I don't want to,' Ditton replied. He glanced over his shoulder at the bar. 'You've got to keep that quiet. Esther doesn't know anything except that Vincent was shot. She can live with that, but not if she knew I was anywhere near it.'

For the next five or so minutes they talked about the events of the week, managing to find things funny that hadn't been anywhere near amusing a few days earlier. Eventually, when their faces were streaked with tears and Vaughn was forced to hold his stomach because it hurt from laughing, Ditton composed himself enough to ask, 'The last time we were here, you were going on about pissing off to the Caribbean. Are you still thinking about that?'

Vaughn shrugged. 'Not actively, at the moment, but it's still an aim, something that I'm going to have to do at some point. What's the point in sitting here and rotting when I could be in the Caribbean living a nice life, surrounded by people who look like me?' He smiled and spread his hands, coughing with slight embarrassment. 'But I've also had a little idea about maybe writing a novel. Who knows if I'll manage it? I don't know, but it's something else to aim for.'

'A novel?' asked Milk with a doubting frown. 'What can you write a novel about?'

'How about the last week?'

Milk took a sip of his drink and looked vacant, but after a pause he began to nod more and more emphatically until he exclaimed, 'Yeah! With me as the star. I can see it now. Well, I can see the film, but the book'll do for now. Go for it, geezer.'

'Why not?' agreed Ditton.

That set them off discussing the week's escapades again, and at times they ended up roaring so loudly that Esther, Michelle and Courtney took it in turns to come across from the bar and tell them to keep it down. After more tear-wiping and aching sides, Vaughn was the most capable of speech. He asked, 'So, have you two thought about what you're going to do with your lives? Any ideas?'

Ditton shrugged and was silent for a while. 'I don't really know,' he said honestly. 'Me and Esther have been talking about some things, discussed a few options, but I haven't made any real decisions.'

Vaughn waited for more, but Ditton shrugged and seemed to be preoccupied with a bunch of keys on the table before him. His fingers lingered on a strange, long black key with a red handle. Ditton noticed Vaughn looking and flashed him a strange smile.

Pointing at Milk with the key, Ditton asked, 'What about you, Milk?'

Milk grinned and scratched his neck, looking from one to the other. 'Well,' he said, hesitantly, 'I've had an idea for a while, but I put it out of my mind—'

'And?' interrupted Vaughn. 'Well?'

Still grinning, Milk asked, 'You really want to know, then?'

'Yes,' said Ditton. 'Yes, we do.'

'Come on,' prompted Vaughn, 'get on with it.'

'All right,' said Milk, still grinning, 'but you've got to promise not to laugh.'

Vaughn sat forward. 'Do I look like I'm going to laugh? Do I?'

Milk glanced at Ditton. 'D, don't be laughing now,' he directed.

'I'm not going to laugh, man. I just want you to spit it out,' said Ditton with his hands spread in a beseeching gesture.

Milk nodded and leaned forward, resting both elbows on the table and coughing to clear his throat. Both Vaughn and Ditton leaned forward too, forming a conspiratorial circle.

'Come on, man,' asked Vaughn. 'Why the suspense?'

Milk raised an eyebrow. 'Impatience, eh? You need to relax, my son.'

'Come on,' urged Ditton. 'Patience is one thing, but you're taking the piss now.'

Milk was grinning from ear to ear and enjoying himself immensely.

'What the fuck is it?' demanded Ditton.

'You're not going to laugh?' confirmed Milk.

Ditton flicked a beer mat in Milk's direction while Vaughn crushed an empty cigarette box and hurled it. Milk ducked and cowered in the corner of the booth. 'All right!' he protested. 'All right, take it easy!'

'Well come on then!' insisted Vaughn. 'Spit it out.'

Milk sat up and tried to keep his face straight while he made certain that nothing else was going to be thrown at him. He cleared his throat again and looked from one to the other before saying, 'A brothel, I'm thinking about opening a big-time brothel.'

Vaughn sighed, blinked a couple of times and took a long swig of his drink, shaking his head as he swallowed. Ditton tapped the table with his keys, groaned and scratched his head.

'What?' asked Milk. 'What?'

Icebox

Mark Bastable

Here's the deal.

Give Gabriel Todd your brain, and you'll live forever. Gabe'll freeze your head in a flask – and three hundred years from now, you'll be reborn in a new, perfect body. You will be immortal.

Unity Siddorn wants in. She has her own plans to save the world – with genetically pumped tomatoes, as you ask – but she's already thirty-bloody-one years old. In actuarial terms, her life is 41.3% over. She'll do anything – ANYTHING – for more time.

Don, her squeeze, is less keen. A pack of smokes and a gambler's shot at seventy years – he can live with that.

Suddenly, Gabe's theories are about to be put to the test – though circumstances are admittedly less than ideal. The police tend to take a professional interest in a freshly severed head. It's not something you can easily hide . . .

0 7472 6839 8

HEADLINE

MITCHELL SYMONS

All In

Steve Ross has had enough. Of gambling. Of losing. Of feeling bad about losing. Of worrying about what he's going to do when he's lost it all (the money, that is, followed by the wife and kids).

So naturally enough he makes a bet with himself. If his gambling account is in the black at the end of the year, he'll carry on. If it isn't, he'll top himself and leave Maggie to cop the insurance. That way, at least the kids are looked after, and he can escape the hell his life is fast becoming.

With Steve's luck it could go either way. But one thing's a dead cert. For the next twelve months he's going to experience the thrill of the ultimate high-stakes games . . .

Set in the twilight world of all-night poker games, betting shop coups and spread-betting mania, Mitchell Symons' debut novel is the darkly funny diary of one man dicing with death.

0 7472 7316 2

review